CODENAME: CHANDLER
THE BEGINNING
THREE COMPLETE STORIES

HIT
EXPOSED
NAUGHTY

J.A. KONRATH
ANN VOSS PETERSON

CODENAME: CHANDLER
THE BEGINNING, THREE COMPLETE STORIES
HIT — EXPOSED — NAUGHTY

August 2014

CONTENTS

HIT

ABOUT HIT

She's an elite spy, working for an agency so secret only three people know it exists. Trained by the best of the best, she has honed her body, her instincts, and her intellect to become the perfect weapon.

CODENAME: CHANDLER

Before special operative Chandler was forced to FLEE, she executed the most difficult missions—and most dangerous people—for the government. So when she's ordered to eliminate a crooked corporate CEO in a manner that looks like natural death, it's a regular day at the office… until she discovers she's not the only assassin hunting this particular prey, and her competition is aiming to make this hit into a political statement that will shake the nation.

HIT

Chandler

"If an obstacle blocks your path," The Instructor said, "pick it up and use it as a weapon."

I threaded through foot traffic crowding the sidewalks of Michigan Avenue, Chicago's Magnificent Mile, a shopping bag from Nordstrom draped over one arm. But despite the new dress I'd just bought and the window displays announcing spectacular August clearances on sandals, I wasn't in the mood for shopping.

Turning on Ohio Street, I strolled west, assuming the attitude and body language of just another shopper heading back to my car after a grueling morning spent searching for the best bargains the Windy City had to offer. The air smelled of hot pavement, car exhaust, and more pleasant aromas drifting from a nearby Starbucks. Two women approached me on the sidewalk with cell phones pressed to their ears, not taking notice of each other, let alone me. An older man emerged from a hotel, suitcase in tow. Cars sped by on the street, an endless, honking race of stop and go. Nothing out of the ordinary.

I turned north on Rush Street and paused at the window, as if admiring the motorcycle jacket in the display. Scrutinizing the reflection of the street behind me, I searched for anyone abruptly changing their travel pattern as a result of my stop. Once I was satisfied I hadn't been followed, I continued along the sidewalk, ducked into the self-park next door, stepped into the elevator, and hit the button for the top level.

This was only my second mission with my new handler, an electronic voice over the phone I knew only as Jacob, and we were both still feeling each other out. So far his choice of drop site was not a point in his favor.

Dead drops made me uneasy on a good day. One in a closed in space with few exits—such as a public parking ramp—made me downright paranoid. But while I could turn down an assassination if there was some reason I felt I couldn't carry it out, picking up this package wasn't optional. Although the government agency I worked for didn't officially exist, it knew I existed. Getting on the wrong side of the powers that be by balking at something as simple as a pick-up wouldn't help my longevity.

The elevator door slid open, and a wave of humid, exhaust-filled heat assaulted me, smelling worse than the nearby Chicago River. I scanned the steep rise of parking spaces, noting the hulking shape of a Humvee taking up several spaces at the end and wondering how anyone had squeezed that thing into the narrow, twisting parking garage. A minivan and three sedans rounded out the rest of the vehicles on this level, with many empty spaces in between. None of the vehicles appeared to be occupied. A quick stop-and-squat to pick up an imaginary coin on the tiled floor gave me the line of sight to prove no one was hiding behind any of them.

I stepped out of the elevator and around the corner.

A teenage kid who looked as if he'd slept under one of the cars stood on the other side of the trash can where I was supposed to find a McDonald's bag, his pants draping so low on his hips that half his boxers were showing. He clutched the fast food bag in his right hand.

"Hey," I called, trying to sound casual. "That's my bag."

"Huh?"

"The Mickie D's bag. That's mine."

"It's trash. I just picked it up from the ground."

"I just set it down for a second. Please. It's my dinner."

He looked at me as if certain I was insane.

Great. He was just a kid. I didn't want to have to hurt him. I dropped my Nordstrom's bag in the elevator's mouth, blocking open the door. "I'll give you money for it." I dipped a hand in my pocket and pulled out a keychain gizmo and wadded up bill.

A hundred. A bit much to pay for trash, but I doubted he had change. I held it out to him.

A suspicious look slid over the kid's face. "What's in this thing anyway?" He held up the bag, started to open it.

I pressed the button on the gizmo—a gift from Jacob—and four parked cars went into ear-shattering alarm mode, wailing and flashing lights, the racket echoing off concrete.

The kid looked around

I didn't.

Lunging forward, I went for his sternum with my left elbow while snatching the bag with my right hand. At the same time, I slipped my left leg behind his ankle, tipping him backwards and onto his ass as gently as I could.

"Sorry, kid." I tossed the bill to him. "There's a McDonald's just down the street. Get yourself something fresh."

I hit the button again and the alarms ceased. Eat your heart out, James Bond. Then I squeezed the bag to make sure it was actually the drop, not leftovers. I felt something hard inside—harder than Ronald ever cooked—and knew I'd scored.

The door had crushed my Nordstrom's loot, but the car was still there. In a moment, I was on my way down to the ground level and out onto the street.

Piece of cake.

Out in the open air, I turned south and took a circuitous route back to the hotel I'd checked into two hours before, located a block east of Michigan Avenue on Ontario Street. I lived in the city, but when on a job, I often operated out of a hotel, the larger and more impersonal the better. That way nothing led back to my apartment and my name.

3

Not that my apartment or anything else was under my real name. In fact, my identity changed like the Chicago weather.

The only constant was my codename: Chandler.

After hopping an elevator to the third floor, I headed for my room, nestled in the building's northeast corner. I unlocked the door, made sure the room was clear, and dumped out the McDonald's bag on the bed.

A cell phone, a small collection of makeup, and a pair of fur lined handcuffs. I picked up the cell phone and hit the send button.

Jacob picked up on the first ring. "Yes?"

"May I speak to Cassie?" I asked.

"I'm sorry, she's in Detroit on business. Would you like to leave a message?"

"Tell her to call her sister in El Paso."

"So who was the kid?" Jacob asked when we'd finished the security verification dance. "Friend of yours?"

So Jacob had been in the ramp. Why didn't that surprise me? "The Hummer? That was you?"

"Of course. Sorry for the unusual drop site, but I couldn't leave anything to chance this time. Had to keep an eye on it myself."

"You call that keeping an eye on it? The kid had it in his hands."

"You were there to handle it."

"And if I wasn't?"

"Then I would have. Lucky for the kid, things didn't go that far. So do you like your new phone?" Even through the voice distortion, I could detect excitement in Jacob's question.

It seemed to be a phone like any other. I wasn't sure what I was supposed to like. "Um, sure."

"Good sound, huh?"

"Sounds like you're sitting next to me." I thought about his presence in the garage. "You aren't, are you?"

"Funny. It's nice, isn't it?"

"It's a phone, so…sure. Nice."

"It's not a phone. Well, it is, but it's so much more. Shock proof, waterproof, virtually indestructible."

"Ahh, I get it. You're still upset that I killed three phones on the Tunisian trip, aren't you? A trip that turned out to be more of a war than a hit, I might add."

"I'm over that. But for the record, I still think you were careless."

"Is that why you felt you had to babysit me in the parking garage? Couldn't this have been done in person, over coffee?"

"It isn't that simple, Chandler."

"I forgot. You're not a field agent."

"We each have our positions. You do yours. I do mine."

"Yet there you were. Are you sure you don't want to switch jobs?"

Silence stretched for several seconds before Jacob cleared his throat and continued. "The phone is also encrypted and much more, but you'll learn the rest later. Guard it with your life. Keep it on you at all times, even in the shower. And answer it every time it rings. Understand?"

"Yes, sir. I'll take care of the new toy. I promise. Now what I really want to discuss are the bracelets." I picked up the pair of fur-lined handcuffs, letting them dangle from my index finger. "I'm guessing my target is a womanizer who likes to dabble in kinky sex?"

"Isn't that true of most of the men I set you up with?"

"Two for two now. Come to think of it, you're shaping up to be a lousy matchmaker."

"If you think you can do better with Christian Mingle, be my guest."

I sorted through the other items. "And what's the deal with the makeup? Hinting that I should freshen up my look?"

"Depends on your definition of freshening. You'll find syrup of ipecac in the lipstick tube and flunitrazepam powder in the mascara. All the help you should need to get your target alone and compliant."

"So are you going to tell me who my target is? Or do I have to seduce and sanction all of Chicago?"

"Ever heard of a company by the name of Bratton BioTech?"

"No."

"They're a defense contractor."

"Let me guess, biological weapons."

"Actually their stated aim is developing immunizations against biological weapons."

"You say potato…"

"You might be closer than you know. Word is the CEO, Dominic Bratton, is in Chicago to pick up something deposited an hour ago in his safe deposit box. It's in a bank on North Clark, put there by an employee. Recently Bratton's been taking calls from people with connections in Russia, Venezuela, and Iran."

"Where is this word coming from?" I usually worked alone, and I liked it that way. Spies were notoriously untrustworthy, and I didn't relish the idea of putting my life in the hands of someone as devious as I was.

"Homeland Security. They have reason to believe he intends to hold an auction. Possibly tonight."

I'd done a variety of dangerous things for my country, but since I despised catching even a simple cold, the prospect of dealing with some sort of biological weapon was not my idea of a good time. "What's in the package?"

"The answer to that is above my security clearance. But I wasn't told to take any special precautions, so that suggests data."

I let out a relieved breath and waited for Jacob to continue.

"Bratton has reserved a private dining room at four and is scheduled to arrive at the bank at closing time, five-thirty. You'll pick him up at the restaurant."

"You don't expect him to bring me along?"

"To the bank? No. To his bed afterwards? If you're good at your job, he will."

"You know I am."

"That's what I'm counting on."

I wasn't accustomed to receiving praise, I had to admit it felt good. My previous handler had been as humorless as a machine and not quite as complimentary. Maybe Jacob and I would end up working well together.

"You're going to have to sell the death as a robbery, and the evidence needs to be solid enough that police won't look any deeper."

I picked up the pair of cuffs with my finger once more and gave it a twirl. "Sounds doable. Is that it?"

"He has a bodyguard with him wherever he goes."

"You might have mentioned that first."

"Problem?"

"Nothing I can't handle. Photo?"

"Sending. Along with a dossier on Bratton."

A light glowed against my cheek and an image appeared on my phone's screen. Bratton was a pug of a man, not fat but soft. A mop of reddish hair streaked with white topped his head. Mean little eyes peered from beneath thick brows.

"I don't have anything on the bodyguard, but Bratton is paranoid for good reason, so assume he employs the best."

"Where's dinner?"

"Across the street. He has a private room reserved for four-thirty."

I peered through the window at the slick, glass building reaching into the sky. On the ground level, two copper lions stood sentry in front of the downtown Chicago location of the Capitol Grille.

"Got it."

With my objective in mind, I signed off, stripped down, and climbed in the shower to get ready for my happy hour "date."

Making a hit appear as if it was part of a robbery was more difficult than it might seem. First it usually meant getting close to a target, a task made complicated by Bratton's personal security.

As a woman I often had an advantage when it came to this step. It was difficult for men to resist the offer of sex, sometimes more difficult for powerful men, who usually saw bedding women as one of the spoils of success to which they were entitled.

Once proximity was won, the next hurdle was the murder itself. When I'd joined Hydra, a man I knew only as The Instructor had put me through intensive training, breaking down everything that made me human and building me back up as a weapon of the government. As a result, although killing wasn't enjoyable to me, I could do it without hesitation. Even when it meant watching the life drain from a man's eyes.

The last challenge was the fact that modern forensic science was frustratingly thorough. Leaving a death scene that looked staged was a path to a full-blown investigation. I couldn't afford mistakes.

Fresh from the shower, I read through the information on Bratton, did a passable job on my hair and makeup, and shimmied into my new dress and sandals. After loading the drugs and kink paraphernalia into a small silver clutch, I packed my clothing and toiletries into my carryon, wiped down everything I'd touched in case I didn't return, and left.

I'd been performing tasks like this for Hydra for years, and while I no longer felt nervous at the thought of playing my part and completing the job, I did note the slight increase in my heart rate that accompanied readying myself for the challenge ahead.

Not a bad sign. A little dose of adrenaline would keep me sharp.

Emerging from the hotel, I turned left toward Michigan Avenue, circled the block, and then took a circuitous route back to the restaurant. When I stepped between the copper lions and through the revolving door, I was certain I hadn't been followed.

The restaurant entrance was warm and inviting, the scent of grilling steak, fresh flowers, and the lingering musk of a guest's perfume reached me. A hostess graced me with a friendly Midwestern smile. "Good evening. Would you like a table?"

"No, that's fine. I'll sit at the bar."

I ran my gaze over the wall of personal wine cellars marked with guests' names on plaques. The restaurant was all mahogany and brass, the dining room decorated with gilded portraits of powerful men, hunting scenes, and race-horses. White linen graced the tables, and warmth flickered from shaded candles and glowed through the amber glass of pendant lights hanging from the ceiling. Diners ate and chatted and raised their wine glasses in celebratory toasts. I didn't catch a glimpse of anyone who resembled my target, but then I'd arrived early by design, so that was no surprise.

I made my way to the rich looking mahogany bar flanked by two eight-point buck heads and featuring a large glass jar filled with fresh pineapple and a clear liquid I assumed was vodka. Choosing one of the red leather covered barstools, I settled into a spot where, between my field of vision and the view reflected in the mirror, I could keep an eye on both the private dining rooms and the entrance.

I ordered a Stoli Doli martini, the pineapple concoction from the glass jar, and sipped it very slowly as not to cloud my senses with alcohol.

It was delicious; lightly fruity without being sweet.

People celebrating an early Friday happy hour flowed in, a few left, nothing out of the ordinary. The bartender chatted with me about the weather, and I told him of my luck on my shopping expedition and perused the menu, ordering an appetizer of Prosciutto Wrapped Mozzarella with Vine Ripe Tomatoes that was to die for. Twenty minutes before reservation time, a man looking nothing like Dominic Bratton stepped through the door.

I wasn't sure why I noticed him at first. At five foot nine, he had a fit build, but not bulky, dark, wavy hair in need of a trim, and a nice looking face that was a touch too rugged to be called handsome. He wore a black button down shirt and tie, a gray jacket that did a good job of hiding his shoulder holster. He was sexy, his movements effortless in the way that suggested a certain athleticism.

He spoke to the hostess, walked to the mouth of the dining room, and swept his gaze through the restaurant before I realized what it was that had drawn my attention.

Each person who had walked through the door previously had brought with him or her a certain vibe or aura, for lack of a better word. Some men oozed authority, others quiet confidence, and yet others stuck out their chests like the nearby portrait of Napoleon, desperate to prove their importance to everyone around them, most of all themselves.

As attractive as this man was, he gave off no vibe at all. If I hadn't been watching the room, I might not have noticed him, and I tended to notice attractive men.

Finishing his surveillance, he walked back to the door and pushed back into the heat. A few minutes later, he returned, this time at the side of Dominic Bratton.

The CEO was shorter than I'd expected. Broad shoulders, cheeks a bit too red despite being lightly dressed in a polo shirt, and his lips a little too smug. Judging by the way he stuck out his chest and peered down his nose at the restaurant staff, he had an inflated opinion of his own importance. As his gaze fell on me, I held it and gave him a little smile.

Nothing.

No reaction. No interest.

I took a sip of my drink. I couldn't remember the last time a man ignored me as pointedly as Bratton had. I was a good-looking woman, and I was not only good at catching male interest, I'd received training in the art of flirting and manipulation. This kind of blatant turn-down didn't happen to me. Bratton was supposed to be a womanizer, so what was it?

I grabbed my purse, and leaving my coat draped on the chair, I worked my way down to the sunken dining room just as the hostess led Bratton and the bodyguard toward one of the private rooms.

Enough with being subtle.

Half stumbling yet still keeping my balance, I fell into Bratton just hard enough to press the length of my body against him.

"Oh I'm so sorry," I said. "Thank you for catching me. If there's any way I can repay you…"

He brought up his hand, and at first I thought he might feel me up right there in front of Mayor Daley's portrait.

Instead he propped me on my feet, stated, "You're welcome," and was on his way.

Damn.

I circled through the restaurant, made a show of asking a server where the ladies' room was, and made my escape. Once inside the very nice restroom, I peered at myself in the mirror.

My hair looked great. Draping to my shoulders, it was swingy and shiny and framed my face perfectly. My body was honed, and the dress showed it.

So what was it? Why didn't he like me?

No time for a bruised ego, I returned to the bar. Two men had joined the party, one muscle bound, dark-haired, and wearing a goatee, the other bald, black, and with a face so battered, it looked like an old football the neighbor kid left out in the rain. Football Face wore a tailored jacket and, like Bratton's bodyguard, a well-concealed shoulder holster.

Judging from their body language, Mr. Muscle was in charge, and he and Bratton drank martinis while the other two settled for coffee.

Judging from their body language, I could tell they weren't old buddies, and this wasn't a friendly meeting. It was business and adversarial business at that.

Buyers for whatever I needed to steal from Bratton? If so, this was a bad development. I needed to speed up my game.

After my bout with rejection, I wasn't sure how I was going to get close enough to Bratton to complete the operation, but I had to figure out something. Slowly sipping my own drink, I groped for ideas.

Just after a second round of drinks arrived at the table, Bratton's bodyguard stepped away from the table and left the room. Using my peripheral vision, I watched him circle the dining room in a wide arc. Half way through his trek, I realized he was heading for me.

There were two possible explanations. Either he'd recognized something about me that made him uneasy—and was therefore extraordinary at his job—or my take on Bratton was off, and he'd sent his bodyguard to invite me to the table.

I obviously preferred the latter.

He sidled up to the bar just behind me, and I caught the scent of aftershave and a hint of his shampoo.

"So you come here often?" he said, a Mexican-flavored accent spicing his voice.

I shot him a tired glance. "Really? That's the line you chose to go with?"

A smile teased the corners of his lips. "You're right. You deserve better. Let me try again."

I answered his smile with one of my own but said nothing.

He rested an arm on the back of my barstool. "Look at this place. A man cave for the rich and powerful. Lions out front. Wood, brass, portraits of expensive horses and influential masters of business and war. Even the spoils of the hunt."

He gestured to the deer trophies behind the bar. "The décor is designed to make the testosterone flow, no? To give men erections as soon as they step through the door."

I smiled, suppressing an honest laugh.

"Or maybe that's a result of being near you."

I fought the urge to roll my eyes. There was another possibility, one I hadn't considered. He was trying to pick me up for himself. I glanced Bratton's way. Sure enough, the CEO was oblivious to our exchange.

"Your time is too valuable to waste on him."

"Excuse me?"

"My employer. A tiresome man."

"I think I can decide whom I'm interested in. And I happen to like rich and famous executives."

"Perhaps, but he won't be interested in you."

"And this from the man who was just coming on to me?"

"I'm interested in you. He won't be. I don't mean to be insulting, *bonita*, but it is what it is."

"Maybe I should ask him."

"You can, if you like. But I can save you the embarrassment."

"Let me guess. You're going to tell me he's gay." If Jacob had missed something that essential to this plan, I would never trust him again.

"Oh no, he's quite a ladies man."

"He only dates blondes?"

"No. Brunettes are his favorites."

"Then it looks as if I should go talk to him immediately."

"You're too old for him, *querida*."

"Ouch." Since when was twenty-nine too old? I thought I had at least another year before AARP started sending me literature in the mail.

"I don't mean to offend, but my employer prefers teenagers. He doesn't understand the finer things in life."

"Such as?"

"Women with brains. Women with fire." He appraised me again, a full body leer, starting at my legs, lingering on my breasts, before meeting my eyes once more. "Women who know what they are doing."

I didn't mind the brazen, cocky approach, and after Bratton's rejection I might admit to even enjoying it a little. But that wasn't why I was here, unless I could somehow get to Bratton through this man.

"And I suppose you do understand women?"

"There are men who want pleasure handed to them. And there are others who know the very best things require effort. Do you know how cattle are killed in the slaughterhouse?"

"So now your pick-up line is talking about how cows die? You know this is a steakhouse, right?"

"Do you know?" He waited, eyes twinkling.

"A bolt is shot into their brains," I said.

"Yes. They are herded into narrow chutes, prodded along until the moment when the steel ends them. Then they are carved into steaks and served on tables covered in white linen." He gestured to the dining room. "From the time those calves are born, they have no chance."

"I'll keep that in mind the next time I have filet mignon."

"Have you ever attended a bullfight?"

"No."

"Do you know what happens in the arena?"

"I know it has something to do with cruelty to animals."

He shook his head. "Raising a steer in a box and shooting a bolt into his brain is cruelty to animals. The bullfight is about honor. The matador can be maimed or killed as easily as the bull."

I didn't think that was precisely true, but in the interest of appeasing the man standing between me and my target, I held my tongue. "So you like bullfighting?"

His eyes locked on mine. "I like a challenge."

And I was beginning to like this guy. He was full of himself, but if I were on my own time, I would enjoy spending it sparring with him, in the bar *and* the bedroom.

"You are a professional, no?"

I didn't react, my core turning cold and hard as ice. Casually I picked up my glass and took a sip, giving myself a moment to consider my next move.

How could he possibly know I was an operative?

And how the hell was I going to deal with it now that he'd made me?

I had a special knife strapped to my inner thigh, but I'd have to hike up my dress to get to it, and it required some assembly—that would cost me crucial seconds. I felt the weight of the glass in my hand and mentally cataloged the other items around me that I might use for weapons.

One of the booze bottles on the rail.

The knife the bartender was using to cut lemons for garnish.

The gun in the bodyguard's holster.

I was accomplished in many forms of martial arts, but if it came down to defending myself, I'd rather not have to resort to bare hands.

"I didn't mean to offend, but don't bother denying it."

I met his gaze but still didn't say a word.

"The world is unfair. I understand that more than most. Men like my boss have wealth. I use my skills to serve him, and he pays me. Why shouldn't it be the same for you?"

It took a second for his meaning to sink in. He hadn't identified me as the professional hit woman I was after all.

He thought I was a prostitute.

I smiled. "I believe in being discreet. That's important to my clients."

"Apologies, *bonita*. Maybe I can make it up to you."

"How?"

"Part of the services I offer my employer involve procuring his entertainment. He has to deal with much tense business this evening. Perhaps you would like to be tonight's feature?"

"You were just telling me I'm too old for him."

"And I can tell you how to fix that problem."

"You're not trying to sell me some expensive skin cream or shoot my forehead full of botulism, are you?"

He laughed, a sound I liked more than I should have. "You are perfection just the way you are. Only a *pendejo* like my employer would fail to recognize that."

"You sweet talker," I said. "You seem to be going out of your way to find a date for this *pendejo*."

"And you wonder why?"

I gave an apologetic tilt of the head. A real hooker probably wouldn't spend a lot of time questioning either the compliments or the promise of a lucrative job. "Does it seem like I'm looking a gift horse in the mouth?"

"I never understood that cliché."

"You can tell a horse's age by looking at its teeth."

He stared at me, as if waiting for more.

"Never mind."

"I told you. It is my job to find his entertainment. But I confess I have more reason than that. I'm hoping something unfortunate happens to him, and then you will be all mine."

I smiled. "So tell me the secrets of Dominic Bratton."

He leaned close and whispered all I needed to know, his warm breath tickling my neck. "You can do that, no?"

"Of course"

"And I will go back to the table and feed him so many drinks he underperforms and overpays, and then you and I will have the rest of the evening."

"I don't even know your name."

He smiled and held out a hand. "Heath Rodriguez."

We shook. "Simone."

"*Encantado,* Simone." With his accent, the name sounded pornographic. "You will be back before we are finished with our steak?"

"I will."

"Don't be late. This meeting will not last long after the food and drink is gone." He brushed his lips to my cheek then turned to leave.

And as I watched him walk back to his employer's table, I almost felt bad using him as a means to his boss's end, especially since he would lose his job out of the deal.

And if he got in my way, his life.

Heath

Heath felt the lovely Simone's eyes follow him all the way back to Bratton's private dining room, but he resisted the urge to glance over his shoulder. The art of flirting was as much about leaving a woman wanting more as it was about showing interest, and Heath was a master at both.

He circled the table and took his chair, sneaking a glance just in time to see Simone rub her fingers up and down the stem of her glass as if she was stroking a man. Then she stood, swooping up her coat and bag, and headed out of the restaurant, the fingerprints on her glass now safely smudged beyond recover.

She was a professional, all right—Heath had identified her the moment he stepped through the door—but she was no sex professional.

Heath recognized an assassin when he saw one.

The signs were obvious if you knew what to look for. Tucked into the corner of the bar, she'd chosen the one seat in the restaurant where no one could approach her unseen, and yet she had a view of the entrance and most of the tables of the main dining room and private rooms. She'd noted his every move without seeming to, expertly positioned herself to run into Bratton, and after having tasted the Capital Grille's pineapple martini drink on his last trip to Chicago, Heath doubted any normal person could manage to sip one so slowly.

And now the attention to fingerprints.

Heath also sensed something about her, a controlled and focused intensity that made the back of his neck prickle and his blood feel alive. He'd known many hot women in his life, but none had affected him this way. This wasn't mere sexual attraction.

She was dangerous.

And Heath could sense it, because he and the *chica bonita* had much in common.

"So did you let the waiter know we need another round?" Bratton asked, the martinis he'd consumed already smoothing the edges off his sandpaper voice.

Heath smiled at his boss like a perfect minion. He'd been working for Bratton for nearly two months now, and had witnessed firsthand what an entitled *baboso* the man was all the way to his core. It had been tough to follow his commands when Heath really wanted to break his neck, but he had managed to be a model employee.

Now that the auction had almost come to a close, he wouldn't have to keep up the charade much longer.

"If you want to enjoy our steak before we must leave for your appointment, I thought it best the waiter bring the wine," Heath said.

Bratton nodded. "See? That's why I pay him. He keeps me on schedule and makes sure I enjoy the finer things."

"It is my pleasure. And I also saw to arrange for your pleasure later."

"You found what I like?"

"*Sí. Muy guapa, muy joven y muy obediente.*"

The Venezuelan, who Heath knew as Pino, and the merc working for him, a former Airborne Ranger named Smith, gave knowing nods.

"Damn wetback," muttered Bratton. "Speak English, will you?"

"Very pretty, very young, very obedient," filled in the American mercenary.

"She'd better be pretty and young. And if she isn't obedient, I will enjoy teaching her."

The men laughed as Bratton downed the last of his martini.

Heath chuckled along, the thought of unleashing Simone on Bratton making the moment all the sweeter.

A chirp cut through the laughter, and the CEO reached for his phone. He glanced at the display, at Heath, and then at the other two in the private room. "If you'll excuse me."

He stood and left. Only when he was safely away from the glass door did he bring the phone to his ear and speak.

Pino pulled his napkin from his lap as if to rise.

"You'll need to stay here for a moment." Heath's words were quiet, but even a radical as far left of Chavez as Pino was took notice of the firmness behind them.

"I was going to visit the restroom."

"Mr. Bratton would prefer you stay here while he is taking his call. *Por favor, acepta mis disculpas.*"

A brittle smile spread over Pino's lips. Then he clapped Heath on the back and took his seat.

A moment later, the bossman returned. The waiter followed behind him with a 1999 Mouton-Rothschild Bordeaux Blend the Capital Grille kept as part of Bratton's private collection. And as the wine flowed and the steak was served, Heath watched the row of clocks on the wall, each showing a different time zone, and counted down the minutes until they had to leave for Bratton's appointment…until he would again see the lovely Simone.

Until he held in his hands the one thing he could deny *El Diablo.*

Chandler

"Those who are used to getting what they want only want what they can't have," The Instructor said. "If you want to become indispensable to your target, be what eludes him."

I made it back to the restaurant just as the dinner party was shuffling out between the copper lions and toward the waiting limo. Heath spotted me first, his eyes crinkling at the corners and lips curving into an appreciative smile. He laid a hand on Bratton's shoulder, directing his attention my way.

Bratton's eyes flared wide. "You outdid yourself this time, Rodriguez."

I smiled and cast my eyes to the sidewalk, as if too bashful to hold his gaze.

A quick trip to Forever 21 on Michigan Avenue scored me a cotton eyelet mini skirt and bejeweled blouse, which I wore without a bra. I'd hated to leave my new dress in the store's restroom, but I kept the shoes, the rest of the outfit change making them look like the Manolo knockoffs that seemed to be everywhere this season, thanks to Sex and the City. As a finishing touch, I'd gone for shimmery pink lip gloss and gathered my hair in to pigtails which now tickled the back of my neck.

A pervert's fantasy. All I needed was a lollipop.

"Hey," I said, looking up at him through my lashes.

Bratton turned to his dinner companions. "I will get back to you with the place and time."

Exchanging knowing looks, the two crossed the street, heading for Michigan Avenue. Heath opened the limo door, ushered Bratton then me inside and climbed in himself. He sat facing us as the limo joined the flow of traffic.

"I'm sorry, *bonita*, but I will have to make sure you have no weapons. It is my job. I'm sure you understand."

I was hoping to get by without him going through my things, but his caution didn't surprise me. The most disconcerting thing wasn't his request but the sharp look in his eyes, all of it focused on me. I wasn't sure if I should read it as suspicion or interest.

"*Bonita?*"

"Of course." I gave him my bag, and he looked inside. He raised his brows at me and pulled out my fur lined cuffs. "You have some surprises up your sleeve, no?"

Bratton put a hand on my breast, pinching my nipple through the fabric as if he was dialing a radio station.

Peering back into the bag, Heath pawed through Jacob's lipstick and mascara, and the sparkly gloss I'd just purchased. When his focus returned to me, it was so intense it made my skin tingle.

The limo turned south toward the river.

"Do you have anything else on your person, *bonita?*"

Heath placed his hand on my inner thigh, holding my gaze as he slowly worked his fingers up. When he reached my garter, he explored further north, finding my weapon. He raised an eyebrow, then tugged out—

"That's mine," I said, snatching it away from him. At casual inspection, it looked like a regular American Express card. But this one, when folded correctly, had a razor edge and firm handle. It could cut through bone.

"Don't leave home without it," Heath said. "Any other hidden surprises?"

"For crying out loud," Bratton said. He grabbed my blouse and gave a yank, popping a few buttons, and exposing me from the waist up. "See? Nothing but firm, young tits here. Now leave her to me and make yourself useful pouring champagne for the lady. I'll have a Manhattan."

As much as ripping open my clothes was an asshole move, Bratton had just done me a favor. My nudity was a handy distraction, not just for Bratton, but for Heath, too. I'd rather have the bodyguard scrutinizing my bare breasts than the items in my bag or my lethal AmEx. Besides, unlike Bratton's pawing and lecherous stares, the small smile on Heath's lips and his quiet appreciation of my body made my breath catch.

If only I'd met him on my own time.

"You are forgetting the stop we must make, Mr. Bratton?" Heath said, throwing my bag on the seat beside him and reaching for the champagne without taking his eyes off me.

"I'm forgetting nothing. Pour the drinks. And…what's your name, sweetheart?"

"Simone."

"Simone here can enjoy a little bubbly while we attend to business. But until then, I'm going to enjoy her."

He cupped a breast in each hand and pinched my nipples as if trying to take them. His hands were clammy and three rings encircled his fat fingers, two on his right hand and one on his left ring finger, platinum and diamonds sparkling in the surrounding city lights.

Heath filled a flute for me and one of the biggest Manhattans I'd ever seen for his boss, extra vermouth. Bratton took his hands off me long enough to chug a quarter of his down. The limo crossed the Chicago River and cruised into the financial district. Streets clear this time of night, it didn't take long to reach the bank.

"Help yourself to the booze," Bratton said, climbing out onto the sidewalk. "When I get back, we'll put that cute little mouth of yours to use."

I formed my cute little mouth into a smile. "I hope you're staying at a hotel close by. I don't want to wait."

"Who said anything about waiting? The drive to Midway Airport is, what, twenty minutes? Maybe less? That's how long you have."

"You're not staying the night in Chicago?"

"Hell, no. I already had my steak, and I'm not in the mood for the blues. Tonight we fly to Vegas." He grinned and glanced at Heath. "I'm feeling lucky."

"Vegas?" I didn't try to hide the surprise in my voice.

"Don't worry, baby. After I get back, I'll give you my undivided attention all the way to the airport." He turned his back and strode for the bank.

Heath poked his head inside. "Cheers, *bonita*," he said, then closed the door, the lock clicking into place and securing me inside the vehicle.

Great.

Apparently the two at the restaurant hadn't come in with the top bid. And with Bratton planning to jet off to Las Vegas, my chance to get him alone was nil. The only way to complete my assignment now was to crash the whole car, taking out Bratton, Heath, and the driver in the process. Too difficult to control all the variables.

Time to move to my back up plan.

The light shifted, the driver tilting the rear view mirror, probably trying to get a glimpse of skin now that he could concentrate on more than the road. I had no reason to believe he would go out of his way to provide Bratton security, but neither was he likely to keep quiet about suspicious activity on my part. So leaving my blouse spread open to keep him focused on the view, I grabbed my bag, zipped it open, and made a show of pulling out my lipstick. I applied a coat of apple blossom pink. Pushing the small button on the side of the tube, I reached to the bar for the bottle of champagne, at the same time tipping a healthy dose of syrup of ipecac into Bratton's Manhattan.

Ipecac's main use in past decades was inducing vomiting in children who'd accidentally ingested poison, although it was no longer recommended for that purpose. Now it was a favorite of the binge-purge crowd. A poison on its own, ipecac caused nausea when taken by mouth. Bratton's profile suggested he was known for fluctuating weight and fad diets to offset his voracious appetite, so traces that might remain in his body was found could be easily explained away. And as a bonus, ipecac was sugary sweet, tasting similar to pancake syrup, a flavor the whiskey and sweet vermouth should camouflage nicely.

I stashed the lipstick tube back in my purse and filled up my glass. Now all I could do was wait.

The men were inside for only ten minutes, and when they returned to the limo, neither one was carrying a thing.

When Jacob had mentioned a package of lab reports, I'd been envisioning a briefcase or at least an envelope. But judging from their free hands, this package must have been small enough to fit in a pocket. And I doubted Bratton would ever let his bodyguard carry something that was valuable enough to warrant a special trip to Chicago.

I needed to get my hands in Bratton's pockets. As luck would have it, my cover identity should make that a piece of cake.

Heath opened the limo door for his boss.

"Left your shirt open, I see. Good." Bratton slid next to me on the seat, his hands immediately going for my nipples, pinching and twisting. "You like showing them off, don't you?"

I forced a giggle. "I like showing them off to you."

I had to figure out a way to kill this bastard soon or I was going to have bruises.

I could feel Heath's eyes on me as he climbed into the seat opposite, and the car started to move.

"How long does it take to get to the airport?" I asked, managing to get a sip of champagne without spilling.

"A few minutes. Plenty of time." Bratton grabbed my free hand and plopped it on his crotch.

Charming.

But a good opportunity all the same, and I took it, feeling up his package while straying to the sides and checking his front pockets for the package he'd picked up at the bank.

Other than his phone, they were empty.

I set down the champagne flute and climbed astride his lap. As I kissed him, I ran my hands down his sides, over his suit jacket, then under.

Nothing.

That left only his back pockets. If whatever he'd retrieved was tucked into his wallet, I was in trouble. Although I could pick his pocket easily enough, I wouldn't be able to verify I had what I needed, not in front of Heath. I had to convince Bratton to check into a Chicago hotel for the night.

"Oh yeah, now we're talking." Bratton unbuckled his belt and lowered his fly. Placing his hand on the back of my head, he attempted to push my face toward his lap.

I was going to enjoy killing him.

"Wait, my mouth is dry." Sliding down to the floor space in front of him, I slipped out from under his palms. I reached for his drink and shoved it into his left hand, the glass clinking against his rings. Then I lifted my own. "Cheers?"

He ignored my attempt at a toast, instead slamming back his drink then plucking mine from my hand. Grabbing a pigtail in each hand, he forced my face into his lap. The rings on his left hand rapped me along the cheekbone hard enough to leave a mark.

With little choice but to play along until the syrup of ipecac took effect, I slipped my hands to his ass. His back pockets felt as empty as the rest, only the square outline of his wallet standing out. Out of the corner of my eye, a ruby set in gold flashed in the evening sunlight slanting in from the west.

Had he been wearing that before? All I remembered was platinum.

The car stopped at a light and I could sense Heath watching me. Trying not to be too obvious, I shifted left to get a better look at Bratton's ring.

A second later, the window exploded.

Pebbles of glass showered me.

I glanced up, recognized Football Face who'd dined with Bratton, focused on the 9mm in his hand. Apparently they hadn't made a deal at the restaurant, and had chosen Option B. I tensed my muscles to throw myself back out of the way. Then Heath was hurtling over me, knocking the pistol back, stabbing for the guy's eyes, falling on top of me.

"Drive, drive, drive!" Heath yelled.

"What?" Bratton sputtered, finally releasing my hair.

Tires squealed, and we lurched forward. Horns sounded from all angles. A sharp pop sounded from outside.

I had to act. I had no gun, but that had never stopped me before. Pushing myself up, I felt Heath behind me.

"I suggest you go back to what you were doing, *bonita*. At least then you'll be keeping your head down."

Right.

I was Simone the prostitute, not Chandler. I couldn't respond to this the way Chandler would. I had to remember that.

I looked at him, not bothering to hide my natural fear. "What are we going to do?"

Another pop, this time it sounded as if a round had hit the rear fender.

"Take the next right," Heath said to the driver.

The car veered, but even with my head down, I could tell the man's cautious driving wasn't going to get us anywhere. Unless I wanted to resort to my first plan of hoping everyone died in the resulting car crash except me, I'd have to jump behind the wheel and blow my cover.

Heath beat me to it.

26

As he crawled through the privacy divider and into the front seat, the driver's side window exploded, and the car veered sharply to the right. Bratton and I slammed hard against the door in a half-naked tangle of thrashing limbs.

Shit. The driver must have been hit.

Or maybe Heath.

A crunch of metal shuddered the air and ripped along the length of the vehicle, but before I had time to speculate about what we might have sideswiped, the vehicle righted itself and accelerated.

I pushed myself away from Bratton. Glancing into the front, I spotted Heath's head above the headrest. The driver slumped against the passenger door, clearly injured, maybe dead.

A groan came from the back.

Bratton.

With the waist of his pants binding his thighs and his complexion the color of dried concrete, he'd looked better. "Are you okay?"

Another groan.

I slid onto the backward facing seat Heath had vacated. Keeping my head low, I reached out a hand for Bratton. "Come on."

He clutched the edge of the seat, not moving.

I glanced out the rear window. From here I could see the car behind us. Football Face was driving, his boss extending a muscled arm out the passenger window, a pistol in his fist.

I looked back down at Bratton—more specifically at his ring, bright gold against pudgy knuckles white from clutching the arm rest.

"Climb up on the seat and put on your seat belt."

Heath took another turn, the CEO tumbling to the right this time.

Great.

"Belt yourself in before you get killed," I yelled. It would save me time and effort, since I was planning to kill him later anyway, but my concern wasn't for him. Riding in the back with him rolling around was like being inside a pinball machine trying to dodge one hell of a heavy ball.

He reached for my outstretched hand just as Heath took another sharp corner. Bratton toppled to the other side, hitting my legs so hard that for a moment, I feared he'd broken my ankle.

Shadow enveloped the car, and I realized we were under the tracks of Chicago's elevated train.

I unhooked my belt and reached for Bratton. "Let me help."

He offered a beefy mitt. I grabbed it with both hands and yanked him up onto his seat. Lunging for the shoulder belt, I pulled it across him and latched it into place.

Heath hit the gas, the car surging forward, its motion pushing me on top of Bratton, my chest landing on his face.

"Oh God, I feel sick," he said, his words muffled by my naked breasts.

Shit. The ipecac.

Sometimes my timing really sucked.

I rolled off him.

The car screeched around another turn, its tail skidding, back tires hitting the curb. I flattened myself to the seat next to Bratton. Grabbing the seatbelt, I pulled it across my chest and secured it just as Heath took another sharp turn.

Now facing front, I could see through the windshield, although a part of me immediately wished I couldn't.

Heath was gunning the limo up a ramp and onto an expressway...an expressway where traffic was heading straight for us.

He met my gaze in the rear view mirror. "They would be *loco* to follow us, *bonita*, no?"

I said nothing, not sure if I was impressed or horrified.

Cars swerved one way and the other, skidding, crashing into their neighbors. Ahead, a pickup barreled straight at us, the driver either not paying attention, playing a demented game of chicken, or looking for a convenient way to end it all.

Heath veered to the side. Bratton slumped into my shoulder, holding his stomach, groaning.

I pushed him upright.

A screeching roar filled my ears, and almost before I could identify it as semi brakes locking up, I spotted the truck. It veered, jackknifed, then flipped onto its side, skidding toward us like a squeegee blade ready to wipe a window clean.

Bratton made a strangled sound deep in his throat. He slumped toward me, and I pushed him away.

If I was going to die, I didn't not want to do it covered in puke.

Heath slammed the brakes and cranked the wheel, pirouetting like some punk doing donuts in the high school parking lot.

"Go, go, go," I yelled despite myself.

He hit the gas and the limo's eight banger responded, flattening us against the seat, the squeal and smell of burning rubber filling the passenger compartment.

Flowing with traffic now and with an open road ahead, Heath gunned the engine. Sirens screamed, the sound audible above the whipping wind.

"Mr. Bratton?" Heath said. "Call Cullen. Tell him to have the plane ready and take off cleared."

Bratton didn't answer.

"Mr. Bratton?" I said.

Bratton leaned over and deposited his steak dinner all over his shoes.

"Take his phone, *bonita*. The number is under pilot."

I fished the phone from the pocket where I'd felt it earlier and did a quick search of recent calls. He'd taken four in the past two hours: one from Heath, one from his wife, and two noted simply as unidentified caller, one bearing the 631 area code I recognized as being from the eastern portion of Long Island, and one sporting Las Vegas's 702 area code.

The winning bid?

"You find the number, Simone?"

"Yeah. It's here." I quickly memorized the two unknown numbers and Heath's number. I could call Bratton's wife and tell her what a creep her husband was, but I was betting she already knew. As long as she was slated to inherit his fortune, I figured I was already doing her a favor.

I hit the number for Cullen.

He picked up on the first ring. "Mr. Bratton?"

"Heath says to have the plane ready and takeoff cleared."

"Who is this?"

"The entertainment."

"Let me speak to Mr. Bratton."

I held out the phone, and Bratton retched again.

"He can't talk," I said. "Something's come up."

Ditching the interstate just as the beat of police and news helicopters started to pound the air overhead, Heath slowed to a more normal pace, Football Face and his muscle-bound boss nowhere to be seen. I leaned my head back, breathed through my mouth, and prayed the ipecac was out of Bratton's system.

I was wrong. Before I could turn away, I couldn't help but wonder what possessed Bratton to eat what had to have been an entire bushel of peas. As I did, the John Lennon song inappropriately popped into my head.

All we are saying... is give peas a chance.

Between bouts of projectile hurling, we reached the airport. As I helped the CEO from the car—which was among the grossest things I'd ever had to do and I'd killed people in horrible ways—Heath spoke to the driver. "You keep Mr. Bratton out of this, and you will be well paid for your trouble. You were carjacked, no?"

"Yes, carjacked." The driver held his limp arm against his body, blood oozing from between the fingers of his other hand.

"*Sí, sí.* They shot you, raced through the streets, almost killed you, but you don't know who these men were."

"I, yes…I understand."

"And you will drive away from here before you call for help?"

"Yes."

"Good man."

Bratton pulled away from me and retched into the gutter.

Circling the limo, Heath gathered two small carry on suitcases from the trunk and stopped in front of me. "And what can I promise you, *mamacita*, for your discretion?"

I had perfected the art of crying on cue. A few thoughts about the death of my parents and desperation of my life in the years after, and the glare of the taillights of retreating traffic grew smeared by tears. "I can't… I'm… oh jesus, I'm so scared."

"They will not find you."

"You can promise me that? I saw them at the restaurant. They saw me."

"If you're careful…"

"Take me with you."

He smiled, as if my request was some private joke. "You want to go to Las Vegas?"

"It doesn't matter where we go. Please. I don't know who those men were, but all they'd have to do to find me is ask around at the restaurant. I go there all the time. Please." I turned up the volume, both in tears and in trembles.

"Very well, but before I take a beautiful woman like you to Sin City, you must make me a promise."

"Anything."

"Give me your word we will stay out of the wedding chapels. I fear you will bewitch me, and my heart will never again be my own."

I sniffled, laying it on thick, and for a moment I wondered who was playing whom.

Heath

Heath had to admit the woman had *cojones*. For her to come out and ask if she could come along to Vegas was not only audacious, it was inspired.

How could he resist a woman like that?

"Do you promise? No wedding chapels?"

Simone smiled through crocodile tears. "I do."

"See why I have to be careful around you, *querida*? You're dangerous."

She reached out to hug Heath. Normally he would have welcomed the contact, even though he knew it was outright manipulation, but this time he held out his palm.

"Later, Simone. As lovely as you are, you are wearing much of Bratton's supper. We should be able to find you a change of clothes on board."

The aircraft was waiting for them, an eight passenger Challenger 300, and it took little time to board. Heath led Simone into the back bedroom and showed her closet full of various outfits Bratton kept for his teenaged girls. Normally Heath felt a stab of pity whenever Bratton violated and humiliated a prostitute. Sex wasn't enough for him. *El chancho* enjoyed the power trip. The debasement.

But Heath did not believe Simone would be debased by any of the clothing she found. If she was an assassin, as Health believed, she would use her wardrobe to her advantage. To distract. To arouse. To control the situation. Had he not hopped into the driver's seat when he did, Heath had no doubt Simone would have.

Something special, this one.

Heath reminded his boss to turn off his cell phone, a task Bratton never failed to complain about, even though it was his own security at stake. Then Heath chose a seat near the front of the plane, next to Bratton's well-appointed wet bar, which boasted some of the best tequila Heath had ever had the opportunity to taste. Gran Patron Burdeos. He poured himself a hundred dollar shot into a brandy snifter and waited for Simone to get dressed.

Bratton settled into a seat near the restroom, a plastic soda cup cradled in his hands. Simone came out wearing a *seifuku*—a Japanese schoolgirl outfit. It was basically a tight-fitting sailor suit featuring a white and blue mini skirt and a low cut, cropped white top with a blue tie.

Heath let out a hiss of breath through his teeth. She'd chosen well.

Simone smiled demurely at him, then leaned over Bratton, handing him a tissue to wipe his mouth. As she did, she gave Heath a long peek at her breasts, braless under the tight top.

Muy bien.

Bratton stared blankly into the bottom of the cup, ignoring Simone.

Heath shook his head. If he ever got so sick that he didn't notice a woman like Simone with perfect cleavage in front of him, then he might as well be dead.

"Best to let him rest, *bonita*. Why don't you come up here and sit next to me?"

She settled into the almond leather seat facing him across a small table, and belted herself in. Minutes later, they were in the air without police making an unwelcome visit or the tower holding up plane.

In sparing the limo driver's life, Heath believed he had made the right call. He only hoped he'd feel the same way about Simone.   •

It was a dangerous thing to do; bringing her to Vegas, and perhaps not so wise to be tempting the devil, as his mother used to say. But the lack of an invitation wouldn't stop her from completing the job she was sent to do. This way, her desire to stay undercover would make her easier to control for as long as he needed.

And it would give him a chance to learn who had hired her.

He poured her Burdeos and refreshed his glass. The plane was cool, the air-conditioning on high, and Heath considered slipping off his jacket and offering it to her. But that would be like putting a sheet over a Degas.

"You can remove the pig tails, if you desire."

"Don't you think he'll notice?"

"I don't think he's noticing anything right now."

"So you don't like my youthful look?" She pouted, and playfully batted her eyelashes. "May I sit on your lap, Papa?"

"I told you, I like a strong woman."

"One with fire."

"One like you."

A smile crossed her lips, seeming genuine. "I don't think you can afford me."

"I'm sure I cannot. But my employer isn't in need of you right now, *bonita*, so you can't blame me for wanting to enjoy a little of your company on his dime. Perhaps we start with you telling me where you're from?"

"Do you want the truth? Or what the johns want to hear?"

"I want what you want to tell me. I find you fascinating."

"I'm from Chicago. Not so fascinating."

"I love Chicago. Did you grow up in the city?"

Her eyebrow rose. "You don't want to know about me."

"But, I do."

"You want to know what I'm after."

"So what are you after?"

"Money."

"I can't believe that's all. You could have taken the money like the driver and saved yourself much time."

"I told you, I was scared."

"Why is it I have trouble believing fear would stop you from anything?"

"I'm afraid of plenty of things."

"Name one."

"Drowning."

Heath thought of what he'd had to endure as part of his training. He had to wonder if Simone had gone through something similar. "That is a wise fear to have. Another?"

"Heights."

"Being in high places? Or falling from high places?"

"Falling. Actually the falling part is fine. It's the landing part that's scary."

"Did you know that is one of the few fears that even babies feel? They are born with it. It's instinct."

"Are you afraid of falling?"

"Only of falling hopelessly in love with you, *querida*."

"Does this Latin Lothario act work on many women?"

He sipped more tequila. "It is not an act. It is who I am."

"You interchange compliments and questions. It is something a pimp does."

For a moment, Heath bridled. He had pity for whores. He had nothing but hatred for pimps. But then he realized she'd managed to steer the conversation back to him, to put him on the defensive, and again he wondered where she'd gotten her training.

"Were you hurt?" he asked. "By a pimp?"

"I've been hurt in ways you can't imagine."

"Are you afraid of being hurt again? As you are of water and falling?"

CODENAME: CHANDLER — THE BEGINNING

Her brow crinkled. "I used to be afraid of catching a baseball. Not a good fear to have when your stepfather is a rabid fan."

"Cubs or White Sox?"

"Him? Sox."

"Let me guess, you like the Cubs."

"We didn't see eye to eye very often."

The way her lips tensed intrigued him. As if talking about her stepfather was akin to poking at a scar that was healed over but still tender deep inside. Real? Or an act?

"The fear, how did you overcome it?"

"I taught myself to juggle. Got really good. Never missed another one of his throws." She gave a light laugh and sipped her drink. "So what are you afraid of?"

"Ah, that is an easy one. Poverty."

"A real mercenary, huh?"

"I make sure I get what I need, just as you do. Unless you expect me to believe you are attracted to my employer for his good looks and charm."

She smiled. "Maybe I just wanted to get to know his bodyguard a little better."

He didn't even have to close his eyes to recall the scene in the limo… only this time he imagined her lips were wrapped around him. "Now you are toying with me, *mamacita*. I can't afford you, remember?"

"We're going to Vegas. Maybe you'll get lucky."

"I'm feeling lucky now." He reached over to the bar and pulled out a deck of cards. Watching Simone, he slipped them from the box and started shuffling. "You play poker, no?"

"Once or twice. Is that the one where I try to get a good pair?"

She leaned forward, giving Heath another glimpse of her breasts.

"Ah, you joke, but you are a shark. I can see it your eyes."

"I could say the same about you."

"*Sí*, yes. We are made for each other."

Chandler

> *"Patience is crucial," The Instructor said. "Doors might close in front of you, but remember if a window doesn't open, you can always kick out the glass."*

I smiled at Heath. With extensive training in reading the emotions of others, poker was my game, and I had to admit, the thought of matching wits with him gave me a little thrill. It also worried me.

Despite my training, I still wasn't sure how to read him. Half the time, I thought he might suspect me. The other half, I was certain he just wanted to get into my pants. Either way, the odds of completing my op were better if I went along, bided my time, and played him best I could until I got my shot at Bratton.

Heath smiled. "Name your game."

"It depends. What are we playing for?"

"We play one hand," Heath said. "If I win, I get to kiss you."

"And if I win?"

"You get to kiss me."

"Nice try. How about a hundred bucks?" After all, that's what call girls were after.

Heath frowned. "A hundred dollars a kiss? In Guadalajara, a hundred dollars would get me three women for the night, plus breakfast the next morning. And a tank of gas. And the car."

"But you aren't in Guadalajara. And I'm not one of those women."

Heath sighed, as if deeply pained.

"I can understand if you can't afford it," I said. "That fear of poverty and all."

He winked. "A hundred dollars it is. What game?"

For pure strategy, poker was the game. Over time the better player would win, even if the cards didn't favor them. I could play poker like a bitch in heat. But playing with Heath, one on one, would be tricky. If he was as good as I suspected, we'd be so into each other's heads I'd lose sight of my main goal—killing Bratton and getting the package.

No, with Heath a game of straight odds would be better.

"Blackjack," I said.

His frown deepened. "Blackjack? That's a game for old maids."

"No, that would be old maid."

"*Que?*"

"Old maid is a card game."

"I would rather play that."

"With blackjack, the house has the better odds."

Under Heath's breath I heard him mutter, "*Ventiuna con Rinconete y Cortadillo.*"

It was a reference to Cervantes, the author of Don Quix-ote. In the particular story Heath mentioned, two cheaters play twenty-one, which was one of the first historical mentions of the card game.

That a Mexican bodyguard knew this intrigued me. But a Chicago hooker wouldn't know it, so I didn't say anything.

"In or out?" I asked.

Part of me was hoping he'd balk.

Another part of me was hoping he'd go for it.

"*Sí*, yes, we play blackjack. But if I win, that better be one heck of a kiss, *bonita*."

He let me cut the cards, then dealt. Two cards each. Both of mine face up, only one of his face up.

I had an eight and a king. Eighteen. The goal was to beat the dealer, by getting as close to twenty-one as possible without going over. The trick was trying to guess what the dealer had, since the player could only see one of his cards. If the player thought the dealer had a better hand, she could ask for another card.

Although the dealer had a slight odds advantage, he also didn't have any choices to make. He had to keep hitting until he totaled at least seventeen. Since face cards were worth ten points, and there were sixteen tens in a deck of fifty-two, it wasn't too hard to guess what the dealer was holding in a single deck game.

Especially since I knew how to count cards.

Heath had a six showing. I stayed with my hand. He flipped over a jack, for a total of sixteen, and had to take a hit according to the rules. He gave himself a seven. Twenty-three. Bust.

A hundred bucks for the *mamacita*.

He dealt again. I got a king and an ace. Instant blackjack. He had two tens, and busted with a five.

Two hundred dollars.

"I do not like this game."

"Would you prefer I deal?"

Heath demurred, dealing again. This time he gave me a six and an eight, and he had a queen showing.

Fourteen wasn't the best hand. But there were thirty-eight cards left in the deck, and only nine or ten of those were tens. Chances were pretty good that I'd draw a low card.

I hit. Got a six. Heath flipped a jack. Tie.

"What do we do for draws?" he said. "I can kiss your neck for fifty dollars?"

I shuddered, hoping I concealed it. The right guy kissing my neck made me weak-kneed.

"It's a wash, you deal again."

This time he dealt me an ace and a five. Aces could equal either one or eleven, meaning I had a six or a sixteen. Sixteen wasn't a good hand, but with an ace the odds said I should take a hit.

Heath, however, also had a six showing.

I stayed. He turned over a queen, had to hit, and busted with a seven.

Three hundred dollars.

"I think it is time for a shuffle, no?" Heath said.

I shrugged as if I didn't care. But I watched his hands closely and caught the son of a bitch dealing from the bottom of the deck.

He was good. Magician-level good. But I knew the same trick and spotted it instantly.

This guy wants to kiss me so badly he'd cheat?

I thought about calling him on it and played out the scenario in my mind. He could admit it, or claim innocence. No harm in either. But if he got angry, that could compromise my mission.

I let it go.

Heath dealt me a twenty and gave himself twenty-one.

"I am out a lot of money, Simone. Make this good."

"How about I give you a hundred dollars back instead?"

I held out one of the hundreds he'd passed to me. His move was snake-quick, so fast he startled me.

In one fluid motion he snatched my wrist and pulled me around the small airplane table and into his lap. I had my hand on my inner thigh, where I'd replaced the AmEx knife while dressing in the schoolgirl outfit, and I was ready to use it, but Heath's eyes weren't angry or threatening.

Jesus. He looks like a lovesick Pepe le Pew.

"You have earned your money, *bonita*. I will not take that from you. But I will take this."

He brought his lips to mine, barely brushing them, close enough for me to feel his breath. One arm had found its way around my waist, and the other lightly brushed my knee. I could smell the tequila on him, a lingering bit of aftershave, and that male smell that I knew was juiced with pheromones.

Heath took my lower lip in both of his, gently, then worked over to the corner of my mouth. I turned my head to meet his, but then his lips were on my ear, and his tongue made the faintest trail down along my neck.

Uh-oh.

His lips brushed my chin, and his mouth opened, as did mine. My tongue rose to meet his, but didn't find it—he'd pulled back. I watched his eyes twinkle in a smile, and then the sneaky little Latino somehow got one of his hands between my legs and began to gently caress me on the outside of my panties just as his tongue met mine with a palpable shock.

My first instinct was to swat his hand away, but I stopped myself. Chandler might be uncomfortable with a move this forward, but Simone would be used to it. And I had to admit the more he caressed and kissed, the more I was beginning to enjoy being Simone.

I couldn't tell if he was better with his tongue or his fingers. The sensations of being explored in both places at once using the exact same motions were as powerful as they were confusing.

I might have moaned a little.

I might have pressed against him.

I don't know if it was the best first kiss of all time, but I would have nominated it for the semi-finals.

And then I gave him a firm but harmless nip on his lower lip, causing him to pull back enough for me to say, "Okay, done."

He smiled, then did something outrageously erotic to me with his thumb. "Done? Your body does not seem to be done, *Chiquita.* It seems like a car just warming up."

I exercised a degree of self-control never before attained in all of female history and said, "The kiss is over, Heath. If you want more, you have to win."

"But I do want more." He moved to kiss my neck again.

I pinched his chest, hard. "Then play the game."

He went from Pepe le Pew eyes to Droopy Dog eyes, and then he had me twirled back to my feet like I was his tango partner. After holding my hand longer than needed, he picked up the cards.

"My turn to deal," I said, sitting down.

"But lady luck was finally smiling upon me."

"Maybe she still will, with me dealing."

Again he placed his hands upon mine, stroking my wrist like he'd stroked me elsewhere. "If you deal, we raise the stakes. Five thousand dollars."

"Against what?" I asked.

"A night with you."

"Do you even have five thousand dollars?"

He shrugged. "We are going to Las Vegas. A man can get lucky, no?"

I'd known few men like Heath.

There were the hot and heavy wham-bam types. The shy ones who didn't have a clue. The over achievers who went down on a girl for so long it became boring. The quick and the fat and the ones who couldn't get hard.

And then there were the kind who treated a woman like an expensive instrument to be played, a gourmet dish to be savored. The ones who truly loved to make love, in every possible sense of the term. They were the fun ones. The ones who made your heart flutter with a look. The ones who made you wet with a single kiss.

Heath was a three day vacation in a ritzy hotel suite, stopping the sex only long enough for more room service champagne and strawberries. What he wasn't was a man to fool around with on an op.

I sometimes had sex on missions, but it was with the target, and although I was able to respond physically it was perfunctory at best. The goal was the hit, not the orgasm. This was a job. A job I was very good at. But I kept it separate from my private life, and never, ever mixed the two.

Heath would have to be the one that got away. Or I'd have to kill him. Either way, our chance encounter wasn't meant to end in a ritzy hotel suite.

My mission, and my focus, was Bratton. And Bratton is where my attention would stay.

"Agreed," I said. Five grand didn't mean much to me. I was well compensated for my service. But maybe it would be a big enough sum to knock the ardor out of the playboy bodyguard. And while he cried in his tequila, I could work on Bratton.

Sorry, Heath. Destiny is a real jerk sometimes.

I did a false shuffle, known as a riffle, riffle, strip. It looked like I was mixing the cards, but they were exactly where I wanted them to be.

I purposely dealt Heath a nineteen.

I had a face card up. My down card was ten. Five grand to the very horny Chiquita. I went to turn my card up, and Heath placed his hand on mine.

"What?" I asked.

"I will take a card."

"You're hitting on nineteen? No one hits on nineteen."

"I have no choice. For some reason I suspect you have a twenty." He trailed his fingers down to mine, then laced them. His thumb found my palm, and began the same movement it had performed between my legs. And I'd be damned if it didn't feel like he was touching me there all over again.

"So all I can do," he breathed, "is pray that lady luck gives me a two and a night with you that I promise neither of us will ever forget."

"You're crazy."

He continued to stroke my hand, and I knew if he kept it up I'd come.

"Crazy to want to make you weep with passion? To see your face when it is so devastated by pleasure it is even more beautiful than it is now? To explore every inch of your body until you plead for me to stop because you can't take any more? Have you ever begged a man to stop, *bonita*? Begged him because you thought you had no more to give, because you were so sensitive the ecstasy was almost pain, only to have him coax more from you until you were sure you would explode?"

"No," I said, barely a whisper, feeling my need throb as he released my hand.

Then I dealt from the bottom of the deck and gave Heath a two, cursing myself as I did it.

Chandler

> *"Sex is a weapon," The Instructor said. "As such, it requires practice, training, and knowledge of when to use it. You never point a gun at anyone you don't intend to shoot."*

We agreed to make good on the debt sometime after Bratton's business in Las Vegas was over. Then Heath turned down the charm a notch, the cards were put away, and my libido returned to status quo. Our conversation meandered to travel. He'd been to almost as many countries as I had. Apparently, before becoming Bratton's bodyguard, he'd done some mercenary work. Odd, because though he seemed capable, he didn't have the gung-ho mentality I normally associated with mercs. If anything, he seemed more like a spy than a grunt.

I admitted to visiting France and Spain, two places a high class Chicago call girl might go on vacation, and that lead to a lengthier discussion of bullfighting, which Heath apparently was passionate about, even to the point of participating as an *aficionado práctico*, or amateur bullfighter, and running in Pamplona.

Bratton woke, and I administered to him, sneaking another dose of the ipecac into a glass of cola this time and sending him back to retching in the tiny bathroom. If Bratton recovered, I'd likely be spending long hours at the casino, maybe only stopping for a quickie, not a lot of time to arrange for his death. If he was sick, he would have to stay in his hotel room, isolated and helpless.

Just where I wanted him.

We landed at McCarran International, and a car was waiting to whisk us to our hotel. I hadn't been in Vegas for a while, and judging from the view out the limo window, it was bigger and brighter and more boisterous than ever. Neon glared in the night, highlighting everything from the pyramid at the Luxor—its beam of light shooting into the sky—to the spires of mythical Camelot that made up the hotel Excalibur, to the skyline of New York, New York, complete with circling rollercoaster. The Bellagio's famous fountain danced across the street from the Paris Hotel's Eiffel Tower. Finally passing Caesar's Palace's columns and the volcano at the Mirage, we reached the Venetian.

The resort itself was built to be a miniature Venice, yet too perfect, too clean, the bridges crisp and new stretching over dyed azure canals. An Italy built exclusively for the rich.

We turned after the replica of the Campanile Bell Tower and entered the resort drive, crossing over a bridge, traffic slowing. Heath lowered a window a crack, letting in a wave of desert-heated night air along with a wisp of *O Sole Mio* from one of the gondoliers on the outdoor canal.

"A tragic song. One of heartbreak. Do you know the words?"

About to answer, I caught myself. Just because Chandler was multilingual didn't mean Simone the prostitute could say the same. I shook my head.

"It is about a poor soul thinking back to the time he was in love, when he had a moment of happiness, before his lover betrayed him."

"That is sad."

"You have no idea."

45

"What's the hold up?" Bratton shouted to the driver just as the car resumed.

We continued over the first bridge and under a copy of Ponte di Rialto, the famous bridge that spanned the Grand Canal in Venice, finally reaching the hotel's expansive, cobblestoned *porte-cochere*. Chandeliers hung from the ceiling of the portico along with reproductions of Italian frescoes framed by gold molding. Even at night, the area bustled with several bell boys dressed in black and white striped duds matching the outfits of the gondoliers.

We didn't have much luggage, I carried nothing but my little purse, and Bratton and Heath only had one carryon size suitcase each, and it didn't take long for us to unload ourselves from the car, through five steps of oven-like heat, and enter the Venetian's lobby.

The first thing I noticed was the scent. Despite the size and throngs of people visiting this time of year, a sweet, floral fragrance tickled the air. A globe fountain dominated the middle of the lobby, water gurgling and sluicing down into the base below. The marble floors held a pattern that played with the eyes, and a map of Venice stretched along the wall behind the reservation desks. As in the portico, the ceiling was covered with more frescoes framed in gold.

"I will arrange for the rooms." Heath said and broke away

I watched him cross to the reservation desk, and start chatting up a blonde who worked at the hotel. He leaned toward her, his body language all flirt, and to my shame, for a second, I felt a tweak of jealousy.

It had obviously been too long since I'd last been on a date.

I didn't have a steady social life. Those in my business never did. But I tried to get out now and then, pick up an attractive guy in a bar, and have a little fun. They never knew my real name, never saw where I lived, and never heard from me again, but it was something, a way to feel close to another human being, a way to wear off a little sexual energy. But it had been a long time since I'd had an opportunity to let loose.

I'd dealt Heath that winning hand in a moment of weakness.

Now that I'd cooled down and was on my way to the privacy of Bratton's suite, either as prostitute or nursemaid, it didn't seem like I'd be able to fulfill that particular debt. And I had to admit, it made me feel a little crabby.

"How are you feeling now?" I asked my john/patient/victim.

He shot me a look of contempt, as if I wasn't even worthy of an answer.

Charming man.

While he was ignoring me, I took a peek at the gold ring, now illuminated by a chandelier the size of a small helicopter. Brushed gold, the band was set with a large ruby surrounded by diamond chips. The more I thought about it, the more certain I was that he wasn't wearing it when he pawed me up the first time. He had to have picked it up at the bank.

So what about this ring of power was so special that Jacob would send me on my own little Frodo errand? Or was the ring superfluous, and the real package was tucked into his wallet?

I supposed it didn't matter. My orders were to make it look like a robbery. I'd take it all.

Moments later, Heath returned, three key card portfolios in his hand. "This way," he said, and we followed him to an elevator, the bellboy trailing behind with the two small carryon bags belonging to Bratton and Heath.

We left the lobby and walked through the Venetian's Grand Colonnade with marble floors and a ceiling reminiscent of the Sistine Chapel, and then we were in the casino, every bit as much of a work of art as the rest of the resort. Like the lobby, recessed ceiling panels bore frescos straight out of the renaissance. Marble floors danced with beautiful patterns, and restaurants of every delicious variety encircled the enormous gaming floor.

In fiction, secret agents, gambling, and subterfuge seemed to go together and spies often seemed to find themselves in casinos participating in high stakes games. But unlike my fictional counterparts, I was not a fan of casinos. Not because I didn't like a little gambling now and then, but because there were too many cameras.

They were everywhere, above each gaming table, in between each row of slot machines, at every choke point in every hall way or escalator. They were meant to keep an eye out for cheats, but they served to record every action and every face on the floor.

I was useful to the government not just for my training, but because I didn't officially exist. I could take care of a target, then fade into the landscape, safe, free, anonymous. Having my image recorded by the dozens of cameras at any one time made me uneasy.

Bypassing the neon and bells, we went straight for the guest elevators.

When we reached our floor, I focused on the double door at the end, assuming that was Bratton's suite. Heath stopped half way down the hall and handed me a portfolio containing a key card.

"And this is for?"

"Your suite." He motioned to the door.

"I assumed…" I glanced at Bratton.

The man didn't even look my way. "I'll let Rodriguez know when I want you."

Not my preference. Also not much I could say about it. "Are you sure?"

Without answering, he continued down the hall with the bellboy.

"I am sorry you are so far down the hall, *bonita*," Heath said. "But you really didn't want to spend all your time with that man, did you?"

I gave a shrug. Of course I didn't. I just wanted to search him and kill him, not necessarily in that order.

"He's paying. Whatever he wants is fine by me," I said out loud.

"Good girl." He pulled a stack of bills from his wallet and shoved them into my hand. "There are shops on the second floor. Treat yourself."

"Thank you."

"You can return that after you have a new outfit. Something less Japanese cosplay, more sin city."

"Sequins and a feather boa? Or what do you prefer? You won our bet."

Couldn't hurt to keep his mind on me and off bodyguarding his boss.

"I prefer a woman to wear nothing but her own perspiration, which I have coaxed from every pore in her body."

Who was distracting whom here?

Heath smiled. "And now I must check the room for Mr. Bratton. I will see you later, no?"

"Of course."

Standing at the door, I watched Heath continue down the hall. My assignment had just gotten a lot tougher. Judging from the CEO's waning interest, he wasn't going to send for me, that much was clear.

I was going to have to find another way to get to him.

After closing the suite's door, I did a quick bug and camera check to satisfy my inner paranoia—a nifty app on my new phone—then called Jacob and engaged in our little security dance.

"The job's done?"

"No."

"It's been hours. What went wrong?"

"Nothing. I convinced him to take me back to his hotel room, but his hotel ended up being in Vegas."

"The Venetian."

"How did… ah. The phone. It has a tracker?"

"No. I don't allow them to be tracked. There's a reason for it. But I turned on the camera when you were in the lobby. Did you use it to sweep for bugs?"

"Don't you know that as well?"

"I have other things to do than monitor your every move, Chandler."

Ouch. Touchy.

"Bratton is already losing interest, but I think I can get at him through the bodyguard."

"So the bodyguard isn't posing a problem?"

"Nothing I can't handle. In fact, it will be my pleasure."

"Let me guess. He's good looking."

"It's as if Antonio Banderas had a younger brother."

"He does."

"He does?"

"His name is Javier. But I'm pretty sure he's not working as a bodyguard for Dominic Bratton."

"You really do know everything, don't you, Jacob?"

"Just doing my job."

"Glad to hear it, because I have a couple of phone numbers for you. Unidentified callers of Bratton's."

"Shoot."

I recited the numbers. "I'm betting the Vegas one is our buyers."

"Nice work, Chandler."

"And while you're in a generous frame of mind, I need a bit more from you."

"Such as?"

"At least a dozen cameras just captured me walking in with him."

"I'll take care of it. Anything else?"

"Wish me luck."

"You're in Las Vegas, Chandler. Home of Lady Luck. What could possibly go wrong?"

Heath

Heath moved through Bratton's suite, clearing each room, as was his usual practice. He didn't find anyone hiding in wait. Only the standard classic furnishings, a sunken living room with a piano, a bathtub big enough for four, three giant televisions, and an amazing view of the Strip. Nothing but the best for Bratton, and more comfort and opulence than most people in the world saw in a lifetime.

Heath had been born in America, but he hadn't always lived in this rich and hedonistic country. In the place he'd spent most of his growing up years, Tijuana, Mexico, life was much different. And every time he visited Las Vegas, he was reminded of the first time he'd used his birth certificate to cross the border into the United States, only to be so dumbfounded by the wealth and glitz that he could do nothing but stare.

He no longer stared, not even in a place like Las Vegas, but he hadn't forgotten that night, either. He would never forget.

"Rodriguez?"

"Yes, Mr. Bratton?"

The CEO settled himself in front of the television, arms stretched along the back of the sofa, the golden ring on his finger reflecting the colors of the television screen.

"That woman...where did you find her?"

"My usual sources."

"Well, you might want to talk to those sources."

"Why is that?"

"There's something not right about her."

"Not right?"

"You know, there's something that just doesn't feel right. Like she's not who she seems."

Could Bratton have seen through Simone? Heath had to admit, he was surprised. He'd never known the man to be aware of anything or anyone but himself. He might have an instinct for business, but all others were lacking. "You believe she's hiding something?"

"Yes."

"What?"

"I think she's older. Maybe even twenty-two or twenty-three."

Heath almost laughed out loud. "Is that all?"

"Isn't that enough?"

"*Sí, sí.* She must have lied about her age. It's outrageous."

"Damn straight, it is. And I'm holding you responsible. Get rid of her and find me someone young. They have high schools in Las Vegas, right? Parents willing to lend out their daughters for a little cash? Or young girls on the streets? I want one that's clean, though."

Bratton disgusted him. He was like so many rich, entitled men. So much like Heath's father. *El Diablo* himself.

"I'm not sure there will be time. You have a meeting coming up tonight, no? With your buyer?"

"Ah shit, yeah." Bratton cocked his wrist to look at his watch. "But not for another three hours."

"I'll need to prepare. How many men will he have?"

"He says two, so probably three or four."

"And you didn't think to tell me this sooner?"

"We're meeting in the middle of the casino. How dangerous can it be? There are cameras everywhere."

"Middle where?"

"Roulette table."

"In two hours?"

"Two and a quarter, to be exact." He tilted his head back and grinned at Heath. "And then I'll have a few extra million in gambling money."

Heath eyed the ring on Bratton's left hand. He'd been hoping the group from Venezuela would come up with the high bid in Bratton's little auction. After all the time he'd spent helping Uncle Sam engineer the coup against Chavez, he knew how this radical splinter group thought, the moves they would make. Even their desperate attack on the limo in Chicago hadn't totally caught him by surprise.

But the Russians were a mystery to him, and since this was a personal project and not a mission for the red, white, and blue, Heath didn't have any resources other than his own.

He had to take care of this and get out before they arrived. "I'll handle everything."

"Good. I'll also need a new pair of shoes."

"Very well."

"And the girl. I want her waiting for me when the deal is over. I want to celebrate."

"I will arrange for it."

Bratton stretched out his feet, plunking them on the table and resting his head back, nice and relaxed. "I want a young one for real this time. Real young."

Heath stopped directly behind him. "*Sí*, Mr. Bratton. That I know."

"And she should be pretty. Fresh. A virgin would be good. Nothing better than busting a cherry, teaching her how to suck."

"Don't worry, Mr. Bratton. I'll make sure you get exactly what you deserve."

"You'd better. It's your job."

"*Sí*." And now that Heath knew the time and place of Bratton's meeting, it was a job he didn't need anymore.

Heath leaned forward over the back of the sofa. Faster than Bratton's brain could function, he snaked his right arm around the CEO's neck, pinching the man's double chins in the V of his elbow and grabbing his left arm below his biceps. Slapping his left palm to the back of Bratton's head, he forced the *cabron's* head down as he pulled his right arm against the man's throat in a choke hold.

The position could be used two ways, both to cut off blood to the brain or air to the lungs. Heath went for the blood, compressing Bratton's carotid arteries in his neck until little could eek through.

Bratton lashed out with his legs, shoes clanging against the coffee table, tipping it over. His hands came up, clawing at Heath's arms, raking in the air for his face.

Heath held him fast. He struggled for only a few seconds, the movements getting more sluggish until they stopped completely, Bratton's brain shutting down, his muscles softened, slumping into unconsciousness.

Heath held him for several minutes longer, and then released him with a sharp twist, breaking the man's neck just to be sure.

For a moment, he stared at Dominic Bratton's body, waiting for some kind of emotion that never came. As many times as he'd visualized killing Bratton over the past weeks, he didn't get much satisfaction from it now. The man was not a challenge. And as much as he disliked him, he didn't feel the need for vengeance.

It was the end of an annoyance, like swatting a buzzing mosquito, no more.

Turning away, Heath walked to the bathroom, gathered a towel and cloth, then returned to the body. He washed the CEO's hands, scrubbed under his fingernails, and lathered up the soap until the golden ring slid free before toweling him off.

Next he took Bratton's wallet, fat with cash and credit cards, slipped it into his pocket, then washed up his own arms. He had a few scratches from Bratton's death grip, and carefully rolled his sleeves down to hide them. Then, wadded up towels in hand, he started for the door.

Heath was reaching for the knob when a knock sounded. He stepped to the side and resisted the urge to peer through the peephole. "Who is it?"

"Simone."

She was here sooner than he'd guessed. A few seconds later, he would be gone and she would be a pleasant memory.

Now she was an obstacle; a beautiful and deadly one.

He opened the door. "*Dios mio*, look at you."

She no longer pretended to be a young girl. Now dressed in a pair of black jeans, sandals, and a blue silk blouse, she looked casual and expensive and good enough to eat. She held a bottle of Patron Platinum in one hand and two snifters in the other. Not quite Burdeos, but still a step above. "Sorry to bother you, but I was concerned about Dominic."

"Ah, yes. I bet you were."

"How is he feeling?"

"Not well. A sore throat, I'm afraid. He's staying in for the rest of the night, *bonita*."

"Staying in? Then shouldn't I—"

"No, no. He doesn't wish to see anyone."

"Not anyone, or not me?"

He pressed his lips into an apologetic line. "He has decided that you are older than you seemed."

"I told you I should have left the pigtails in."

"*Sí*, and you were right. But what's done is done. Still you are in a nice hotel and have a nice suite, no?"

"It's beautiful."

"So this whole experience, it's not so bad. You have a pleasant vacation, try your hand at some blackjack for real, and you don't have to see Mr. Bratton again."

"In that case…" Holding up the bottle, she handed him a snifter and shot him a coy smile that made his blood pressure step up a notch. "Want to share?"

"I thought you brought that for Mr. Bratton. It is an expensive gift for a bodyguard. I hate to see you throw away all your money."

"If it makes you feel better, I charged it to my room. So you can thank Mr. Bratton for it, not me."

Heath let a smile creep over his lips. "You never cease to arouse me."

"Good. Because I was also hoping I could settle up my blackjack debt."

Stepping out of Bratton's suite, Heath closed the door behind him. He needed to disappear before the Russians arrived. With work left to do and only two hours until the meeting, he might be cutting it close, but the risk would be worth it and not just because he'd wanted to bed this woman since he first laid eyes on her. It would also give him a chance to tie up a few loose ends.

The first: discovering who Simone worked for.

The second: Simone herself.

"I was hoping you would feel that way, *querida*, because I am in the mood for a challenge."

Chandler

> "In the world of an assassin, there is no place for mercy," The Instructor said. "Strike first, strike hard, and strike lethally. Kill or be killed. There is no other way."

Heath zigged to the side and tossed a couple of towels into a maid's cart before leading me to his suite one door over.

Within striking distance of Bratton's.

All I had to do was take Heath out and get my hands on his key card, and this op would be as good as in the bag.

Heath's suite was much larger than mine. We crossed an Italian marble foyer and stepped into a carpeted dining area.

Beyond I could see a sitting room looking out over the bright lights of the Strip, and to the right, an open doorway led to the bedroom.

"I'm pleased with the Platinum, but would you prefer something else?" He gestured to the wet bar and held out his hand for the booze.

"The Platinum is fine. I'll pour. Would you mind getting some ice?"

"You are not going to put ice in good tequila."

I gave him a smile. "Of course not. The ice is for something else."

As I'd hoped, he grabbed the ice bucket off the bar and made for the door immediately.

So far, so good.

I fished my mascara out of my purse, twisted off the cover, and tapped a good dose of powder into one of the highball glasses. Flunitrazepam, more commonly known as Rohypnol, roofies, or the date rape drug, came in pill form, but to get the substance to dissolve quickly, grinding the tablets into a powder was necessary. The pills were commonly dyed blue to prevent people from sneaking it into an unsuspecting victim's drink, but Jacob had gotten me the uncolored variety, and he'd done such a good job of turning the pills to powder, that they dissolved as soon as I splashed tequila into Heath's glass.

Flunitrazepam acted as a hypnotic, inducing sleep, but it also had the nifty side effect of causing anterograde amnesia. With the dose that I'd given him, Heath would sleep for a good long while and have a hard time remembering what happened after he ingested the drug. Instead of having to kill him, I would merely leave him with a bad hangover.

Just as I was pouring a healthy shot into a second glass, the door rattled, and Heath returned. He passed me, heading straight into the bedroom, and set the ice bucket on the nightstand.

I followed with both drinks and handed him his glass.

"To debts paid," I said, raising my drink.

"To a challenge." He reached up and unfastened the buttons of my blouse with one hand, spreading the silk open and revealing my bare skin. Then instead of drinking, he dipped his finger in the tequila and circled a nipple.

My body tightened, chills fanning out over my body.

"So responsive." He followed with his mouth, warmth chasing the alcohol's cool, first soft with his tongue, then sharp with his teeth.

An involuntary squeak issued from my throat.

"You like that, don't you?" He dipped his finger again and started playing the game with my other breast.

At this rate, it would take him forever to finish his drink and start to feel the effects of the flunitrazepam. But with his mouth doing delicious things to me, I was having trouble convincing myself a small delay was a bad thing.

"It killed me to see Bratton's hands on you when I knew you were meant for me."

As if to prove it, he skimmed his fingers up my side, over my chest, and cradled the back of my head in his hand. Then he claimed my mouth.

His touch was gentle. His kiss was not.

He pressed hard against me, hungry, demanding, as if he wanted everything I had to give and still it wouldn't be enough.

I tangled my tongue with his, the kiss more fight than tenderness, more desperate than loving. I fitted my body hard against him, every inch, and clawed his tie free with one hand. The buttons on his shirt came next, until we were finally standing skin to skin.

Next I went for his pants. My drink still in one hand, his fly took longer than I liked, and by the time I tried to ease it down, his erection pressed tight against the zipper. I lowered it as much as I could, and then reached inside and pulled him free.

I rubbed my abdomen against him and moved my hand to the back of his pants, as if to push them down his legs. When I slipped the wallet from his pocket, he didn't seem to notice.

Moaning, he pulled away from me. "Drink."

I downed the rest of my tequila and handed him the empty snifter.

Carrying my glass back to the bar in the dining room, he tipped back his head and downed his tequila, and I tucked the wallet between the cushions of a nearby chair.

He returned with a filled glass and gave it to me. In his other hand, he held the bottle. "It is more convenient this way, no?"

We each took a swig, then he set down both glass and bottle next to the ice and kissed me.

The taste of him mingled with the bite of tequila, and before I could think about it, our kiss had again taken on a force of its own.

Heat.

Hunger.

Desperation.

I wanted more.

I wanted everything.

When Heath finally pulled away, we were both out of breath. "You kiss like you are on fire, no? Are you on fire, bonita?"

He didn't wait for my answer; instead he swept his hands up my sides and skimmed my open blouse off my shoulders. My jeans came next, and my panties. Then he took off his own clothes, quickly and efficiently.

I watched him undress. He was as fit as I was, defined and lean, almost as many scars and miscellaneous scrapes and scratches, and I felt a pressing need to touch every part of him. As far as sex drives went, mine had always been strong, but I was still surprised at my visceral reaction. I often felt the need for sex after completing an op. But sex in the middle of an op, at least sex with a man I really wanted to sleep with, was a bit more unusual. Whether it was the adrenaline or the man that had me this turned on was hard to say, but Heath was right.

I was on fire.

This time when I kissed him, I took him in my hands. He was already hard, and I reveled in the size of him, the weight. I pushed him backward until he hit the bed. Letting out a laugh, he sat on the mattress.

I sank to my knees, edged between his legs, and captured him with my mouth. Taking him deep into my throat, I moved my tongue down the underside of his shaft then slowly pulled back until I was flicking at the tip. All the while, I watched him, looking directly into his eyes, showing him how much I wanted him.

I knew many women disliked giving head, but I loved it. There was nothing more exciting, more empowering, than looking into a man's eyes and knowing I had complete control. That for as long as I wanted, he was not only my plaything but my willing slave. The power rush was a turn on with normal men.

With Heath it made me feel invincible.

I circled him with tongue and lips then devoured him again. The third time, I brought my hand to him, stroking him, fondling his balls. I took an ice cube from the bucket and slipped it into my mouth, then took him as well, working the cold around him, over him, and then warming him again with my mouth. I arched my back and slipped him between my breasts, moving up and down his length, the tip of him emerging only to sink back down.

His eyes looked glazed, the muscles of his jaw slack. He let out a moan, a muffled *querida*, and several nasty curses in Spanish.

He grasped my shoulders, lifted me up onto his lap, and fitted my body over his. I sank down onto him, more than wet, more than ready, and as I took in his full length, an orgasm seized my muscles and shuddered through me.

But I didn't stop. He wouldn't let me.

He thrust up into me as I plunged down onto him. As the first orgasm subsided, another built. Sweat slicked my skin and stung the corners of my eyes. My breasts bounced with our movement, and he nipped and licked one nipple then the other.

I could feel his muscles tense, feel him start to shake, to shudder, then he grabbed hold of me and buried his face in my chest.

I clung to him, held him, shaking as hard as he was. Then our breathing slowed, and I could feel him relax inside me.

For long time he was still, and I wondered if he'd finally succumbed to the flunitrazepam. I kissed his forehead. "Heath?"

"Just regaining my strength. You took it out of me." He rolled over and laid me on the bed, my head on the pillows. Stretching length to length, he kissed me deep and slow. He littered kisses down my neck and over my chest. "You have bewitched me, no? I need to taste all of you, *querida*, see all, so I can remember."

Taste and see? Sure. Remember? Not so much.

He kissed me again, and then pushed himself up from the bed. Picking up my glass from the nightstand, he handed it to me, grabbed the bottle for himself, and took a chug.

I settled for a sip. Heath should be feeling his roofie cocktail pretty strongly by now, and I needed to keep my mind sharp, not clouded with alcohol. I hadn't eaten since the appetizer in Chicago, and I could already feel my first drink sending a warm shimmer through my muscles.

Or maybe that was Heath's still-hungry stare.

"Open, *bonita*. I want to see you."

I spread my legs for him, cold air rushing over heated skin.

For a long time, he just stood there, exploring me as intimately with his gaze as he had with fingers and tongue and cock.

I had a great body, if you didn't count the many scars I'd earned over the years, and I liked the feeling of showing it off to men. But somehow this was different, hotter, more intense than any exhibitionist thrill I'd ever had. I felt out of breath, maybe even a little dizzy.

It had been way too long since I'd had this much fun. I wanted more. "Come back to bed."

"In a moment, *querida*. Right now I am too mesmerized by your beauty to move."

"You're so full of shit."

"Am I?"

I was starting to get impatient. "Yes. Now get back here and fuck me."

"So demanding."

"Afraid you can't keep up?"

"I've already given you three orgasms, my greedy *chica*."

"Afraid you can't manage four?"

"I can manage more than that."

"Prove it."

He took another swig from the bottle, then mouth still fresh with tequila, he climbed between my open thighs and brought his mouth to me.

The first touch of his tongue sent ice through me, then as he slowly licked and teased, the sensation turned to flame.

It had been a long time, all right, and I felt giddy with sex, drunk with it.

I leaned my head back, savoring the warmth of his mouth, the grit of whiskers against sensitive skin, the fat, lazy strokes of his lips and tongue. The pressure built, only for him to pull away, and then kiss and caress and torment until it built again.

Another orgasm claimed me, coaxing a scream from my lips before I could choke it back.

"You are so beautiful." Heath laughed, a warm sound, a nice sound. He moved up my body, grasped my chin with one hand, and claimed my lips.

His mouth tasted like the two of us, mingled until we were one, and for a second, I let myself give in; to the kiss, to the man, to the longing I tried never to acknowledge.

Then I felt the handcuff click around my wrist.

I yanked my arm back, but he'd already fastened the bracelet to the bed.

How did I not notice that?

"What? You don't like your kinky game now?"

Of course, the handcuffs were from my purse, the ones I'd intended to use on Bratton if the need arose. I eyed Heath. If he passed out, and I was still cuffed to the bed like this…

"Let me go, Heath."

"You don't like?"

"No. I only use those if the john likes to be tied up."

"Where did you get this?" He smoothed a hand over my abdomen and traced the small, white scar on the lower part of my belly button.

It took me a second to figure out what he was asking, my thoughts sluggish, as if trying to fight through bats of cotton jamming my skull.

Too long.

He caught hold of my free hand, and before I could react, that wrist was secured to the other side of the headboard, this time with his tie.

My head swam, dizzy, and my tongue felt clumsy in my mouth. All along I hadn't been reacting to the booze or the sex or Heath's charm.

The bastard had drugged me.

I wondered if it would be hypocritical of me to feel outraged.

"What did you give me?" I asked.

He straddled me, sitting on my thighs, making it impossible for me to move. "You should know, *mamacita*. Whatever it was came from the glass you poured for me."

Memory flashed like pictures in my mind. Heath painting my nipples with tequila. Heath taking my glass and downing his as he walked back to the dining room for more.

Only he hadn't actually drunk it.

"Fuck."

I craned my neck to glimpse the tumbler on the nightstand. There was still a good amount of tequila left. I hadn't had much. Maybe I could fight the effects, keep from losing consciousness.

"Who trained you, Simone?"

I glared at him, naked and astride me, his erection recovering quickly. "Trained? Trained in what? Giving you a hard on?"

"Answer the question."

I shook my head. How had I been bested by a bodyguard? It wasn't possible. But then… the thought escaped me. Whatever it was, my brain was too sluggish to keep up. Better not to say anything at all than something I would regret.

"Who trained you, *querida*? Did you call him The Instructor?"

Heath

Heath watched the slight flinch of recognition in her eyes, not that he needed the verification. They were the same, Simone and him, He'd felt it the moment he first saw her and now he knew at least part of the reason why.

The Instructor had taught them both how to think, how to kill, and most of all, how not to feel.

That lesson had never sunk in with Heath, but then he'd come to The Instructor with fire for revenge running in his veins. After witnessing Simone's passion, he guessed that lesson hadn't fully taken root in her, either.

But that didn't mean he could trust her.

He leaned over Simone, bringing his face close. "Did he send you after me?"

A small crease dug between her eyebrows. "You?"

She was feeling the effects of the drug, so he would make it simple. "Are you here to kill me?"

"Why would I be sent for you?"

"Don't pretend with me. By now you know I am no more a bodyguard than you are a hooker. You should really be more careful about pillow talk. It gave you away."

"Pillow talk? I... I didn't say anything."

"I wasn't listening to your words, *querida*. I was reading your body."

Heath traced a finger over the tiny white line, clearly visible against her smooth belly. He didn't know what the scar was from, but he knew where she got it.

Because he had one as well.

It was there at the bottom of his navel, just like hers, a little white smile. But while her skin was smooth, he had the hair of a man, making the scar hard to see unless you knew where to look.

Her eyes focused on his for a moment. "What are you, some kind of spy?"

Did she not know?

He concentrated on the feel of her body beneath him. Her heart was pounding hard. She hadn't had enough of the tequila to succumb quickly to whatever she had laced it with, but she was having trouble regulating her reactions and thinking things through. He had a sense for this woman, a visceral understanding of her, and right now he judged she was telling the truth. She hadn't been sent for him.

And that meant The Instructor must not know he was here.

Heath needed to keep it that way.

"I'll pay you to let me go." She said, her tongue slightly fumbling over the words.

Heath smiled. "You can't afford me."

She bucked her hips.

Still straddling her, he rode the wave of her body. "If you are trying to arouse me even more, it is working."

"Fuck you."

Simone might be drugged and naked and tied, but she was not beaten.

She was *magnifico*.

"So you have come for Bratton, no? I will not stand in your way. But I'm afraid I must leave you here, bound and beautiful. I can't have you following me."

"Give me the key, and I won't follow."

"I might be in love with you, *mamacita*, but that doesn't mean I trust you."

He sprang off her, getting clear of the bed just in time to dodge a kick directed at him.

"So fiery and passionate. You make me wish I never had to leave."

"So don't."

Heath still had some time left, so he sat on the bed and began to stroke her once again.

She spread her thighs and gave him a smile he could feel in his groin. "Let me go. I want to touch you, too."

"Just seeing you, feeling you is more than I can take, *querida*."

She pulled against her bindings, tried to close her legs, but by then he knew her body. Knew how to make it react.

"Your struggle only makes you more beautiful, Simone. Let me make you come once more. As a way to say goodbye."

"You're a bastard."

"*Sí*, yes."

"I hate you."

"I know."

He continued to touch her, adjusting the rhythm, gauging her expression, reading her level of passion, until she finally gave in and didn't try to retreat any more. Until she pressed against him. And then he teased, touching her with less pressure, pulling his fingers away as she stretched for him. When she began to groan with frustration, no doubt hating him even more—more than desiring him—Heath pushed two fingers deep inside her and massaged her with his thumb, flicking as fast as he could, making her cry out.

He watched her face, watched the turmoil there. The anger. The betrayal. The hunger. Watched the orgasm build, watched her shuddering release, and thought there could be no better thing in life than to do this, over and over and over.

But, sadly, he had to go.

Reluctantly he withdrew his hand from her body and gave her a kiss on her damp forehead.

"Don't leave me," she said with a touch of that smile.

Never giving up, not his *querida*.

As he pulled on his pants and shirt, he let his gaze wander over her body once more, slowly, savoring the view in case it was the last time.

"If only we had met under different circumstances, *mi amour*. Now if you don't mind, I'm running out of time, and I must avoid keeping an appointment."

By the time he grabbed his carry on suitcase and left the room, it was after eleven. The casino was slightly out of his way, but he headed down to the ground level anyway.

The place was crowded with gamblers, plugging slots and playing games. Bells and whistles, beeps and chimes rose from the banks of machines. The air smelled slightly floral and sweet, like a woman's perfume, and the fragrance mixed with a whiff of food now and then from the restaurants that were still open.

He turned down a row of slot machines, adopting the persona of just another gambler hoping to hit it big. The ring felt heavy on his hand, more valuable than any riches he might win here, and also more terrible. To Bratton, it meant money. To Heath, it was far more personal.

A shout rose over the din.

Heath did not have to speak Russian to recognize the language. They were gathered around the roulette wheel, just as Bratton had said they would be. Three of them. The man who'd shouted scooped up his winnings. Taller than Heath, twice as wide, muscle not fat. The shirt he wore was the size of a four-person tent and covered with pictures of dolphins leaping from white surf. Heath couldn't spot a weapon, but he would bet it was there under the folds of fabric.

The second and third men gathered around the wheel were smaller, but not by much. The first had hair so short it looked like yellow baby fuzz. Blemishes pocked his face, and along with a neck as thick as Heath's thigh and arms nearly bursting the seams of his blazer, Heath pegged him as a steroid enthusiast.

The third man was much more average. Thin compared to his compatriots, he had brown hair and a forgettable face. Perfectly average, until he smiled. Half his teeth seemed to be knocked out, the others chipped and filed to ragged points.

Heath glanced around the casino, picking out four more men hovering near the chokepoints of the casino floor. The two closest had hands marked with tattoos, one featuring various letters, the other the head of Satan. The two others were too far away to spot details, but their body language told Heath all he had to know.

At least seven men. Overkill for a friendly business exchange.

Pinche mierda, Bratton really had no idea what he'd started.

Heath kept moving, reaching the main entrance, a grand area with the ornate ceilings rising over twenty meters in the air. The exterior façade was a copy of the Doge's Palace, and the marble floors and grand scope of the entrance was truly beautiful.

Escalators reached to the second floor shopping area, and Heath jumped aboard. He seemed to have gotten past the Russians without being recognized, but they were early and looking for Bratton, not a random Latino playing the slots.

Of course, soon they would get restless. Heath had to make sure he was long gone by then.

He had one more task.

Reaching the top, he stepped off the escalator. Located on the second floor, above the casino, were the Grand Canal Shoppes, an indoor shopping mall like no other. The mall floors were cobblestone streets, the ceiling was a painted sky glowing as if it was early evening, and the store facades were buildings in the Venice streets. But the most unique feature of all was the canal running through the mall's center. At 400 meters long, the waterway was spanned by arched bridges connecting the shops on either side. And down the center floated gondolas giving rides to tourists, the gondoliers piloting the boats singing songs of love and loss, just as they had been outside near the entrance driveway.

Heath picked up his pace, moving along the faux streets and weaving between shoppers. Beyond the replica of St. Mark's Square, an area in the middle of the mall boasting more shopping, restaurants, and entertainment, he would find the ballrooms of Congress Center and the hotel's business area. At this time of night the business center was closed, but that was no challenge. He carried a set of picks and a torsion wrench. He had planned every step, and nothing would stop him now.

He dipped a hand in his pocket for Bratton's wallet. Gone.

Nothing would stop him... except Simone.

He shook his head and might have laughed if not for the frustration of it. She was a true challenge. A woman after his own soul.

Turning in his tracks, he headed back down the escalators and through the grand colonnade. At least she was no longer a concern. Because as much as he admired her, if she got in his way again, he would take her life.

And that would be such a waste.

The lobby had cleared of tourists in the late hour, but guest registration was still open. Heath stashed his carryon on a luggage cart then approached a thin, pale man whose submissive body language suggested he'd been put on the earth to serve others. According to his little gold badge, his name was Gene.

"Hello, sir. Welcome to the Venetian. How may I help you?"

"Thank you, Gene. I checked in to this fine hotel a short time ago, and I have made a very grave mistake."

The man's eyebrows shot toward his hair line. "A grave mistake?"

"I came down to the casino to try my luck, and I'm afraid I left my key card in the suite."

"Oh, that kind of grave mistake."

He let out a little laugh, and Heath joined him, making it into a bonding experience. One or two more shared chuckles, and they would be like brothers. "Not as grave as choosing the wrong lady to blow on my dice, no?"

The man laughed again at the innuendo, and they were on their way.

"What is your room number?"

Heath gave him Bratton's room.

"Ah yes, Mr. Bratton. I hope your suite is to your liking."

"Please Gene, call me Dominic. And the entire hotel is beautiful, as always."

"I'm glad to hear it. Now let's get you back inside it, shall we?" He laughed, and Heath chimed in. "All I need is some identification."

Heath gave his new brother a grin. "My key is in my wallet... which is in my room."

"Of course it is," said the desk clerk. "But I'm afraid I can't just give you a key without knowing who you are."

"But you do know who I am. You have my name right there on your computer."

He shook his head, no laughter now. "I'm sorry, but I can't give you a key without identification."

"And I can't get my identification without a key."

"That might be true, but the rules are the rules."

"But sometimes it is necessary to break rules, no? Especially to help a friend?"

"I'm sorry, sir. I can't. Following the rules is very important."

So much for being the *amigo* of this *cabron*. Gene might have been put on the earth to serve others, but it turned out those others were the rule makers.

"I see you checked in with two others. Would they be able to vouch for you?"

Heath thought of the current states of Bratton and Simone. "My companions are... indisposed at the moment."

"I'm sorry to hear that."

"Yes. I could hear them moaning all the way down the hall. I think someone else might have been in the room with them, too. Some people are so loud."

Gene gave him a deadpan look, sticking to his rules about rules.

Heath paused for a moment. There had to be another way, and as he glanced around the lobby, he found it. "But if you ask the pretty blonde at the end, an angel by the name of Karen who checked me into the hotel, she could vouch for me, no?"

Chandler

"If you're poisoned," The Instructor said, "you have a choice. Find the antidote, or puke."

Fog filled my head, my thoughts slow and sluggish. My mouth felt dry, my head starting to throb behind my eyes, my stomach queasy.

I imagined the most disgusting thing I could. A toasted maggot sandwich, slathered in curdled mayonnaise, with cigar butts in it and a side of raw, rotten beef liver being fed to—

The tequila came up, along with the roofies. I hacked, spit a few times, and then got angry.

How had I let him fool me?

Not only had I ignored signs that he was an operative, I'd let him use my own drug against me. I was lucky I wasn't dead. I was also lucky I hadn't had more of the tainted tequila than I did.

I worked my wrist back and forth against the neck tie, the silk loosening until I could slip free. Unfortunately escaping the handcuff wasn't going to be so easy.

I shifted my legs to the side, angling my body until my feet were off the bed. Using my toes, I groped the carpet, my arms stretching to their limit, the cuff cutting into my wrist. My heel hit something near the bed's edge. There it was. I gripped the fabric with my toes, then using my stomach muscles, I scissored my body and brought the panties to my free hand.

Sitting up on the bed, I brought the garment to my bound hand and skimmed my fingers along the elastic band until I felt a hard piece of wire sewn into the fabric.

When I'd bought the jeans and blouse from the boutique in the Canal Shoppes, I'd thought about buying sexy underwear to go with it. Fortunately for me, I hadn't. As the only garment that wasn't new, the panties were properly prepared, two lengths of wire sewn into the seam between elastic and lace, along with a rolled up hundred dollar bill.

I worked the wire free. Seconds later, I had the cuffs unlocked.

Heath's wallet remained wedged between the chair cushions, and before I took time to pull on a stitch of clothing, I checked inside.

Not Heath's wallet at all. The driver's license of Dominic Bratton stared up at me. And inserted next to a collection of credit cards and wad of hundreds was a key card for the Venetian.

This wasn't over yet.

My heart rate accelerating, I opened my purse and pulled out the bikini I had also purchased on my newest shopping expedition. Far from a fun vacation buy, the swimsuit was my insurance. If I found myself in a tough spot, I could always take off my street clothes, slip into one of the many pool areas along the Strip, and fit right in. I put the suit on instead of underwear, and then dressed in the jeans and blouse. Slipping the rolled hundred from the seam in my panties, I stuck the cash, the wires, and the lingerie in my pockets, stuffing my phone and Bratton's wallet in my purse. Later I'd ditch the underwear in a public trash can.

My head throbbed, but the fog seemed to be lifting in my mind, adrenaline sharpening my senses despite what was left of the drug in my system. I didn't have much hope in catching Heath. He was probably long gone. But I still had the rest of my job to do.

I poured the rest of the three hundred dollar bottle of Platinum on the sheets, destroying whatever DNA evidence I'd left. Wiping the room of my fingerprints, I collected the handcuffs and tie and left the room. The hall outside was vacant, most guests probably at a casino, a show, or a nightclub. I paused outside of Bratton's suite and listened for a few seconds. Hearing only the faint drone of television news, I used the key card to let myself in.

CODENAME: CHANDLER – THE BEGINNING

Bratton's suite was as large as Heath's and mine combined. Keeping on the balls of my feet, I moved silently over the entry's marble floor. Light from the television pulsed straight ahead, the glow of neon filtering in from the bank of windows beyond. I ducked into a powder room on my left, waiting for the sound of voices or footsteps or any kind of movement at all.

Nothing.

If Bratton was awake, he'd be surprised to see me. I would have to act fast, before he suspected the reason I was there, before he could gather his thoughts enough to react.

I peeked through the powder room door. In the glow from the boob tube screen, I could see him leaned back on the sofa, not moving.

Stepping out, I padded across the remaining marble and into the carpeted sitting area. The suite opened up to the right, a full dining area behind Bratton, all of it dark and quiet. Slipping to the right, I circled the spot where the CEO reclined, watching for any flinch, any sign he knew I was there.

Something was wrong.

For a few heartbeats, I wasn't sure what, and then it hit me.

The smell.

It was light, barely there, but unmistakable. Not the fleshy, sweet blood odor that surrounded a shooting victim. But the acrid stench of urine, voided at the moment of death.

Heath had beaten me to it.

The towels he'd disposed of on the way to his room, the scratches I'd noted on his arm, Bratton's wallet in his pocket, it all added up.

I approached the body, taking in the slight subconjunctival hemorrhage staining the whites of open eyes, the slightly off tilt of the neck.

Leaving him, I moved through the suite. I was fairly sure Heath had killed Bratton before our tryst, but it never hurt to

74

be thorough. The last thing I needed was an unwelcome surprise. Clearing the bedroom, bathroom, closets bigger than my apartment, and workout room, I returned to the sofa and pulled out my phone.

After verifying our identities, I launched right in.

"Bratton is dead."

"Good, then—"

"I didn't kill him. The bodyguard did."

"Where?"

"In his room."

"Who knows he's dead?"

"As far as I know, no one other than me and Rodriguez."

"Are you in the room now?"

"Just me and the corpse."

"Does Bratton have a flash drive on him?"

"It wasn't in his wallet." I did a quick search of the dead man's pockets, but he hadn't added any items since the car ride in Chicago. "I have a cell phone here, a wallet, with over two thousand in cash, and a condom, thankfully unused. Wait—"

I checked his hands. The three platinum rings were there, his fingers swelling around them, but the ruby ring set in gold was gone. "Could this information be hidden in a ring?"

"A ring?"

"After the meeting in Chicago, he was wearing a ring I'm pretty sure wasn't on his finger before."

"Take it."

"That's the problem. I don't have it. I'm betting the bodyguard does."

"Then you know what you need to do."

I did. "Recover the Precious. But I don't know where Rodriguez went."

Silence hummed over the phone, then the clack of fingers on a keyboard.

"Jacob?"

"Leave that part to me. Does he have anything else with him? Suitcase?"

"One." I returned to the master bedroom. Finding Bratton's carryon in a closet, I plopped it on the bed and rifled through it.

"Anything?" Jacob asked.

"Not unless you're interested in condoms. The guy has a drug store's entire inventory in here."

I wiped down all the surfaces I'd touched, not just for security reasons but sanitary ones as well, then returned to the sunken living room. A memory niggled at the back of my mind, although it took a couple of seconds for me to grasp hold of it—the lingering flunitrazepam, no doubt.

"Shit."

"What is it?" Jacob asked.

"Heath Rodriguez." I paused. I wasn't sure if Jacob was familiar with the training I'd gone through, but as my handler, I suppose I had to trust him. There was no one else. "He mentioned The Instructor."

"The Instructor? Are you sure? And you didn't think to bring that up until now?"

"I was... I've had a few problems."

"What did he say?"

"He asked if The Instructor trained me."

"Why would he ask that?"

I tried to recreate the memory in my mind, but it was no use. I wasn't sure if it was the flunitrazepam or the orgasms, or a combination of the two, but the whole experience shifted and blurred as if something from a dream. "I don't know. He also wanted to know if The Instructor sent me to kill him."

"Did he say anything about Hydra?"

"No."

Only the sound of computer keys clacking came from the other end of the line.

"A couple things he said make me think he might be an operative. Could he be working for someone The Instructor wants dead?"

"You've got to find him, Chandler."

I hadn't expected a clear answer from Jacob, but the way he ignored my question and changed the focus made me uneasy. "In all of Vegas? That will be easy."

"He's on the second floor in the Grand Canal Shoppes, just entered St. Mark's Square."

"What, are you magic now?"

"Casinos are full of cameras. And I know how to access them."

"So in a word, magic." I said, already on my way out the door. I slipped the Do Not Disturb sign over the knob and broke into a run. "There isn't any way you can use some of that witchcraft to zap me up a gun, is there?"

"Sorry. There you're on your own."

Heath

Heath threaded through the crowd jamming the replica of St. Mark's Square, moving quickly yet casually enough not to attract attention. Scanning the crowd as he went, he skipped over singers and stilt walkers, jugglers and human statues dressed in costumes from the *Commedia Dell' Arte,* and the obligatory Bermuda shorts-wearing tourists. He was good at reading body language and intent in faces and barely had to take the time to really look at them. And that was a good thing. The trip to the lobby for another key card to Bratton's room had taken more time than he'd hoped. Too much time.

By now, the Russians would be getting restless.

On the far side of the square, doors opened to the ballrooms and convention center. A crowd of nearly all women milled the halls, the lanyards around their necks and piles of books in their arms suggesting some kind of booklovers' convention.

For what might be the first time in Heath's life, he shifted through the currents of women without paying them the attention they so richly deserved, keeping his mind focused and feet moving.

The business office was a quarter of the way down the long hall, situated between two ballrooms. He glanced through the side panel window and as expected, it was closed for the evening. What casino would want executives faxing at midnight when they should be in the casino, blowing money?

Any sane person would probably hesitate before breaking into a locked room amidst a crowd like this, but Heath slipped his tools in his hands and walked up as if he belonged there.

People tended to defer to confidence.

Even with thousands of dollars of computer equipment in the room, the door was little more than a courtesy lock, and he had it open in just a few seconds. He closed it behind him, turned on the lights, and reset the lock before moving into the room. Passing a fax machine, he sat down at the first computer and snapped on a pair of nitrile gloves. Then he booted it up and logged in using Bratton's key card and the access code to his room's Wifi.

The rest went quickly. Hacking was one of Heath's specialties, and he spoke binary as fluently as he spoke English. Within minutes he had accessed the hotel's mainframe by using a USB stick to upload a Trojan horse—a malicious code he'd worked on for quite a while—which began a brute force password attack. Then he sat back and waited.

The casino's security was good. The Trojan was better. In eight minutes, Heath had his password, and two minutes later he was remotely spliced into the Venetian's command center, peering at the images caught by cameras all over the hotel. Since he didn't have a monitor array, he had to cycle cameras manually, made a little easier by twelve thumbnail images per page.

As he'd guessed, the Russians looked uneasy, though as long as he avoided the casino, he should be able to sneak past, quiet as a gentle wind.

More concerning was an image showing a bank of elevators on the second floor. She moved so quickly and casually, he almost didn't spot her, just a flash and she was gone. But he couldn't push back the smile that bloomed on his lips.

"How did you wiggle yourself free, my *chica bonita*?"

She was fast, but she still had a long way to travel. Maybe he could still get away without killing her.

He switched the feed to the next batch of cameras, people playing blackjack, the front escalators, and…

A shot of adrenaline dumped into his system as he watched Pino and Smith stride through the Doge's Palace façade's main door.

Heath performed a quick check of his cell phone, but it was safely turned off, the battery removed as always. There was only one way those two could have followed Bratton's plane to Las Vegas and then their car to the Venetian Hotel. Bratton's phone. If the *pendejo* wasn't already dead, Heath would kill him again.

Time ticking away, he attacked the keyboard and uploaded the other program on his USB stick; a system restore malware virus.

One by one, the camera feeds went dark. What the clever little program did was reboot the entire surveillance system using yesterday's data. It would infect every hard drive in the network, erasing all newly recorded video and replacing it with the most recent back-up. Then it would infect the back-ups and do another reboot, erasing everything.

Once begun, it couldn't be stopped, and they'd be dark for at least an hour. By then he'd be gone, and no one would ever know he'd ever been there. Not the authorities, not the Russians, not Pino and his group of Venezuelan radicals.

And most of all, not The Instructor.

Heath pocketed the key card and found his way back into the throngs of chatting readers, the decibel level of the women's excited talk camouflaging the thunk of the door as he closed it behind him. As expected, hotel security had already mobilized, men in suits with ear-mics walking past in a big hurry.

No one gave Heath a second glance.

He made his way back to St. Mark's Square and ducked into a shop selling Venetian masks. Simone would be here soon, and he needed to be ready when she arrived. Only after he made it past her was it even worthwhile to worry about Pino and Smith.

Chandler

> *"When you can't escape,"* The Instructor said, *"plain sight can be the best place to hide."*

The Grande Canal Shoppes were on the second floor of the hotel, and I took the elevator straight there. Although in the real world it was almost midnight, the ceiling of the shopping mall resembled an incredibly realistic-looking sky and carried the soft glow of early evening. Plenty of shoppers still milled, street singers sang, and living statues statued. The scents of food still drifted from the many restaurants, and the nightclubs and the casino downstairs were just getting heated up. A gondolier boomed O Sole Mio, shuttling one of the last pairs of lovers for the night down the fake canal, and I thought about Heath's earlier comment about the song.

I hated being manipulated. Ironic since I was trying to manipulate him at the time, but the truth nonetheless. I'd killed men I'd fucked before—my job required it—and I wouldn't hesitate this time, either. The bastard more than deserved a little payback.

I wound through the pristine faux streets and took one of the bridges arching over the canal, finally making my way into the St. Mark's Square portion of the indoor mall. The place was jammed with late night diners, shoppers and tourists. Street performers sang and mimed and juggled, all dressed in elaborate masks, gowns, capes, and hats straight out of a medieval carnival.

A clown-like Arlecchino, or harlequin, walked past me on stilts, and two living statues posed nearby among throngs of tourists, wearing the elaborate costumes and masks of the *Commedia Dell' Arte*; one dressed as the sharp nosed Capitano, the other donning the shriveled face and rich robes of Pantalone. Beyond them, another sported a Bauta mask and tricorn hat, as if Casanova himself had taken up residence in Las Vegas.

The place was huge, the ceiling soaring to a false sky several stories above and rimmed with shops and restaurants that looked out over elegant balconies. I walked with the flow of traffic, scanning as I went, but there was so much going on it was difficult for me to take it all in, even with my training.

If I was going to find Heath in this haystack, I'd need more assistance from Jacob. I reached for my phone and called. We used an abbreviated exchange code and got right to it.

"I'm in St. Mark's square. Point me in the right direction."

"I can't."

Despite the voice distorter, I could hear the alarm in Jacob's voice. "Can't? What happened?"

"The security video. It's gone."

"For St. Mark's Square?"

"For the whole hotel. The entire system is rebooting and the back-ups were wiped."

"That's not a coincidence."

"No kidding. It's also not easy."

My computer hacking knowledge was limited compared to Jacob's, but I remembered the story of a twosome in Australia who'd hacked into a casino's security cameras and used them to spy on the opposition's cards. In that case, the gambler and his accomplice were discovered right away.

"There's no trail?"

"Oh, there's a trail. It leads to a computer in the hotel's business center and to Bratton."

"Smart."

I watched the living statues change positions. Two Arlecchinos in the balcony above started to sing, and another standing on a giant ball surrounded by the type of velvet ropes you see in movie theaters, started to juggle.

"But wouldn't there be a username? A password? Something?"

"Sure. There's an Internet access code assigned to each room. In this case, Bratton's. The password for the control center was hacked. It's one thing splicing into a live video line—we've all seen that in a hundred movies. But your boy somehow got a Trojan to do a blunt force attack. I saved part of the malware code, but I don't think I can trace it."

"I guess Heath thought of everything."

"Chandler?"

"Yes?"

"Who the hell is this guy?"

Good question.

Capitano and Pantalone moved to the side, getting ready for their part in the song, and for the first time, I noticed Casanova was dressed in a black shirt and dark gray sports jacket. But more than the clothing, I recognized the body underneath it. The way he moved.

"You want to know who Heath is, Jacob? How about I ask him?"

"He's still there?"

"Right in front of me."

He was at least twenty meters away, on the other side of a dining area for one of the restaurants, closer to the mall. I must have walked right past him, and I was sure he was watching me now.

He'd see me coming long before I could reach him.

"So what are you waiting for?"

"You to wish me luck."

"You don't need luck, Chandler. Go kick his ass."

Tucking my phone into my pocket, I glanced around the square and focused on the juggler. Balancing on top of a large ball, he rolled in tiny circles as he tossed red, yellow, and blue balls in the air, catching one only to toss again in unending movement. A small group surrounded him, chattering and nodding with appreciation.

I moved closer, infiltrating the group and pushing to the velvet rope separating him from his admirers. Feeling the rhythm of the tosses and catches, I gave the large ball he was standing on a shove with my foot. The harlequin scrambled for balance, staying on top but abandoning his juggling act.

I reached out and snagged the smaller balls midair.

One.

Two.

Three.

"Hey, what are you—"

Spinning in one motion, I pulled back my throwing arm and fired them at Casanova.

The first hit him in the shoulder.

The second knocked his mask off.

The third pegged him in the side of the head and sent him sprawling to the ground.

Gotcha motherfucker.

"Those are my balls!" The Arlecchino yelled. "She stole my balls!"

People scattered, screaming and cursing and threatening to call the police.

I raced around the dining area, dodging the stilt man and two giggling college girls eating cannoli. I was fast, but by the time I reached Heath, he had already scrambled to his feet.

Damn. I was hoping I'd knocked the bastard senseless.

"Good throw, *bonita*. I'm sorry I don't have more time to play catch."

I walked toward him, watching his hands. Light from a nearby light post glinted off a gold ring set with a ruby on his left ring finger. Bratton's ring.

"You don't want to get in my way, *querida*."

"Oh, I'm pretty sure I do."

"Why? Because I did your job for you? Don't worry. I won't tell anyone."

"Give me the ring."

He waggled his finger. "Oh *mamacita*, it was a marriage of convenience. She means nothing to me. Not compared to you."

His joking was beginning to piss me off. At least the fact that he'd taken the ring confirmed it was the item Bratton had retrieved from his safe deposit box in Chicago. My best bet was that a microdot was hidden somewhere on the gold band or under the ruby, although that part really didn't matter. Not to me. My job was recovering it. Jacob could figure out the rest.

"Seriously, you should let me go. I do not want to kill you."

"Pretty sure of yourself, huh Heath?" I brought my fists up, ready for whatever he threw at me.

He raised his right hand, holding a HK45 Compact Tactical pistol.

That'll teach me not to focus so much on a man's ring. "You're going to shoot me?"

"It is sad, but I seem to have no choice."

"Not here. Too many innocent people."

"So you have a heart, too. I'm impressed, *querida*. I have fallen in love with you, and I do not even know your real name."

"I'll trade you. My name for who you work for."

"What if I told you I was freelance?"

"Even freelancers have bosses."

"Not always. But I see what you are doing. Stalling until hotel security arrives. A noble effort."

He grabbed my right upper arm and snugged the gun barrel into the side of my rib cage.

"Any noise louder than a whisper, I will end you," he said. "It will pain me to do so, but do so I shall."

Steering me back toward the mouth of the square and the indoor canal, he nodded at the people cowering and gaping.

"No worries. I have the offender under control. Go back to enjoying this beautiful evening."

"So full of shit," I said. But I took his threat seriously and kept it at a whisper level.

Out of the corner of my eye, I could see him smile.

The juggler stopped in front of us, blocking our path, his harlequin makeup smeared, the diamonds over his eyes looking more like the mask of a raccoon. Maybe he hadn't been able to balance as well as I thought.

He extended a shaking finger, pointing at me. "She grabbed my balls."

I could feel Heath's chuckle through the gun's barrel.

"Lucky man. Should I be jealous, *mamacita*?"

"I mean it. She stole them. I want my balls back."

"While I'll admit this *chica* has *cojones*, I sincerely doubt they belong to you." Heath shoved past the man.

With my peripheral vision, I could see Heath's eyes shifting, taking in the crowd on all sides, as if looking for someone. Or trying not to be found.

The Arlecchino juggler jumped in front of us again, blocking our path. "The bitch owes me."

"*Chingado*. Get out of our way."

"Not until she pays me for my balls."

An idea blossomed in my still sluggish mind.

I hated involving an innocent, especially one I'd dragged into this mess, but I wasn't crazy about letting Heath escort me outside and shoot me, either. Besides the guy could have gone back and picked up his balls in the square himself.

Instead he chose to be an asshole.

He stepped closer. "You hear me? You're going to find them for me or buy me new ones."

"All right," I said. "I'll go back with you and look for them right now." I moved as if to step toward the juggler, instead stumbling into Heath. He released my elbow and slipped his arm around my waist, propping me up.

What a gentleman.

And that's when the stupid harlequin reached for me.

Twisting to the side, I came down on Heath's gun arm with my now free left hand, a knife edge strike to his radial nerve, forcing him to drop the weapon. At the same time, I grabbed the juggler's outstretched hand and fitting the back of his hand into my palm like a nesting doll, I swooped down, grabbed Heath's crotch, and squeezed.

Heath doubled over while his weapon clattered to the cobblestone.

Leaving the juggler gripping Heath's *huevos*, I jumped back a safe distance from the men.

"There. Have some balls," I said, trying to locate the pistol among the dozens of onlookers' feet scrambling to get out of the way.

Heath recovered quickly, sending his knee into the juggler's head, casting him to the ground. Then he turned to face me. The muscles of his face taught with pain, he attempted to give me one of his flirty smiles and failed miserably.

"*Muy bien, querida*," he said. "Now let me see what else you can do."

He brought up his hands, dancing up on his toes like a boxer looking for an opportunity to strike. But when he finally did, instead of a punch, he launched into a spinning kick, connecting with my shoulder.

I rolled with the motion of the blow, but it still shuddered through my spine and sent me flying to the side, my head connecting with a wrought iron railing. My ears rang, an ache seizing my head

I could smell blood, and when I touched the spot where my scalp hit the rail, my fingers came away red. The crowd cleared the area around me. Shouting rose in the distance along with the alternating squawk and static of two-way radios.

Struggling to catch my breath and clear my mind, I saw Heath readying himself to come at me again. I preferred martial arts that relied on kicks and lower body strength. But the quickest way to neutralize a kicker was to use his weight and momentum against him, so I lowered my center of gravity, preparing to throw him on his ass when he attacked again.

He didn't. At least, not right away.

Heath glanced to one side, eyes rounding a touch.

Figuring he was trying to fake me out, I didn't look.

Good call.

He came at me with a whirling movement, combining an evasive maneuver with a spinning kick. Originating from the Brazilian martial art capoeira, the *meia lua de compasso* packed a wallop. I'd once seen a MMA fighter use it to take out a much larger opponent a mere twenty seconds into the fight.

I managed to evade, lunging to the side and getting hit only by the wind as his leg streaked past. His momentum carried him beyond me, and he was out of range before I could strike back.

But instead of turning around to come at me again, he kept going, leaping over a series of railings and steps.

I set out after him, reaching the canal just in time to see him jump over the last rail and down to the water.

Voices sounded behind me. I expected security to be on us by now, or even the police, but these voices were neither. They spoke Spanish, one tinged with an accent I'd just recently heard.

I glanced back, spotting Football Face towering over the crowd. Judging from the panic of the crowed surrounding him, he was armed and not being too subtle about showing it.

How had they followed us from Chicago?

I turned my attention back to Heath. He was already on the other side of the canal, pulling himself up on the railing, his clothing perfectly dry.

The guy could walk on water now?

I scanned the area, quickly realizing what he'd done. Just as the first gunshot exploded in the air behind me, I jumped over the rail and into the canal.

Heath

Heath had just made it over the railing on the other side of the canal, when the shooting started. Pino and his man Smith.

Chingado!

He'd seen them enter the square, seen the moment they spotted him, seen them draw their weapons.

Pinches pendejos! It wouldn't be long before Las Vegas PD's tactical team would be swarming the place.

Heath had to get out of here.

It was his own fault. He should have killed Simone in the suite. Then he would have been able to disappear, clean and free. Women had always been his weakness, but this one... she seemed to flow in his veins, as hot as his own blood.

Keeping low, he raced down the corridor. People shrieked around him. Shop owners slammed their doors. And behind him all hell broke loose.

Simone would likely not survive, and for that he was sad. But life was short, as always. And he knew she had lived hers well. A woman as passionate as she could not help it.

Heath would light a candle for her next to the one for his sweet mother.

He reached the bend in the canal, the faux street opening up to the escalators. Three hotel security guards ran past him, rushing toward a situation far over their heads. A group of shoppers crowed to get on the down-flowing side for the moving staircase. Three women in front stepped on board, standing still and letting the escalator carry them down, apparently oblivious to the trauma everyone else ran from.

Heath turned away, intending to find the elevator.

Just then, a group of police officers headed up the hall, blocking his path, leaving the escalator as the quickest way out.

He stepped on board.

Shouts came from the floor below, and as he started down the escalator, the Russians stormed around the corner. One by one, they filed onto the ascending escalator,

Too late to reverse course, Heath stared straight ahead, trying to make himself as still and unnoticeable as possible. He focused on reading his surroundings. The fragrance of flowers piped in through the ventilation system of the hotel. The beeps and bells of the slots in the casino below from people refusing to leave their winning machine, even if all hell was breaking loose one floor above.

Heath had to admire their dedication.

The first man pulled even, the behemoth wearing the dolphin shirt, him gliding up, Heath gliding down.

Heath could feel the man's scrutiny and the accompanying rise in his respiration and heart rate. He could hear the low rumble of their conversation, even over the screaming back in the Grand Canal mall. He forced his breathing to deepen, forced his pulse to slow.

The first man passed him. Next came the one with fuzz covering his head like yellow feathers on a baby chick.

The third was the average-looking *cabron*. Heath was again struck by how unremarkable he was. If he'd passed him without the others, even he might not have picked the man out as a threat.

Then the man turned his head, glanced at the ring on Heath's finger, and smiled, lips pulling back to show those hideous teeth.

Chandler

> *"Training will save your life," The Instructor said, "but so will instinct. The more you train, the better your instincts become."*

The drop into the canal wasn't far, less than four meters, but when my feet hit the gondola it bucked as if I'd dropped from fifteen. I absorbed as much of the concussion as I could with my knees, but the craft tipped and bobbed anyway, leaving the gondolier with arms outstretched like a tightrope walker, struggling to keep his footing.

"Hey," said a skinny older man in the back of the boat. "What are you—"

I didn't answer, instead grabbing the oar from the gondolier's hands. Channeling my inner Olympian, I jabbed it to the concrete bottom of the shallow canal and half-pole vaulted, half-jumped to the next boat.

Raised voices sounded behind me, and I didn't have to look back to confirm I'd been spotted by Muscle Man and Football Face.

The next two boats were close enough for me to leap from one to another without any help from the oar. Two bounds and I dove for the far wall. Grabbing the bottom rail, I pulled myself up, scrambled over, and fell flat to the cobblestone on the other side.

I crawled along the floor on my belly. At the bend in the canal, I struggled to my feet, just in time to see Muscles crossing over one of the bridges, heading me off.

He leveled the barrel of a Glock 19 at me.

I raised my hands. I might be good under pressure, but even I got a little nervous when a gun was pointed at me by someone obviously not afraid to use it, even in a crowded mall.

"Where is Bratton?"

"In his room."

"You will take me there."

I shook my head and turned my body so he could see the blood matting my hair and trickling down the side of my face. "I'm hurt."

"You will take me there."

"I can give you the number and the key."

"So you can send me to the wrong room? I don't think so."

"Why would I do that? I don't care about Bratton. He's just a john. Please, I'll tell you everything I know. Just let me find a doctor. This really hurts. I'm starting to feel dizzy."

"*Muy guapa, muy joven y muy obediente.*" His mouth tilted into an ugly sneer. "And you expect me to believe a hooker can fight like that?"

Shit. He'd seen me sparring with Heath.

I glanced over my shoulder, looking for a way out, a place to take cover close by.

Football Face closed behind me, having taken a different bridge.

Double shit. They had me hemmed in.

There was only one way out.

I flung myself over the rail and plunged head first into the shallow water.

Heath

When Comrade Sharkteeth raised his OTs-23 Drotik, a Russian-made machine pistol, Heath's fist had already started its arc. He hit the man with a hammer blow to the side of his head, the force shuddering up Heath's arm and sending his attacker spinning to the side just as he pulled the trigger.

A three-round burst sprayed the frescos.

Screams shrilled from the crowd around him, bouncing off marble and ornate moldings.

People scrambled on the moving steps, jostling, falling, a chaos of fear.

Comrade Dolphin Shirt and Comrade Chick Fuzz pulled their weapons, but Heath was already on the move. He swung his feet up, landing his ass on the escalator's moving railing. Then with a mighty shove, he leaned back, feet first, and slid down to the first floor, kicking panicked people out of the way.

With only three of the Russians accounted for on the up escalator, he wasn't surprised to find two more of them at the entrance, the tattooed *cabrones* he'd noticed earlier. One stepped out in front of the doors, blocking Heath's way. His hand darted to the small of his back, no doubt grabbing the pistol he had stashed there.

Heath didn't wait for him to draw the weapon.

He loved capoeira for its rhythm, its art. But this time, he forgot all that and went straight for a *martelo de estalo*, or cracking hammer, a roundhouse kick that utilized the top surface of the foot.

He connected solidly with Tattoo's ribs, and the man crumpled to the side, breath whooshing from his lungs.

Heath kept moving, racing through the doors and out of the building before the second man even knew what was happening.

Several police cars filed into the entrance of the Venetian, and Heath slowed down, hoping the flashing light bars and sirens in the distance would prevent the Russian geniuses behind him from opening fire. But at only midnight on a Friday night, plenty of people moved by on the street, gawking at the first responders.

Heath crossed the arched bridge to the boulevard and mixed with the rubbernecking crowd, hiding behind a gurgling fountain.

A few seconds later, the man with *El Diablo* tattooed on his arm emerged from the doors, two others behind him, their weapons tucked discreetly away. Following the path Heath had taken, the three fanned out, sifting through the crowd.

Time to *adios*.

Flowing with the crowd, Heath crossed South Las Vegas Boulevard at the light. The night was cool, the desert in summer, and a barely there breeze ruffled the leaves of palm trees in the median. A crowd gathered on the opposite sidewalk, and he mixed among them, drawing several venomous stares from people. When the volcano show began, he understood why.

A mixture of fire and water, music and explosions, the volcano outside the Mirage Hotel was blindingly spectacular.

It also might provide exactly what he needed.

Heath blinked, trying to clear the ghost of the fire's brilliance from his eyes. He wound through onlookers, moving closer to the lake and the cauldron of fire in its center. He was sure it would be hot enough. All he required was 60 degrees Celsius. Just slip the ring from his finger, give it a gentle toss, and let the fire show and a little time solve the problem for him.

So close. So easy.

He darted to the front of the crowd…and ran smack into an iron wall of a man.

The man muttered something that sounded like *izvinite*, and Heath froze.

Although Heath was fluent in several languages, his area of expertise was focused in Mexico, South and Central America, Western Europe, and the Middle East. He had little experience with the languages of Eastern Europe or Asia, but it didn't take much to recognize the Soviet ring of the word.

He glanced at the man out of the corner of his eye, noting how the orange of the volcano flame reflected off the yellow fuzz on the man's scalp.

Chingado.

The man's giant mitt of a hand closed around Heath's arm.

Lifting his knee and quickly extending his leg in a *ponteira*, Heath delivered the simple front snap-kick hard and fast into the brute's groin. Although the man tried to protect himself, he was too slow. He doubled forward, releasing Heath's arm.

All Heath needed.

He spun and shoved his way free of the crowd. Where Chick Fuzz was, he knew the others would be also, and he ran like *El Diablo* himself was on his tail.

Up ahead, a bright light caught his attention, shooting into the sky like a beacon.

The laser streaming from the tip of the Luxor pyramid.

It was far down the Strip, but if he could catch a taxi, he might be able to make it, before the Russians or the Venezuelan or, if she was still alive, sweet Simone caught up with him.

It was worth a try.

Dodging groups of tourists and clumps of palm trees, he made it to the end of the block, then crossed against the light, picking his way through traffic to reach the Roman columns of the Forum Shops at Caesars Palace. Heath kept going, past fountains and grand entrances and rows of arborvitae, his breathing settling into a rhythm. The men chasing him were big and armed, but he was thrifty, fast, and smart.

He liked those odds.

Shouts erupted behind him, along with the trample of heavy, running feet. But as he turned on the speed, the distance grew.

Soon the muscles in his legs started to burn, his lungs hungry for oxygen. The sweat came quickly, but it didn't do much to cool him in the desert heat. Even at night, Vegas was an oven. He kept moving, dodging around tourists and hand-billers passing out pamphlets, jumping over the occasional drunk passed out on one of the sculpted sidewalks. He was in spectacular shape, but even he couldn't keep up this mad dash forever. Already he could feel himself tiring, his strides slowing, growing shorter.

Although Heath could no longer hear the Russians, he knew they wouldn't give up so easily. They'd catch up, weapons ready. And when they did, he had to make certain they wouldn't be able to find him.

He crossed the boulevard again at the intersection of Flamingo Road, this time taking the escalator up to the foot-bridge connecting the Bellagio to the tube-like entrance of Bally's. He kept moving, searching for a place to stop, to hide, a spot where he could keep an eye on his surroundings and yet no one would think to look.

He passed Bally's and looked up, his gaze tracing the glorious architectural lines of an Eiffel Tower two thirds the size of the real one.

Heath smiled.

He'd always loved Paris. It must be the romantic in him.

Chandler

"Fear is debilitating," The Instructor said. "Never let your enemy know what you fear. If he's worth his salt, he'll use it against you."

Although I could swim just fine, I hated water. I'd done countless laps in training, learning to use my arms, my legs, my torso, and my breathing to move through the water as quickly and efficiently as possible. I'd trained in survival, spending hours in cold, deep water with only my jelly fish float and thoughts for company. I'd practiced lifesaving techniques, those focused on saving others and myself, until I could perform a cross body carry or tired swimmer's assist in my sleep.

But none of it, not all those hours, all that practice, all that training, had rid me of my deep-seated fear of drowning.

There were several reasons for this; the interrogation resistance I had to endure in training, an unfortunate chapter in my life before that. I tried to push all of it from my mind as I entered the canal.

It didn't work. Not entirely.

Even though I knew that in this shallow canal I was in more danger of breaking my neck on the bottom than of drowning the conventional way, I was still seized by a moment of sheer panic.

I arched my back, curving upward in the water as soon as I hit with a painful belly flop. Even so, my momentum took me to the bottom. I turned my head to the side, the floor of the concrete canal scraping my cheek and then my chest before I was able to arc back in the direction of the surface. The water was piss warm, dyed blue, and stung my eyes with chlorine.

Changing the curvature of my body again, I straightened my path, preventing my head from emerging. A few good dolphin kicks, and I was careening downstream, the shadow of a gondola passing overhead.

When I felt I'd gone far enough to surface without gun-fire greeting me, I did, gasping in air.

The canal was shallow enough for me to stand, and I found a spot under a bridge and tight to a wall where I could rest for a second and assess my surroundings. My priority was finding Heath, but if he'd gotten clear of the hotel, I'd be hard pressed to track him down on the streets of Las Vegas.

I could only hope he'd run into as many problems as I had. If not, I'd have to guess he'd flag down a cab on the Strip and hightail it to the airport and who-knew-where, so he could sell who-knew-what information was in that ring.

I had to find him before he reached the airport.

Clinging to the wall, I listened to the activity around me. People seemed to be running everywhere, barking orders, static bursts from two-way radios, security or police, I wasn't sure. With law enforcement on the scene, the Venezuelan and his merc would be stupid to stick around. At least my odds of being shot had dropped considerably.

I pulled myself from the water and climbed over the rail-ing. Keeping my head down, I wound through the canal shops and blended with the frightened crowds, making my way to the escalators, the air conditioning raising goose bumps under my wet clothing.

Two security officers stood at the door, but they had ap-parently given up trying to stop the exodus of gamblers and shoppers. I walked in the shadow of an older man, and stum-bling, I reached for his hand. Like a gentleman, he grabbed hold of me, and we swept out the door right under the noses of police, side by side.

I let go of him on the bridge arching over the outdoor canal.

"Thank you so much. I can take it from here."

He looked at me, concern evident on his face. "Are you sure? Someone was shooting in there. Better to—"

"Yup," I said, pulling free from his hands. "Gotta find my husband. Big guy. Really jealous."

Leaving my protector, I searched the area for any sign of Heath in the crowd. But like I feared, he appeared to be gone.

Red and blue lights from emergency vehicles lit up the night, competing with the neon. I stopped at the fountain marking the entrance to the Venetian resort. If Heath was trying to get to the airport, he'd go south, so at the light, I crossed to the south-bound lane, stopping next to a clump of palm trees outside the Mirage's volcano.

The show was over, the crowd breaking up, and from the look of it, catching a cab wasn't going to be an easy feat. I eyed the flow of traffic. Coming toward me was a truck pulling a narrow trailer designed to hold a moving billboard. This one advertised "Hot Babes Direct 2 U," and I figured that was as good an opportunity as I was bound to get.

The truck stopped at the intersection, and I made my move.

Springing back out into the street, I wove through parked cars until I reached the billboard. I grabbed the side railing and climbed aboard just as the light changed. The truck continued down the street, hopefully bringing this Hot Babe Direct 2 Heath.

The warm desert wind dried my clothing and hair. Everywhere on the Strip, people seemed to be partying, taking in the carnival atmosphere, not a care in the world. Neon blazed, turning darkness into twilight. I whizzed past Caesars Palace on one side, Harrah's and the Flamingo on the other, the big resort casinos interrupted by small shops advertising tours of the Grand Canyon and Hoover Dam.

At the intersection with Flamingo, near the Bally's on the opposite side of the street, I noticed a group of four men walking down the sidewalk. Even from this distance, I could see two of them were armed, yet their body language suggested none were cops. In fact, I'd lay down a sizable bet that none of them were American either.

But they were obviously searching for someone, and I had a pretty good idea who.

The truck slowed to merge with traffic flowing from Flamingo Road, and I jumped off my billboard trailer and took the pedestrian bridge to the other side of the street. I didn't know precisely who these guys were, but I was certain I didn't want to attract their attention.

I followed them to the Paris resort and stepped over a low rail and into the outdoor seating area of the Mon Ami Gabi bistro. Slipping into a vacant table scattered with empty dessert plates and coffee cups, I hooked my finger into the handle of one, pretending to be indulging in a little after dinner caffeine.

The men spread out, scrutinizing the diners, the trees, and the casino entrance under one leg of the Eiffel Tower. Two more men joined them, moving down the Strip to the next hotel.

Six men versus Heath. Not a fair fight, but I wasn't sure for which side.

The waiter approached my table, making his rounds. Surprise crossed his face when he saw me pretending to sip on my coffee.

I raised the cup. "Can I get a little warmer upper, please?"

He frowned, clearly realizing I wasn't supposed to be there. But instead of ordering me out, he grabbed the tip tucked under one of the plates, nodded and slipped back inside, probably to call the manager or security.

Time to bring an end to dessert.

I stood and passed by a large tray filled with cleared plates. On one side lay a thin, stainless steel stick, twenty centimeters long, pointed on one end and forming a ring on the other. The skewer was designed for grilling shish kabob, satay, or since this was French cuisine, brochettes. It wasn't going to protect me against the firepower the men following Heath had on them, but since beggars can't be choosers, I grabbed it off the tray and slipped inside my jeans, its length trailing down my thigh, the ring sticking out of the top of my waistband.

I jumped back over the railing. The six men had moved off down the sidewalk and had almost reached the end of the block, and I started walking, eager to keep them in my sights.

I wasn't ready for the beefy hand to grab my wrist and twist my arm behind my back. He jammed the barrel of a gun into my ribs.

"Why are you following?" he asked.

I pegged the accent as Russian, and thought of Jacob's briefing. Bratton must have been taking competing bids from the Venezuelans and Russians. The only guests Jacob had mentioned who were missing at the party were the Iranians, unless of course, that was who Heath was working for.

"Idiot," I said in fluent Russian. "Release me or you'll regret it."

"Huh?"

"You obviously don't have it yet. I was sent to help. It appears you need all the assistance you can get."

He lowered the gun. "I wasn't aware that—"

I didn't wait for him to finish, instead I turned sharply to the left. Bending my knees, I dipped my head forward and spun under his left arm. Then I struck his left elbow in an upward jab with the palm of my right hand grabbed his gun hand and twisted the weapon to the side, and as the coup de grace, I followed up with a knee to the groin.

He doubled over involuntarily, and I wrenched the gun free. He hit the ground, and I drove my foot into the side of his head three times before he lay still.

People who had watched the exchange stared wide-eyed, some murmuring to one another, some reaching for their cell phones. I glanced down the sidewalk, but the other six were already passing by the Arc de Triomphe replica on their way to the Aladdin.

The pistol was an OTs-23 Drotik with a fourteen round magazine. Relieved to come up with a little weapon conjuring magic of my own, I stuck the machine pistol into the back waistband of my jeans and pulled the tail of my blouse over it.

I don't know what made me look up. It wasn't a sound, between the traffic noises, the crowds of people, and the music and roar of water across the street as the dancing fountain show started at the Bellagio, I couldn't hear a thing. Maybe Heath had been right. Maybe we were connected on a deeper level, a psychic level, because I looked up at the replica of the Eiffel Tower, and the first thing I saw was Heath standing on one of the girders above me.

I reached for my newly procured gun, and then he was plummeting toward me.

He hit me with a wallop, knocking the weapon from my hand and flattening me to the ground.

"Oh querida, I should have known you'd be the one to find me."

I rose to my knees, coming up at him with a good old fashioned uppercut. My fist glanced off his chin and sent him jerking backward.

Capoeira could be fought at normal standing height or low to the ground with moves reminiscent of break dancing. So I wasn't surprised when Heath threw a *rabo de arraia* at me, a low version of what seemed to be his favorite kick, the m*eia lua de compasso*.

I hugged the concrete in an evasion move called a *negative de solo*. Low fighting required a lot of arm strength, and although I could take out any woman in that kind of a matchup, I wasn't confident in my ability to best Heath.

I leaped to my feet, but as fast as I was, he was my equal. I came at him with a couple of kicks. He ducked them with easy, then countered with another *Meia Lua de Compasso*. This time I failed to evade, and his foot hit me in the shoulder with such a wallop that it sent me spinning into a planter, then bouncing into the street, my head cracking against the pavement.

Horns honked and tires squealed, a classic red Corvette missing me by inches. I turned back to the sidewalk, expecting to see Heath running away. Instead he raced right past me and into the street. It only took a second for me to figure out why.

The six Russians were half a block away, but having spotted their prey, they were closing fast.

I struggled to my feet, my shoulder and head aching, and set out after Heath. Dodging traffic slowed him down, and I caught up as he reached the opposite curb. I leaped on his back, snaking my arm around his neck, the joint of my elbow pinching his throat. Gripping my left arm, I tightened the pressure on his carotid artery, trying to stop the blood flow to his brain.

He spun around, raking at my face and hair with his hands, trying to shake me from his back.

People crowding in to watch the fountain show pushed back, attempting to get out of our way.

I saw what he was about to do a split second before he did it, and my words to him in the airplane echoed through my jangled mind.

"Why is it I have trouble believing fear would stop you from anything?"

"I'm afraid of plenty of things."

"Name one."

"Drowning."

Heath dove over the rail, taking me with him.

The water hit me with a cold slap.

The panic hit me harder.

And among the roar and flashing colored lights of the fountains and Frank Sinatra's voice belting out "Luck Be a Lady", I realized I was going to die.

Heath

Sometimes Heath got tired of being right all the time.

Just as he'd foreseen, Simone had been the one to find him. And just as he'd known, she'd been an admirable foe. The fact that he had to kill her now, in a way she had confessed she feared most horribly, bothered him.

But not as much as her killing him.

He only wished he knew her real name. Simone was a nice one, but it didn't fit her. She would be called something sexy but stronger. Fierce. Brave. As was her nature.

He would have to be satisfied remembering her as *bonita*.

He dove deep into the fountain pool, Simone's arm still wrapped around his neck, dragging her with him. Although under the water, he could no longer hear the music, the fountains persisted, loud as explosions.

BOOM!

BOOM!

BOOM!

He felt lightheaded, his limbs growing sluggish, Simone doing a good job of restricting the blood to his brain. He grabbed her arm, trying to pull it away from his throat, but she was strong.

A worthy adversary. His perfect match.

If she kept her grip, he would be unconscious soon, and once that happened, she could release his throat and let him drown. If she gave in to her fear, he could twist away, embrace her under the surface, wait until her panic made her gasp and take water into her lungs.

Sad their love story had to come to this.

Tragic as Romeo and Juliet.

Chandler

"Show no mercy," The Instructor said. "Because in the spy game, no mercy will be shown to you."

My heart pounded in my ears, louder than the shooting fountains of the Bellagio. Water closed around me, pressed in on me, clamored for me to take a breath.

Just one breath.

No.

I didn't want to kill Heath. He'd had ample opportunity to kill me and had stopped short, and I felt I owed him the same professional courtesy. I just wanted his damn ring. But even more than that, I wanted to breathe. I wanted to live.

I let go of his neck.

He let go of my arm.

As soon as my head broke the surface, I felt as if I'd entered a war zone. The relentless explosions continued, even louder now. Sheets of water rained down on my head. I opened my mouth, trying to breathe, and got as much water as air. Coughing and sputtering, I focused on the neon glowing around the pool's edge and started swimming.

As I neared dry land, a spotlight shifted over me, the glare bouncing off waves and hurting my eyes.

An amplified voice boomed over the music and fountains. "Please get out of the water. Get out of the water, immediately."

Heath reached the edge before me, and two police officers fished him out, pulling him over the rail and onto the sidewalk. Then it was my turn, hands gripping my arms in the darkness, towing me out.

"Down on the ground, both of you. Face down."

I couldn't see who was giving the order, but I complied. Shivering, I lowered myself onto my belly, water pooling on the concrete around me. Out of the corner of my eye, I could see Heath doing the same.

"Put your hands on the back of your head."

I did, my hair wet and matted beneath my fingers, my scalp battered and aching.

"Cross your legs at the ankle."

I did that, too. The position was awkward and uncomfortable, but as far as the cops were concerned, that was part of the point. If Heath or I wanted to move, we would first have to uncross our ankles and lower our hands, giving the forces around us plenty of time to see our movement and stop us before we could rise.

I knew what would come next. They would cuff us and book us into jail. Jacob would get his ring. As soon as it had been logged as one of Heath's possessions, it would disappear, if not before.

But I wouldn't be as lucky.

Working for an agency that only a few people knew existed had its downside, one of them being that officially I didn't exist either. Once I was taken into custody, Jacob wouldn't help me. The government would turn its back. And if I told anyone who I was and what I did for a living, I would get my throat cut in my cell for a reward.

I could see and hear four officers total. Not an army. Not nearly enough to contain both Heath and me, if we had the element of surprise on our side. But I didn't like the idea of hurting cops. I was supposed to be one of the good guys, on the same team as the boys and girls in blue.

"Put the cuffs on."

If I was going to make my move, I had to make it soon, before I was wearing bracelets. An officer moved over me.

And that's when the first burst of gunfire raked the trees around us.

The Russians.

The police had already cleared the area of civilians, but a collective panicked scream bounced off concrete and water and hotel anyway. The cop about to cuff me collapsed onto my back, and I could feel the warmth of his blood seeping through my wet blouse. Around me, the other three officers dropped into a defensive stance, taking cover behind a parked car, a tree, anything they could find, forming a perimeter and returning fire.

I turned my head, glancing in Heath's direction, only to find a wet shadow on the concrete where he used to be and a trail of drips leading toward the street.

Rolling the wounded cop off my back, I made for the street myself, slinking behind a parked car, and leaving Las Vegas's finest to deal with the Russians on their own.

I moved low and fast, using the cars to shield me from view. Flashing lights filled the night. Sirens rose over the gunfire. I made it all the way to the end of the block before I caught my first glimpse of Heath. He stood in the street, trying to flag down a cab, a shopping center featuring Louis Vuitton, Prada, and Tiffany's looming behind him.

Fortunately for me, the cabbie was in no mood to pick up a desperate-looking Latino who happened to be soaked to the skin.

Heath spotted me and abandoned the cab search, instead running down the sidewalk.

We were in a footrace now and I sprinted flat out, fast as I could. As long as I could see him, I was okay. He wouldn't be able to get away or hide and get the drop on me.

Heath dashed into the street, angling his way through traffic. I lost sight of him for a second as he crossed the median, his silhouette obscured by palm trees and other foliage, then he appeared in the oncoming lane, a dark form against the glare of headlights and glowing neon. He crossed into an area of strip malls advertising dream car rentals, discount show tickets, and helicopter tours.

I pushed my tired muscles to move faster, my breath roaring in my ears. There were few places to disappear in the area flanked by the big resorts, but in this hodgepodge of smaller buildings he could easily slip through an alley, and I'd have a hard time tracking him down.

I heard the faint sound of an engine while I was still several buildings away. A light flicked on in front of a tattoo parlor and oxygen bar, under a sign boasting the "Best Ever Tours." Then in a streak, Heath buzzed out onto the sidewalk, riding a scooter.

So much for our footrace, the cheater.

I made a beeline for the row of red rental scooters. The business was closed, all the little bikes chained together plus individually fastened to the steel rack. Heath had already unlocked the larger chain's padlock, and the smaller bike locks were no contest for me.

I reached into my pocket, pulling the little wires I'd gotten from my panties from my pocket. Taking a knee beside the closest bike, I had her free in under a minute. A little jimmying with the ignition, and I was on Heath's tail.

Horns blared as I cut across traffic, jumped the median, and folded into the south moving lane. Heath was a good distance ahead now, and I pushed the bike to its limit, weaving between cars in an effort to catch up. I swept by the Monte Carlo hotel on the right, the light changing to red at the intersection with Rue de Monte Carlo.

Sitting back on the scooter, I rushed the curb, yanking back on the handlebars just in time to thunk up onto the sidewalk.

People scattered, and I narrowly missed a fire hydrant. Dropping my foot to the concrete, I pivoted the bike and accelerated, taking the crosswalk.

Ahead, in front of the fake Manhattan skyline of New York, New York, I spotted Heath stuck in traffic. A glance back at me, and he swung off the road, too, dodging pedestrians and racing onto the replica of the Brooklyn Bridge.

I followed. His failure to act sooner had cost him his lead, and as we raced past little Italy, a Broadway box office, and an upper east side brownstone, I pulled even with his back tire.

He shot out a foot, bracing on the front of my scooter and giving me a shove.

I swerved, nearly crashing into the pilings of a faux wharf before regaining control.

He darted under a pedestrian bridge that spanned the boulevard.

I followed, racing as fast as I could. Rounding the corner, I spotted him driving into an elevator that reached up to the crosswalk above. I gunned my scooter, flying over the first few steps of a staircase and jolting down rest. I made another corner and reached the elevator.

"Too late, *querida*," Heath called, smiling at me through the last open inches as the elevator door closed.

Damn.

I pivoted and gunned the scooter, making a sharp turn and racing to the end of the escalator. Twisting the accelerator again, I drove straight up the moving stairs. The bike bucked and strained and for a moment, I thought it was going to flip over on top of me and career back down. Remarkably, it didn't, and I reached the pedestrian bridge only a few seconds after Heath had buzzed out of the elevator.

Heath raced across the bridge, me only inches behind. Reaching the other side, he opted for the stairs.

I took the escalator.

The way down was smoother than the way up, and with the extra speed the movement of the steps gave me, we were even when we hit the sidewalk, racing past the MGM lion and into the street neck-and-neck. He swerved around a couple of pedestrians, and I focused on the gold ring, still glinting from his finger.

Heath kicked out with his right foot, hitting the main body of my scooter, but before he could push me into traffic, I leaped.

I landed on the back of his bike, wrapping my arm again around his throat. This time he was ready, snaking a hand under my arm and prying me free, then he sent an elbow back, slamming me in the ribs.

Gasping for breath, I held on.

He thudded over the curb and swerved into the street, racing kitty corner across the intersection. Horns blared. A truck skidded to keep from hitting us, sliding sideways into a SUV.

On the other side of the street, we bumped up onto the sidewalk, the spires of the Excalibur Hotel's version of Camelot a blur. Heath accelerated, the scooter's bumble bee engine whining, pushed to its limit.

Scissoring his body between my thighs, I held on with my legs, clawing at his face with my left hand and trying to pull the brochette skewer free from my wet jeans with my right. The denim was tight and the stainless steel slippery, and every time I thought I had a grip, Heath hit me with an elbow or butted me with the back of his head. Finally it started to slide out, one centimeter, two...

He swerved the bike hard. Then slinging his left leg over the seat, he flung himself off and into a cluster of plants.

I lunged at the handlebars, but by the time I reached them, the bike was already starting to slide. I pulled my right foot up to the seat, staying on top as the scooter screeched flat on its side along the concrete.

Jumping free, I landed on the sidewalk at a run, the hard surface jolting up my legs. I'd landed in front of the Luxor Hotel, a few meters from the obelisk that served as a sign post, but when I looked back at the spot where Heath had leaped, he was gone.

Struggling to catch my breath, I scanned the area. Palm trees towered around me, and behind them, a giant sphinx guarded the mouth of a thirty-story glass pyramid. At the apex of the pyramid, a laser shot a beam into the sky.

The area around the Luxor was relatively flat, composed of parking lots and a bulldozed lot across the street that was waiting for new construction. The only other big hotel was the Mandalay Bay complex further down the boulevard. But if Heath had headed there or anywhere else besides the Luxor, I should still be able to see him.

My body shaking and my ribs aching where Heath had driven his elbows, I walked back to the spot where he'd bailed off the scooter. A path led from there to the hotel and I took it, walking between two rows of statues then angling to the front entrance.

Doormen flanked the entrance to the hotel, an older man climbed from a cab, a clearly drunk couple staggered out the door, on their way to another casino. Like any other Friday night in Las Vegas.

No sign of Heath.

It wasn't until I heard a woman walking down the sidewalk gasp and saw her point, that I looked upward.

Twenty meters from the base of the pyramid, Heath climbed slowly up the slanting glass.

I eyed the top of the structure, thirty stories high, tilting my head back to take in the view.

Great.

Since drowning hadn't worked, it seemed Heath had decided to test another one of the fears on my list.

Heath

The *chica bonita* was everything he thought she would be and more.

Brave.

Strong.

Fierce.

Tenacious.

Not to mention sexy.

And now she was beginning to get on his nerves.

He kept his eyes focused forward. Putting one foot in front of the other, he climbed one pane of glass at a time, up the 39-degree angle. He'd left his shoes at the bottom of the pyramid, nestled in a group of plants, his bare feet doing a better job of sticking to the glass than hard soles. He hunched forward, gripping the edges of the glass and metal framing with his fingertips, finding holds where there seemed to be none.

The going was meticulous and slow.

Pane by pane.

Story by story.

The rooms inside the Luxor pyramid ran along the walls. Although he couldn't see much through the dark bronze glass, he could imagine whatever guests were in their rooms on a Friday night would have quite a surprise.

And he was sure there would be more to come.

Whatever happened, as long as he got to the top before Simone caught up with him, his plan would work out fine. All he would need to do was buy a little time, and the problem would be solved.

He kept climbing, his fingers aching, the bottoms of his feet already starting to feel raw. The light ahead grew blinding, filling the night and shooting into the heavens. Twenty meters away, he could feel the heat. Ten meters it burned his fingers, his feet. Five and it was almost unbearable.

He kept going, kept climbing. He couldn't turn back now.

Sweat rolled down his back and stung his eyes.

A cramp seized his back, his arms, his legs.

The dry air and heat sucked the moisture from his body and parched his tongue.

Finally he reached the pinnacle, the light too bright to see, the heat too much to bear. He slipped Bratton's gold ring from his finger and tossed it onto the illuminated glass, the stone which wasn't a stone taking the super-heated rays full blast.

Then he turned back around and went down to meet his lovely Simone.

Chandler

"It isn't over until you've won, escaped, or died,"
The Instructor said. "Shoot for won *or* escaped.*"*

I trudged up the pyramid's steep incline, trying not to think too hard about how high I had scaled and the slick slope behind me. It was impossible for me to climb while looking up the glass. Not only was the light at the top blinding, but with every glance, I felt like I was tumbling backward, and I had to stop, trembling, to catch my breath.

My last glance upward had told me Heath had reached the top. Why this was important to him, I couldn't guess. From the first, his actions hadn't made sense.

If he knew I was an operative, why had he allowed me to board that plane?

Then once we arrived in Vegas, why had he killed Bratton?

And even more confusingly, why hadn't he killed me?

But the kicker was this pyramid stunt. When he'd raced down the Strip, I'd assumed he was trying to get to the airport, attempting to get away. That made sense to me. But this?

Why in the hell would he climb the Luxor?

I glanced up at him again. This time he was easing himself down the glass on feet and hands, facing up.

"I'm coming for you, *mamacita*," he sing-songed. "Did you miss me?"

"Are you off your meds or something?"

He laughed. "Do you not know why I'm doing this?"

"I don't know why you're doing anything."

"Oh, you will. And once you do, you will see you have helped me immeasurably."

Not what I wanted to hear.

Two meters from me, he pushed himself onto his feet and brought his hands up in a defensive stance, his legs bent, ass almost touching the glass.

I readied myself for his attack. The slant of the pyramid was more suited to grappling and throws rather than the kicks, evasion, and trickery of capoeira. I wondered what other skills he had in his arsenal.

I focused on his hands. In any fight, body language could betray the fighter's plans. The shifting of weight here, angling the body to protect and injury there, all of it could give away the fighter's plans and weaknesses. But the most important part of the body was the hands. Heath wouldn't be kicking now, not on this incline. As long as I watched his hands, I'd be ready.

Wait.

I zeroed in on his left hand ring finger, but where Bratton's gold ring used to be, there was nothing but a reddened mark.

"What did you do with the ring, Heath?" I asked, watching his eyes.

Unfortunately they were locked on me and didn't give away his hiding place.

"Be patient, *bonita*. I will give it to you in time. I'm sure The Instructor will be quite impressed with you."

"How do you know The Instructor?"

"Many know him."

"Really? I haven't seen him in years."

"Then you should count yourself fortunate."

"Who do you work for, Heath? The Venezualean?"

"Pino? No."

"I know you don't work for that group of Russians."

"Definitely not."

"Then who? Why are you doing all this?"

"I would tell you, my *querida*, but then I would have to kill you."

He sat down, sliding toward me, feet first.

I tried to shift to the side, make him miss, but I couldn't control the movement, and in a heartbeat, his right foot hit me and I was sliding too.

"This is fun, no?" he yelled. "Like a children's game."

"Fun?" I grabbed his bare foot, grasping his second toe with one hand and his third with the other, I pulled them in opposite directions until I could feel a crack.

He bellowed, lashing out with his heels, hitting me smack in the head.

Lights swirled around me. I flattened my belly against the glass and slid another three meters before I finally stopped, my head throbbing in time with my pulse.

"This will all be over soon, *bonita*. You must have patience."

I looked up from where I was sprawled on the glass and shook my head. "You already used up my patience."

I started crawling on my belly, elbows moving in time with my knees.

"And what are you going to do if you reach me? I don't have the ring."

I peered up at the top of the pyramid, the beam of light shooting out of the top and into the sky like some sort of supernatural beacon. If Heath really didn't have the ring, it was either up there or he had stashed it before he'd started to climb. Since no matter how nuts he seemed, I didn't buy that he'd climb all the way up this thing for no reason, I decided to put my money on the top of the pyramid.

I climbed to my feet as best I could.

Then I scrambled up the glass to try to get above him.

He reached for me, and I dodged his hand, pushing harder. Fear be damned, I was faster, more agile, and once I passed him I could—

Something caught my ankle, making me gasp, causing me to fall forward my chin smacking the glass.

"The view from up here," Heath said. "*Magnífico.*"

I stared down at him and saw he wasn't admiring the Vegas strip. He was staring at my ass.

I tried to kick his hand, and he yanked me down until I was alongside his body, his arm on my waist. A position strangely reminiscent of one we'd shared in bed earlier.

The son of a bitch was smiling.

"You think this is funny," I said.

"No, *querida*. This is a smile of admiration. I am in awe of your skill, your determination, and your beauty."

"If you haven't noticed, we're trying to kill each other."

"Indeed. But not trying as hard as we might, no? We have difficult jobs. Now we are at cross-purposes, and I truly do not know how this will end. But I do want to thank you for one of the most memorable days of my life."

His fingers stroked my thigh.

I drove my elbow into his nose.

That knocked the playfulness out of Casanova, and he pushed me away, hard.

My feet skidded out from under me, and I plummeted down the glass. I spread my arms and legs, digging in toes and fingers until my momentum slowed... stopped. Then I gathered my feet and hands under me and started to climb once again.

"Bring it on, *chica*." He touched his nose, but unfortunately I hadn't hit it hard enough to break it. "I can do this all day."

I moved my legs under me, ready to strike again, when something stiff running from my right hip half way down my thigh impeded my movement.

My improvised weapon. With all that had happened since I'd procured it, I'd almost forgotten it was still stuck down the leg of my jeans.

Staying flat on the glass, I reached into my waistband. My jeans drier now, I managed to loosen it but left it sheathed. Then I struggled to my feet.

Heath loomed above me, master of the high ground.

The problem with this high ground is that the footing was as bad as the spot where I stood.

I stepped toward him. Then instead of attacking his face or torso, I dropped back to my belly and lunged for his feet.

We both went down, skidding down the glass.

I grabbed his legs, going for his crotch with my left hand.

He blocked me, driving a heel into my chest.

Gasping for air, I climbed up his body, hand over hand, until we were side-by-side again. But there was no flirtation this time. Heath looked as panicked as I felt.

He grabbed my left hand, immobilizing it, then went for my right.

Too late.

As we slid down the glass, gaining speed, I pulled the brochette from my jeans. If he didn't let go of me, we were both going to die. Pointing it in the direction of his head, I came down in one swift stab.

The stainless steel blade plunged into Heath's eye.

He screamed and released my hand, clawing at the skewer. Now free, I splayed my hands and legs, using every part of me, even the side of my face, to stop my downward skid.

My slide slowed and stopped.

Heath slowed, but not enough.

By the time he hit the pyramid's base, hard, I could see police cars screaming into the Luxor's entrance. Several on-lookers waving their arms to direct them to his landing spot.

I turned my attention back to the laser.

My climb was tough. Story after story, slipping and making up the distance. But finally I approached the top. The last few panes soaked my hair with sweat and seared my skin where I touched the glass, and I hadn't even reached the top.

The heat was unreal. Over two hundred degrees Fahrenheit, easily. And staring into the light was impossible. This close, it was brighter than the noonday sun in a cloudless sky.

The idea of reaching onto those lighted panes and groping around to find the ring, was comparable to sticking my hand into a blast furnace. Forty billion candlepower? No way in hell I was touching it.

But Heath had been in this spot before he'd descended the pyramid to meet me. The ring had to be close.

Squinting, I stripped down to the bikini top and brushed my silk blouse over the super-hot, illuminated glass like a windshield wiper. There was a hissing sound over the hum of the Xenon lamps—my wet blouse sizzling into steam, but there was also a faint tinkle. Like metal clinking against a window.

On my first try, my blouse had connected with the ring and swept it off the lighted pane—sending it skidding down the side of the Luxor.

I didn't think. I reacted, reaching out, snatching it in my thumb and index finger, burning them as if I'd touched the heating element of a stove. I couldn't hold on. Releasing the ring, I sent it rolling out of my reach, then dove face-first after it.

During training and on missions, I'd bungee jumped. I'd rappelled. I'd jumped out of helicopters and airplanes and off buildings, bridges, and cliff faces.

But nothing matched the sheer terror of body surfing down the Luxor pyramid, picking up speed crazy fast, staring down at such a steep angle it made my bladder clench.

A scream welled up in my chest, panic not far behind, but then my training kicked in and I splayed out my arms and legs to slow my descent. As I got a grip on my fear, I spotted the ring, the goddamn Precious, rolling only a meter ahead of me. Focusing on that and not the ground, I streamlined my body and picked up some speed. I was halfway down the hotel's face, and it had only taken a matter of seconds. But now I concentrated on the goal and once it was within reach, I snatched it up, cupping it in my palm and spitting on the hot metal, feeling it burn, switching hands and spitting on it again to cool it down, and then I was spread-eagled and pushing down with my free hand, causing me to spin as I slid.

I hit the ground hard, two policemen waiting for me, but I rolled through their outstretched arms, got to my feet, and ran for it. I jumped some hedges, went quickly over a fence, and found myself in the pool area.

Tucking the ring into my pocket, I forced myself to slow down and reconnoiter. The warm night meant lots of people at the pool, and my entrance hadn't gotten any attention. I rolled up my jeans, wrapped a hotel pool towel around my waist, and parked on a chaise lounge, getting my heart rate and breathing under control.

Cops came. Cops left. I was invisible, just another tourist.

When ten minutes passed, I picked up a pair of forgotten flip-flops, beelined into the casino, and spent an hour plugging quarter slots.

I won thirty dollars.

Then as the hubbub subsided, I walked out the front door and climbed into a taxi. "Take me to the cheapest hotel in Vegas, off the Strip."

Chandler

"It's best not to focus too much on the past," The Instructor said. *"Not if you want to clearly see the present."*

The Sunny Family Motel was $34 a night, and had a vacancy. After that and the cab, I had enough money left to buy some shorts and a shirt at a nearby gift shop.

I called Jacob to report, and asked him to FedEx me a passport, new ID, and cash. In Chicago and a few other states, I had rental lockers where I kept essentials like that, but didn't have one in Vegas. So I waited sixteen hours for my package to arrive at the front desk.

I spent much of the time sleeping.

I spent some of the time thinking about Heath.

I spent more of the time trying not to.

When my package arrived, I took a cab to the airport and boarded a six pm flight to Chicago. Once I landed at O'Hare, I took the train downtown to the Grant Bark Park, a dog friendly area tucked behind the Chicago Park District Maintenance building. I placed the ring and Bratton's wallet and water-logged and now worthless cell phone into a poop bag, as I'd arranged on the phone with Jacob, then leaving the bag on the ground outside the receptacle, I walked to the nearby tennis courts and pretended to watch two middle aged couples play doubles.

The truth was I hardly saw them. Instead I kept watch on the dog park, waiting for Jacob or someone under him to make an appearance.

I spent even more time trying not to think about Heath.

After thirty minutes ticked by, I'd seen a little tennis and a lot of people, but no one had looked remotely like the way I'd pictured my handler. I walked back into the doggy portion of the park to check my package.

The bag was gone.

Impossible.

How had I missed seeing Jacob? Or had I seen him?

I pulled out my phone and punched in his number. Glancing around the park, I waited for someone's phone to ring, but I couldn't detect a sound over the kids playing Frisbee and the dogs barking in the adjacent free run area.

We recited our codes and Jacob was first to speak.

"I received the package. Nice work."

"Already?"

"I'm good at my job, Chandler."

"So which one were you? The jogger? The kid on the skateboard?"

"You were spying on the drop site?"

"Well, I *am* a spy."

"Funny."

"You were watching me at the parking ramp drop site."

"From a distance. I didn't see your face."

"Your loss."

I couldn't resist a little flirting any more than I could resist getting a glimpse of my new handler. Even if he was cute, I knew any kind of relationship with Jacob would lead to complications I didn't need. But rolling the thought through my mind was entertaining anyway.

Anything to wipe Heath from my memory.

"The guy with the Weimaraner? No, wait. The old man in the wheelchair, right? That was you."

"I'm a voice on the phone, Chandler. Believe me, it's better that way."

"You weren't the nun, were you?"

"Chandler..."

"You were! Wow, nice job. You really looked like a woman."

"I wasn't the nun. I'm not talking about this anymore. And I strongly suggest you don't try this again."

"Or?"

The silence that followed was chilly.

"You haven't asked about Heath Rodriguez," he finally said.

I hadn't. And I wasn't sure I wanted to hear about him now. "Did he die?"

"The ambulance never made it to the hospital. The Las Vegas PD found it a few blocks away from the Strip, everyone inside unconscious, sedated, or strapped down. And Heath, or whatever his real name is, was gone."

I couldn't say I was surprised, but that didn't mean I was happy. I hadn't wanted Heath to die, but any chance I'd run into him again at some point, made me more than a little uneasy.

"So who was he working for?"

"I don't know. Not yet, anyway. But the two of you sure left Vegas in a mess."

"I thought whatever happened in Vegas stayed in Vegas."

"Some of it. You'll be happy to know your Russian friends are either in jail or the morgue."

"Who were they?"

"No one is talking, but several have ties to the Russian mob operating out of the Ukraine."

"And the Venezuelan?"

"He's in the wind. We're doing our best to sort through the rest."

"So what's the whole ring thing about?"

"Don't know yet."

I wasn't often eager to know the details of the fallout after a hit. But this one was different. The men at the restaurant, the Russians in the casino, I had to admit I was itching to know what these groups were after.

"Whatever you learn, let me know, okay?"

"Sure." Jacob said, his tone not remotely convincing.

"It's beyond my security clearance, isn't it?"

"You know how it works."

I did. As a field operative, it was too risky for me to know much. I could be subjected to interrogation, torture, or any number of ways they could force me to talk. Best I not have anything too important to say.

But that didn't mean I wasn't curious.

"Now go home. Get some sleep. I hate to send you back to O'Hare so soon, but there will be a plane ticket waiting for you. You're flying out Monday."

"Where am I going?" I asked.

"Times Square. The Marriot Marquis hotel. This assignment is a bit of a rush, so I'll have to let you know more after you check in."

"Not even a hint?"

"After what you've just been through, this should feel like a vacation."

I liked the sound of that. A vacation in the Big Apple, the real one this time, not a scooter chase through a themed casino in Las Vegas.

I could go for a little reality. Things being even remotely what they seemed would be a refreshing change of pace.

"Bring it on."

Senator Ratzenburger

The junior senator from the great state of Arizona wasn't a man who enjoyed attending weekly worship services. The music was too loud, the pastor too long winded, and the coffee during fellowship afterwards was almost always as weak as water. But he went nonetheless, every week like clockwork, no matter where he was. Holidays as well, of course.

His opponents liked to say his churchgoing was an election ploy, but anyone who knew him realized his motivations went much deeper than that. The senator was a holy man. He might not enjoy the service the way he enjoyed a baseball game, but he was willing to put in the time and effort to ensure his understanding of God's will was the correct one.

Today, of course, was different.

Not only was he in church for a sparsely attended Saturday evening service, but he was alone, and he was here for more than the good word.

He took his seat in a pew three from the back and waited, looking at the backs of the few worshippers in front of him, thinking of tomorrow afternoon's golf outing with two fellow members of the Senate Defense Committee.

He didn't notice the man sitting in the pew behind him until he spoke.

"The item was recovered."

The organ launched into "Am I a Soldier of the Cross", and Ratzenburger pulled a hymnal from the back of the pew in front of him and opened it with trembling hands. "And Bratton?"

"Taken care of."

His knees felt a little weak. He'd stuck out his neck for Dominic Bratton. When he'd learned the man was attempting to sell his research to the highest bidder, research bought and paid for by Uncle Sam and was meant for righteous things, Ratzenburger had feared the worst.

"So we have what we need?"

The organ soared, drowning out the voices of the few parishioners in attendance. The man sitting behind didn't answer.

"Do we have what we need?" Ratzenburger repeated.

"During the recovery attempt, the blood sample set in the ring was subjected to a great deal of heat."

"Destroyed?"

"Yes."

Heaviness settled over Ratzenburger's shoulders. Years had gone into his plan. For it to end when it hadn't really had a chance to begin was hard to bear. "So it's over then."

"Not quite."

Bracing himself, he waited for the man he knew as The Instructor to continue.

"We were able to get a Long Island phone number from Bratton's phone. A microbiologist named Pembrooke. I'll be in touch with him soon."

Ratzenburger smiled down into his hymnal. "You'll keep me informed?" he asked. And when no one answered, he glanced back at the empty pew.

Heath

Sitting in the dark of an apartment in the heart of Tijuana, Heath poured over his computer, sifting through a series of reports he wasn't meant to see. There were few as good at hacking as he was, and while one of them had designed the cyber security guarding the confidential files of a secret government agency called Hydra and cost him countless hours, he had found a backdoor entrance in the end, no doubt built by the designer of security himself.

"*Soy tu dueño, cabron.*"

I own you.

Heath leaned back in his chair, enjoying the hard won victory. His head ached with a pain no pill would cure, the socket where his eye had once been covered by a bandage. He rubbed his good eye, took a healthy swig of Patron from the bottle next to him—not Burdeos or Platinum but a respectable Anejo—and focused on the report.

There was no mention of him, only of a Latino spy who had killed Bratton and stolen the items he'd been trying to sell at auction. As far as anyone could prove, he'd been at a beach house in Puerto Penasco, Mexico, also known as Rocky Point, recovering after losing his eye in an amateur bullfight.

He'd be going back there, to the housekeeper, Analisa, who was beautiful and warm and wonderfully talented with her mouth. But even though she was everything he could ask for and more, she wasn't Simone.

Heath scanned the screen, looking for any mention of the operative who'd recovered Bratton's ring, but there was nothing.

Not until he dug a bit deeper.

There, three quarters of the way down on a sub report issued by her handler, a man named Jacob, was a single name. It was obviously a codename. But even her codename was everything he could have hoped for.

Chandler.

He said the name out loud, caressing it with his tongue the way he had caressed the most intimate parts of her body.

His soul mate.

His nemesis.

The love of his life.

She hadn't beaten him—he'd destroyed Bratton's research before she'd taken it to The Instructor—but in all of his career, from the moment he agreed to be a soldier to this very second, no one had ever come as close.

Heath wouldn't forget her. And not just because she had taken his eye. That was just one of his many regrets.

He could see it now, looking at the Hydra reports. He'd believed destroying Bratton's discovery was the right thing, the just thing, but he should have known the world wouldn't make things that clear and easy.

There was never an end to evil. Heath might have obliterated one incarnation, but *El Diablo* would counter by simply coming up with another. He should have seen that possibility, should have recognized the relentless march. If there was anything he'd failed to do, it was that.

The fight was far from over.

Next time he got his hands on something of this magnitude, he would protect it, keep it, use it to fight back. He would win justice for those who had none. And he would let no one get in his way.

Not even his Chandler.

EXPOSED

ABOUT EXPOSED

She's an elite spy, working for an agency so secret only three people know it exists. Trained by the best of the best, she has honed her body, her instincts, and her intellect to become the perfect weapon.

CODENAME: CHANDLER

Before special operative Chandler was forced to FLEE, she executed the most difficult missions—and most dangerous people—for the government. So when she's tasked with saving a VIP's daughter from human traffickers, Chandler expects the operation to be by the numbers...until she uncovers a secret that will endanger the entire population of New York City, and possibly the world.

EXPOSED

Death is in her blood.

Don't blame her. It's in her blood.

Prologue

Her eyes open to the steady *beep ... beep ... beep* of a heart monitor machine.

She's in a hospital bed. Alone. Wearing one of those flimsy gowns.

She has no idea how she got here.

An overdose? Did she take too many downs?

She concentrates, tries to remember.

Her last memory is of ...

Of what?

Walking somewhere. To the dealer?

No. To the free clinic. Ashamed, hoping her STD was something that could be treated with a pill.

She talked to three different doctors. They took her blood. Made her wait a long time.

And then ...

A shot. They gave her a shot. She touches the spot on her arm, then notices the IV tube snaking from the back of her hand, the sensor pads stuck to her chest.

They gave her a shot, and now she's in the hospital?

She glances around the room. White walls, no window, not even a television. This place doesn't smell like a hospital. It smells like a garage.

Where is she?

She looks for a call button, can't find one, and then begins to yell for the nurse.

She yells several times.

No one comes.

Was anyone there at all?

Beep ... beep ... beep ...

She sits up, feeling absolutely normal. No pain beyond the tug of the needle in her hand. No dizziness. So why is she here?

"Someone answer me!"

No answer.

She's thirsty. She has to pee. She needs to know what's going on.

Using her fingernails, she picks the edge of the tape on her hand, then peels it back and tugs out the IV, wincing as the blood beads up. Then she reaches under her gown and tears the sticky pads from her skin.

The machine by her bed stops beeping, giving way to a sustained tone. Like someone just died.

Still no one comes.

There's a drawer next to the bed, but her clothes aren't in it.

She stands, the white tile cold under her bare feet, and pads over to the door.

Opens it.

This isn't a hospital.

It's a warehouse. A big warehouse, with concrete floors, steel walls, forty-foot ceilings. There are pieces of medical equipment on carts, several tables and chairs, some cages along the far wall, and ...

Oh, sweet Lord.

Dead people.

Lots and lots of dead people.

Many are in white lab coats, stained with blood. Others are in what look like military fatigues, equally soaked in red.

A dozen. Maybe more. Lying on the ground. Propped against a chair. Sprawled out on a table. Two crimson figures, arms around one another, bruised faces forever frozen in agony.

Then the smell hits her.

She chokes back a sob and begins to run, past the cages, which are filled with—dead monkeys?—heading for a door at the other side of the building, praying it isn't locked, skidding to a stop when it suddenly opens wide and an army guy stands there with a big rifle pointed her way.

"Help me. I don't know what's happening."

"There's been an attack," he says. His eyes quickly scan her, stopping on her hand. "You're bleeding."

She glances down at her hand, where the IV needle had been. A slow trickle of blood snakes down her index finger.

"It's just—"

"Hold still," he orders. Then he pulls something off of his belt, and before she can react he's spraying her hand with some sort of foam. It dries almost instantly, forming a hard crust.

"What is—"

"A liquid bandage. Quickly, come with me."

He has an accent she can't place, but she doesn't care where he's from. He's there for her, there to help her. She takes his gloved hand, and he leads her outside, into the blinding sunlight.

Water laps a shoreline to the left and to the right.

An island?

She smells salt riding the air, the scent familiar. The Atlantic Ocean.

There's a sound, too, beating in her ears, a helicopter on a landing pad, its blades whirling. The soldier nods at the two army guys standing guard and then takes her to it.

She's scared, confused. But she wants to get out of here, to get away from all the dead people. As they buckle their seatbelts, she's very close to crying. Then the soldier smiles at her.

"You're very beautiful," he says.

His words surprise her. She thinks she must look terrible. That tacky gown. No make-up. Her hair all messed to hell. But she knows she's pretty. She's been getting by on her looks since she was twelve.

"I want to be a model," she says. It's a weird thing to say, but she doesn't want to talk about the dead people.

He nods, appears to think it over. Then he says, "You know, I have a friend, works for a modeling agency. I bet he could help you."

"Really?" This has to be the most surreal moment in her entire life, and she almost wonders if it's all a dream.

"Do you have family? Someone who would be worried about you?"

She hesitates, then shakes her head.

"I'll call my friend. You can stay with him. He's very famous. Did covers for *Vogue* and *Elle*. He rescues models all the time."

The chopper lifts off and zooms over water. A larger island unfolds beneath them, Long Island, the vague haze of New York City barely visible in the distance.

Despite not wanting to think, she wonders what's going on. Why she's here. Why all those people are dead.

She wonders if they cured her STD.

But all of that pales in comparison to what the army guy said.

She came to New York to get discovered.

Now, maybe, she finally would be.

Chandler

Several years ago ... before I had to FLEE ...

"To a special operative like yourself," The Instructor said, "it can be tempting to rely on your physical training and strength. But some missions will call

for more than that. Many times, knowing how to fit into your surroundings, understanding human behavior, and plain old acting skills will be more effective than brute force. Learn to be a chameleon, and you have a better chance of being successful."

I have always preferred formulating my own explosive with household chemicals to creating a smoky eye in the makeup mirror. So when I pulled the barely-there dress and four-inch Jimmy Choos out of the FedEx package the bellman had brought up to my hotel room, my stomach gave a nervous flutter.

Not a good sign in a spy who had been trained to control her emotions.

I returned the cell phone to my ear and frowned, hoping my new handler could sense my attitude as it bounced off New York City's cell towers.

"So where does this op take place, Jacob? A strip club?"

He laughed, the sound a slightly robotic, electronically disguised version of his real voice.

Not that I'd ever heard his real voice.

"If you want, I can call around, see if any of the area clubs have an amateur night."

I couldn't help but smile, at least a little. Jacob and I hadn't worked together long—this was only our third operation together—and I was still trying to figure out if I trusted him. On the positive side, I was a sucker for humor.

But that didn't mean I appreciated his fashion sense.

"I can't conceal a weapon in this outfit. You realize that, right?"

Pushing my dark hair over one shoulder, I held the dress against my body with my free hand and peered into the Manhattan hotel room's mirrored closet door.

Okay, so it was hot. Damn hot.

Maybe I could make due with a knife strapped to the inside of my thigh.

It would have to be a very short knife.

"You can't be carrying. They'll search you before they let you inside."

"And my cell phone? Where am I supposed to stash that?" Jacob had just sent me a new encrypted cell, and I was under strict orders to keep it with me at all times, no exceptions. It was even waterproof, so I could take it into the shower.

"Did you notice the bag? Check the lining. Like the dress, it's been prepared for you."

I took another look in the box. A small, cross-body purse lay at the bottom, black sequins and tassels. I opened it, running my fingertips over the interior and feeling the familiar shapes of two rolled bills and two small wires. I had emergency cash and lock picks sewn into the hems of all my clothing. Being prepared wasn't only for Boy Scouts.

"The strap has a steel wire in it," Jacob continued. "It can be used as a garrote."

I tugged on the strap, feeling the bite of the wire inside the leather. "Talk about a killer handbag."

"So now that we have your wardrobe covered, care to hear what you'll be doing?"

"Shoot."

"That's it, actually. You'll be going to a photo shoot."

"As in a modeling photo shoot?" Not a typical day in my line of work. "Explain."

"The Bradford and Sims Modeling Agency is a front for—"

"Let me guess. Porn."

"Too easy, but yes. And human trafficking. They promise stardom to young girls, then ship them overseas and sell them."

"Sexual slavery. Nice."

"We're still gathering information on the group."

Gathering information? In our first two ops, Jacob had been all about preparation. He'd known everything about everything. That he was sending me in before he really knew what I was facing made me uneasy.

"Is this a rush job?" I asked.

"Marked urgent, and we only have a small time window, so we'll need to keep in close contact in case the situation changes."

"These traffickers, you want me to read them bedtime stories?" Before I put them to sleep.

"They aren't the important thing here. They've recruited the eighteen-year-old daughter of a VIP. You are to return her to her father unharmed. Not a scratch. The orders are specific about that. She cannot be harmed in any way, not even slightly. I'm sending her photo. She's using the name Julianne James."

A babysitting job. A first for me. I glanced at the phone, and a picture of a pretty blonde came up on the screen.

"Who's her daddy?"

"I don't have that information."

It had to be someone important if they were sending me in. There weren't very many agents in the world with my kind of training.

"Where is the shoot?"

"North of the Hamptons. Your contact is working as a driver for the modeling agency. Your exchange is *E-B-P-D*."

"Got it."

"He'll introduce you as new recruit Claire Thomas."

"Claire Thomas," I repeated, trying on my new name. I used and discarded identities like Kleenex. The only constant was my codename: Chandler. My real name was nobody's business.

"You're twenty-five years old, an aspiring model from Brooklyn. Your contact will get you in. After you get the girl, text your location to this number, and he'll pick you up."

A number appeared on the screen.

"He'll be at the curb in twenty minutes. And Chandler?"

"Yes."

"The girl thinks she's getting her big break. She might need some convincing before she'll be willing to leave."

"And if I can't convince her?"

"Just get her out of there in one piece. Unharmed." Jacob signed off.

I got dressed and did my best to channel my inner Max Factor while I sank into the role. I was a wannabe model. Several years younger than my actual age. Pretty. Spoiled. Used to getting my way, but still naive about men. I was looking for my big break. I would do whatever I could to get it.

I went heavy on the make-up, dark eyes and too much pink lip gloss. The dress fit as if it was designed for me, and the shoes made me feel like sex on a stick.

"I'm Claire Thomas," I said into the mirror. And I believed it.

I slipped my phone into the purse, then headed down to meet my contact.

Human voices, background music, and the clack of heels on marble floors all rose to greet me before I reached the ground floor. The scent of coffee drifted from the resident Starbucks, and a woman passed me wearing enough perfume to enchant half of Times Square.

I personally disliked big anonymous hotels. But due to my frequent need to be anonymous, I stayed in them often. Sometimes the best place to hide was in a crowd. Even so, negotiating the revolving door and stepping out into summer's hot chaos on the flashing neon streets of New York overloaded my senses. The smell of hot dogs on the street corner and falafel down the block warred with exhaust and teeming humanity. The jangle of car horns and voices and the thump of a bass guitar assaulted me from various angles. The late morning was warmer, stickier, than the hotel lobby, a bit of autumn cool threatening to make an appearance but chickening out.

I paused and forced myself to focus, cataloging each noise and smell and sight, becoming grounded in the now. At the same time, I shut off part of myself—the part that worried about applying makeup and got an ego boost from a good dress and sexy shoes—and I let the other part take over.

The part that had been trained to kill people for the government.

Dismissing the white noise and glitz and big city smells, I ignored what belonged there and singled out what didn't.

Someone was watching me.

I glanced north to 46th Street.

A man stared at me, standing with his hands at his sides, on the curb next to a black Lincoln Town Car. He was in his mid-thirties, handsome in that GQ kind of way, dressed in a dark suit and sunglasses. It wasn't his appearance or the car that raised my notice—in midtown Manhattan, the only type of vehicle more common than a black Town Car was a yellow taxi cab, and many of the chauffeurs dressed as if they were auditioning for a role in the *Men In Black* sequel. No, it was his air of calmness, of stillness, of total focus, that was strong enough to raise the hair on my arms.

And in that split-second assessment, I judged him to be a dangerous man.

My contact, no doubt.

I made a quick visual sweep of the street to be certain he was alone, and then I walked to the car. As I approached, he climbed out, circled to the curb, and reached for the back door handle with his left hand.

"Miss Thomas?"

I nodded. "Hello, Eddie."

"Going to the ballet?"

"How about the park?"

"Yes. They have ducks."

I suppressed a smile, amused that the only noun beginning with the letter *D* he could manage on the fly was *ducks*. His danger vibe went down a notch.

He opened the door and I settled into the leather seat, then he circled back to his spot behind the wheel, and soon we joined the flow of cabs, limos, and delivery trucks.

Traffic moved well, and it took less time than I'd estimated for us to get through midtown, take the Queens Midtown Tunnel under the East River, and hit the Long Island Expressway. Industrial landscapes gave way to shopping malls and carefully managed green space, then on to nature preserves, beaches, and country clubs. I inched the window open. The scents of salt water and fresh cut grass tinged the air and the screech of gulls rose over the whistling wind. The expressway dwindled to winding roads and the housing seemed to range from vacation mansions to vacation palaces.

"These aren't nice men, you know." The first words he'd said since I'd climbed in the car.

His face tilted up to the rearview mirror, and I met his stare.

"I'm not nice, either."

I watched his lips turn up in the barest hint of a smile. "I know we're strangers, but can we get on a code-name basis?"

"Call me Chandler."

"Call me Morrissey."

I wished I could see his eyes, but they were hidden by his sunglasses. "Thanks for the tip, Morrissey."

He swung the car into a long drive that wound through a copse of salt-stunted trees.

"They aren't going to let you take her. Not without a fight. And they're armed. You're not."

"How do you know I'm not?"

"Your purse doesn't have anything heavier than a cell phone in it. I can tell by how it hangs. And that dress ... you couldn't conceal anything in that dress."

"Just make sure you're ready to pick us up when you're called."

"I'll be ready for more than that."

The car emerged from foliage, and I caught my first glimpse of the house. All contemporary angles, glass and sprawl, it looked cold and hard and expensive. The blue of the water beyond held the unreal look of a movie set.

I scooped in a breath of salt air. *My big break. Photos on the beach. My name is Claire Thomas, and The Bradford and Sims Modeling Agency is going to make me a star.*

"Remember," Morrissey said out of the corner of his mouth, "she can't be harmed."

That again.

I was going to ask him what the deal was with that when the front door opened, and a man wearing a blue polo shirt and gray trousers stepped out. Shoulders as wide as a line-backer's, he squinted blue eyes into the sun, his scalp pink under blond stubble. He stood at the top of the staircase, a Tec-9 submachine gun hanging under his arm on a strap.

What kind of modeling agency required that much fire power?

"Follow my lead." Morrissey gave me a final look and stepped out of the car. He circled the Lincoln and opened my door. Like a good chauffeur, he offered his hand to help me from the car.

I took it. His skin felt rough, a man used to doing more than driving for a living. Jacob hadn't told me anything about him, but most likely his work was similar to mine. Though I didn't let on, I liked that he noticed my dress. After all this, maybe we'd have an opportunity to get together. There was no room in my life for a real relationship, but that didn't mean I had no needs. Someone like him might be just the ticket. No strings, no complications.

He hauled me out into the sun and released my hand. I allowed myself to look him over as I followed him up the steps. The stillness I'd noticed earlier left his body, and his stride took on the swagger of a man who fancied himself a player. He tossed a look over his shoulder, pride with a hint of ownership in his gaze, as if he'd just won a hand of blackjack in Vegas and I was his prize.

I had to wonder if I changed that drastically when settling into character. Probably. It was hard to know who another person really was, but in this line of work it was damn near impossible.

I'd be smarter to stick to the usual outlet for my sexual energy; random men picked up in bars.

Morrissey stopped in front of the burly sentinel and cocked one leg. "Hey, Udelhoffer. How's it going?"

The behemoth eyed me. "Who is this?" His accent carried hints of Eastern Europe but with Brooklyn overtones, suggesting to me he'd been in the States for a while.

"Nice, huh?" Morrissey said, continuing with his schtick. "Your boss said if I found girls to model, he'd give a bonus. If they had something special clients liked, a little extra."

"This is a closed shoot."

"Not what I heard."

The big man gave Morrissey a dead-man's stare. "You heard wrong."

I kept silent. A young girl in my situation wouldn't dare be too forward, not with her dreams on the line. If Morrissey couldn't pull this off, I'd find another way.

Morrissey thrust out his hand, palms up. "So, what? You expect me to turn around and drive all the way back to the city?"

Another stare for an answer, silent this time.

Morrissey shook his head. "Not gonna happen. I was given promises. I stuck my neck out here. This one?" He motioned to me, "A favor for Tony D'Angelo."

The man didn't even spare me a glance but kept his attention on Morrissey.

"You know who D'Angelo is, right?"

A nod from the hired help.

Morrissey continued, punctuating his words with thrusting waves of his hands. "I said I'd help her get a job, know what I mean? He's not going to like it if I don't come through on my word. He might even call some of his friends, you know? And I ain't going to take all the blame."

Udelhoffer let out a heavy sigh. "Wait here." He stepped into the house and closed the door behind him.

I did a quick scan of the doorway and eaves. No closed circuit cameras. Probably not needed with an armed guard at the entrance. Even so, I kept my voice low, paranoid about bugs.

"D'Angelo? Let me guess. Gambino family?"

Morrissey gave a curt nod. "I needed to make it easier to let you in than turn you away."

"And you think they'll buy that I'm some mistress he needs to get rid of?"

"That depends on how well you sell it."

When I'd assumed a cover identity in the past, I had prided myself on preparation. Knowing everything about who I was supposed to be and who I was dealing with had saved my ass more than once. This operation had been rushed from the beginning, and now I was supposed to be the pawn of a mob figure I knew nothing about. I had to wonder if, in getting me in the door, Morrissey had just handed me a death sentence.

"I can sell it."

I would have to. Not only was my life dependent on it, but so was a girl's future.

The door swung open and Udelhoffer motioned me inside. As soon as I stepped into the marble foyer, he held up a hand, blocking Morrissey. "You'll hear from me if she works out."

Morrissey nodded and the door closed in his face.

I was on my own.

The man stared down at me with the dim look of hired muscle. "You wanna be a model, huh?"

I channeled eager. "More than anything."

He shrugged a shoulder and heaved another sigh. "Yeah. We'll take care of you. Purse."

"Huh?"

He grabbed it without asking, digging a paw inside, fingering my phone and make-up. If he noticed I was conveniently missing a wallet or any kind of ID, he didn't give me any indication it made him suspicious.

"Come with me."

I followed Udelhoffer to the back of the house, taking note of my surroundings as I went. The house was furnished in a modern, generic style, the pieces and arrangements big on price tags but low on originality or warmth. I smelled gardenias from the back porch, a hint of some sort of animal musk, and the distinctive oniony, deep-fried smell of McDonalds coming from the kitchen and breakfast nook. A police scanner erupted in fits and starts, blending with a faint Latin beat drifting from somewhere in the house.

"How many girls are you shooting today?" I said without selling the obvious irony.

Udelhoffer kept walking, not bothering to answer. He led me out to a patio surrounding a kidney-shaped pool. The air smelled of salt water and fish, and beyond the pool, sunlight shimmered on Long Island Sound. Three other men stood near the diving board. They weren't armed that I could see, but I wouldn't be surprised if they had weapons nearby. The blonde in Jacob's picture perched on a chaise lounge, dressed in a miniskirt and tee, a small carry-on suitcase on the paving stones in front of her sandaled feet.

No one even pretended to be snapping photos.

Udelhoffer stopped in front of a swarthy man with a hawk-like hooked nose, and they shared a few hushed words.

Too quiet for me to hear, but I'm a fair lip reader. I saw *Gambino*, *favor*, and *ice*.

Even though the big man towered above, it was clear from their body language that Hawk Nose was in charge. Dressed in a button-down open at the neck, he looked more like a South American businessman than a thug, except for the shoulder holster under his jacket.

The third was average height and skinny, yet judging from the sinewy muscles in his arms, as strong as steel wire. He had ex-military written all over him and reminded me of a man I'd killed in Columbia. Tight shirt, and I didn't spot his carry until I noticed the bulge on his right ankle.

The fourth was portly, with sweat stains in the armpits of his Hawaiian shirt. He wore khakis and loafers, no socks, and I couldn't spot a pistol on him. An investor, maybe? Or a perspective buyer?

Udelhoffer finished his briefing, and Hawk Nose slowly walked over to me, a smile on his face that was pure mockery. "So … you ever model before?"

I pegged his accent as Venezuelan. "I've done some—"

"Then you know how this works."

I had no clue. But since I doubted he did either, I gave him what I hoped was an enthusiastic nod and motioned to Julianne James, the real reason I was there. "Should I go sit down with the other model while you get ready?"

"In a minute."

His smile widened. He grabbed a nearby bag, rummaged inside, then held up a skimpy bikini.

"Put this on … for the pictures. And since you're a model, you should be used to dressing and undressing at the shoot."

These men might not be overly concerned about selling their modeling agency cover, but they weren't stupid. Making me strip in front of them provided more than a cheap thrill. It let them check if I was wearing a wire. Or a weapon.

"Sure."

I unslung my purse. Leaving my heels on, I pulled the dress over my head. Next I slipped off my bra, stepped out of my panties and stood in front of them totally nude.

The fact that four men were staring didn't bother me. After all, I was a model, used to being gawked at. I tried on a playful smile and held out my hand for the bikini.

After a lengthy pause, the man in charge handed me a scrap of a swimsuit.

I pulled it on, keeping my voice steady. "Let me know when you're ready for me," I breathed, then wiggled across the patio and took the chair beside the blonde.

"I'm Claire."

"Julianne."

I peered into her sunglasses, but only my reflection stared back.

"Are you going to be part of the shoot?"

A slow shake of her head.

"They say I'm going to Paris." She didn't seem convinced, and the syllables took too long to roll off her tongue. From all appearances she was under the influence of something beyond the lust for modeling stardom.

"Really?" I forced awe into my voice. "To model? When?"

"They said soon."

Jacob might not have a lot of information about this operation, but what he did have was correct as usual. Now I only had to figure out how to get her out of here before "soon" rolled around.

"Have you signed a contract?"

Another head shake. For someone who'd been told she was about to go to Paris to model, Julianne was acting incredibly detached.

"I know an attorney. He told me what to look for. You know, just to make sure you're getting what you're worth."

I didn't know if an eighteen year old would care about something as practical as contract negotiation, especially when she was sailing on whatever drug they had given her. But I needed to lure her away from the pool and the men watching us, and beyond physically dragging her, I had few options. "If we could go somewhere private for just a few seconds, I'll fill you in."

"No, thanks."

"It'll just take—"

She lowered her voice. "They aren't going to like you talking to me."

Then I understood. I wasn't hearing disinterest in her voice. I was hearing worry.

"Why not?" I asked.

She leaned in closer. "They haven't taken any pictures of me. They won't let me leave. I can't even make outside phone calls."

"You're the only girl here?"

"No. There are others. But they're doing X-rated stuff."

"Have they made you do any?" I asked, feeling myself grow cold.

"They haven't even asked. No one has tried anything." She shook her head, like she was denying an accusation. "Men have always liked me. I've never been around guys who didn't try to hit on me."

My first thought was surprise that these men hadn't tasted the goods.

My second was that maybe there was a reason.

"Julianne, are you a virgin?"

Virgins fetched top dollar on the slave market.

A crease dug between her eyebrows. "What?"

"Are you?"

"Not since I was fourteen." She lowered her sunglasses, staring into my eyes. They were glassy, but there was panic dancing beneath the dope haze.

"Have they hurt you? Threatened you?"

"They mostly ignore me. I thought maybe they were gay, but I saw two of them messing around with the other girls."

I considered repeating what Jacob had told me, that she was going to be sold. But I didn't see how scaring her even more would improve the situation. Besides, something wasn't adding up.

"I don't think they're taking me to Paris," she said.

"So why are you here?"

"I don't know." Her eyes focused on me, and she lowered her voice to a whisper. "I'm scared."

"I can get you out of here," I said. "Do you want me to?"

She nodded. "Will you? Please?"

"Leave it to me, okay? Just be ready when I tell you."

"Thanks." She reached over, squeezed my hand.

I squeezed back.

Movement, in my peripheral vision. Hawaiian Shirt had left the other men and was now circling the pool to where we sat, an expensive-looking digital camera around his neck. He motioned to me, the tip of his tongue flicking out and running across his bottom lip.

"Okay, you. Miss Hot to Trot. Come on."

I didn't want to let Julianne out of my sight, but I couldn't exactly refuse my chance to become a big star. A few bikini shots in the sand would still give me a chance to keep an eye on her. I scrambled to my feet, doing my best to look excited.

He turned in the direction of the house.

"I thought we were going to shoot on the beach, since I'm wearing a swim suit and all."

He opened the patio door and ushered me inside. "Trust me, honey. This will be better."

Inside he made for the staircase to the second floor.

I could guess what kind of pictures he was planning to take. A guess that was confirmed as we went deeper into the mansion. A long hallway opened at the top of the stairs, doors flanking both sides, most standing open. I peeked into the first, hearing moaning.

The lighting—a simple klieg on a tripod—was strictly amateur hour. And so was the talent. But what she lacked in professionalism she made up for with enthusiasm. I guessed this shoot could have been called, *I Love Fruit*, because that's what the girl was doing.

"Now the Bartlett, babe," the cameraman cooed as he snapped away. "And put the strawberry up to your lips. No, your other lips."

The next door down was a video production of the more vanilla variety. Guy on girl, pretty standard stuff.

Scratch that. An animal musk odor made me look closer, and I noticed a miniature donkey next to the bed.

I'd call that production, *A Piece of Ass.*

"You like to watch?" Hawaiian Shirt asked, leering over his shoulder.

"I'm more of a doer than a watcher," I answered, hoping my grin looked real.

We passed another door, saw another video shoot.

I'm pretty shock-proof, but my cover persona, Claire Thomas, wouldn't be.

"Yuck." I gave a shudder. "That's gross."

"Gotta keep upping the ante," Hawaiian Shirt said. "We're calling it *Three Girls, One Cup.* You want to join in?"

"No, thanks. I already ate. And I don't want to eat *that.*"

We were almost to the end of the hall when a sound caught my attention. More a beat in my chest than a noise, but I recognized it immediately.

A helicopter.

Many millionaires had vacation homes in the area and few suffered the inconvenience of traffic snarls on their way back and forth to Manhattan. Around here, helipads were as common as tennis courts. But as much as I told myself all these facts, my gut said the arrival of this particular aircraft was no coincidence. It was here for Julianne, and I was stuck modeling for nudie shots with this chubby Seymore Butts wannabe.

He chose the last bedroom on the left.

The room was large, furnished only by a king size bed. It smelled of new paint and sheets that needed changing. Windows looked out on the Sound, and I spotted a purple Bell corporate-type helicopter approaching the beach.

"Let's try a few on the bed. Take off your top, show me those sweet tits again."

I struggled to look unsure.

"Come on, all the famous bitches did nudes. Marilyn Monroe did nudes. You want to be famous like her, right?"

I chewed my lower lip and pretended to think it over. "Well, okay, I guess."

I set my purse on the nightstand, perched on the bed and untied the bikini top. I needed an opening, some way to escape my photographer without the men downstairs finding out and greeting me with gunfire.

I let the top fall to the bed.

He snapped a few shots then paused, stretching his neck.

"Stiff neck?" I asked.

"It's nothing. Arch your back more. Show me what a hot little slut you are."

I'll show you something else instead.

"I can help you with that," I cooed. "The stiff neck. I used to date a chiropractor."

I climbed to my knees. Sitting back on my heels, I spread my thighs wide and patted the bed in front of me. "Why don't you come over here."

The smile spreading over his fat face had nothing to do with spinal adjustment. He put down the camera and sat where I'd indicated.

I massaged his shoulders for a few seconds, then unbuttoned his shirt, revolted that his boobs were even larger than mine.

"You really do want a modeling career, don't you?"

"More than anything." I pressed myself against his back, skin on skin. Circling my arms around his shoulders, I snaked one hand down to his crotch.

He moaned, deep in his throat.

"I can adjust this, too," I said.

"Oh, yeah, baby. Here I thought I was going to have to slap you around. I still might. Horny bitch like you would like that, I bet."

Charming.

I cradled his head between my breasts then smoothed my right hand around his shoulder and massaged up the back of his head to his scalp. I could feel him relax, goose bumps rising on his back.

I collared his neck with my left arm, and then before he realized what was happening, I grabbed my right elbow, pushed his head downward into the V of my left arm and flexed my biceps, applying pressure to his carotid artery.

He tensed, but even though he had weight and strength on me, it only took seconds before he was unconscious. Stopping the blood supply to the brain will do that.

I slipped out behind him and let his body fall back on the bed.

Breaking someone's neck isn't as easy as it looks in the movies. It also isn't lethal 100% of the time.

Breaking someone's trachea and cutting of their air supply is simpler, and more effective. It's possible to survive a broken neck. Survive not breathing? Not so much.

I chopped the sex-trafficking pig in the windpipe, not sticking around to watch him suffocate. Grabbing my scrap of a bikini top, I slipped the memory card out of the camera and into my purse and closed the door behind me.

I had finished tying the top around my back and slinging my purse across my chest by the time I reached the patio. The *whump whump whump* of the helicopter blade pulsed in the air. The sun glared off the water, making me squint. Raising my hand to shield my eyes, I scanned the chairs surrounding the pool.

The other men were gone.

So was Julianne James.

"No operation is simple," said The Instructor. "Things can invariably go wrong, and like any good soldier, you have to be ready to improvise, adapt, overcome."

I started down the steps, leaving the door open behind me. Once the helicopter left the ground, Julianne would be lost, and I'd be damned if I was going to let that happen. She had taken up with some bad people, which made her more like me at that age than I wanted to admit. But I'd been given another chance.

She deserved one, too.

"Where are you going?"

I hadn't spotted Udelhoffer standing behind a hedge that separated pool from lawn, but now he stepped out from the right, coming at me fast for such a big man.

Adrenaline spiked my blood, making everything slower, clearer. Udelhoffer's movement. The drum of my heartbeat. The smell of the water and screech of the gulls. I stopped and held up my hands. "I was just wondering where everyone went."

"What happened to Ronnie?"

"He's taking a breather."

Udelhoffer's eyes narrowed. His beefy fingers twitched. I could see him thinking it over. Asking himself, is this just some dumb bimbo, or is something going on here?

His training kicked in.

His hand went for the Tec-9.

I anticipated the move and kicked to the side, my right foot striking just below his knee cap. I followed the blow through, scraping the side of my shoe down his shin, drilling the stiletto heel into his instep.

He bellowed like a bull.

Without pause, I brought a knife hand blow to his forearm, targeting his radial nerve just below the elbow. Localized strikes are hard to pull off on a moving target, but I was fast.

The Tec-9 fell from his grip and swung on its sling. I grabbed the strap, dropped, and jerked it off his shoulder, twisting as I did. Then I released. The machine gun skittered across flagstones without going off.

I moved to follow-up with a chin jab, missing and hitting his chest. High heels were effective weapons, but they also made balancing trickier. By putting so much of my weight behind the stab to his foot and the blow to his arm, I'd left myself unbalanced.

I saw him aim the palm of his hand for my chin, but I couldn't reverse my momentum fast enough.

My head snapped backward, the blow clanging through my skull. My brain stuttered, overtaken with too much stimuli at once. I staggered, almost going down. Motes of light swirled in my vision just as the pain came.

He lunged at me again, slamming a fist into my solar plexus.

Air burst from my lungs, and I doubled over and tried not to puke.

He came at me again, an old-fashioned right hook this time.

I twisted out of the way, causing his attack to bounce off the top of my skull. But even though it was a glancing blow, the force clanged through my head like a fire bell. I was able to get in close and respond with an elbow strike, snapping it up under his chin, but I wasn't sure the behemoth even felt it.

"That's enough."

I heard the unmistakable sound of someone racking a semi-auto.

Udelhoffer and I both stumbled to a halt. Above us on the steps, Hawk Nose glared down, a 9mm pointed at my chest.

Another dark-haired man emerged from the house, one I hadn't seen before. Wearing a white Scarface suit, he held an automatic pistol.

Outnumbered and outgunned, I dropped my gaze and rounded my shoulders, looking submissive.

"Take her inside. Think you can handle that, Udelhoffer?"

The brute grumbled, breathing hard. He wrapped his left arm around my right like a bridegroom escorting me down the aisle, then grabbed my hand, locking me into place by his side. It was a hold often used by police to convince unruly ci- vilians to come along without a fuss. Just a little pressure and he could easily bring me to the ground or break my elbow.

I gasped as if he was hurting me. "Let me go. Please."

He forced me back in the direction of the house.

The pulse of helicopter blades speeding up their rotation registered somewhere in the back of my mind. If that craft lifted off, Julianne was gone.

I couldn't let that happen.

The man's training and size would enable him to counter any move I threw at him. My only shot was suckering him into underestimating me. I thrashed against him ineffectively, hoping to convince him this was all I had left to give.

"Knock it off." He put pressure on my wrist, and I let out a cry of pain that wasn't entirely acting.

I let him lead me past the pool, and we started up the shallow flagstone steps. Above us, Hawk Nose lowered his pistol. Apparently satisfied that Udelhoffer was under con- trol, he and the other man turned and slipped into the house ahead of us.

Halfway up, I stumbled a little, getting out of step, throwing him slightly off balance. Then I made my move.

I veered toward him and reached down with my free hand, grabbing his balls and yanking them like the handle of a Nautilus machine.

He released my arm, buckling over with a grunt. No matter how much hand-to-hand training a man had, when you went below the belt he forgot everything and tried to protect the goods.

As he leaned forward I slipped to the side, grabbing his shoulder, using his momentum to carry him forward and introduce his head to the stone planter at the top of the stairs. He hit it with a dull *thud*, then crumpled to the ground.

I didn't know if I'd killed him or merely incapacitated him, and I didn't wait to find out. I raced down the stairs and past the pool, kicking the shoes from my feet as I ran for the helicopter.

I wasn't exactly sure what I'd do once I reached it. I had no weapon, no plan. The aircraft was a purple Bell 427, under ten years old. Twin engine, light utility, seated eight. Through the cabin doors I saw four people inside, one of them the pilot, one Julianne. I'd been trained to fly several different varieties of chopper, including more common types used for corporate flying, but I didn't think they were just going to hand over the keys because I asked nicely.

Voices erupted behind me, but I didn't turn to look. I ran in a zigzag pattern, waiting for the pop of gunfire, but it never came.

Then I heard grunting behind me; a runner, giving chase.

I straightened course and pushed more energy into my legs. The grass was stiff and harsh against the soles of my feet, jabbing and slicing. The copter backwash was hot, smelled like exhaust, blowing faster and louder every step closer, until I couldn't hear my pursuer anymore.

But I knew he was still there.

Ahead the helicopter shifted to one side, then started to lift.

I hit a dip in the ground and stumbled to one knee. Pushing off, I righted myself and ran harder.

I could feel the man behind me now, feel his footsteps gaining. I was fast, but in a few strides he would overtake me.

I was nearly upon the aircraft. Sand particles pelted my skin, stirred into the air by the blades. Hair whipped across my eyes. The chopper was now three feet in the air, rising fast.

There was only one thing I could do, and I couldn't believe I was actually going to attempt it.

Once I passed under the chopper, I leaped for all I was worth. My fingertips hit the right skid. I grabbed on, one hand slipping. The helicopter swayed and bucked and for a moment, and I thought the whole thing might come down on top of me. I made another swipe with my loose hand, and this time my fingers held and the helicopter lifted me into the air.

My pursuer was right beneath me. His arms closed around my legs, binding, holding tight. It was the Tony Montana wannabe.

I twisted, fighting to break free.

The chopper tipped and veered to the right.

I pulled a foot loose and kicked, hitting him in the forehead with my heel, but he wouldn't let go.

The blades canted, dangerously low to the ground. One hit and it would be over for all of us. I'd seen a bird cartwheel before. They never found all the pieces of the dead.

I pummeled Scarface with my bare heel, the force shuddering up my leg. His hold slipped. He clawed at my knee, locking my ankle in his armpit, but I kept up my assault, driving my foot into his head, his face, as we ascended.

My grip was one of my best skills. I could crack walnuts barehanded. Once, during training, I hung onto an iron bar for six hours.

But I didn't have an extra hundred eighty pounds gripping my ankles, or the extra g-force of liftoff. Unable to hold on, my left hand slipped off the skid.

My right wrist turned, and I felt like I was being pulled in half. I chanced a look down, saw the ground blurring beneath me, and got a straight shot of fear.

Fear was an ugly, destructive thing. It enveloped you, made you doubt yourself, clouded your thinking and muddied your ability to act.

But human physiology also provided a plus to counter all of those minuses. The fear kick-started my adrenal cortex, and I got a pop of adrenaline that made me feel like my muscles had been electrified.

Screaming against the pain, the weight, I slapped my loose hand up against the skid and doubled my kicking efforts, aiming for my assailant's nose, feeling each impact shudder up from my heel to my palms.

Say! Hello! To! My! Little! Friend!

Scarface finally let go when we were high enough for the fall to break his neck.

The helicopter rolled in the other direction, and it was all I could do to hold on. The air swirled around me, beating like fists. Tears filled my eyes and streaked my face. Hair lashed my cheeks.

If I lived through this, I swore I'd shave my head.

The copter leveled and rose into the air. My shoulder and chest still ached from Udelhoffer's blows, and I groaned as I performed a pull-up and hooked my elbows over the skid. Below, the ground receded, and soon we were flying over Long Island Sound.

Vibration from the rotors knocked my teeth together. Pressure squeezed my chest, making it hard to breathe. I had never been fond of heights, but that was nothing next to my hatred of water. I'd never forget the feeling of it closing over my head, trapping me, filling my lungs, pulling me down ...

Another shot of fear overtook me, so powerful I almost panicked, and for a moment I thought I might fall.

I closed my eyes, blocking out the sparkling blue below. I couldn't let myself think of the water, the height. I had to focus on getting control of the helicopter. I could land this one in my sleep. I just needed to get inside.

That meant I had to get the other passengers outside.

I kicked one knee over the skid and looked up into a side window just in time to see the barrel of a rifle—AR15 or M16—staring at me.

I pushed myself forward and flipped head first, diving between skid and the body of the craft. A piece of cake in the gym. A bit more complicated hanging from a helicopter.

Swinging from my hands, I jackknifed my body toward the bottom of the bird, not thinking, just acting on muscle memory. Finding the bracket where the skids connected to the craft, I pulled up and caught it with my knees. I hung wildly like that for a second, upside down, wind beating me, before I could find a handhold and right myself.

I looked up. A gun barrel poked under the fuselage. Then a boot followed, bracing on the skid.

I didn't wait for him to get a shot lined up. I switched my grip to my hands. Using my stomach muscles, I swung my body as before, and on the second swing, aimed both feet directly at the boot. My heels hit hard, and the boot slipped, followed by the man. The rifle jarred free of his hands and hung by the strap around his shoulder. He caught the skid with his elbows, his legs dangling right beside me.

The craft bobbed then dipped like a rollercoaster, and for another stomach-lurching moment, I thought we were going down.

We locked eyes, his aflame with fear and rage. He kicked out, hitting my thigh, causing me to swing again. My strength was ebbing. Another kick like that, and he'd knock me off the skid.

Hand over hand, I moved away from him. Then I switched my handhold and turned around, eying the other skid, opposite me, about seven or eight feet away.

I looked back at my attacker. He gained hold of the rifle, pointing it in my direction.

I jackknifed my legs and swung, hard and fast, like a gymnast getting ready for her dismount.

Gunfire crackled behind me.

I eyed the opposite skid—

—and let go.

The brief moment of weightlessness, soaring through the air under the chopper, seemed to play out in super-slow motion.

I felt the wind, cold and sharp, invading every pore on my body. Heard the rotors and the shots, impossibly loud but surprisingly easy to ignore. Stared up at the blue steel underbelly of the helicopter as my body became parallel to the fuselage. Waited for my legs to hit the other skid, waited so long that I had plenty of time to second-guess my aim, sure I'd missed my mark, sure I'd plummet to the ocean where I'd shatter my body and drown.

But then my knees found the opposite skid, my legs bending over it, my hands reaching up and locking on.

Before I could celebrate, I caught a hot burn across my shoulder, like I'd been touched with a branding iron.

Shot.

I'd been shot.

I turned around, still able to hold on, facing the man who shot me. He had one hand on the opposite skid, the other on the rifle, pointing at me.

He was too far away for me to kick him, but, incredibly, I noticed I still had my cross-body purse hanging from my shoulder.

Hanging from one hand, I pulled the purse strap off my shoulder and made a quick slipknot around my ankle.

He fired, bullets breaking to my right.

I swung at him, kicking out my legs.

My handbag continued forward on its strap, and hit him right where I was aiming—square in the nose.

He cried out through closed teeth, the sound driven away in the whipping wind, and his grip broke. He followed his assault rifle into the water.

From this height, it was like hitting concrete. He wouldn't be swimming back to shore.

The wind was slamming against me so hard it was difficult to breathe, to think, and for a moment all I could do was hold on and wait for the helicopter to stop its roll and pitch.

I'd only seen one other man at the house with Julianne, the skinny guy from the pool. Since I didn't recognize the guy who had just gone into the Sound, Skinny was probably inside with Julianne, along with the pilot.

I pivoted my hands, swung my legs over the opposite skid and pulled myself into a sitting position. Then I wound my purse back over my shoulder, simultaneously checking my wound. Barely a nick, not even worth a stitch.

I was banking on my hunch that the second armed man would be focused on the door his buddy had just exited. It took most people a moment to recover from something as traumatic as watching a human being plunge to his death. I'd put in countless hours to shorten my own reaction time.

I felt the door open above me.

Apparently someone else had shortened his reaction time as well.

I saw the gun barrel first, but instead of putting a foot on the skid to gain balance and see what he was shooting, this guy just pulled the trigger.

Even in the roar of the wind and the rotors, the crack of the rifle was deafening. I had no place to go, nowhere to run, and bracing yourself against gunfire was impossible. If he hit me, it would hurt, and I'd fall to my death. Or maybe it would kill me instantly. Either way, I had no defense.

But luck continued to be on my side. The man fired eight rounds, none of them even coming close.

I grabbed the rifle barrel. It was hot as a stove, and in the back of my mind I was aware of my palm burning. But I had a lot of practice ignoring the somatic reflex and hung on tight, shifting my body to the side to get out of the way in case he pulled the trigger again, tugging with all my strength.

Like the first man, Skinny had the gun strapped around his shoulder, so when I pulled, I didn't just get the weapon. He came with it.

I released the searing barrel and let the whole package fall. I didn't wait to see him hit the water. Instead, I climbed to the outside of the skid and lifted myself into the passenger compartment behind the cockpit. I pulled the door closed behind me.

The cabin was separated from the crew's compartment, and the first thing that struck me was how quiet the space was inside. I could still hear the blades making the classic *whump whump* sound, in fact it was still far too loud to carry on a normal conversation, but thanks to the trauma my ears had suffered and heavy soundproofing, the noise barely registered. Three leather seats lined each wall, three facing forward and three back, each complete with a headset hanging above.

Julianne was slumped in the middle seat, her vacant eyes suggesting she might have had a little extra medication for the journey, or perhaps whatever they'd given her earlier was fully kicking in.

She opened her eyes halfway, and I gave her what I hoped was a reassuring smile.

"What ... how did you do that?"

"A little training, and a whole lot of fearing for my life. You ready to get out of here?"

"How?"

It was a good question.

Process. Evaluate. Segregate. Then take control of the situation.

The sun shifted through the windows, the pilot turning the craft around, heading back to the mansion. I touched the wall between passengers and pilot, soundproofing material backed with steel. A check for parachutes, weapons, or anything else I might use came up empty.

To get to the cockpit, I would have to climb back out of the craft and access a separate door, a door that would be locked. Not the best plan. But I couldn't wait for the craft to land. No doubt the pilot had used his radio to arrange for a welcome party to greet me.

And by greet I meant kill.

I finished scanning the compartment, spotting speakers but no cameras, and then I brought my attention back to Julianne.

My assignment was to get her out of this mess, unharmed.

I'd get her out. But the *unharmed* part probably wasn't going to happen.

A dip in altitude and a glance out the window told me we were approaching the mansion, the bay where it nestled already in sight. I had to make my move soon, or I wouldn't get to make it at all.

"You got shot," she said, pointing an unsteady hand at my shoulder.

"Just a little bit."

I grabbed the bottom cushion of the seat opposite me and pulled. The Velcro holding it in place made a ripping sound, and it detached. I ripped another free then released Julianne's seat belt.

"What are you doing?" Her words came out in a slow ooze.

I didn't answer. After the sound of the Velcro and her muttered question, no doubt the pilot was listening over the intercom and would be wondering the same thing. I didn't have much time before he figured it out.

My heart hammered hard enough to break a rib.

I grasped the door handle and shoved it open. I moved quickly, not only hoping to catch the pilot off guard, but Julianne, too. Even in her state, she would resist if given the chance.

Hell, I was resisting it myself.

Holding the seat cushions by their built-in straps, I pulled Julianne out of her seat and looped her left arm around my shoulder and my right arm around her waist. I needed the perfect moment. Low enough so the impact didn't injure us, but not so close to shore we hit bottom. Or worse, land.

"What are you doing?" she repeated.

When we descended to thirty feet, the beach coming up fast, I made my move. Scooping in a deep breath, I held Julianne tight against my body and jumped.

She screamed all the way down.

"There will be times when you must work with other operatives," The Instructor said. "Rely on your counterpart to put his mission first, always, and you do the same. As long as you share the same goal, you don't need to worry about trust."

The water hit my feet first, slapping them hard, the force shuddering up my legs and through my spine. Cold enveloped my body and closed over my head. Moments after we submerged, I lost Julianne.

I was only under for a few seconds, just enough time to stop my downward trajectory and fight my way to the surface, but it felt like forever.

It felt like I was going to die.

I almost—*almost*—freaked out, but peeking through the water, eyes stinging, I could see the sun glinting off the waves above me, and my arms and legs scrambled hard and fast, like I was crawling up out of a grave.

When my head broke the surface, I gasped too soon. Salt water filled my mouth, making me gag and cough. Above, the helicopter blades continued to beat out their rhythm.

Julianne's blond head broke the surface just two feet away. She stared with panicked eyes. Reaching out, she clawed at me like a frightened kitten.

I grabbed her hands and did my best to control her, keeping us both afloat with a scissors kick. I knew how to swim well enough, and once I got myself beyond the terror of being plunged into water, I could do okay. But that didn't make it easy. Julianne's grabbing and thrashing made keeping my own fear in check more challenging.

When panicked, a drowning swimmer can pull down anyone attempting a rescue. If this kept up, I would have to dive deep, forcing her to choose between holding onto me or self-preservation. Once she let go, I would be able to secure her with a cross chest carry.

I preferred it wouldn't go that far. I'd drowned once before and didn't care to risk repeating the experience.

"Julianne, I have you. It's all right." I looked straight into her panicked blue eyes and kept repeating the words. Finally she focused, and I seemed to break through.

I caught sight of a seat cushion carried on the waves, too far away to justify the effort to fetch it. Instead I placed Julianne's hands on my shoulders, so I could perform a tired swimmer's assist.

"Lean back and float."

Miraculously she did as I said, her legs coming up on either side of me. Moving my arms and legs in a modified breast stroke, I pushed us both toward shore.

When I finally touched sand, my muscles were so fried I wasn't sure I could walk. We emerged from the water and limped up on a strip of land flanked by a crowded, summertime beach and a waterside restaurant, its parking lot nearly empty in the hours between lunch and dinner.

Julianne leaned against me, her steps uneven as we wound through swimmers and sunbathers scattered along the beach's edge. People eyed her dripping clothes, but no one spoke or tried to help.

Overhead, the helicopter hovered high in the sky, its blades still beating staccato. No doubt the pilot had seen us come out of the water. Hawk Nose and whatever men he had left would be descending on the beach soon. We needed to be gone when they arrived.

I dipped a hand in the purse still slung diagonally across my chest and brought out my phone.

After locating a sign proclaiming the beach's rules, I texted the name to the number Jacob had given me.

I sure as hell hoped Morrissey was close. If he didn't arrive soon, we'd have to make a run for it and hope there was a train station nearby. At least I had the cash Jacob had stashed in the purse.

"You ... threw me out of a helicopter," Julianne said. Her tone was belligerent.

"It was the only way."

"I'm sure there were other ways. There had to be other ways."

"There weren't."

"You're crazy." She yanked her arm away and stumbled on her own for a few steps.

I caught up, grabbing the crook of her arm.

"I'm here to help you."

"Get the hell away from me."

"Those men weren't working for a modeling agency, Julianne," I said. "You were right to be afraid of them."

"You threw me out of a helicopter, you crazy bitch."

Standing there with her hands fisted by her side, she reminded me of how young she actually was. And how stupid.

But I couldn't be too angry. After all, as many mistakes as she'd made, I was still about half a dozen up at her age.

"Those men are human traffickers, Julianne. Ever hear of sexual slavery?"

She shook her head.

"They sell girls. They were planning to sell you."

"What?"

"You think normal modeling agents carry guns around? They're going to sell you to some rich asshole overseas, where you'll be raped and killed."

Her eyes went out of focus. She stammered something I couldn't decipher.

"What are you on?" I asked, squinting into her eyes. "What did they give you?"

"Leave me alone."

Her pupils looked normal. From the slightly slurred speech, and the lack of coordination, I guessed it was something in the diazepam family, Valium, maybe Xanax.

"Julianne, you have to listen to me and do whatever I say. We're not safe here."

"If you don't leave me alone, I'm gonna start screaming."

I saw her take a deep breath. Screaming would draw attention, which would draw Hawk Nose.

I raised my hand and slapped her, hard, wet palm against wet cheek.

Her eyes went wide.

"I don't give a shit if you don't believe me, or you're confused, or the drugs are clouding your head. These are dangerous men, Julianne. You're in trouble, and if you don't do exactly what I say, when I say it, I'll knock out every one of your teeth, and then any chance you might have at a modeling career will be gone. Got it?"

She nodded quickly. "I ... I ..."

"Shut up and come with me."

I took her by the hand and led her into an overpriced gift shop in the beach parking lot. After spending a minute working the rolled up fifty dollar bill out of my purse lining, I bought each of us a Red Bull and ordered Julianne to drink hers. They didn't have first aid kits, and the bandages they sold were too small for my wound, but they had the next best thing—super glue. I dripped half a tube onto the bullet burn, effectively stopping the bleeding. It was ugly, but effective.

The limo pulled up just as we walked back outside.

Morrissey lowered the window. "I think everyone east of Oyster Bay saw you jump out of the helicopter. Cops will be here any second." He eyed my shoulder. "Are you bleeding?"

"I was. I took care of it."

"Is she?"

"No."

"You sure?"

I pulled on the door handle. It was locked.

"Open the goddamn door, Morrissey."

"Are you sure she isn't hurt?"

"I'm fine," Julianne mumbled.

The door unlocked. I pushed Julianne into the back seat of the car and slipped in beside her. Morrissey hit the gas, flattening us against leather. I fastened my safety belt and made sure Julianne did the same. The air conditioning raised goose bumps on my nearly naked skin.

We wound along twisting, tree-lined streets dotted with quaint Victorians that probably cost half as much as my apartment building back in Chicago. I spotted a dark blue van turn onto the street behind us and caught a glimpse of Hawk Nose behind the wheel.

They had automatic weapons. If we got stuck in traffic, we were dead.

"You spot 'em?" I asked Morrissey.

"Yeah. See the bar back there?"

I glanced at a leather-covered compartment just to the right of Julianne's footspace.

"I stashed something in the ice bucket for you."

I opened the little cubicle. Tucked into the insulated bin was a Glock 22. Fifteen .40 rounds in the magazine, one in the chamber.

Julianne made a mewing sound in the back of her throat.

"Hold on." Morrissey swerved across traffic and onto a ramp leading to the expressway. Tires squealed and horns honked.

I glanced out the back window in time to see the van complete the same risky maneuver.

"You didn't shake them."

"I see that." Morrissey's tone was dry, as calm and still as I'd noted when I'd first seen him outside the hotel.

He drove on, a mile, two, five humming by under the tires, Hawk Nose and his boys still following.

I held the gun in my lap, my index finger stretched along the side of the trigger guard, thinking. So many parts of this assignment didn't add up. So many details didn't make sense. A whole house on Long Island Sound and only one girl loaded into the helicopter? At least five highly-trained and armed men to watch over her? Pornocopia central but no one laying a finger on her?

After I'd jumped with Julianne, things must have gotten immeasurably messy for The Bradford and Sims Modeling Agency. They had no idea who I was, who I worked for. The smart move would be to cut their losses, wipe down their rented house and disappear, not go on a high speed chase to ... do what? Recover one girl? Or erase three witnesses while potentially creating many more?

The whole thing seemed foolhardy.

"Who are these guys?" I asked Morrissey.

He shrugged a shoulder. "I know as much as you."

"Haven't you been on this case for a while?"

"Working for the car service, not the modeling agency."
He accelerated, weaving through a caravan of slower moving
cars. "I do what I'm asked, just like you."

My turn to nod. And seeing that I'd already delivered Julianne to Morrissey, my part of the operation was over.

Not that now would be a convenient time to take my
leave.

"Where are you taking her?"

"Somewhere safe."

I sensed Julianne's glance from Morrissey to me. I met
her eyes. "It's going to be all right."

"How do I know that?"

"We're the good guys. We were assigned to protect you."

"Protect me? You threw me out of a helicopter."

"I did it in a protective way."

She eyed me as if I was crazy and she was afraid it would
rub off. I thought once more about Jacob's orders, that she
not be harmed in any way.

Was this really human trafficking? Or something else?

"Who is your father?" I asked her.

"What?"

"Your dad. Who is he?"

Some of the fear went away, replaced by anger. "It doesn't
matter."

I had lived up to my end of the op. I had no control over
what happened to her from here on out, and I had no business
knowing anything more. Any curiosity I felt, any sympathy I
had for this girl, were meaningless to the mission. So rather
than push it, I clammed up and turned my attention back to
the men chasing us.

The green whipping past the windows fell away to
shopping centers, and finally, industry. Ahead, the Manhattan skyline shivered in the glare of the afternoon sun like a
mirage.

I heard a pop. The car lurched and skidded.

I threw an arm over Julianne, forcing her down.

"Are they shooting at us?" she squealed.

Morrissey regained control, but the car shuddered and bucked with each rotation of the punctured tire.

Ahead, a sign directed us to the Queens Midtown Tunnel. Morrissey took the turn.

I couldn't believe it.

"Tell me you're not heading into the city with these guys on our tail."

He glanced at me in the rearview mirror. "You have a better idea?"

This chase along the expressway was one thing. Once we were in the city, traffic would be slow, sometimes standing still. What would prevent Hawk Nose and his boys from walking up to the limo and taking a shot?

"Yeah, drive somewhere else. Unless you want to make us a slow-moving target."

"I get the idea that you can move pretty fast when you want to."

"What are you planning?"

"I'll take care of the guys behind us. You have the girl at Columbus Circle at six o'clock."

I didn't ask how he was going to take care of them. I had a feeling he'd find a way, and that I'd know what action I had to take when the moment came.

We moved through the EZ Pass toll and plunged into the tunnel.

Traffic moved steadily in two Manhattan-bound lanes. The air held the odor of trapped exhaust. The shiny, cream colored ceiling reflected headlights, their glare adding to the artificial lighting and neon-bright speed limit reminders every hundred feet. There was a cacophony of horn honking, helpful New Yorkers trying to tell us we had a flat, as if the sparks being thrown off the bare rim weren't obvious enough.

"Hold on and be ready to release your seat belts."

Julianne's fingers circled my free hand and clenched. I braced my legs wide.

The Town Car's wheel screeched, metal on pavement. The drivers around us fell back, apparently not wanting to get too close. Only the van stayed glued a few feet behind our bumper, close enough for Hawk Nose to glower at me, close enough to take a shot.

So why didn't he? He might hit the girl?

Morrissey slowed the car and inched toward the center, straddling lanes. Horns echoed off concrete. Surrounding cars fell back farther. A few more seconds passed.

He hit the brakes and the car skidded sideways.

Tires screeched all around, the sound amplified in the tunnel.

"Now. Go."

Before the car had reached a complete stop, Morrissey was moving. He pulled an assault rifle from under the seat and slid across to the passenger door.

I was moving too, pushing Julianne in front of me, over the seat, out the door. The cars ahead kept moving down the tunnel, leaving both lanes free and clear. I grabbed Julianne's arm and ran. The soles of my bare feet slapped pavement. The muggy air smelled of exhaust and burned rubber. Angry voices and horns behind us gave way to bursts of gunfire and screams.

My heart was a hummingbird trapped in my chest. With all the training I'd had, the sound of gunfire was still a viscerally frightening thing, especially at my back. I was sure it was much worse for Julianne. To her credit, she kept up as best she could, her sandals pounding the concrete behind me, her breath coming fast and rhythmic.

I wasn't sure how long one man could hold off Hawk Nose's entourage. In a firefight, numerical superiority usually won out. I had to wonder if we'd see Morrissey again, but I pushed those thoughts from my mind and kept running.

Finally I picked up the faint smell of fresh air, the first sign that we were near the end.

An explosion shook the tunnel around us.

Julianne screamed.

I looked back, over my shoulder, back to where we'd left Morrissey. The tiled walls and shiny ceiling reflected the orange glow of flame. The smoke came fast, like an acrid thunderhead.

Unlike in the movies, gunfire doesn't easily cause car explosions, but explosives wired to the gas tank could. They also caused one hell of a traffic mess when detonated in a tunnel. And one hell of an emergency response that criminal types would be eager to avoid.

I had a feeling Morrissey was going to come out of this just fine.

By the time Julianne and I reached the end of the tunnel, sirens echoed from everywhere and the smell of burning car coated the back of my throat and infused my hair. I pulled her up on the walkway to the side of the two traffic lanes and concealed the Glock along my leg. We made it to the mouth of the tunnel and walked out onto the streets of Manhattan. The area was swarming with cop cars, and I jammed the pistol into my tiny bag.

We walked to Grand Central station, stopping at a Banana Republic in the terminal to pick up a dress to pull over my bikini, a change of clothing for Julianne and gym shoes for both of us. The clothing wasn't pricey, but the purchase still took most of the money Jacob had stashed in the purse. Two subway fares took the rest.

"Why are we going to Columbus Circle?" Julianne asked.

I thought of the glorified roundabout marking the southwest corner of Central Park. It offered continually flowing traffic, access to streets leading in several directions, and the cover of crowded sidewalks. A decent place for a hand off.

"It's just a meeting place. We're trying to get you somewhere safe."

If I thought it was hot on the streets, I was mistaken. Descending into the subway tunnels felt like burrowing into humidity hell. Exhaust and the odor of hot humanity swam in the air. I heard the click of heels and rumble of voices, nothing but ordinary subway sounds.

We moved into a wide area of red quarry tile rimmed with scarred wooden benches. Live music echoed off walls and floors, zamponas, charango, guitars, and percussion, a distinctly South American sound, maybe Peruvian. I'd only been to Peru once, but I'd spent significant time in Columbia, Brazil, and Venezuela, the last time I remembered seeing a Tec-9, until today.

I had to wonder ...

I led Julianne down steps and through platforms only to cross over tracks and double-back. The third time we passed the Andean band, she spoke up. "Are we lost?"

"I'm making sure we weren't followed."

She glanced around, as if the bogeyman himself might jump out from the nearby newspaper stand.

"Were we?"

"No."

She let out a long breath, but still looked far from re-lieved. "What you said back at the beach, was it true? Were they really going to sell me as a sex slave?"

I nodded, although my doubts were adding up fast. Ju-lianne was pretty and blond, but there was simply no way a criminal enterprise could make enough money selling one girl. Bradford and Sims was no modeling agency, their little porn operation aside. But I was becoming less and less sure they dealt in human trafficking, either.

"Well, thanks. I know I didn't seem like I appreciated you saving me at first, but I do. I was just a little, you know, shaken up."

She was sounding better, clearer. The combination of caffeine and getting shot at was working against the drugs in her system.

"Understandable." I gave her a smile and led her past the band one last time and up a sloping ramp toward the S train that would take us to Times Square.

"Who are you, anyway?" Julianne asked, once the band was far enough behind us to hear one another speak.

"Not important."

"It is to me."

"Then just think of me as a friend."

She frowned, a tiny crease forming on her lineless forehead. "I ... I don't have a good track record with friends."

I knew the feeling. "Okay, how about a bodyguard? I was sent to keep you safe."

"You and the driver."

"Yes."

"Sent? By who?"

I said nothing.

"Please?"

"I shouldn't have told you that much."

Not that my explanation would hurt anything, but I'd learned, when dealing with civilians in the field, it was better to keep things simple and them at arms' length. I was already starting to like Julianne more than I should.

"If someone is looking out for me, isn't it better that I know who?"

The platform was crowded, the rush hour stampede starting to heat up. The S train ran between Grand Central Station and Times Square every fifteen minutes. We wouldn't have long to wait, but I still felt as if it couldn't come fast enough.

"I've never really had anyone who has looked out for me before. Not really. Not since my mom died."

I didn't react, not outwardly anyway. Inwardly I was struck again by how many similarities there were between the two of us.

"I had friends and stuff, but no one ever seemed to be there when I needed them, you know?"

"You're trying to manipulate me."

She had the nerve to give me a little smile. "Maybe."

"It's not working."

"My mom used to love me. At least I remember thinking she did. She died when I was sixteen."

I focused on the rumble of the train approaching. I had been ten when I lost both parents. At least Julianne still had her father.

"I've kind of been on my own after that."

"What about your dad?"

"He's not important."

I didn't believe her. There was more to this than human trafficking. If her dad was a VIP, like Jacob said, this could be a kidnapping for ransom. Or leverage. Take a senator's daughter, and you own him. That could be useful for certain corporations. Or certain foreign governments.

The train rolled in, the sound too loud for words. Doors opened, releasing crowds of commuters, then we stepped on and they sucked closed behind us. I stood, holding onto a pole.

Julianne stood next to me. I scanned the crowd around us, looking for potential trouble. We remained quiet until we emerged from the 42nd Street subway station and joined the steamy, neon hubbub of Times Square.

She broke the silence. "Being alone, not knowing who you can trust, it's not fun. You don't know what that feels like."

Actually, I did. Not that I was going to share the dark times of my life with Julianne James.

But I could see her point.

Everyone needed someone to rely on. I had Kaufmann, the parole officer who'd been there for me when my life fell apart at age fourteen. He still checked in with me from time to time. He had no clue about the nature of my real job, my real life. But just knowing he cared made all the difference.

"Tell me why you're helping me," Julianne said, "and I'll leave you alone."

I let out a deep breath. When it came down to it, I really didn't know much, and Jacob hadn't said anything about keeping what little I did know from Julianne. "Your father sent us, sort of."

She narrowed her eyes. "What?"

"Your father pulled some strings to make sure you were safe."

"You think that's funny?"

I shook my head. "Listen, I don't know the history between you and your father. You don't want him involved in your life, take it up with him."

"My father left my mother before I was born," she said, voice flat. "I've never met him. Whoever sent you, it wasn't him."

"You are a weapon," The Instructor said. "You are a tool of your government. You'll have to make calls in the field, snap decisions, but don't let that seduce you into believing you decide anything. You may turn down an assignment, but once you accept, your job is to carry out orders, no more. Your handler will aim you, fire you, and it is up to you to make sure the bullet hits its mark."

I let her words sink in the rest of the walk to the health club and focused on my usual security precautions, doubling back, watching for tails.

The place was called Stretchers, a nationwide chain exclusively for women. I didn't have my membership card, but I gave them my fake name and address and they confirmed my ID on their computer. Julie waited in the lobby, and I popped into the locker room and opened my rented locker. From the duffle bag I took a clean driver's license and a credit card in the name of Heidi Orland, a thousand in cash, an S&W tactical folding knife, and a spare charger for my cell. I still had Morrissey's Glock, but I figured I might have to return it, so I added a compact Ruger .380 LCP of my own and two extra mags, cramming everything into my purse until it was so stuffed it refused to close. Then I secured the locker and led Julie to the nearest hotel.

Once we were inside the room and I'd searched the place for bugs using an app on my phone, I allowed my thoughts to turn back to what she'd told me.

"So you don't know your father."

"Never met him, have no idea what he even looks like."

Julianne stepped to the floor-to-ceiling window. Crossing her arms over her chest, she looked down on Times Square. She looked small, lonely. Behind her, the clock on the Paramount Building read four o'clock, a half hour slow.

"My name isn't even Julianne. It's Julie. I just thought Julianne sounded more like a model."

I attempted to run a hand through my hopelessly tangled hair. While I had recovered from my earlier desire to shave my head, as soon as this operation was over, I was definitely getting the mess cut short enough to keep it out of my eyes.

"What do I call you? I'm guessing your name isn't Claire."

No harm in telling her my codename. "Chandler."

"Chandler. That's cool. Like on that show *Friends*."

I preferred comparison to the dead mystery writer, but I supposed it didn't matter.

Normal, not-a-model Julie turned from the window and looked at me.

"So now what, Chandler?"

"Nothing has changed. My assignment is to make sure you're safe, whether your father is behind it or not doesn't really matter. Okay?"

She gave a little nod, but she looked less than convinced.

"You're going to be fine. I'll make sure of it. I promise." I gestured toward the bathroom. "Now why don't you get cleaned up?"

As soon as I heard water hiss through pipes, I called Jacob. We engaged in our usual security dance. By the time I was able to speak, I felt like crawling out of my skin with impatience.

"Who is the VIP, Jacob?"

He paused for a moment. "I hear the extraction didn't go as smoothly as we hoped."

"She's here. She's unhurt."

"But you left a nasty traffic snarl in the Queens Midtown Tunnel. The media is calling it a terrorist attack."

"Couldn't be helped. Who's the VIP?" I repeated.

Another pause. "All I was told is that he's the girl's father."

I was getting used to Jacob's altered voice, but there were times I still wished I could hear his natural inflections, or better yet, look into his eyes, gage his expressions.

"She says she never knew her father, insists it couldn't be him."

He paused, then said, "Interesting."

"That's all you have to say? Interesting?"

"Does she have any ideas?"

"She says she has no one, and I think she's telling the truth."

I went on, filling him in on Julie's real name and my suspicions that our fake modeling agency was also a fake when it came to the human trafficking business.

"You think they're some kind of intelligence operation?"

"It seems so. Several are South American. I'm guessing Venezuelan, although they all might be mercs."

"And that means there's more to Julie than the fact that she's daddy's little girl," Jacob said, summing up my thoughts.

"Right. I might have something on the Bradford and Sims Agency. I took the memory card from one of their cameras. It got wet, but if it works I'll upload it to the dropbox as soon as I can."

Jacob and I often communicated via a series of secure Internet drop boxes. It was a convenient system for trading various types of files no matter where I was in the world.

"Even if it's damaged, I might be able to recover the data."

"I'm not sure anything useful is on the card. But at the very least, you'll be able to ogle some topless photos of me."

"You weren't kidding about the strip club, huh? I don't know how you find the time."

I smiled despite myself, and it felt good. I might never meet Jacob in person, but that didn't change the fact that we seemed to 'get' each other, important when my life depended on his communication skills and willingness to watch my back.

"You sure you can't find out more about this VIP?"

"Chandler ..."

"Right. You'll let me know when you know." I paused, trying to come up with some other approach we could take. "How about my contact, Morrissey?"

"Morrissey? I have a dossier on him. He's an experienced field operative. He has a clean record, is reliable, has been working undercover as a driver for a Manhattan car service for about four years. Has provided Uncle Sam with all sorts of intel."

Four years of driving a car. I thought of his rough hands, his calm and deadly demeanor. I wasn't sure I really suspected Morrissey of anything—actually I liked him, more than a little—but it never hurt to be thorough. I wouldn't be surprised if he did a similar background search on me.

Not that he'd find anything. According to government records, Morrissey was undercover. I, on the other hand, didn't exist.

"Military record?" I asked.

"Nope. Former FBI Recruited by NSA"

That didn't seem right. Morrissey had combat training. He was a fist, not an ear. Sticking him in a limo service seemed like a waste of his talents.

"What else?" I asked.

"Not much. Parents deceased. Lives in an apartment on Staten Island."

"Previous operations?"

"Classified."

"I thought classified doesn't apply to you, Jacob."

"Are you asking me to dig?"

"Indulge me, will you?"

"You have your assignment, Chandler. Deliver the girl to Morrissey unhurt. The rest isn't your concern."

"Maybe not, but I'll feel better."

For a moment I wondered if we'd been cut off. Then Jacob cleared his throat.

"I'll see what I can find."

We ended the call. Jacob was right. Worrying about this was not my job. I was trained to follow orders, a weapon to be deployed. I'd saved Julie from the fake modeling agency and now I was to turn her over and walk away.

The rest didn't matter.

I had suspected from the beginning that I was given this assignment precisely because my teen years were similar to Julie's. Because of those similarities, this didn't feel like any other mission to me. I cared about what happened to her, but that didn't mean I could allow my personal feelings to skew my judgment.

If there was reason to worry, Jacob would find it and let me know.

The drone of the hairdryer ended. Time being short, a shower for me would have to wait. I focused on accessorizing, strapping the folding knife to the back of my left thigh, under the dress. On my right thigh, I donned a Velcro holster for the Ruger. A brush through my tangle of hair, and I was out the door.

Even without my taking time for a shower, we were pressed to upload the camera images to the dropbox and make it to Columbus Circle. I would have preferred to walk, since it was much easier to spot tails by foot, especially in rush hour, but since we were short on time, I opted for a subway ride to Lincoln Center. Backtracking one avenue and four blocks, we reached our rendezvous spot.

I checked my phone. Twenty minutes before six, just as I'd planned.

Jacob hadn't called back.

I focused on my surroundings. I hadn't picked up any evidence that we were being followed during our walk, and I didn't spot any shadows now. I smelled exhaust, hotdogs from a nearby food cart, and the tang of horse manure wafting from the park. A woman passed by, the scent of some sweet vanilla coffee concoction trailing in her wake. Behind us, a small group of men offering pedicab rides through the park spoke in broken English, trying to talk tourists into paying a small fortune for an evening jaunt in the half-bicycle, half-cart contraptions. Horns honked and cabbies yelled, typical New York City on a summer evening.

When I spied the Town Car, my nerves surged.

He was early.

The car swung to the curb and Morrissey stepped out. He was tall and lean and calmly dangerous, and I felt that same little burst of edginess mixed with lust as when I'd first met him this morning. This time he wasn't wearing his sunglasses, and I caught a flash of ice blue eyes that just added to his allure. Like the perfect chauffeur, he climbed out and circled the vehicle.

CODENAME: CHANDLER – THE BEGINNING

"Nice car," I said. "This one rigged to blow, too?"

One side of his mouth lifted in a crooked smile. "You did a good job."

"You, too. Want your Glock back?"

"Sure. At least until the next time you'd like to borrow it."

He stepped close to me to shield the exchange from on-lookers. He smelled of Giorgio Armani For Men's *Acqua Di Gio*.

At least someone had gotten a chance to properly clean up.

I took the gun from my purse. When he pulled me into a hug, I placed it in his hand.

"Take good care of her, okay?"

He brushed my fingers as he took it from me, lingering a moment too long, then he slipped the weapon into a holster on his left side.

"She'll be safe. And if you need to get in touch with me, you have my card."

"I do?"

Morrissey's hand slowly made its way down my side, then up under my dress. He slid a business card into my thigh holster. His breath on my neck was hot, and for a brief moment I could practically feel his lips on my bare skin.

He pulled away, then glanced at Julie and opened the back door. "Ready?"

We exchanged a quick hug, her grip a lot tighter than mine.

"Thanks," Julie said. "For everything."

"You bet," I told her. "It's all going to be okay from here on out."

When she climbed into the limo, Morrissey shut the door behind her and circled to the driver's door.

"I hope we get to work together again," he said.

"Me, too." But I actually had play on my mind.

On impulse, I took out my cell phone, miming making a call. Instead, I took a quick picture of him.

It was natural to be horny as hell after a mission, especially after almost being killed. It was an affirmation-of-life kind of reaction. If I wasn't going to get laid tonight, I could at least have a photo to get myself off. And fantasy sex was safer than real sex, especially in my profession.

He smiled, then slipped behind the wheel and pulled into traffic.

I watched them follow the flow around the circle and head uptown on Broadway. My role in this was finished, another assignment completed successfully. Soon I would be on my way back to Chicago or on a plane bound for who-the-hell-knew. My thoughts would be on other things, my focus riveted to threats from other quarters. I would file this experience into its compartment in the back of my mind and go on with my life.

The cell phone buzzed against my hip.

I answered.

"I need to speak to Ursula," Jacob's electronic voice said.

The code signified urgency, and I could feel a dose of adrenaline surge into my bloodstream.

"I'm afraid she has already left for the hospital."

"You've met with the contact?"

"He just took Julie." I peered at the cars flooding around Columbus Circle and up Broadway.

"Damn. He's early."

"What is it?"

"You were right to have me check him, Chandler. He's not Morrissey."

Oh, shit.

"What do you mean?" I knew the suspicion was originally mine, but Jacob's words carried a shock wave anyway.

"Morrissey's body was found—or at least part of it was—a week ago in New Jersey. He was mutilated, no face, no hands, so we didn't identify him right away."

"But you're sure it's him?"

"Yes."

I didn't ask how or when. Worrying about that was someone else's job. "So this guy, who is he?" I was already walking, rimming Columbus Circle, waving my hand for a cab.

Goddamn rush hour.

"We have no idea. Can you describe him?"

"I can do even better."

I forwarded the photo to Jacob, pleased that being horny might have actually come in handy for once.

"Hmm, he's cute." Odd thing for Jacob to say. "I'll run it through facial recognition software. Hold on."

I squinted into the distance, breaking into a jog. The limo was still in sight—thank you bumper-to-bumper—but getting further away. As I ran, I fished the business card out of my knife holster.

No name on the card. No phone number either. Just a generic Hotmail address.

I took another scan of the roundabout, searching for a vacancy light in the flood of cabs. A green SUV caught my attention. Rental plates. Five men inside. Not South American, maybe of Middle Eastern origin. But it wasn't the vehicle or their ethnicity that caught me. It was the intensity behind their eyes, the way they assessed the crowd ... just the way I would if I were searching for someone.

Maybe I was being paranoid, but I doubted it.

Keeping my expression neutral, I glanced at the cars beyond, not letting on I'd made them.

"Got a match," Jacob said after only thirty seconds. Jonathan Kirk. Former special forces. He fell off our radar about a year ago. Apparently he's been operating without a leash."

"Merc?" I eyed Broadway, but I'd lost the car.

"Yeah." Jacob paused, but I could feel what was coming next. "Most recently, he's been doing wet work."

"No matter how well you've prepared or how thorough you are, sometimes you will make mistakes," The Instructor said. "The important thing is that you identify the mistake immediately and take steps to salvage the mission. Stay aware, use your brain, your handler, and anything around you to set the operation right. If repair is impossible, cover up your involvement and get out of there."

I ran, picking and dodging between people on the sidewalk, the phone still pressed to my ear.

"Was Morrissey part of the package?" I asked.

"Yes. Came with the deal."

A hum rose in my ears. I'd invested myself in protecting Julie, not just because it was my assignment, but because I'd started to care. The possibility that I might have been set up from the beginning to deliver the girl to her death made me grind my teeth.

"Jacob? Are we being used here? Who's the VIP?"

"You're thinking Kirk was brought in on purpose?"

"It occurred to me."

"We don't have any evidence that Kirk's working for the VIP. A third party could have intercepted Morrissey before our agency was brought in."

Of course, Jacob was right. But often playing devil's advocate could help sort through confusing or complicated situations like this one. I was hoping that strategy would work now, because I was confused as hell.

I kept moving, rimming Columbus Circle, my mind racing as fast as my feet.

"Or Kirk could have taken out Morrissey himself, maybe with the VIP's blessing."

When we'd been in the limo, Kirk had a chance to kill Julie and me. But that would have been a mistake. First of all, driving around with two dead chicks in your car wasn't safe. Second, killing me would have brought a shit storm down on him and whoever controlled him. Better to wait until the heat died down and let me deliver her, thinking the op had ended there.

"He must need her alive," I said.

"Agreed. Kirk has had sniper training. He could have taken her out without involving you at all. Or you could have been ordered to do it."

I hesitated. Could I have killed Julie if that was my assignment? Probably not. But there were other female assassins they could have assigned in my place, women who didn't have a history similar to Julie's and wouldn't hesitate to complete the job.

"So why lie to us about the father?"

"It's the government, Chandler. I think lying is merely the default setting."

"I don't like being lied to. Or used."

Jacob paused for a beat before replying. "I do have one thing. The assignment was routed through the defense department."

"So the VIP is someone in the Pentagon? Or is it the Pentagon itself?"

"Don't know. I'm trying to find more."

And maybe, if I could catch up with Kirk, I could do the same from my end. "Thanks, Jacob."

"Good luck."

I stuffed the phone back in my pocket and eyed the streets leading off the circle.

I wanted answers.

I also wanted to make sure Julie was safe.

But apparently I wasn't the only one looking for her.

The SUV holding the men I'd noticed earlier was just inching onto Broadway.

Cabs clogged the flow of traffic like cholesterol in a fat guy's bloodstream, but not one had its light on indicating it was for hire. Even if I could flag down a ride, traffic was moving so slowly, I'd never catch the men I'd pegged as Middle Eastern operatives, let alone Kirk. He'd be long gone and so would Julie.

I needed to find another way, and running wasn't cutting it.

The jingle of a bell caught my ear, followed by a voice speaking heavily accented English.

"Out of the way. Move!"

I spun around just as a bike/cart combination drew even with me, one of the pedicab drivers I'd noticed earlier taking a couple of tourists into the park. I shot out a hand and grabbed the handlebars, wresting the vehicle to a halt.

"Get off," I said evenly.

He stared at me as if I'd lost my mind.

"Get off. Now."

I grabbed his left hand and jammed his wrist backward. Using the leverage, I twisted his arm and his whole body moved to the side and off the seat.

"Okay, okay, take it," he said.

He also held up his wallet. Only in New York.

I released him, climbing onto the seat.

"Hey, you can't do that, lady!"

The couple in the cart. I'd almost forgotten them.

I shot the man a hard look. He was in his fifties, soft around the middle, with a bulbous nose, sitting next to a woman who had the exact same face, only twenty years older.

"You and your mom get out," I said. "This is your only warning."

"You're stealing this man's bike! I'm calling the cops!"

"Call them, Walter!" Mom chimed in. "And make a citizen's arrest!"

Neither got out.

"Your choice."

I drove the balls of my feet down on the pedals. Pedestrians in the crosswalk scurrying out of the way, I cut across Central Park West and skirted the edge of the circle and onto Broadway.

"Stop!" Walter yelled. "You're under arrest!"

North of Columbus Circle, Broadway turned into a boulevard, traffic flowing both up and down town. The faux Morrissey had headed uptown, I suspected on his way to the expressway and maybe the Bronx or New Jersey.

I couldn't let him make it out of Manhattan.

"Tell her to stop, Walter!"

"Stop!"

"Tell her again!"

"Stop!"

"She didn't hear you! Tell her again!"

"I said stop!"

"My son said stop!"

Ahead, vehicles choked the street, barely moving. Brake lights flared red. I cranked the bike to the right and jumped the curb onto the sidewalk. The bike's front tire shuddered, and it was all I could do to keep the handle bars steady. The back cart followed, jolting, and the couple let out squawks of surprise.

"She won't stop, Ma! I told her to stop, but she won't stop!"

Forcing pedestrians to dive out of the way, I skirted two food carts and bounced off the edge of a trash can.

I regained my balance and thrust down on the pedals with all my strength, gaining speed. The cart rattled behind me. People shouted obscenities and threats in my wake. Heat poured off the concrete in waves, and sweat soon slicked my back and stung the corners of my eyes. My breathing settled into a rhythm, in and out, in and out, in time with the pump of my legs.

"She's going faster, Walter! Tell her to stop going faster!"

"Stop going faster!"

"Walter!"

"Stop going faster!"

I went faster.

Trump International Hotel and Tower flashed by on my right, the SUV I'd noticed earlier on my left, screaming from the cart behind me. I'd been trained to pick out details, focus on them, isolate them, and as I whipped past the SUV, I could hear the men inside exclaiming excitedly in a language that sounded like Farsi.

They were Iranian? That conjured up all sorts of new questions.

"Tell her again!"

"Stop going faster!"

"Tell her again!"

"Stop going faster! Ma! She's still going faster!"

"Walter, I'm getting sick!"

"My mother is getting sick!"

I heard the sound of Walter's mother getting sick.

"My mother got sick all over me!"

I bet those two were a real hoot at home.

A bus shelter loomed ahead. I swerved to the right.

A group of slow walkers blocked the sidewalk.

"Move!" I ordered, but they ambled on, oblivious to the world around them.

Walter's mother got sick again. From the sounds of it, she'd had a big lunch.

"Please stop! My mother got sick again!"

"On my new outfit!" Walter's mother wailed.

"She got sick on her new outfit!"

I cut back toward the street. A phone booth came up fast at the edge of the curb.

A phone booth? Who uses phone booths anymore?

I veered hard to the left. Not fast enough. The cart hit the corner and bounced to one side. We careened off the sidewalk and into the street. Car tires squealed. I counter steered. The cart whipped around and sideswiped a tow truck. Drivers shouted through open windows. Something that sounded like weeping came from behind me, and the odor of Walter's mother's lunch mixed with the scents of exhaust and hot pavement.

Regaining control of the pedicab, I swung back in the direction of the sidewalk and again jumped back onto the curb. It seemed safer.

A whimper came from the back seat. "Please let us out!"

"I tried." I barely avoided a line of newspaper boxes.

"I'll pay you!"

"Walter, I'm going to wet myself!"

"My mother is going to wet herself!"

"Walter, I just wet myself!"

"My mother just wet herself!"

"Walter, I'm going to be sick again!"

"My mother is going to be sick again!"

Walter's mother got sick again.

"You have to turn around! My mother got sick and lost her dentures!"

I considered pulling my Ruger and killing them both, but lucky for them my purse was out of reach.

I streaked past an electronics store and two outdoor cafes. I couldn't pick out the Town Car yet, but I had to be gaining on it. Traffic crawled, traffic stopped, traffic crawled again.

There it was.

With all the identical cars clogging the street, I didn't know why I was so certain this was the one. But my gut reaction had been right so far. It was time I listened.

I stood on the brakes, leaping off the bike and breaking into a sprint, listening to Walter yell behind me, "She stopped, Ma! I made her stop!"

I wove between cars. He probably wasn't expecting me, and surprise was my best weapon. I ducked behind a produce delivery truck and, grabbing the back door handle, rode its bumper until it halted at the next light.

Then I made my move.

Circling the truck, I stayed in its lee as long as I could. I only had seconds once I emerged. The man I'd known as Morrissey was sharp. Even though I doubted he'd be looking for me, he would be alert, and since I had no weapon beyond surprise, I had to make this count. I needed to get inside that car, and the best way to do that was to make sure his attention was focused front.

The light changed. The truck started inching forward.

Now.

I swung around the truck and landed on pavement, knees flexed, legs already moving. It only took seconds for me to make it to the driver's door, and I pulled out my phone as I ran.

My phone had been designed for a multitude of functions, and on one corner, the titanium casing tapered to a conical, seemingly harmless nub. Reaching the car, I rapped that nub against the driver's window, the full force of my blow concentrated on that small point.

The glass shattered, showering tiny pebbles.

His eyes met mine, the first time I'd seen him anything but calm.

I thrust my arm inside to the shoulder, going for his gun.

He grabbed my arm and held. The cars started to move, and he hit the gas.

I scrambled to stay on my feet, trying to keep up, retain my balance, but it moved too fast. I stumbled and fell, my gym shoes dragging along the pavement, their rubber soles getting rapidly eaten away. The edge of the door pressed into my side, making it hard to breathe.

I caught a foothold for just a second and surged forward, smacking him in the nose with a head butt.

He grunted and his grip loosened slightly.

I reached, my fingers hitting Kirk's left leg, his holster.

I acted quickly, making a grab for the gun, but his recovery was equally fast. His hand closed over mine, wrestling, hitting, prying at my fingers.

I sensed we would hit the car ahead a split second before impact.

The crunch of steel shuddered through my spine. The car jolted to a dead stop. I hit the hot pavement in a roll, breath exploding from my lungs, head smacking hard. My vision exploded in stars. Tires screeched. I heard the Glock skitter, but where it ended up, I couldn't guess.

A heartbeat and the car door opened, and Kirk came down on top of me.

I struggled for breath.

Kirk's hands found my neck, my throat. He had my arms pinned under his knees, so I couldn't reach either of my weapons. Heat enveloped me. His grip was strong, squeezing, closing off my trachea, stopping the flow of blood to my brain, making my vision dim, go dark.

The crack of gunfire exploded in my ears.

Kirk bellowed. His hands released me, and his body lifted from mine.

I gasped, coughed, and gasped again.

A scream shattered the air around me. Not me. Not Kirk.

I forced the darkness back, forced my eyes to see, forced my body to function.

It was Julie. She held the Glock.

She had shot him.

Kirk staggered away from me. Julie raised the gun again but he batted it away, sending it through the air. Then he gripped Julie's arm, steering her toward the car. He moved awkwardly, each stride jerking, and it was then I noticed the dark glisten drenching one leg of his black trousers.

I pushed up from the street. Pain seared my hands and knees, but I forced it to the background, forced myself to concentrate, adrenaline and training taking over.

Kirk was too focused on Julie and the bullet in his leg to notice me come up fast behind him.

Using the knife edge of my hand, I delivered a sharp blow to the side of his neck, below and slightly in front of his ear. I rotated at the waist, driving all the power I could muster into his carotid artery, jugular vein, and vagus nerve, following through.

His body seized, muscles going rigid, then he slumped forward.

I wasn't sure if he was unconscious or merely stunned for a few seconds, but either would do. I looped my arm under his and across his back as he crumpled.

"Open the back door."

Julie stared at me. "Is he … is he dead?"

"Just do it."

I glanced down Broadway. Although I couldn't see them, I was sure the Iranians would be here on foot at any moment. Cops too, after the gunshot.

"Unlock the back door. Now."

She reached in and unlocked it from the inside.

I threw it open and shoved Kirk into the back seat. A quick search of the glove box scored me a handful of zip ties. I used one to secure his wrists in front of him.

He groaned and tried to lift his head, already coming around.

Traffic moved around us, horns blaring from behind, a few idiots even having the nerve to yell obscenities. I tugged my Ruger from the holster and set it on the dashboard. The driver from the car we'd back-ended stepped out onto the street, glimpsed the gun, and climbed back behind the wheel.

I shifted into drive and veered into the parking lane. Steam rose from under our hood, accompanied by the odor of scorched coolant. I doubted the Town Car would be running for long.

Ahead, traffic stopped again.

Iranians and cops would be on us any second. Disappearing was my first priority, getting Julie out of here as fast as we could. But if I hoped to find out what was really going on and why I had been lied to, I would have to take Kirk with us.

I assessed the surrounding cityscape. We weren't far from Lincoln Center.

"Come on. We're taking the subway."

I shoved the car into park and climbed out, pulling Julie with me. Opening the back door, I yanked Kirk to his feet, keeping the gun on his head.

"You, too."

We made it to the sidewalk, him dragging his feet the whole way.

"Faster, Kirk."

"She shot me."

He was gimpy, but he could still walk. I had no sympathy.

"Suck it up, unless you want *me* to shoot you this time. I won't aim for your leg."

"And I thought we liked each other."

He moved a little faster, grunting as he hobbled, sweat beading on his brow.

I didn't know if he was working with the men I'd seen in the SUV or not, so I kept my mouth shut. We'd covered about a block when I caught my next glimpse, three of them, running up the sidewalk. They weren't holding guns, but I saw bulges under their sports coats.

We needed to hurry.

We reached the next crosswalk, the Iranians closing the distance behind us disturbingly fast.

Sirens cut through the air, and a squad rounded the corner, probably sent to check out the disturbance we'd caused. The car stopped just twenty feet from where we stood.

As much as I'd like reinforcements to deal with my Iranian problem, I couldn't let police complicate my operation, and that included letting them take Kirk to the hospital for his injury or me to jail for the Ruger I had in a death grip.

I eyed Julie. "Quiet, hear?"

To my relief, she nodded.

I circled my arms around Kirk and gazed up at him in obvious adoration, the gun to the back of his head.

"If you signal them in any way, you're dead."

He returned my loving smile with one of his own.

"Don't worry, sweetheart. I want the cops involved about as much as you do."

Halfway down the block, the Iranians slowed to a walk, noticed the police car, and then ducked into a bistro with outdoor seating.

The light changed, and the cops passed by.

We continued across the street with the other pedestrians. I kept one arm around Kirk, both helping and steering him, his hands still bound in front of him with the twist tie. We moved quickly, coming as close to a run as Kirk could manage. As soon as the officers drove by the bistro, the Iranians would be back on the street and in pursuit. I had to take advantage of the short delay.

We reached Lincoln Center, rushing by the famous fountain in front of the Metropolitan Opera House without a sideways glance, then plunged down into the oppressive heat of the subway.

I bought three fare cards, and we pushed through the turnstiles. The Iranians had been delayed, but they had to guess we'd make for the train. They would catch up within minutes, maybe seconds. I had to make sure we were not where they expected by the time they came calling.

The Lincoln Center station was accessible to those with disabilities, and while Kirk was still mobile, handrails and ramps made navigating much faster than it would be in some of the less accessible stations. But though we reached the platform in record time, no train was waiting, and I couldn't detect any rumble to suggest one would be approaching in the next few seconds.

The blood on his leg was obvious, but those who noticed purposely turned their backs to it. I kept a watchful eye out for Good Samaritans. None attempted to get involved.

I needed to find a place to hide. A place the Iranians would be unlikely to expect me to go. A place I could extract some answers.

I steered Kirk and Julie into a men's restroom.

The place smelled like piss, mildew and those sweet pink deodorizing cakes that never really seemed to work. The bank of urinals and sinks weren't being used. Dipping low, I noticed one pair of feet under a door. I directed Julie into the large stall on the end and pushed Kirk in after her. After depositing Kirk on the toilet, I flattened him to the tile wall behind him, my forearm snug up under his chin, and waited for the lone man to finish up and leave.

Kirk wisely stayed silent, watching me. Although his skin was pale and sweat beaded on his brow, he was still giving off that calm, deadly vibe.

Too bad for him I was now immune to his charm. Trying to kill me tended to dampen my ardor.

I held the gun against his forehead. When I actually decided to end him, I would opt for the garrote in my purse strap, but there was nothing quite like the barrel of a gun to convey you mean business.

"You killed Morrissey."

"I didn't."

"Then who did?"

"My employers. I was brought in to take his place, rendezvous with you and get the girl. I'm just the hired help."

"Who are you working for?"

"An interested party from Moscow."

I narrowed my eyes on his. "Try Iran."

"The Iranians? I wondered how long it would take them to catch up. Have the Venezuelans rejoined the party yet?"

I hadn't seen Hawk Nose and his boys since the tunnel incident, but I felt no need to answer. Knowledge was power, as they say, and right now Kirk had all the answers. I wasn't about to let him start asking the questions.

"You expect me to believe you don't work for them?"

"I work for whoever pays. Sometimes it's even Uncle Sam. Today it happens to be the Russians."

"Then how did they find us? Manhattan is a big place."

"Who? The Iranians or the Venezuelans?"

I gave him a cold stare.

"You want me to guess?" he asked.

"Give it your best shot."

"The Venezuelans have a passion for police scanners."

I thought of the scanner I'd heard at the house on Long Island. Great. If they were using the police scanner to find us, after our street shooting, they might just be on their way, too.

"And the Iranians?"

He gave a shrug. "If they found me, my best guess is they had the same intel that you do. Eyes on the street. Or maybe in the sky."

Satellites. I liked that answer a little better. If it was true, we could lose them in the maze that was the New York subway system.

"How about the Russians?"

"They don't have anyone else in the game. I'm it. That's part of my deal."

I considered this for a moment. I didn't want to trust Kirk, and yet every sign he was giving suggested he was telling the truth, that he was a gun for hire and had no stake in any game other than a paycheck. As a bonus, the story jived with the profile Jacob had dug up on him.

"And what are the Russians paying you to do?"

"Same thing as you're being paid to do."

"My job is to protect Julie."

I shot her a glance. She leaned against the stall wall, her eyes large and sunken, a child who'd witnessed more trauma than she could absorb. Graffiti etched the paint behind her.

"Protect her," Kirk continued. "Deliver her unharmed. Bingo."

"Why would the Russians care if Julie is harmed? What value does she have to them?"

"Ask what value she has to you." He shook his head. "Scratch that. I can see you're the protective type, at least where she's concerned. So instead, ask what value she has to your employer."

A fair question.

"She knows something."

It was a complete guess on my part. Since I had no idea who the VIP was or even if there was a VIP, a shot in the dark was all I could manage. I looked Julie's way, this time in question.

She shook her head. "I don't know anything. I swear."

When I brought my focus back to Kirk, he was smiling.

"Okay, spill," I said. "What does she know?"

"She doesn't know anything. She told you herself."

"So what are you getting at?" I gave him a hard stare, waiting for the punch line.

"It's not what she *knows*. It's what she *is*."

Now I was really confused. "What she is?"

"I'm going to be on the level with you, Chandler. Okay? This is just a job to me. I don't have anything to hide. If it matters, I wasn't trying to kill you. I could have shot you at any time. I was simply knocking you out."

"Just spill it, Kirk."

He took a deep breath, let it out slow. "Ever heard of an asymptomatic carrier?"

Where the hell did that come from?

"It's someone who has a disease and can spread it but never actually gets sick," he said.

"What?" Julie not only looked in shock now, she appeared as confused as I was.

"And you're telling me Julie is an asymptomatic carrier?" I asked Kirk.

He nodded.

Julie shook her head. "I am not. What are you talking about?"

Kirk's gaze flicked to her. "You really have no idea, do you?"

"Idea of what?"

The girl was getting distressed now. I could hear it in the rising pitch of her voice.

"Don't cry," Kirk warned. "Do not cry."

Julie's chin trembled, but she held back the tears. "Chandler?"

I pressed the gun barrel against his temple, hard enough to leave a bruise.

"You have two seconds to explain."

He spent his first second frowning at me, his next uttering a single word.

"Ebola."

"Many things can happen in the field, developments no amount of training can help you understand or absorb," said The Instructor. "In the face of such

*trauma, knowing how to compartmentalize extrane-
ous thought and emotion can save your life."*

Heat rushed to my face, and I felt lightheaded. I lowered my arm from his throat, freeing him to sit normally, and
rocked back on my heels. I wanted to believe it wasn't true,
that Kirk was lying, but it all added up. It all made sense.

A laugh bubbled up inside me, but I held it back. I felt
giddy, on the edge of hysteria. This girl I'd been protecting—
who I'd thought of as a younger me and even started to care
about—was the host of a disease that could wipe out all of
Manhattan.

Hell, it could wipe out the entire world.

Ebola was known as a filovirus, and it was probably the
deadliest and most virulent little critter on the planet. Also
known as hemorrhagic fever, Ebola basically invaded cells
and chopped them into bits. Victims bled internally—and
ultimately externally—through every opening in their body,
including pores.

All bodily fluids leaked by someone with Ebola were
highly infectious. Including tears.

If Julie was a carrier, she could spread the disease without getting ill herself.

She cannot be harmed in any way, not even slightly.

I took a step back, fear making my shoulders bunch up.

Every moment I'd been with Julie, I'd been on the verge
of disaster. The bullet wound on my shoulder was like a wide
open door. Add in all the cuts and scrapes I'd sustained, and I
was just begging to be infected.

"How did she contract the virus in the first place?"

Kirk looked at Julie.

It took several seconds before she opened her mouth.
"The free clinic."

He nodded like an encouraging teacher whose student
had found the right answer.

"I just went there to get some antibiotics, you know? They took a blood test and then they gave me a shot, and I woke up in a hospital, only ..."

Her eyebrows dipped low, and worry dug lines in her forehead.

"Only what?" I prompted.

She focused on the grimy floor, her hands clasped.

"It wasn't a hospital. It was some kind of ... warehouse. On an island."

"Plum Island," Kirk said.

I knew Plum Island, AKA *Plum Island Animal Disease Center*, off the coasts of Long Island and Connecticut. There were actually several facilities on the island, and there had been rumors for decades it was a front for US biological weapons research.

"What happened there, Julie?"

"I don't know."

I studied her, the way her fingers fidgeted, the flush to her skin, and I had to wonder if she couldn't remember or just didn't want to.

"You must know something. How did you wind up at the mansion?"

"I got up out of bed ... and ... and ... there were doctors and nurses ..."

"Only," Kirk filled in, "the nurses and doctors were dead."

Julie's face crumpled. "They were beat up and shot. Murdered."

"No crying." Kirk ordered.

She looked to the ceiling and fluttered her eyes, trying to drive back tears.

Kirk continued. "It might have looked like that to you, skin purple with bruising, blood everywhere."

Julie nodded.

"They were infected by the virus. They got sick, crashed and bled out within hours."

I almost choked. "That fast?"

A chill moved through me, chasing the heat. I was somewhat familiar with the symptoms of Ebola. The red eyes, the way the virus replicated and ate away at a person's body until nothing was left but a bloody soup of more and more virus. But hours?

"I thought it took days."

"Not this particular strain. It had some help. A little genetic tinkering."

I let the new snip of information sink in.

"So I'm sick?" Julie said. She hiccupped a little.

"You're not sick, but you can kill others."

"Typhoid Mary," I said.

"Exactly. Your body is a factory for a powerful biological weapon, a virus that couldn't be produced without killing its host … until now."

Julie slumped against the stall wall. She looked stunned, almost catatonic. But to her credit, she didn't cry.

I had to report this to Jacob, only I was afraid what he'd say. It was probably a tossup; finish the op by delivering her to the government, or destroy her.

What the hell was I going to do?

I now understood why the defense department was concerned about Julie. If she was a living, breathing, hot zone capable of killing people within a few hours, every government and terrorist group on the planet would want her. She'd be worth billions.

Because she could kill billions.

Kirk cocked his head to the side and looked at me as if he'd just finished discussing a Broadway play or a film he'd seen at the local multiplex.

"So, where are we off to now?"

"We?"

I struggled to shut away the voice in the back of my mind that was screaming *Ebola, Ebola, holy shit, Ebola,* and focus on my surroundings.

If possible, the smells of mildew and urine had gotten worse, mixing with the scent of stress emanating from the three of us. One of the faucets dripped, and somewhere in the walls I heard a clunk in the pipes.

Something inside me shifted, as if I could physically feel myself locking away the shock and fitting back into my skin.

"Morrissey has a personal car. I can take you to it." Kirk raised his brows, trying to sell the suggestion.

I answered with an emotionless frown. "Actually, this is where we part ways."

He didn't seem surprised. He answered with a sideways sort of smile, of all things.

"You made me run all this way on a bum leg just to kill me?"

"Sorry for the inconvenience."

"Do I get a last request?"

"Depends. What is it?"

"Kiss me."

I hadn't seen that one coming. Facing death, and still flirting. Had to hand it to him.

"Seriously?"

"Ever since I laid eyes on you, I've thought about kissing you. Could I ask, out of professional courtesy, for one kiss before you kill me?"

A kiss. After handing Julie off to him at Columbus Circle, that's precisely the path my thoughts had taken. A kiss. Hot sex. That seemed like forever ago.

Now I was bodyguard to a biological weapon, and I had to single-handedly keep her away from Iranians and South Americans who wanted to use her blood to wipe out their enemies.

"How about it, Chandler?"

I blinked, bringing my thoughts back to Kirk, an idea starting to form.

"How much did they pay you?" I asked. "The Russians?"

"Fifty grand. Twenty-five up front. If I don't deliver, I have to return it."

Killing him was no doubt the safer move, but I didn't kill unless I had a very good reason for it. So far, Kirk appeared to have been upfront about everything.

Besides, I could use some help.

"Tell you what. You return the money, come back to working for us, and Uncle Sam will give you sixty."

Kirk smiled, full out this time. "I like that deal."

"Of course you do."

"You think you can trust me?"

"I think you're a whore for the money. You'll serve whoever's paying you."

"True. So what about the kiss?"

Cocky bastard. "If we get out of this alive, I'll give you more than a kiss."

"I'll hold you to that."

"Now where's Morrissey's car?" I remembered what Jacob had told me about the murdered spy. "Staten Island?"

He nodded. "The St. George ferry terminal. Just need to take the number one train to the ferry."

I hiked up my jeans, slipped the small blade from my ankle sheath, and used it to cut the zip tie on his wrists.

"Give me your jacket."

"Undressing me? You rethought that whole waiting-to-see-if-we-lived thing?"

"You're not that cute."

"Sure I am."

Yeah. He was. But I was the one with the gun. I pointed it. He handed me the garment.

I tore off a sleeve and hiked up his blood-soaked pant leg. I was right, the bullet hadn't hit bone. In fact, the wound looked more like a deep cut than a gunshot. Still, flesh wounds, as they call them in the movies, were not something to scoff at. They hurt like hell, could render a muscle ineffective, and caused significant blood loss.

"Julie, can you … um … step back a bit?"

She nodded, putting both hands over her mouth as if her very breath was infectious. The dazed expression in her eyes was different than the drug buzz. She looked to be in shock.

I used the jacket sleeve to wrap Kirk's leg and slow the bleeding. Ebola or not, this was a mission like any other. My life was in danger. Other lives were in danger.

Anyone who got in my way was in the most danger of all.

"Killing is part of your job," The Instructor said. "You must know when to do it and be able to follow through without hesitation."

The creak of the bathroom door hinges dumped another dose of adrenaline into my bloodstream. I peered through the space between the stall walls and door and spotted a flustered looking man carrying a briefcase. Judging from the way he moved and his obliviousness to his surroundings, I pegged him to be just what he seemed, a guy who needed to pee.

He sidled up to one of the urinals, just about to open his fly.

I held the Ruger against my leg where he wouldn't be likely to spot it, but yet it would be ready in case I was mistaken, and opened the door.

Kirk limped out of the stall behind me, followed by Julie.

The guy's eyebrows jutted upward, then an *attaboy* smile spread over his lips.

I caught a low chuckle coming from Kirk.

Boys.

We moved to the door. I inched it open, checking the area outside before emerging. I remembered red dots on the signs marking the platform and wound back to it. Sure enough, the number one was among the train lines posted.

Now we just needed the train to make its appearance before the Iranians did.

I focused on our surroundings. Exhaust hung in the air like thick fog, along with the usual mix of body odor and too much perfume. Still, compared to the smells in the bathroom, the air was positively fresh.

Tiled floors and walls bounced the clack of footfalls and rumble of voices until they meshed into a general roar, each sound almost indistinguishable from the other. A brass quartet played *New York, New York* further down on the platform. And finally, getting closer, I detected the low roar of an approaching train.

I almost didn't hear the voice.

Farsi.

I turned toward the sound, scanning the crowd. One of the men from the SUV raced down the steps toward us, a cell phone in his left hand, his right tucked under his sport coat, most likely concealing a weapon. His eyes were trained on Julie and Kirk.

The rumble grew louder. People shifted on the platform, positioning themselves for closest access to the doors once the train arrived.

I eyed Kirk. His leg injury would slow him down, but he could still help me. I could no longer afford to sit on the fence. I either had to trust him or not.

I slipped out the pistol and handed it to him. Then I drew my knife from its sheath and opened the serrated, black blade.

"Get her on the train. You cross me, I'll find you."

"I would expect nothing less."

I stepped to the side. The crowd closed in around Julie and Kirk, filling the spot I'd vacated.

Avoiding or heading off a dangerous situation was always preferable to dealing with a threat once it arrived. As an operative, much of my training focused on being aware of everything around me. Not just sight, but sounds and smells and attention to subliminal clues—what most people liked to think of as hunches or intuition. Awareness prevented surprises. It also staved off the sin of tunnel vision.

My Persian friend might be very good with whatever weapon he held under his jacket, but when it came to being aware, his training was lacking.

I circled to the right, moving purposefully but slowly enough not to gain notice. Reaching the benches lining the wall at the back of the platform, I wound through the crowd, keeping watch on the back of my target's head, moving closer.

My hair clung to the back of my neck. The train's roar grew louder, drowning out all other sounds, even the patter of my own heartbeat.

I stepped up, only inches behind him.

He didn't know I was there until I had my left hand on his mouth, fingers bruise-tight across his lips, thumb over his nose, squeezing down. I yanked his head back, to my right shoulder, and at the same time, thrust my knife low and buried it hard into his back, punching through his ribs, penetrating his heart.

He arched and cried out against my hand just as the train swept into the station, the rumble drowning out everything. I held his mouth and kept the blade in his body, feeling it twitch with his heartbeat.

One ...

Two ...

Three.

The doors whooshed open and the crowd shifted to one side to allow commuters to clear out of the cars.

I moved with the crowd, stepping away and letting him fall, trying to pull my knife back. But the S&W didn't have a blood groove, and suction held it fast.

By the time he hit concrete, I had blended into the sea of commuters. I wasn't worried about fingerprints—the knife handle had been treated to resist latents—but I didn't like being unarmed.

Screams cut through the ambient noise. People pushed and scattered. I saw a dark-haired man ramming his way through the crowd, moving quickly from my right. Trying to help? Afraid of missing the train?

No. Another Persian assailant.

How did all of these assholes get into the country? Didn't TSA have a goddamn *no fly* list?

The people departing the train cleared the doors, and the crowd surged forward. I caught a glimpse of Kirk ushering Julie into a subway car.

The new arrival noted the same thing. He veered in the direction of the train.

I angled my trajectory to head him off, bouncing between harried commuters. A voice said something over the public address system, impossible to decipher.

One woman elbowed me as I tried to pass. "Hey, wait your turn."

I refused to give ground. "You don't want to get on this train."

She gave me a sour look but wisely allowed me to squeeze past, not that she really had a choice.

I reached the door a split second before the Persian did and jumped inside, taking two running steps and then grabbing the pole used for standing commuters. Channeling my inner stripper, I whirled around, leading with my feet, ankles together.

As the Iranian stepped onto the train, I plowed into him with both heels.

He flew backward, flying into the sharp-elbowed woman and sending both of them sprawling onto the concrete platform.

I fell to the floor of the train, landing hard on my hip.

He recovered before I did, rising to his knees, pulling a pistol out of a shoulder holster, pointing the barrel square at my chest.

The explosion was deafening, bouncing off steel and cement.

I flinched, expecting the impact, expecting the pain.

The Iranian flinched, looking surprised.

A moment later he slumped to the ground, trying and failing to plug the bullet hole in his chest with his hands.

I guess Kirk was trustworthy after all.

The subway car erupted, screams, crying, stampeding people. I grabbed the pole to keep from being swept out, peering past the surge and into the car, searching for Kirk and Julie. Kirk had concealed the gun and was moving with the crowd, pushing Julie toward the open door, acting as if they were part of the panic.

I did the same, getting to my feet and rushing through the door in front of me. With a gun going off and two dead on the ground, there wasn't a chance in hell the station agent in the booth would let the train go on as usual. We'd have to find another route downtown.

The sharp-elbowed woman lay on the ground behind the dead Persian spy. She looked up, staring at me with shell-shocked eyes.

"You should have listened to me," I said as I stepped over the body and blended with the crowd.

I caught up with Kirk and Julie at the closest subway newsstand.

"The two of you. Put these on," Kirk shoved a Yankees baseball cap, and *I LOVE NY* tee shirt, and a pair of fuchsia sunglasses into my arms.

I grabbed Julie and ducked into the bathroom. Suppressing my Chicago Cubs fan sensibilities, I shoved my hair up under the hat.

I gave Julie the tee and glasses. She was listless, her jaw slack.

"You hanging in there?" I asked.

She stared at me like she hadn't realized I was standing next to her.

"You should get away from me." She bit her lower lip.

"My job is to protect you, Julie."

"I could make you sick."

"I'm willing to take that chance."

She looked ready to burst into tears, but choked it back.

"You're going to be okay," I said.

"Really?"

"Yes," I lied.

She reached out to hug me, then caught herself and shrank back.

Poor thing.

When we emerged, Kirk was waiting for us, dressed in a dark blue NY tee. He gave me his white button down, and I pulled it on as an over shirt and rolled up the sleeves.

As far as disguises went, it wasn't much. I doubted it would fool the Iranians or the Venezuelans or whatever additional intelligence agencies happened to be after us, but it might keep the cops off our tails. Eyewitnesses in stressful situations tended to remember the simple things, if they remembered anything accurately at all. Changing the general look of our clothing and length of my hair would hopefully get us off the NYPD's radar.

One concern in a mile-long list.

"We need to get out of here," I told Kirk. "Think you can hoof it for a while?"

He looked about as excited about the idea as I expected.

"The ferry terminal is at the tip of Manhattan. That's a long damn way."

"Then let's shoot for the Columbus Circle subway station."

He nodded. "Ever get the feeling we're retracing our steps?"

"It has occurred to me."

We emerged from the subway to find rush hour still in play and Lincoln Center's fountain rimmed with summer tourists and New Yorkers alike. The faint beat of helicopter blades sounded overhead, and my stomach seized until I spotted it. Police this time, not ideal, but at least it wasn't Hawk Nose and his friends.

I eyed Kirk. In the sunlight I could detect the sheen of fresh blood darkening his pant leg, seeping through my makeshift bandage. If we had to do much walking, I wasn't sure he would last.

Ditto if Julie sneezed on him.

I had to admit, I was relieved to have Julie away from mass transit. Ever since finding out who she really was, what she really was, the knowledge that her blood could wipe out much of the city weighed heavily on me. The odds of getting her all the way to the tip of Manhattan, then across the harbor to Staten Island, seemed astronomical and growing. Even if she died, she still represented a threat.

It was something I would have to deal with, sooner or later.

"Come on," I said.

Kirk nodded, sweat already soaking his hair and trickling down his forehead. He picked up the pace, his lips tight with pain.

"You'd better take this." He handed me the Ruger.

He'd proven himself a good shot, but he was probably right. Running on a bad leg didn't improve marksmanship. As long as he could shepherd Julie, I'd take care of the rest. I slipped it into my holster just as my phone buzzed.

"Is Ginny there?" Jacob's electronic voice asked.

"I'm sorry, she left for Phoenix yesterday," I said, giving the appropriate response.

"Tell me you're not near Lincoln Center."

We kept walking. "Are you asking me to lie?"

"That's what I was afraid of. Get out of there."

"The police are on their way, I know."

"The city is on lockdown. They're calling that tunnel explosion a terrorist act, and some dead Iranians were just discovered in the subway. They're buttoning up Manhattan. National Guard has been called."

Shit. So much for our plan to get to Staten Island. I needed to come up with another way out of the city, and I had to do it quickly.

"Listen, I found out some interesting things about our Julie."

After I filled him in, Jacob was silent for a good ten seconds before speaking.

"What are you going to do with her, Chandler?"

I wished I knew. "I'm not sure. Get her out of New York, for one."

"You know the threat she represents."

I glanced at Julie. She looked beaten. Afraid. Confused. It wasn't her fault our military turned her into a germ warfare incubator.

But life wasn't fair, and the needs of the many outweighed the needs of the few.

"I know," I told Jacob. "I haven't decided yet."

"If the enemy gets her, or even if Uncle Sam gets her and she's brought back to Plum Island …"

"I know, Jacob. Right now, my main goal is getting her away from here."

"How?"

I glanced up at the NYPD chopper overhead. It was a long shot, but with Kirk's help, I might be able to make it work.

"What's the closest helipad to Lincoln Center?"

I heard the clacking of a computer keyboard over the phone despite the traffic noises all around me.

"Probably your best bet is the Port Authority Helipad at 30th Street and the Hudson."

"Thanks, Jacob. Oh, and Mr. Kirk is now working for us."

"You turned him."

"His deep-rooted sense of patriotism won out in the end."

"So you offered him money."

"How do you know it wasn't my feminine wiles?"

"Was it your feminine wiles?"

"Partly. We also owe him sixty grand."

"I'll make arrangements. I trust your judgment, Chandler, and hope this doesn't have anything to do with him looking like Colin Farrell."

"I can't entirely rule that out."

"Hmm. Well, maybe you two will have a chance to hook up."

"Maybe."

"If you live long enough."

"If any of us do." I ended the call and squinted at Kirk. "We need a cab."

He glanced back over his shoulder, and we spotted the men at the same time. More Iranians. Two of them threaded through the pedestrians, each with a hand hidden under their jackets, eighty meters away and rushing toward us at an alarming speed.

Shit. That hadn't taken long.

"We need to get the hell out of here," I said, but we were already running, weaving through pedestrians, Kirk gimping along with his arm behind Julie, gingerly guiding her in the right direction. Traffic flowed by on the street, cab after cab with silhouettes in back seats, vacancy lights off, and not a pedicab to be found.

Each equipped with two good legs, the men were closing fast.

I felt the beat of chopper blades in my chest and scanned the sky between buildings. A purple Bell 427 hovered overhead.

Welcome back to the party, Hawk Nose.

We had to get some wheels or this would be over far too soon.

Our trio hobbled along for another block before a cab with an empty back seat passed us. It stopped at the next intersection, its vacancy light off, signaling it wasn't looking for passengers.

Not that I was going to let that stop me.

I raced into the street. Grabbed the back door handle.

Locked.

The front passenger window was open, so I reached through, found the handle, and yanked it open.

"Hey! Hey! What do ya think you're doing?"

"Get out," I ordered.

"I'm off duty," he said.

"You see this?" I asked, reaching my hand under my skirt.

"Hell, yeah!" he said. Then he saw I was holding a gun. "Hell, no."

"Unlock the door."

"You're holding me up?"

"Take your cash. I just want the car."

He frowned. "Look, lady, I got a wife who's a fat, lazy bitch, a kid in a gang who sells smack, the landlord just served us papers, and this morning I found out I have diabetes. You kill me, you'd be doing me a favor."

I had barely registered the crack of the gunshot when the windshield spiderwebbed, and the driver gurgled and slumped against the wheel. The bullet had just missed me.

Julie stared, mouth open, as Kirk forced her down behind the cab.

"Get in," I yelled, ducking inside and hitting the unlock button.

Kirk pushed her into the back seat, climbed in behind her, and shut the door. He slipped his hand behind her back and bent her forward at the waist, out of the line of fire.

I didn't have time to undo the seat belt and pull out the body, so I slid onto the dead man's lap and shifted into drive.

The light stayed red. Cars boxed us in from all sides.

I found the two Iranians behind us with my mirrors. The one who had taken out the cabbie crossed the street in front of us, weaving through standing traffic.

Here I'd been totally focused on the pursuers behind and missed the man in front.

I couldn't miss him now.

He walked closer and closer, until he was just off my left bumper.

Just when I was convinced I'd made my last mistake, the light changed to green, and the river of cars started to inch forward.

Not fast enough.

The man in the street raised his hands, the pistol in his fists pointed at my head.

I cranked the wheel and hit the gas.

He bounced off the hood with a sickening thud and hit the street.

I kept going, gunning the engine as the cab lurched and bumped over him.

Tires squealed around us. Horns blared. Cars rushed by.

Some New Yorkers didn't let anything get in their way.

We cleared the intersection, traffic in front of us still moving. In the rearview, I could see the remaining two men race across the street.

Judging by the purpose with which they moved, I assumed their SUV was close by. They'd be back on our tail soon. And if Hawk Nose did even a passable job keeping track of us from the sky, the Iranians weren't our only concern. Even so, it was the best head start we'd had all day, and I'd take it.

The West 30th Street Heliport rested on the bank of the Hudson River. More than thirty blocks away. Traffic was crazy, due to the tunnel being closed, the subway incident, and presumably the dead man now lying in the center of 9th Avenue, emergency vehicles everywhere.

I drove like all of our lives depended on it.

The SUV appeared, too soon for my comfort, ten car lengths behind.

We played stop and go, street light to street light. Sometimes I gained a few meters. Sometimes the Iranians did. At each red, we watched intently to see if they jumped out of their vehicle to rush us. So far, so good.

It took ten excruciating minutes to reach 49th Street, and I got the hell off of 9th and turned right, heading for 12th Avenue, our pace slightly faster than a snail surfing on molasses.

"You guys okay back there?" I asked, eyeing my passengers.

Kirk had distanced himself from Julie as much as he could, leaning against the passenger side door.

"Never better," he said, winking at me.

I couldn't see the SUV behind us anymore, but wasn't optimistic I'd lost them. This op had been nothing but one bad break after another, and the only thing I was optimistic about was the fact that our luck was terrible.

I blew through a yellow light and swung left onto the boulevard that was 12th Avenue, the vast blue/black of the river running parallel to us, filling my nostrils. Coming up on the right was the USS Intrepid, moored there since 1982.

The once mighty aircraft carrier was now a museum, a relic of wars past.

Once again I checked the rearview, eyeing Julie.

The Intrepid was still a sight to behold, over two hundred fifty meters long, weighing thirty thousand tons, armor four inches thick in parts. A fearsome weapon.

But not as fearsome as what I had in my back seat.

Traffic was better on the boulevard. We passed the Silver Towers, the sprawling Javits Center, and finally reached our destination. A long, concrete platform edged the water, enclosed by fencing and a few no-frills trailers, the heliport was built for function, not fanciness.

Lucky for us it wasn't built for security, either.

Best yet, a small, sightseeing helicopter sat on the helipad, as if waiting for us.

Maybe our luck had begun to change.

I swung the cab into the entrance. We didn't have much time, and normally I would ram the cab straight through the fence instead of risking involving civilians. But considering Julie's state, things weren't so simple. If a flying bit of glass should cut her or she happened to bump her nose, a city full of civilians wouldn't just be involved—they'd be dead.

I double-parked, and we headed for the trailer promising helicopter tours of the Big Apple. I took the lead, Kirk hobbling behind me with Julie at his side. Still no sign of the Iranians.

The inside of the trailer was about as posh as the outside. Indoor/outdoor carpet, particle board furniture, and the smell of well-aged cigarette smoke from before the recent indoor smoking ban gave the place an ambiance all its own. At least it was clean.

"Can I help you?"

The young woman behind the counter peered over her glasses at us. The evening sun streamed through the window and reflected off the diamond stud in her right nostril.

"We need to take a helicopter."

"I'm afraid there's a couple going up right now. We prefer you make reservations, but I have some paperwork here that—"

I met Kirk's eyes, and we brushed past the desk and made for the door leading out to the helipad.

"Wait! You can't—"

But we could, and we did.

Leaving the woman yelling empty threats in our wake, we reached a blue helicopter—a single engine EC120—emblazoned with the tour company's logo. Smaller than the corporate craft used by Hawk Nose, this bird offered only one compartment, forcing the pilot and the passengers to cram together in the tiny space. The pilot stood with his back to us, instructing an older, well-dressed couple in how to fasten their harnesses.

"I'm sorry, but you won't be sightseeing today," I told them.

The tourist couple stared at me as if I was speaking another language. The pilot frowned.

"Who are you?"

"Homeland Security. We're commandeering this aircraft. Now I need you to get out and return to the trailer immediately. Oh, and keep your heads down."

The pilot shook his head. "Can I see some sort of ID?"

Overhead I could hear the *whomp, whomp, whomp* of chopper blades in the far off distance, the sound bouncing off buildings. I could only hope it was another tour coming in to land, but I had a bad feeling I was just fooling myself.

I pulled out the Ruger. "The helicopter. We need it. Now."

The pilot backed away from the door. The couple scrambled, almost tripping over each other to get out. Some part of me registered that this was the third mode of transportation I'd stolen in the last hour.

I nodded to Julie and Kirk. "Hurry."

Julie looked as if she'd rather do just about anything but go on another helicopter ride, but she stepped up into the tiny craft anyway.

Behind Kirk, the pilot turned around, and I caught a gleam in his eye, that little surge of adrenaline people felt just before they were about to do something very stupid.

I opened my mouth to shout a warning.

I needn't have bothered.

Kirk twisted at the waist, throwing his body weight into a well-aimed punch.

The pilot crumpled onto the concrete.

"Nice," I said.

He cocked his head and shot me a half smile. "I'm a lover, not a fighter. Wait 'til I show you my real talents."

Still no Iranians, but in the distance I saw a chopper heading toward us, still too far to tell if it was Hawk Nose, or just a tourist craft.

I climbed into the pilot's seat, Kirk slipping into the seat next to Julie.

Moving fast, I familiarized myself with the interior: collective control stick, cyclic control stick, rudder pedals, RPM gauge, altimeter, airspeed indicator, manifold pressure gauge, vertical speed indicator, fuel gauge, oil pressure and temp, cylinder head temp.

Then, Kirk: "Above us!"

I was just reaching for the ignition when a round crashed through the upper windshield and dug into the main instrument panel. More bullets peppered the fuselage. I dropped to the floor.

Apparently Hawk Nose had realized Julie's corpse was nearly as valuable as taking her alive.

Shitastic.

Julie hunched forward. "Oh my God. Oh my God."

"Are you hit?" Kirk yelled at Julie.

For a second, I couldn't breathe.

"They're shooting at us," Julie screamed over the noise.

"But are you hurt?"

"No, no. I'm okay."

"No crying."

Another full magazine of automatic weapon fire punched through the roof, pinging off the metal floor. While the layered construction of the hull and windshield was made to withstand the occasional run in with a seagull or even a goose, it couldn't hold up to bullets. And I couldn't risk lifting off, provided the instrument panel was even operational at this point.

"We have to evacuate. Find cover."

I swung the doors on both sides of the cockpit open.

The roar of another engine caught my attention, then the shuddering clang of steel.

I had hesitated at running through the fence. The Iranians hadn't. The green SUV screeched to a stop less than twenty yards away, between us and our yellow cab.

"The river." Kirk gave me a look. "Can you keep them busy?"

I nodded, fitting the Ruger into my hands, wishing I had a rifle. "Move."

Kirk and Julie scrambled out of the cockpit and crouched on the helicopter's off side. I climbed out as well, kneeling low, trying to gain as much cover as I could.

I gave Kirk a look, then squeezed off several rounds, first targeting the helicopter, which was too high to hit, and then the Iranians' SUV.

Bullets flew, from the ground, from the air, until it was impossible to tell who was shooting who, the only thing I was sure of was that Julie and Kirk had made it off the edge of the platform and into the river.

I didn't think I would be so lucky.

The chopper lifted higher, flying out of range of my .380.

Something moved in my peripheral vision.

I swung the pistol back in time to see one of the Iranians advancing along the concrete pad that jutted into the water, just ten feet away.

He wasn't out of my range. I put a round in his throat.

The Persian went down, made a few twitching movements, and then lay still, his rifle still slung across his shoulder.

A gift.

Firing off my last few rounds, I scooted toward the man I'd just killed. I yanked the rifle—a Madsen LAR—over his head and tugged the strap free of his heavy body.

The weapon was hot to the touch, and by my mental count he'd used about half of his thirty round AK magazine. I squeezed off a burst of three at the SUV.

No one returned fire, but I could see movement.

The beat of the blades crescendoed, coming in for another assault.

I couldn't hold off the chopper and the SUV, not without more ammunition, and in a few more seconds, my chance to make a break would be gone.

I fired another three rounds, then made my dash for the river.

My feet slapped pavement, trying to get traction, adrenaline humming in my ears.

Five steps to go.

Four.

Three.

A gust of wind hit me, sending my Yankees cap flying, knocking me to my knees.

The purple helicopter dropped in front of me, hovering, cutting me off.

I propped myself up, raised the rifle, took aim, fired.

My first shot cracked the windshield. My second missed entirely.

The chopper turned to the side. The passenger compartment door gaped open, my old buddy Hawk Nose raising his rifle, putting me in his sites.

I squeezed the trigger and held it, giving him everything I had left.

But I didn't aim for Hawk Nose.

I aimed for the back rotor, and I hit it square.

The helicopter whirled around, spinning, spinning. It veered to the side, smacked into the far side of the platform, crumpling like an angry god squeezed it in his fist. Flames began to curl out from the engines.

Tires screeched, drawing my attention. It was the SUV.

The last Iranian was driving away, fleeing the scene.

But why?

I scrambled to my feet, dropping the useless rifle and heading for the water's edge. The helicopter exploded in a brilliant fireball, heated air and the smell of burning fuel washing over me.

Adios, Hawk Nose. Maybe you'll luck out and they'll have donkey porn in hell.

I spotted Julie and Kirk twenty meters away, hovering on the edge of the platform, clinging to the concrete pilings that anchored the pier-like helipad to the river floor.

My purse vibrated, and I slapped my cell to my face.

I traded codes with Jacob. It was a miracle I could remember the appropriate response.

"Chandler, I'm watching via satellite feed. They're coming."

"Who?"

"The DoD. They're treating you as hostiles."

"How soon?"

"Now. Get out of there."

"Nice shot," Kirk said, peering up from the water as I approached.

The river smelled, of fish, of rot, of petroleum and garbage. The air smelled of smoke. Something moved at the base of the pilings, and I had a creeping feeling it was probably rats.

"We need to go."

"We can swim downriver, steal a boat or a car."

"Let's do it." I squatted, preparing to slip into the water, and squinted past Kirk. "Ready, Julie?"

"I ... I can't." Julie stared into the darkness under the platform.

"Don't think about them," I said. "Rats won't hurt you if you don't hurt them."

"No, no, it's not that." Her voice was soaked in tears, and I glanced at Kirk, waiting for him to warn her not to cry.

Kirk was facing the same direction as Julie, but they weren't staring at the rats. They were staring at the red blooming all along Julie's arm and streaming into the water.

A hum rose in my ears. Bright motes swirled in front of my eyes, and I wasn't sure if I wanted to throw up or cry.

Kirk was the first to recover. "Get out of the water. Now."

He grabbed Julie by the arm and dragged her around the helipad and up the shore.

I pushed all thought, all feeling into the back of my mind and forced myself to follow, my body relying on training and muscle memory to function.

We ran for the closest trailer. The door was locked, so I broke it down. Once inside, I pulled off Kirk's button down, wrung it out and handed it to him. We moved quickly and without talking, him wrapping the cut on Julie's arm, me checking the trailer's perimeter.

The hum in my ears gave way to a beating sound, more helicopters, two of them, black this time. Four matching SUVs roared through the broken gate and rimmed the perimeter of the heliport, reflecting light from the burning chopper like dark mirrors. Soldiers wearing black CBRN suits deployed from the vehicles, assault rifles at the ready. They moved from trailer to trailer, clearing each, approaching ours.

I knew what was coming but had no ideas of how to stop it. I had no gun. Even if I did, shooting was risky. Of course, they would have to choose their targets carefully. Julie was too valuable to harm.

Unfortunately, I doubted Kirk and I would come out of this alive.

But then, we already knew that.

I met Kirk's gaze, pressing my lips into a bitter smile.

He lowered one lid in a wink. "I only wish we'd taken time for that kiss."

I did, too. I had just opened my mouth to say so when a window shattered, and I heard the hiss.

An incapacitating agent.

Yeah, that's what I would have done.

I started to feel the effects before I realized I'd taken a breath.

"As an operative, you must learn to live in the moment," The Instructor said. "Not just while carrying out an assignment, but in every aspect of your life. There's no point in putting things off when the future may never come."

When I woke, I expected to be bound.

Scratch that—I expected to be dead.

I was wrong on both counts.

Beyond that, my thoughts were scrambled. Images drifted through my mind in snips and snatches. Fire. Water. Subways and helicopters.

Blood.

Swirling blood.

I forced my eyes open, pushed back the confusion long enough to concentrate on my surroundings. I was lying in bed, wearing a flimsy hospital gown and nothing underneath but heart monitor pads stuck to my chest. An IV tube snaked from my hand and led to a bag hanging from an adjustable metal pole attached to the bed frame. Cloth tape held a square of gauze to the outside of my left upper arm.

My skin felt hot, my stomach uneasy. I could smell river water and rubbing alcohol and the dusty scent of concrete. The area looked like a hospital room, white floors, blank, white walls, but there were no windows.

And I was not alone.

As soon as I saw Jonathan Kirk, I knew who he was, but it took a little longer to remember why we were here.

The river. Jacob's warning. The cut on Julie's arm.

He was in a bed hooked to monitors, same as me.

I wondered where they'd put Julie. Wondered how long we had to live. I watched Kirk in silence until his eyelids fluttered.

"Hey," I said.

He opened his eyes fully and frowned at me, obviously as confused as I had been.

I sat up on my stretcher. A little dizzy at first, I planted elbows on knees and cradled my head in my hands.

"I think we're in some kind of lab."

A minute or two passed, and I could see the thoughts shifting around in his mind, just as they had in mine. Finally Kirk sat up and glanced around the room.

"Plum Island."

"You've been here before?"

He shook his head. "Just a guess."

"Probably a good one."

He swung off the side of the bed, slid onto his feet, and grimaced.

"Damn leg."

Bandages wrapped his gunshot wound, ankle to knee.

"There's a camera in the corner." I pointed out the small device hugging the ceiling.

Kirk gave it a sneer. "They're watching us, waiting to see how we die."

In my line of work, dying was an occupational hazard. But I'd often speculated about how I'd feel when the time came. I'd faced death before. I'd fought it. So far, I'd won. But this time I had no one to fight. This time the enemy was inside, and no tool or training or sheer will to survive could save me.

I probably should be frightened. Instead I felt nothing at all.

"You're awake," a male voice said.

I followed the sound to an intercom speaker, embedded in the wall.

"Why are we here?"

"You've been infected with a virulent disease."

"A virulent disease?" That might be the understatement of the year. "You mean Ebola."

"Yes."

"Where's the girl? Where's Julie?"

"She's here. Thank you for bringing her back where she belongs."

I looked up at the camera. "You're the VIP, aren't you?

"VIP?"

"The one who requested this operation. The one with ties to the DoD."

"Weapons are the purview of the defense department, it's true."

It was neither a confirmation nor a denial, but I didn't need either. I knew the answer.

"What is your name?"

"Pembrooke."

"I want to see Julie, Mr. Pembrooke."

"It's Dr. Pembrooke, and she's serving her country. You two have an opportunity to do the same."

"An opportunity?" Kirk guffawed. "Does that mean we can refuse?"

"No."

"Didn't think so."

"You both had injuries. Being in close proximity to Miss James meant a very high likelihood of infection."

"So now you're watching us to see how well your new biological weapon works?"

"All weapons must be tested."

"So that means what?" Kirk asked in a dry voice. "You kick back and watch us die, while chomping on popcorn and Raisinets?"

"We aren't doing this because we find it entertaining, Mr. Kirk. This is science."

"Maybe we weren't infected," I said.

There was no reply.

Then I understood.

"You son of a bitch. You made sure we were infected. Didn't you, Pembrooke?"

"Why?" Kirk asked. "To keep us quiet?"

"The genie can't be put back into the bottle, Mr. Kirk. Our concerns are more immediate than you spilling government secrets. We have a weapon, and we need to know if we can properly manage it."

"Manage it? How can you manage a ..."

But then I knew. I knew it sure as anything.

"You're testing a cure." As soon as I'd said the words, my hands began to shake.

"Yes, we are testing a cure. A DNA vaccination, to be more specific."

"Well, what're you waiting for?" Kirk said. "Shoot us up."

"We administered it while you were unconscious."

I scanned Kirk's body, my own arms and legs. "And is it working?"

"We'll see."

I wasn't very attentive in middle school, but I did remember a few things from science class.

"If this is an experiment, there has to be a control group."

"Yes."

My stomach dipped. "So you only gave one of us the cure …"

"And the other was given a placebo shot. That's correct."

I closed my eyes. Pressure assaulted my chest, making it hard to breathe. I wanted to look at Kirk, see how he was handling this, but I was afraid if I did, my shaking would increase. Or worse yet, I'd start to cry.

Kirk was the one who summed up the obvious. "So one of us will die and the other gets to watch."

"That will be true if the vaccine works."

"And when one of us starts showing symptoms? Will you give the vaccine then?"

"That will be too late. Once the virus has replicated enough to be symptomatic, the vaccine is no longer effective."

"You've done other tests?"

"Only with chimps. The vaccine was not effective once symptoms began."

I forced my eyes open, remembering the dead doctors and nurses Julie had described. I had to wonder what the prick on the intercom had done with the bodies. What excuse he'd given the families to explain why their loved ones weren't coming home from work.

"How do you know the vaccine will be effective if it's given earlier?" Kirk asked.

"We don't."

"So we could both die."

"Unfortunately, yes."

"Unfortunately?" I let out a bitter laugh. "I'm sure your heart bleeds."

"I'm defending our country. Defending our way of life from those who seek to destroy it. Every war has casualties."

"Don't give us that *war on terror* bullshit, Pembrooke. And don't give us that goose-stepping *just following orders* bullshit, either."

"If we didn't do things like this, the other side would."

"If you didn't do things like this, the other side might not hate us so goddamn much. You're a monster."

I wasn't naíve. I'd done a lot of morally questionable things, murdered a lot of people, all in the name of my government and keeping my country safe. But I killed players. Politicos. Military. We all signed on for it. Creating a biological weapon, which would no doubt kill millions of innocent civilians ...

I reached under my gown and pulled the sensors off my chest, causing the machine to flat line. Then I ripped the tape off my hand and pulled the IV needle out of my vein.

"The morphine drip is to help you with the pain. And we need to monitor your vitals to—"

"You need to shut the fuck up." I slung my legs over the side of the bed.

"You really should—"

"I'd listen to her if I were you," Kirk said.

I didn't feel any effects of morphine. My head was clear, my body as achy as ever. Even so, my first steps were wobbly, a few remaining effects of whatever they'd gassed us with. I was steady by the time I reached the door.

Locked.

"There's no way out of that room, not until we come in and get you."

"You'd better hope not, Pembrooke. Because if I get out of here, the things I'm going to do to you will make Ebola look like hay fever."

I tried the door with a couple of kicks, then moved on to the perimeter of the room, testing walls, ceiling, and floor until I had no sane option but to acknowledge the voice was right. There was nothing left to do but die.

Or watch the other die.

My stomach felt hollow.

I walked back to the bed where Kirk had just disabled his heart monitor. He was a few years older, a formidable man, a mercenary forged by the same type of red-hot violence that had hardened me. And when I looked at the calm in his eyes, I wondered how many times he had recognized the possibility of his own death.

"Ever dreamed it would happen like this?"

He gave me a crooked smile. "Never thought about it."

"Not once?"

He shrugged.

"It doesn't bother you to die in a laboratory as part of some sick experiment?"

"Better than a men's can in the subway." He gave me that bedroom eyes stare. "And I couldn't ask for better company."

I let out a small laugh at his bravado.

It had to be bravado.

He couldn't be serious.

Right?

I looked at him, studied his face.

Jesus, he actually was serious.

My stomach jittered again, but this time it was a good kind of jitter.

"I took a picture of you," I said.

No reason not to be brazen.

"What for?" he asked.

"For me. If I never saw you again."

"But you don't need a picture. Here I am."

"Here you are."

I stepped close and circled my hands around his neck. This morning I hadn't known him. Just a few hours ago, I'd been ready to kill him. Now it felt like we were the only two people in a brutal world, and only one of us would see tomorrow.

I brought my lips to his.

He opened to me, his hand cradling the back of my head, pulling my mouth hard against his.

Heat spiked my blood.

Lust.

Life.

I wasn't sure how long the kiss lasted, but when we broke apart, I knew it wasn't enough. I wanted more. Needed more. If I only had minutes left on this planet, I would damn well make them count.

"I know how I want to go out," I whispered.

He tilted his head to the side, studying me, a smile playing at the corners of his lips. "And our friend on the other side of that camera?"

I glanced up at the lens peering down at us. "Let the bastard break out his popcorn and Raisinets."

I thought Kirk's little grins and sideways looks were sexy before, but I didn't have words to describe his expression now. He pulled me tight against his body and kissed me again, hard, needy. Beyond the river water, his skin still smelled of that Armani cologne, and a warm scent that was all his own.

I breathed him in, wanting to take everything about this man deep inside.

Our hospital gowns were off in seconds, and our battered bodies intertwined. At first we just clung to one another, kissing, probing. A dusting of hair covered his chest, and I ground my breasts against him, the sensation zapping through my nipples like an electric charge.

Then I was pushing him back on his bed and climbing on top of him.

233

He was erect, and I rubbed against him until I was wet enough to take him inside. I came on my third stroke, waves shuddering through me. I arched my back, still thrusting, and he buried his face in my chest.

I hardly knew Jonathan Kirk. And now I never really would.

But right then, he symbolized everything to me.

Sensation.

Connection.

Life itself.

I wanted to explore all of him, feel things I never had before. I wanted this to last forever, and knowing it wouldn't made each second, each moment, each thrust and sigh and whimper all the more profound.

I sensed the muscles in his thighs tensing, trying to hold back the coming release, and slowed my motion.

Nuzzling my breasts, he looked up at me.

"What do you like most?" I breathed.

His smile was a wicked thing. "Let me taste you."

"Me first."

I moved down his body, littering kisses over his chest, his belly, my hair fanning over him in my wake. I trailed my tongue up the length of him, then took him full in my mouth. I tasted myself on him, the flavors and scents mingling, intoxicating.

We were good together, me and him. I'd sensed it from the first. So much alike, yet different enough to add spice. It was a cruel joke that our time together would be so short.

I didn't let myself think of that, though, but only of the sensations. The feel of him in my mouth. The hair on his legs rubbing rough on my skin.

Our first time together.

Our last time together.

When he'd reached his climax, he found my arms with his hands, guiding me upward until I was straddled over his mouth. He teased me at first, going too slow, pulling back, torturing me with gentleness, until the tension built and built and I was thrusting myself on him, trying to capture his fluttering tongue, begging for release.

"Please ..." I gasped. "Please."

He grabbed my hips, pulling me closer, taking me firmly. Devouring me.

I shuddered, the pleasure so intense it was almost pain, the first ripple in a building, rising wave that reduced me to nothing but pure sensation.

I could only hope the taste of me, the sound of my screams, gave him as much satisfaction as he gave me.

When my leg muscles could take no more, I moved back down his body and brushed his lips with mine.

He peered at me, his cheeks flushed, his eyes bright.

I slipped next to him in the bed and fitted my body against his.

"You were amazing," I breathed. "Just as I thought you'd be."

"You, too."

I shook my head slowly, the sadness creeping in. "I wish we had more time ..."

"Time?" He grinned. "Babe, we got the rest of our lives."

His hand moved between my legs and began to stroke.

I had no idea how my body had any more to give, but again I began to respond, despite the specter of death around me.

Or maybe because of it.

Sex affirms life.

He shifted, moving on top of me, keeping his weight on his elbows. I wrapped my legs around him, sighing as he entered me, burying my face in his neck as he began to thrust.

We were the only two people in the world.

Only one of us would see tomorrow.

I couldn't think of a better way to go out.

When we finished, we held each other.

Held each other, and looked at each other.

The afterglow faded.

Dread crept back in.

The looking at each other became watching each other.

I saw it first, and it felt like a punch to the gut.

Just a small bruise on the back of the hand.

But it hadn't been there a moment ago.

Small. Black. Harmless looking.

Then it began to grow, spreading out, taking only a few minutes to double in size while we both silently stared.

The nosebleed came next. A trickle at first. Then a steady stream.

"Aw ... Chandler ..." Kirk said.

I reached for the IV needle.

Hooked up the morphine.

Tried to be brave.

"It's okay," Kirk said, staring at me so hard he must have seen my soul.

The whites of his eyes were bright red.

Subconjunctival hemorrhage.

"It's not okay," I said. "Not at all."

I held his head to my chest.

After that, things happened quickly. The progression of the virus, which normally took days, unfolded in under an hour, right in front of my eyes.

Coughing.

Coughing blood.

Vomiting blood.

Kirk didn't despair. He didn't complain. He didn't cry. He didn't do any talking, other than two softly whispered words.

"Kill him."

I promised I would, wanting to squeeze his hand, not being able to because his skin tore as easily as tissue paper.

By the time I moved to sit on my own hospital bed, Kirk didn't even notice. He stared into space, his red eyes blank, the muscles of his face slack. The parts of his brain that made him who he was were gone, liquefied by the virus. Only the illness's final stage remained.

Death.

That word echoed through my mind as I witnessed the last moments of Jonathan Kirk.

> *"When it comes to survival, violence often isn't the best option," said The Instructor. "But when you choose to use it, strike hard and fast and destroy your enemy. There is no winning and losing in a fight, only living and dying."*

The room smelled like a slaughterhouse.

There was a sink, and I did my best to wash Kirk's blood off me.

I checked myself for new bruises.

Didn't find any.

Chilled, I pulled my hospital gown around my naked skin. My hands trembled, events of the past day catching up to me, overwhelming me. Tears brimmed my eyes, turning the world into a blurry mosaic of white and red.

I blinked them back.

Focus.

I am ice. Cold. Hard. A blow torch couldn't thaw me.

The camera eye stared down from the ceiling. The heart monitor had been turned off, the room silent now except for the drip of Kirk's blood on tile.

And a soft hiss …

A soft, smoky hiss, coming through the overhead vent.

I scooped in a breath, held it, then staggered and collapsed to the floor.

The hiss continued, long after my lungs had started to scream for oxygen. But I was damn good at holding my breath, and soon the tone of the sound changed to the hum of a ventilation system at work.

I let my air out slow, made my lungs take in big, deep breaths like I was asleep.

A short time later, the door opened, and four people in full, pressurized hazmat gear lumbered into the room. I heard the soft sound of wheels, as if they were pushing a tray or gurney, and the suck and release of their SCBA.

"Put her on the bed. I need some blood."

The voice was muffled, but I could tell it was the same voice that had spoken to us over the intercom.

"Then where do you want her?"

"In the room with the girl."

"And him?" another asked.

"You can clean that mess up later."

Two sets of hands lifted me from the floor and dropped me onto the mattress. I caught a glimpse through my lashes, a tray filled with needles and vials. One of them grabbed my arm and wrapped a rubber tourniquet around my biceps. I felt the sting of a needle on the inside of my elbow, then a clumsy shifting as they filled tubes with my blood.

"Okay, got it. I don't want her waking up. Stick that IV back in and get her sedated. And tie her hands to the bed rails this time. No sense in taking chances."

I would have preferred to let them take me to Julie before making my move, at least then I'd know her location, but I couldn't let them put me under. Still if I could bide my time, take them by surprise, hope that some left to perform other jobs, I'd have a better chance. If even one stepped out of the room, I'd increase my odds by twenty-five percent.

I stayed put, picturing the room around me in my mind's eye, cataloguing what tools were at my disposal. Once the man at my bedside replaced the catheter in the back of my hand, he would have to reconnect the drip. For a second, he would be facing away from me, and that's when I would make my move.

He stuck the needle in the back of my hand, and I braced myself against the pain. For several seconds he poked and jabbed, searching for a vein. Finding none, he slid the needle out and tried again.

Still no luck.

And no one had left the room. Although my eyes were closed, I could hear four distinct respirations, four sets of shuffling movement. I didn't know if these guys were medical personnel, lab techs, or soldiers, but judging from the skill set of the one prodding me, I was leaning toward soldiers. They would know how to fight.

But when he stuck the needle in for a third time and started digging around, I knew I couldn't take it any longer.

Focused on poking the hell out of my left hand, my torturer didn't see my right until it was too late.

I brought the heel up fast and plowed it into his nose, driving upward.

CBRN suits are designed for soldiers to wear in combat. Hazmat suits, like these, were not.

The face shield collapsed under my blow. The guy made a grunting noise and flew backward, hitting the floor hard.

A human being's reaction to a swift violent assault is to freeze. Like a deer in the headlights, the body biologically seeks to hide in plain sight in hopes the predator will pass them by. It takes years of training to shorten this natural reaction. Even then, training wasn't the same as engaging in the real thing.

I'd engaged in the real thing more than I liked to think about.

I was moving before they'd realized the first man was down.

Grabbing the stainless steel IV pole—a solid bar with some serious heft—I pulled the adjustable portion from the bed and started swinging.

The second man hadn't had the chance to turn around, and I hit him hard in back of the neck, connecting with the cervical vertebrae. He went down immediately, leaving me with only two to go.

The odds were getting better.

I went after the third.

He managed to step backward, making my next swing miss. Then threw a right hook. The move was clumsy, the suit slowing him down, and I blocked the blow and retaliated with an elbow strike that dented his face mask and exploded his nose, coating the inside of his visor with blood.

The fourth man—the oldest of the group—ran from the room.

The first man had staggered to his feet. He came at me from behind with a bear hug.

I drilled the back end of the pole into his gut. He doubled over, choking and gasping.

I went after him again, clanging him in the head with everything I had, putting him out before man number three tackled me from behind.

I sprawled forward, hitting the floor on hands and knees, the brute landing on top of me. Air was sucked from my lungs. He grabbed my hair, lifted my head with a yank, then smashed my forehead against the tile.

Sparks of light blossomed behind my eyes.

I had to get him off me. One more hit to my brain pan and I wouldn't be able to function.

Face pressed to the cold floor, I willed the dizziness back and searched for something I could use as a weapon.

There.

I reached out my hand, skimming it over the tile until I hit something slick and wet—the remnants of Kirk.

Then I snaked my arm back to the hand tangled in my hair. The hazmat suit was thick and strong, made in layers to keep out the smallest biological agents, viruses. But the gloves were attached with nothing more than duct tape.

I sank the bloody IV needle into the meat of his wrist.

A bellow echoed through the room. He released my hair and scrambled off my back.

The door opened, and the man who'd fled stepped back inside, a pistol in his gloved hand.

"Dr. Pembrooke! She put an infected needle in my arm," the one I stabbed began to scream. He didn't move, just kept screaming, even as I got to my feet.

"Stop," Pembrooke said. "I don't want to have to shoot you, but I will."

The man I'd stabbed with the needle started to sob.

"Get in the decon shower," Pembrooke ordered.

"But she got the last dose of vaccine—"

"Get. In. The shower. Now."

The sobbing man hurried out of the room.

And then there was one.

Of course, the one remaining—the doctor himself—had a pistol pointed at me. And even though he looked to be inexperienced with a firearm, a man with a firearm was still a man who had to be respected.

But only as long as he still held said firearm.

Careful not to take his eyes or the gun barrel off me, he stooped to pick up one of the syringes from the floor. He tossed it to me. I caught it and stared at the fluid inside.

"It's a sedative. You know how to give yourself a shot?"

I couldn't suppress a laugh and didn't try.

"You expect me to knock myself out so you can, what? Study me?"

"Study how your body managed to avoid contracting the Ebola. Yes."

This guy was a piece of work. People could die all around him, and all that mattered were the next tests he might be able to perform.

I supposed it was handy for a scientist who worked on biological weapons to also be a psychopath.

An awful scenario washed through my mind.

"Am I a carrier now?"

"With biology, you can never be sure. But, I don't expect you are. A blood sample should prove it, one way or another."

"So test it," I said.

"I will, after you give yourself that shot."

"I'm not letting you put me under."

"You're not in a position to be making deals."

"You're not very experienced with handguns."

A brief flash of uncertainty flinched behind his eyes. He recovered quickly, but he'd told me what I needed to know.

I took a step forward.

"I hope your first shot is a good one," I said softly. "Because you won't get the chance to take another."

He extended the gun, aiming right at my center mass. "I can perform my tests on you whether you're dead or alive."

There was only a meter between us, and he wouldn't miss. I was fast, but bullets were faster.

This wasn't the moment. I had to catch him off guard.

"Why Julie?" I asked. "Why is she the carrier?"

Ask a man about something important to him, and he'll never shut up.

"She's one in a million. One in a billion. I theorized that someone with her unique genetic markers might exist. Someone who could carry the virus and remain asymptomatic. You have no idea how much blood we tested, how many false starts we had."

"You tried this before," I stated. "With others."

Pembrooke nodded, seemingly proud of the fact.

"Many others. Those free clinics are funded by tax dollars, but used by those who contribute nothing to this country. It's about time those freeloaders gave something back."

I'd met a few psychos in my time, but never one who looked like someone's grandfather.

"How many people have you killed while trying to find a Julie, Pembrooke?"

He shrugged. "You know the saying. To make an omelet, you have to break a few eggs. Now inject yourself."

I shook my head. "No way."

"Either you let me sedate you, or I kill you."

I held the syringe in both hands—

—then snapped it in half.

"That did nothing. I have more."

"So go get it. I promise I'll stay here and wait for you."

I could see him working it out in his head, wondering what to do next.

I was wondering the same thing.

Then the obvious hit me.

Pembrooke wasn't a pro. So I didn't have to treat him like one.

I looked over his shoulder at someone who wasn't there and made my eyes wide.

"Do it!" I yelled at my imaginary savior. "Now!"

I sold it well. And like any amateur, Pembrooke bought the act, craning his neck around to see who was there.

I moved forward, to the side of the gun, putting my palm on the hammer and squeezing so Pembrooke couldn't fire, then twisting my body around and snapping my elbow against Pembrooke's faceplate.

He went down, falling onto his ass as he released the gun.

I pointed it at his head.

"How many people are at this facility?"

"What?"

"Who else is here?"

"No one. Just us."

"No guards?"

Pembrooke motioned to the men on the floor behind me. "Those were the guards. Them and Johnson, in the decon shower."

"If you're lying to me—"

"I'm not lying. The full team won't be here until tomorrow. We have to take steps to make sure there are no accidents, like there were last time."

I searched his face, judged him sincere.

"Where's Julie?"

"The other side of the facility. She's sedated."

"Thanks. That's all I need from you."

His eye went wide, and I had to admit to some base satisfaction watching him piss himself.

"Please! You can't kill me. Our country needs me! I'm the only one who can protect us! I'm a brilliant man!"

"You're not brilliant, Pembrooke. You want to know what you are?" I put the gun to his eye, let him see his own death down the barrel. "You're an omelet. And I'm about to break a few eggs."

"NO!"

I raised the gun, then clubbed him across the side of the head. He collapsed onto his side.

I checked the two men I'd put down earlier. They were both gone. I searched them, found some plastic zip ties.

I pulled Pembrooke over to Kirk's bed, and bound his wrists to the railing.

Then I took Kirk's hand—the one that an hour ago was touching me—and jammed the blood-soaked fingers into Pembrooke's mouth.

"There you go, Kirk," I said. "I didn't have to kill him. You did it yourself."

I found Julie where Pembrooke said she'd be. As he'd also stated, there didn't seem to be anyone else at the facility. By the time I found Johnson, in the decontamination shower, he was already starting to hemorrhage from the virus.

I put a bullet in his head to ease his passing.

Then I went back to Pembrooke.

He was awake. And unlike Kirk, he despaired. He complained. He cried.

He also had two last words.

"Kill me."

"Doctor," I said. "Heal thyself."

I stayed until he crashed and bled out.

My phone was in Pembrooke's office, along with my clothing. I took a decon shower before dressing, and then got to work. I was apparently immune to Ebola, but I didn't want to spread the disease to anyone else.

It took me less than an hour to do what needed to be done.

There was only one final loose end.

Julie.

I tugged my purse over my shoulder. My purse, with the wire garrote in the strap.

Not such a bad way to go, being strangled while under sedation.

I went to her, stood at the foot of her bed.

And I did the only thing I could do.

"When an operation goes wrong, thorough cleanup is a must," The Instructor said. "Your value to the program depends on few people knowing you exist. If you can't preserve this secrecy, others will be called in to clean up for you, and you will be part of the mess to be cleaned."

My phone rang when I had the MH-60M Black Hawk helicopter in the air over the island. I connected it to my headset and answered the call.

"May I speak to Sheila, please?"

"Sheila is visiting her sister in Pensacola. Would you like to leave a message?"

"Jesus, Chandler. You're okay. You scared the hell out of me."

I smiled at the relief evident in Jacob's slightly robotic tones. "Did you expect anything less?"

"I obviously shouldn't have."

I gave him the Cliff's Notes version of all that had happened since I'd last talked to him back at the West 30th Street Heliport.

After I'd finished, he was silent for several beats. "Do you have the vaccine?"

"I am the vaccine," I said. "From what I could gather, Pembrooke believed he could use my blood to vaccinate others."

"I've got an eye in the sky on Plum Island. Is that you in the chopper?"

"Affirmative."

"The director?"

"Dead."

"Any survivors?"

"Negative."

"You have the medical records?"

"I destroyed them."

"The computers?"

"Likewise. What's left is going to burn."

I stared down at the facility, smoke already beginning to leak out of the roof. With all of the flammable chemicals on the premises, the firefighters were going to have a helluva job putting this one out.

"Ebola is a horrible weapon," Jacob said. "One that can't be controlled, no matter what people like Pembrooke believed."

"I'm glad we're on the same page." I hesitated, waiting for the other shoe to fall.

"How about the girl?"

I hesitated, feeling sick in the pit of my stomach, unsure of what to say.

I trusted Jacob.

But more importantly, I needed him.

"She's with me."

"She's alive?"

"Yes."

"Chandler. This needs to end."

My conscience was telling me the same thing. As the Typhoid Mary of Ebola, Julie was too dangerous to exist.

But that didn't mean I wanted to listen.

Silence stretched so long, I was beginning to think he'd hung up. Finally he answered.

"There's the ocean."

I closed my eyes. I was a trained killer. I lived with death every day. I dealt it out to others like a losing hand of poker. As traumatic and horrible as Kirk's death had been, that was his reality, too. Kill or be killed. Every day balanced on the edge of a knife.

It was what we did. It was who we were.

But Julie wasn't from that world.

She'd never signed up for this. She'd had this horror forced upon her. Did she really deserve to be cast into the ocean for being in the wrong place at the wrong time?

Could I be the one who pushed her from the aircraft?

"I won't do it, Jacob. I won't let them turn her into a biological weapon, but I won't kill her either."

"If you don't, I'll have to send someone else to do it."

"They'll have to kill me, too. Do you have anyone that good?"

"She can never be a part of society."

"I know."

"That's no way for a young girl to live."

"I know."

I stared at Julie, sleeping in the back seat.

"The ocean may be the most humane thing to do."

"I know," I said, trying to swallow the giant lump in my throat. "I know."

Six Weeks Later

"Sometimes," the Instructor said, "you'll do things that will be hard to live with. You might never be able to forgive yourself. There's no advice I can give you for when this happens. I'm sorry."

The wind off the coast of Maine was as cold as the water was rough. Between the blue sky, autumn leaves, gray rock, white lighthouse, and adjoining red keeper's house, the place looked as colorful as an image from a postcard.

Picturesque but lonely.

Maine had over sixty lighthouses along its shores and nearby islands, some so remote that even tourists and photographers hadn't discovered them.

This was one.

I hefted box after box out of the fishing boat I'd rented and set them in the trolley next to the dock. Rails ran to up the steep, rocky face to the lighthouse and keeper's house, an efficient system of delivering supplies that had been in place for a hundred years. It took me nearly a half hour, but finally the trolley car was full and my boat was empty.

Except for one box I would deliver myself.

I lugged it to my hip and started up the narrow path. The first time I'd been to the lighthouse had been the summer night after Plum Island. Now the ocean wind carried with it the crisp slap of fall.

I reached the crest of the hill, my back slick with sweat and the muscles in my legs pleasantly warm. The countless blood tests I'd had since contracting Ebola had all shown I was virus free, and every day since I'd fully appreciated how alive I felt, how strong.

This had been Jacob's idea. He and I were only two of three people in the whole world who knew about it.

The third person opened the screen door and skipped down the steps, running toward me.

"I didn't expect you until Saturday," Julie said, all smiles.

I set my box on the ground and took her in my arms. She felt good, and when we finally ended the hug, I had to blink back a few tears.

Julie looked me over. "Your hair looks great."

I raised a hand to my head, still a little surprised that my tresses no longer reached my shoulders.

"I'm still getting used to it."

She eyed the box. "You brought me presents?"

"I have a whole trolley load waiting to be hauled up."

Her eyes widened like a little kid at Christmas. "What did you bring?"

"Supplies, of course. Food, toiletries, that kind of thing."

"Anything fun?"

"Of course."

"Movies? Books?"

I nodded. Loading up boxes of the thrillers and romantic suspense novels Julie loved had just about broken my back. I couldn't wait for the time when e-readers were common and buying a new book would be as easy as pushing a button.

"I've started writing, too. You wouldn't believe how fast time flies when I'm busy making up stories."

It was a relief to see Julie was adapting so well to her limited life. After our escape, I'd spent two weeks here with her, helping her adjust. Since then, I'd spent many sleepless nights worrying about my decision to hide her rather than cast her into the sea. Now I felt like I could finally breathe a little deeper.

"I can't wait to read your stories."

She grinned. "Maybe I'll publish them someday."

A tentative scratching noise came from the box at my feet.

"Okay, Chandler. What's in the box?"

"You really want to know?"

She gave me a pointed look. "Duh."

"Okay. Open it. Gently."

She popped open the lid in two seconds flat.

"Oh my God." She pulled out the little brown pup and squeezed him to her chest. "What kind is he?"

"A mutt. He's a rescue dog."

"Like me." She beamed, then the smile faded. "He won't get sick, will he?"

"No. Dogs who have been exposed to Ebola produce antibodies and become immune. Epidemiologists test the blood of dogs in some areas in the world to trace areas of virus outbreak."

I could tell her more, having reassured myself before bringing the pet to Julie, but she didn't care. She was too busy petting the little guy and keeping him from nipping her fingers.

"I also included some puppy training books."

She laughed. "Good idea."

"All that's left is for you to name him."

Her eyebrows bunched together. She opened her mouth, then closed it without speaking, hugging the squirming puppy to her chest as if he was everything. And once again I was struck by how young she was, barely eighteen, this girl who'd seen too much, who'd been sentenced to live the rest of her life in isolation.

She leaned forward and kissed the pup's head.

"I think I'll call him Kirk. Do you think he'd like that?"

I had no idea. When it came to normal life issues like whether or not he liked dogs, I knew little about Jonathan Kirk. I had only seen slices of who he was. The brutal part that enabled him to do unspeakable things for money. The sly humor. The bravery in the face of death. The love of life that he was able to reveal, and able to reveal in me. How I never really knew him, yet missed him so terribly.

"Do you like it, Julie?"

Eyes glistening, she gave a nod.

"Then he would, too."

NAUGHTY

ABOUT NAUGHTY

She's an elite spy, working for an agency so secret only three people know it exists. Trained by the best of the best, she has honed her body, her instincts, and her intellect to become the perfect weapon.

CODENAME: HAMMETT

Before special operative Hammett became a mercenary, she executed the most difficult missions—and most dangerous people—for the government. When one sanction turns into half a dozen dead, the agency Hammett works for realizes she's gone rogue. And there's only one way to deal with rogues; eliminate them with extreme prejudice.

But this target has other ideas…

NAUGHTY

There's nothing to fear but fear itself. And her.

LOS ANGELES, 2007

Hammett

> *"No one can argue that some people simply need to be killed," The Instructor said. "Our job is to figure out how to do it."*

His new name was Roddy "Whiteboy" Simmons. Hammett had broken into his home seven minutes earlier, having picked the deadbolt on his back door and disarmed his burglar alarm with the use of a drill bit, a dental mirror, wire cutters, and a 9-volt battery. Child's play. But what came next was anything but.

She stood in his living room, letting her senses report. The house was dark and quiet, save for the hum of the refrigerator coming from the kitchen down the hallway. The scent of lemon wood polish was strong, and there was a lingering odor from the microwave lasagna he'd eaten for dinner several hours ago. As her eyes adjusted to the darkness, she scanned the room, first for his computer, which was nowhere to be seen, then for the cat. Last Thursday she had gone through the garbage he'd left on his curb and found several empty cans of Friskies.

Hammett liked cats, and was curious what kind this one was.

After ten minutes of standing in place, no cat showed up to greet her. So she began to explore the rest of the house.

Roddy Simmons was especially careful on the web, probably due to his previous bust. She'd tried all of her Internet tricks in an attempt to track him, but he'd spoofed his MAC address and was getting online through a virtual private network.

So Hammett set up a MySpace social networking page, pretending she was a twelve-year-old girl, complete with a cute pic of a fresh-faced kid with braces and pigtails. Then she spent two days friending real tweens and answering endless, banal surveys about favorite movies and music and ice cream flavors and Twilight, which she'd never read but now considered herself an expert on.

After that she wasted a solid week of ten-hour days, finding every MySpace user under the age of sixteen named after some variety of "Rod." She chanced upon Roddy Simmons after more than two hundred misfires. He was masquerading as a thirteen-year-old boy, and his predator camouflage was good enough that his account looked exactly like a teen's should, including several dozen photos.

Hammett didn't want to think about where he got those photos.

Roddy "Whiteboy" Simmons, under the previous aliases Rod "Wigger" Thompson and "Hot Rod" Klein, had killed two children before coming to the attention of the agency she worked for. He'd done things to those kids that sickened even her lead-lined stomach, and had been clever enough to leave no physical evidence at the crime scenes.

She had to begrudgingly admire Rod for that. Law enforcement had grown increasingly sophisticated over the past decade. Vacuuming for hairs and fibers. Using alternate light sources to illuminate bodily fluids. Sexual assault and murder usually left trace evidence, even if the perp was careful.

Roddy was very careful.

So was Hammett.

She wore a black unitard, latex gloves, and a hairnet. Though she fancied Mark Fisher heels for playtime and Doc Martens for work, today she'd opted for stealth and gone with soft-soled ballet shoes. They were silent on hard floors, and didn't leave distinct footprints on plush carpeting. Plus, Hammett liked the feel of the ground underneath her feet when she was in stalking mode. It kept her in touch with her inner predator.

Strapped around her waist was a canvas tool belt, with four leather pouches containing everything she needed for this job. The lock picks. The silk rope. The pliers. The ball gag. The duct tape. The vials of cyanoacrylate. The cup of jacks. The scalpels, wrapped in microfiber cloth so they didn't clang together.

Creeping into the kitchen, Hammett found the cat's food and water dishes on the floor in front of the sink. Remnants of liver *pâté* clung to the bowl, still emitting a pungent odor.

The kitchen, like the living room, was fastidiously clean. Roddy was as meticulous in his housekeeping as he was with his Internet activities.

She allowed herself a small smile at the observation.

Sometimes, no matter how careful you are, there are still things outside of your control. Like the woman in your house about to murder you.

She wasn't sure how Rod came to the attention of the agency she worked for. Hydra assassinations were usually international and political, and Rod was a local boy, uninvolved in world affairs. But now that Hydra, and Hammett, knew about him, his minutes were numbered.

On the countertop was an old fashioned phone; a model that still had a cord attached to the receiver. It was expected. Unless you understood how to encrypt the radio waves that cordless phones transmitted, it was safer to stick with corded models. Hammett slowly unwound two feet of duct tape, picked up the receiver, and wrapped it around the earpiece, setting it on the counter. When that annoying beep began indicating the phone was off the hook, it was barely audible.

From the kitchen she prowled into the carpeted hallway, passing a bathroom, coming to a door. From the layout of the house, Hammett knew it was the bedroom. A quick check of the knob found it locked. But unlike most suburban households, this wasn't a cheap, hollow-veneer door, or a press-button privacy lock. This door was metal, the lock serious. Whoever slept behind it was careful about security.

Of course he was. He had secrets to hide.

Hammett reached into the first pouch on her belt, removing a black box half the size of a cigarette pack. After switching it on, she placed the ear bud in her right ear, and the contact microphone against the door, and was rewarded with the sound of steady, rhythmic breathing. Satisfied he was asleep, she traded the listening device for her lock picks, selecting a Z-shaped tension wrench and a tool with a small hook on the end. Knocking back the tumblers was child's play, and she had the door open in under ten seconds.

The strategies for entering a room varied, depending on the situation. Going slow made less noise, but the chances of being noticed increased as time passed. Going quick drew more immediate visual and audible attention, but could catch the target unaware. Hammett took it slow, easing the door over the shag carpeting an inch at a time, holding her breath while listening for his, opening it just wide enough to slip her slender frame through, then closing it again behind her.

Hammett paused, standing in his bedroom, watching him sleep. The only light came from the blue LED of his bedside digital clock, which bathed his chubby, shaven face. With his balding head, he looked almost cherubic.

She slowed her breathing until it matched his, and then traded her lock picks for the two vials of cyanoacrylate. Then she approached the bed, taking a step with each breath. There wasn't any professional reason for this. She simply liked to prolong the moment. The lovely calm before the lovely storm.

Rod made it easier for her by sleeping on his back. She uncapped the vials, brought them to his face, and squeezed them over his eyes simultaneously.

One of several things would happen next. Perhaps he would remain sleeping and not react at all. Perhaps he would try to open his eyes. Perhaps he would touch his eyes, either in sleep or while waking up. Or perhaps he would wake up instantly and attempt to flee or fight. Though she'd never actually had the last one occur in the many times she'd done this, Hammett kept her hands defensively in front of her and her feet in a solid, centered stance.

Rod stirred when the superglue hit his eyes, and after a few seconds he lifted his hand to rub them, bonding his fingers to his lids.

When he jerked into a sitting position, Hammett pulled the cup from her belt, popped off the top, and dumped the contents onto the bed behind him. The contents were several dozen metal jacks, like those used in the child's game with the red rubber ball. Except these were made of stainless steel, and each prong ended in a barb, like a fish hook.

After pouring out the jacks, she clipped Rod under the chin with the heel of her hand, knocking him back onto the bed. The barbs embedded themselves into his back, and into the sheets and mattress, pinning him there better than any rope.

He struggled, screamed, none of it mattering a damn.

She tied his free hand to the bedpost with a length of strong, silk rope. Then she tied his legs, and yanked his glued hand from his face (taking the eyelids with it) and bound that as well. When she was sure he was properly restrained and escape was impossible, she went to work with the scalpels and the pliers.

Roddy "Whiteboy" Simmons had done terrible things to children.

Hammett made sure the things done to him were even worse.

She never said a word about why she was doing this. He knew his crimes. Hammett saw no need to remind him. But she did ask for some intel. Information above and beyond what was required of her. Passwords. Names. URLs.

Hammett got all she asked for. Then she gagged him, because the screaming and begging was giving her a headache.

He died sometime before dawn, probably hypovolemic shock, though she'd done what she could to staunch the blood loss. When she was finished she placed her bloody gloves into a plastic bag, snapped on a fresh pair, picked up the laptop he had on his nightstand next to the bed, and locked the bedroom door behind her.

Leaving via the back door, she was met by a black cat with gorgeous blue eyes. Hammett crouched, held out her hand. The cat rubbed its face against her knuckles and purred.

"We need to find a new home for you, baby."

She scooped the cat up and held it to her chest, the laptop in her other hand. This was a risky proposition. The cat hair clinging to her could be connected back to the crime scene. The cat might also be chipped, which could lead back to Hammett in all sorts of ways.

But even though this was an outdoor cat, it still needed a home. And what kind of human being would Hammett be if she let some poor kitty starve?

"You should do what is asked of you on a mission, no more and no less," The Instructor said. "Doing less makes you worthless to the organization. But doing more could make you a liability."

After calling in a successful mission to her handler, Isaac, Hammett stopped by a no-kill animal shelter, the cat's collar tied via rope to the sign outside that said ABSOLUTELY NO AFTER HOURS ANIMAL DROP-OFFS. She'd done this before, knew they'd take the kitty anyway. That was one of the reasons she'd donated many thousands of dollars to the place. And if the cat did have a tracking chip implanted, it wasn't as if calling the owner would do any good.

She showered in her hotel suite, and then watched the sun rise, exhausted but wired. Part of her wanted to get onto

Hot Rod's laptop. A bigger part of her wanted to get laid. As usual after an op, she was horny as hell. Though she wouldn't call torturing a man to death—even a pedophile who'd deserved it—a turn-on, the fact that she'd gotten away with it left Hammett buzzing. Too early to pick up a guy at a bar, she sat naked on the bed and leafed through the Los Angeles phone book, discovering a whole section of escort services offering straight men. She called the one with the biggest ad, asked who was available at a short notice, and made a date.

Hammett played with herself until her rent-a-stud arrived, and when he did she answered the door in her bathrobe.

She wasn't disappointed. He had the L.A. metrosexual look down to a science. Trendy facial hair with a close cropped anchor mustache and a pointy Van Dyke. Hair short, black, and gelled. Heavy aftershave. A tailored silk jacket and pants, light blue, and a dark blue shirt unbuttoned to the navel, showing a chest that looked like a two hour per day gym addiction.

He smiled at her with his mouth, and when he took notice of her body in the open bathrobe, he smiled with his eyes. No doubt he'd popped a few Viagra or Cialis before the date, in case she was a heifer. But while Hammett had more scars than most Hollywood types, her body was toned and curved in all the right places.

She grabbed him between the legs, pulled him inside, and then kissed him when the door was closed and locked. He tasted like mint floss, and his teeth were as perfect as his face and body. After a very hot meeting of tongues he bent down to pick her up, and became confused when she braced her legs and placed a hand on his chest, throwing off his balance and leverage just enough to make it impossible. While Hammett knew his only intention was to carry her to the bed, she wanted to stay in control, especially with someone almost twice her weight. So instead she led him to the bed, lay back with her knees apart, and let him dive in.

He was better with his mouth than she'd been with her fingers, obviously happy in his work. He read the subtle movements of her hips and her moans to know when to apply more pressure, and when to back off. A real pro, he used his mustache to highly pleasurable effect.

After several orgasms she beckoned for him to undress, and he followed her silent commands for how fast and hard he should fuck so she could come again. When she did, she let him take the lead for a bit, turning her this way and that, varying depth and speed, maintaining exceptional control until she found herself growing less interested in him and more interested in what was on the laptop.

She allowed him to come—something she sometimes refused to allow escorts to do because she liked to see them break character and pout or beg—but he'd been good enough that he earned that. Then, when he was half-hard with his condom still on, she ordered him to immediately dress and leave.

He did, without having said a word the whole time. Which worked for Hammett, because when a man that good looking said something, it was usually vapid and ruined the whole fantasy.

Maybe the guy had a PhD in philosophy and would have been thrilled to discuss Nietzsche's Zarathustra, but Hammett guessed he'd rather talk about how the Lakers are doing, why Adam Sandler was hilarious, and how he wanted to see her again. Yawn.

Content and wonderfully sore, she locked the door behind him, booted up Roddy's laptop using the passwords he had so generously provided, and delved into his private email account.

It was a good thing Hammett had gotten laid before tackling the computer, because it took less than ten seconds for her to dry up and go cold. After viewing some of the images of violated, crying children, she might have killed her handsome escort had he still been in the same room with her, just for the crime of having testicles.

Jaw set, she surfed through the jpg attachments, and went to work on tracing where they'd originated. Not an easy task when senders spoofed their IP address and used VPNs. But Hammett kept her hacking software online in a file locker, so once she downloaded it to Rod's computer and did a quick installation, a'hunting she did go.

It took thirty minutes to trace the first of Rod's pedo buddies to an address in Beverly Hills. A man named Stuart Lupowitz. He liked little boys.

Protocol dictated Hammett get on an afternoon flight to her apartment in Columbus and wait for her next directive. Protocol also insisted that after an op, staying out of sight and lying low was mandatory. Drawing undue attention, or engaging in risky behavior, was forbidden. Hydra, like the many other shadow organizations the U.S. government no doubt funded, survived because of secrecy.

So when Hammett dressed and headed toward Beverly Hills instead of LAX, she knew it was a severe breach in procedure. One that could have major consequences.

As expected, L.A. traffic was almost as horrible as what she'd done to Rod only a few hours ago, and an eight-mile drive took forty minutes. The weather was hot and smoggy, and Hammett was wearing a red unitard, having tossed the black one in the hotel's lobby garbage. Over it she had a white mesh swimsuit cover-up which would have looked out of place anywhere but Hollywoodland. A floppy white hat, oversized Prada sunglasses, and her ballet shoes rounded out her ensemble.

After spending ten more minutes looking for a spot on Rodeo Drive, she parked five blocks away from Lupowitz's house and fed the meter to the maximum limit. Then Hammett began to walk, tuning into her surroundings. Traffic sounds, a dozen people on the sidewalks, most shopping, one roller blader, a jogger across the street. Fresh coffee smells from a bistro. The stench of smog and exhaust mixed with the dry heat. She passed one designer store after another—stores that normally drew her in like a kid to candy. But Hammett hardly paid them any mind.

She was in stalking mode.

Taking a circuitous route, backtracking twice to check for tails, she made her way out of the shopping district and into the residential areas. Hammett knew to be careful here. Celebrities and the uber rich got extra police protection, and sure enough she spotted a patrol car in her peripheral coming up when she crossed Santa Monica Boulevard. She ducked behind a pine tree, letting the cop pass, and then continued on to Carmalita Avenue. Every house was a mansion, every mansion a burglar-proof fortress. Lupowitz was some sort of hotshot producer when he was not jerking off to kiddie porn, and no doubt breaking into his domicile would be a lot harder than getting into Rod's.

Which is why, when she found the house, Hammett simply walked up and rang the doorbell. The obligatory Mexican maid answered, and Hammett asked, in Spanish, if Señor Lupowitz was in. He was at work, naturally, so Hammett gave her the SD memory card she'd prepared—pictures and emails he had sent Rod, along with a hundred dollars for her trouble. After an exchanged *muchas gracias*, Hammett wandered back to Rodeo and spent a few hours trying on ridiculous outfits and shoes and handbags that cost more than her first car. Dior, Gucci, Prada, Fendi, Vuitton. Fashion gluttony. Turning fifty cents of cow leather into five thousand dollars on stilettos.

Hammett adored it.

But she was traveling light and not making any purchases. So she disappointed shop girl after shop girl, because although she had the airs and bearing of a rich bitch, she didn't help anyone land a single commission, even though she was feted with champagne and caviar and a lovely brie that was the best Hammett had eaten outside of, well, Brie.

When she grew tired of playing Beverly Hills Barbie, she found a pastry café where the cupcakes cost as much as a steak dinner in New York and killed another hour sipping cappuccino and watching the rich, overfed, clueless gentry pass by in an endless decadent parade. Hammett mused, briefly, about being one of them. Staunch patriotic killing machine becomes kept woman for some ultra hunky movie star. But she knew that after the fourth or fifth banal Hollywood party, she'd no doubt take up killing again out of boredom. Or perhaps she'd specifically target studio heads who insisted that sequels, remakes, and movies based on old TV shows and comic books were the only way to sell tickets.

Six o'clock rolled around, and Hammett made her way to the Starbucks on Wilshire. Upon walking in, she instantly spotted an obviously agitated Stuart Lupowitz. Ten years older than his IMDb.com picture, gray and soft and scuzzy looking even in a five thousand dollar suit, he stood next to the men's toilet, fidgeting and looking a lot like a pedophile who'd just been caught.

Which is exactly what he was.

"Mr. Lupowitz," Hammett met him with a big smile and a surprise embrace, brushing the gun he'd placed in his jacket pocket, ruining the lines of his tailored Ralph Lauren. "So pleased to meet you. Did you bring a car?"

He nodded, then began to say something. Hammett put a finger to his lips, than slipped her arm around his like they were old friends.

"We'll talk in the car, where it's private."

He nodded, then put on a brave face and gave the parking attendant a ticket. Hammett had to smile.

Beverly Hills. Of course Starbucks has a valet service.

He drove a Mercedes S-Class, white, a new model. When it pulled up and Stuart fished out his wallet to tip the driver, Hammett slipped the revolver from his pocket. A .38 snub nose Colt Cobra. Older, reliable, but far from the luxury firearm a man like Lupowitz could afford.

"What is it you want?" he asked once he took the driver's seat. "Money?"

"Drive," Hammett said, studying the car's instrument panel. "Head to West Hollywood. We'll talk on the way. And buckle up for safety."

Lupowitz fumbled with his seatbelt. Hammett left hers off. If he tried anything stupid, like running into a tree, she figured the Benz's airbags would be enough to save her.

After driving in silence for half a minute, Lupowitz nervously and obviously patted his jacket pocket.

"Looking for this?" Hammett pulled the .38 from under her cover-up. She opened the cylinder, saw it was full, and also noticed scratches on the crane where the serial number should have been.

"Nasty little toy you've got here, Stu."

"I… I just wanted to scare you."

"Sure you did. And see how scared I am?" Hammett smiled wide, genuine.

"Look, lady, I'm… I'm important in this town."

"And you wouldn't want your buddies at the studio to find out your extracurricular habits."

He squeezed the steering wheel so hard his knuckles faded to white. "It's not like that. I just have a couple of pictures on my computer. I never hurt anyone. I'm married, for chrissakes."

Hammett went cold inside. "Do you have kids?"

"No."

Lucky for him. She would have shot him in the head right then.

"But you like kids, don't you, Stu?"

"It's… complicated. You don't know how it is to be… I mean, imagine if you did something you thought was normal that society found reprehensible?"

You have no idea.

But Hammett wasn't going to explain the differences between killing scumbags for the government and violating innocent kids for kicks.

The silence that followed must have made Lupowitz uncomfortable, because he quickly followed up with, "What do you want from me? I have money. I can pay."

Oh, you'll pay all right.

"I want names, Stu. Where you got the pictures of the children."

He glanced sideways at her, eyes narrowing.

"Are you a cop?"

"No. Cops follow rules. I'm not arresting you. And I'm not blackmailing you, either."

"So what do you want?" She saw hope flit into his eyes. "To star in one of my movies? Are you an actress?"

An interesting question. Hammett did consider herself an actor, but not the kind Lupowitz usually associated with.

"I want names, Stu. Who sent you the pictures. Who you sent them to."

They came to a red light. Hammett kept the gun at hip level so passersby didn't see it.

Lupowitz's eyebrows creased, as if he was in deep thought. "No one uses real names online," he eventually said. "We don't know each other."

"There's no annual conferences? No meet-and-greets with a secret pedo handshake?"

"Jesus, no! I mean, the secrecy, the security. Everyone is extremely careful. It would be easier to hack into the Pentagon."

That made sense. Unfortunately, it wasn't what Hammett wanted to hear.

"Somehow you got into one of these groups. How?"

Lupowitz's lips pressed together.

"I bet a big wheel like you knows someone. If I were looking to score some kiddie porn in this town, who would I talk to?"

The light turned green. Lupowitz didn't move. Hammett slipped the scalpel out of her fanny pack and palmed it. She also kept her head down—lots of intersections in L.A. had cameras. If they recorded her, all they'd see was her floppy hat. Cars behind them honked.

"Can't think and drive at the same time, Stu?"

He stepped on the gas. Hammett watched the gears turn in his head.

"And if I give you a name, you go away? How do I know you won't hold this over me forever?"

"You're a smart guy. You can get rid of your computer, delete your online accounts. Since I contacted you, I bet you've already done that. I've got the laptop computer you sent those pictures to. It's got the emails on it. A unique IP address. You give me some names, I give you the laptop and let you go. Promise."

Her offer made no sense. She could easily copy the emails, or the hard drive. And if he thought about what she was asking for—information and not money—he should have been questioning her motive, following it to the inevitable conclusion.

But Lupowitz was looking for a way out, and desperate men didn't think clearly. Which is why the pervert had called one of his seedy friends and bought himself a throwaway piece, no doubt to use on her. What a charming man.

Apparently Hammett's acting skills were good enough for him to believe her, because he said, "Tex Darling."

"Tex Darling? That's his real name?"

Lupowitz made a face like a bad smell had entered the car. "I doubt it. He's a porn producer. But he's connected. And I've gotten certain... um... *materials*... from him that aren't for sale through regular channels."

"Does he shoot these materials himself?"

Lupowitz went silent again. Hammett gave him a quick jab in his thigh with the scalpel, in-and-out like a snake striking. It took a moment for the pain to register, the blood to come. But when it did, Lupowitz acted appropriately surprised.

"JESUS CHRIST! YOU STABBED ME!"

"Press your palm to it. Keep pressure. I may have hit an artery, and you could bleed to death. Plus, think of the upholstery."

He pressed a hand to the widening circle of red on his leg.

"Now I'll ask again, and I'm done with your lengthy pauses. Does Tex shoot these materials himself?"

"Some of them."

Hammett noted in Lupowitz's expression and tone that he'd gone from worrying about his secret getting out to worrying about his life.

"Have you ever been in one?"

"What? No! Are you nuts? Me, being in a video?"

"But you bankrolled a few of these productions, didn't you, Stu?"

Lupowitz hesitated only long enough to glance at the scalpel again.

"I gave him some money, cash, no record of anything."

"And he made a movie just for you?"

Lupowitz's eyes began to get glassy. Perhaps he was finally realizing what a monster he was, but Hammett guessed it was self-pity.

"I gave you a name, like you asked." His lower lip trembled. "But... but you want more than just a name, don't you?"

"Gas station, on the right. Turn in."

He did. Again Hammett kept her face down, away from the pump cameras.

"The automatic carwash. Pull up."

He stopped the car next to a credit card kiosk, which allowed a person to pick the wash they wanted.

"You're a rich guy, Stu. Get the Ultimate Wash. Comes with an undercarriage cleanse and Turtle Wax. Seems like a good deal."

"My credit card is in my wallet."

"So whip it out, stud."

Hands shaking, wincing in apparent pain, he reached for his back pocket and managed to pull out an AmEx Platinum from a calf leather wallet. The kiosk thanked him in a robotic voice, saying his Ultimate Wash would take three minutes.

"Roll up the window and pull in," Hammett ordered.

"You're going to kill me."

"I'm going to give you a chance to live, Stu. That's the truth. Now pull into the goddamn carwash."

He drove into the Y-shaped conveyor track which caught his left front tire.

"Put it in neutral."

He did, full-on crying now. The conveyor engaged with a mechanical whir, pulling them into the carwash. Foamy soap dripped onto the windshield in obscene clumps.

"Now unzip your fly," Hammett told him.

"What?"

Hammett stabbed the scalpel into the top of the dashboard.

"You have exactly sixty seconds to castrate yourself, Stu, or I'll shoot you in the head."

Lupowitz stared at her, jaw dropping open.

"Fifty-five seconds." Hammett raised the .38.

Lupowitz glanced at the scalpel, then reached for his car door. He got it open, but his seatbelt prevented him from jumping out, just as she'd anticipated. Hammett jabbed the barrel of the gun under his flabby neck.

"Close the door and start cutting. Fifty seconds."

Lupowitz closed the door, some foam speckling his expensive suit.

"I... I can't," he blubbered.

Hammett kept her eyes on him, seeking the radio with her free hand. She turned it on and cranked the volume up. Some obnoxious Top 40 crap.

She continued to count down in her head.

When she got to thirty, Lupowitz unzipped his fly.

At twenty, he tugged the scalpel out of the dashboard.

The car passed through the mitter curtain—hanging cloth strips that undulated across the foamy windshield.

With ten seconds left, Lupowitz surprised Hammett and actually began to cut.

The music covered his screaming. It also covered her shot to his temple, because he didn't finish in time, only managing to complete half the job.

Hammett took his wallet and cell phone from his jacket, putting them into her pack. During the rinse cycle, Hammett opened her door and stepped out into the steamy waterfall. She walked back the way she came, tucking the gun into her fanny pack, and strolled out the carwash entrance. Head down, she walked off the gas station property before Lupowitz's car made it through the other side.

In the California sun, she was dry within three blocks.

By the time she'd walked back to her parked rental car, she'd ditched the floppy hat, tossing it into a sidewalk garbage can. She should have also wiped down and ditched the gun. Getting caught with it would be an instant conviction, and the agency she worked for would no doubt deny she existed. Also, because she hadn't used gloves, there were microscopic powder burns on her hand from when she'd fired it. A simple test could link her to the gunpowder residue on what was left of Stu's head.

Yet she kept the weapon. In expectation of things to come.

It had been a sloppy hit. But Hammett was beaming just the same. While she should have been exhausted, she felt even more alive, more wired, than when she'd killed Rod.

And she was just getting started.

"Stick to the op," The Instructor said. "As long as you do, you're an asset to be protected. Once you stray, you become a liability."

The room Hammett found in L.A.'s Chinatown was one normally rented by the hour. Hammett knew Chinese, and *Hóu hòisàm gindóu néih* was the Cantonese pronunciation of the characters on the marquee, which meant *pleased to meet you.*

The Pleased To Meet You Motel. A perfect name for a dive where Triad gangsters pimped their recently acquired hookers. Prior to arriving, Hammett had found a Fredrick's of Hollywood shop and bought some appropriate slutwear. Fishnets, thigh high stilettos, a black PVC micro mini skirt and a black lace bustier. She rounded out the ensemble with a peaked PVC dominatrix cap, the kind brought into vogue by the military during WWII.

She paid for the room in cash, which was another reason for her seedy choice in lodging. All legitimate hotels demanded ID, and her current fake driver's license and credit cards were traceable by her employer. Her handler, a man on the phone with an electronic voice modulator she knew only as Isaac, wasn't one to fuck around with. If he knew she'd gone off-mission, there would be consequences. Better for him not to know.

It was the kind of motel where there was no lobby, and all the rooms faced the parking lot. As expected, her accommodations were bare bones. Cheap bed, cheap dresser, missing tiles in the shower, a TV that used quarters to turn it on. But it had an L.A. phonebook in the nightstand, and Hammett quickly found Tex Darling's studio number under *adult video production.*

Using Lupowitz's cell phone, a Motorola RAZR, she called the number and wasn't surprised to get Darling's answering service. Hammett hung up without saying anything. Then she went out to the rental car and found some quarters in the cup holder that she'd been using for toll roads. Back in her room Hammett pushed a few into the coin-op TV and flipped through a few porno stations until she found local news about the car wash murder. She watched for a moment, but apparently they hadn't released the victim's name.

She only had a small window of time, but Hammett decided to go for it.

Besides the coin-op adult movies and bedbugs infested with STDs, this motel offered free WiFi included with the room. Hammett logged onto the Internet, then entered Hydra's backdoor to the U.S. Treasury Department. A minute later she had Tex Darling's last three years' 1099s, along with his current address and two phone numbers, and she assumed one was his home and the other his cell.

She tied her hair in pigtails and laid out on the scuzzy bed, bra down and nipples exposed, one arm over her head to make her breasts flatten out to look less developed. With her other hand she took a pic of herself, chewing her lower lip, using Lupowitz's RAZR. Then she texted the pic to both of Darling's numbers, followed by this message.

It's Stu L. Got a PYT that's hot to trot. Vid for $$$?

In pedophile parlance, PYT was *pretty young thing.* If this didn't get Darling's attention, she could always pay him a visit at his home. But Hammett didn't know if he was there. He might be out for the night, or the week. He might be having a party with twenty gangsters. He might be home alone, but with a killer burglar system and a footlocker full of constitutionally protected Second Amendment ordnance. Luring him out was easier, and allowed Hammett to control the setting.

She waited, watching Asian pornography on the pay-per TV until her change ran out. Though Hammett felt empowered by her sexuality, even when used in the line of duty, she believed porn was a small step down from stripping and a small step up from prostitution. Lots of exploitation and victimization there. That didn't bother her. Adult women were free to make their own decisions, even bad ones. Children, on the other hand, were innocent. There was a difference between making poor life choices and being abused under the age of consent.

Eighteen minutes later, Lupowitz's phone buzzed with a text reply.

Have camera, will travel. Where?

Hammett punched in the motel's address, and gave her room number.

C U in 30, Darling texted back.

Perfect.

She changed out of her slutwear and into steel toe combat boots, relaxed fit chinos, and a tight shirt, replacing her pigtails with a ponytail. She kept the PVC military domme hat. Any possible witnesses would remember the distinctive hat, not her face.

Then she went out to her rental car and hunkered down with Lupowitz's cell phone and gun, waiting for Darling to arrive. She was only mildly surprised when an SUV screeched into the motel parking lot, and four guys piled out.

None had movie equipment. All were armed.

Either Hammett had violated some sort of code of contact by impersonating Lupowitz, or Darling had gotten wind of his murder and had come prepared.

She would know soon enough.

Hammett watched them approach her room, handguns out. The three men in dark suits were standard muscle. Maybe mafia, or Darling's bodyguards, or maybe he'd gotten them at rent-a-thug. They were semi-pro, scoping out the parking lot, covering the guy who kicked in the door.

Darling stayed back a few paces and watched. His suit was different than the hired help, loud and flashy, a slick lavender color that matched what had to be a custom-dyed Stetson on his head. He was soft in the middle, and had a bulge in the back of his belt where he kept his gun. Or, considering Darling's appearance, he probably called it a *roscoe*.

It took them less than a minute to case the tiny room and determine she wasn't inside, and then they engaged in a henchmen huddle, apparently deciding one would stay behind and wait while Darling and the other two went back to their vehicle.

That's when Hammett stepped out of her rental. Adopting a rock-solid Weaver stance, she dropped the three goons with head shots and Darling by blowing out his right knee.

Four down in less than two seconds. Darling clutched at his leg and screamed rather than trying to reach his piece. Idiot. Hammett was on him in ten strides, kicking him in the face, stepping on his neck, and picking up his gun.

"I have money!" His voice was high pitched, frantic.

"It won't help. I want information. Your distributor."

Darling made a face like a dog who didn't understand a command. Hammett placed her boot on what was left of his right knee and gave it a little weight. When Darling finished screaming, Hammett tried again.

"Who distributes your kiddie movies?"

"His name is Guterez! He's in Tijuana!"

"Call him. Set up a meeting for tonight."

Another confused expression. Another pain motivator. Darling quickly got the hint and dug his cell phone out of his silly, expensive suit jacket.

"Speaker phone," Hammett ordered. "Tell him you've got some hot stuff to give him."

He nodded, frantically dialing a number. Hammett checked the periphery. So far, no cops or onlookers or triad members looking to protect their whores. She muted out the ambient city noises to pinpoint any police sirens, but didn't hear any. Even so, Hammett figured she had thirty seconds, tops, before she needed to leave the premises.

"Fernando? It's Tex. *Que pasa, amigo?*"

"*What you want, cabrón?*"

"I've got a... uh... hot property for you."

"*So call my people, set up a screening.*"

Hammett shook her head and raised her boot over Darling's knee.

"No! It's... um... it's too hot for that, Fernando. I need to get this to you right away. Tonight."

"*It better be worth my time, pendejo. Jack's. One o'clock.*"

Fernando hung up, and a dial tone came through the speakerphone.

"What is Jack's?"

"Bar. In Avenida Revolución, the Zona Centro. They have a mechanical bull."

"Describe Fernando."

Tex hesitated. He obviously knew that his life would be over once he told Hammett that bit of info. Hammett got on one knee and bent over, staring into Tex's wide, fear-filled eyes. Then she kissed him, her tongue darting in fast, her free hand on his head under his Stetson.

"It's okay, lover," she said. "I'm not going to kill you yet. I still need you. Now describe Fernando."

Tex's voice came out in a rasp, but his face relaxed a bit. "Short, maybe 5'6". Mustache."

"You've just described the entire male population of Mexico."

And some of the women, Hammett thought. Didn't they know about waxing south of the border?

"He drives a stretch Caddy, black, with horns on the grill. Always wears silver tipped boots. Rattlesnake. Lucchese. Expensive as hell."

Hammett knew the brand and owned a pair, though she preferred her Tony Lamas.

"Is he armed?"

"Always. And he has bodyguards."

"How many?" Hammett asked.

"Two. Sometimes four."

She shook her head slightly. "No. How many children have you videotaped getting raped?"

Tex's eyes rounded again, the whites showing all around his cornea.

Hammett emptied Stu's gun into Tex's crotch, then hammered the butt of the gun against his face enough times to take most of the flesh off. She finished him off by smashing both of his eye sockets to mush. He was still breathing when she used his shirttails to wipe her prints off the gun. If he lived—which was unlikely—he wouldn't be harming any more kids. Not blind and with his junk blown off.

Hammett scooped up his gun, and the weapons dropped by his henchmen. She also took their shoulder holsters, pleased that one was left-handed and one right-handed.

There were still no police sirens.

Too bad for the residents. Criminals were free to do what they wanted.

"Shitty neighborhood," Hammett said.

In the trunk of the rental she had a box of baby wipes. Hammett got the blood off her hands, discarded the wipes in the parking lot, and then got in the car and headed south.

"When operatives go rogue," The Instructor said, "they become a threat to the organization. All threats shall be dealt with. Lethally."

Getting into Mexico was cake. It was getting out that would be a problem.

Hammett buzzed down the San Diego Freeway through the border checkpoint in a briskly moving line of cars. She'd been driving for three hours, stopping once to refuel and pee, and the long period of inactivity had made her antsy.

She exited in Tijuana, on Benito Juárez y/o Segunda, and was looking around for a hotel when she stumbled across Jack's Taberna on the corner of Avenida Miguel F. Martinez. Hammett passed the bar—it was only ten in the evening—and wove her way through Baja streets until she found El Motel Del Sol. She parked and checked in, the proprietor happy to accept American dollars, and found her room to closely resemble the one she had in L.A.'s Chinatown, from the bare carpet to the same model pressboard nightstand. The only difference, Hammett surmised, was the roaches here spoke Spanish instead of Cantonese.

She killed some time by field stripping and cleaning all the weapons she'd acquired. Tex might have been a scumbag, but he knew enough to equip his men with quality firearms. His guards had been carrying Ed Brown Special Forces 1911s—around $3k each. Tex himself had chosen a S&W M&P 340 for his carry. Double action, concealed hammer, Tritium sights, five .357 Mag rounds in the cylinder. Nice.

Hammett made a boresnake out of some paracord she used as shoelaces, and was running it through the 340, cleaning out residue, when the phone rang. While this didn't surprise her—she was always tuned in to her surroundings, even when asleep—she was curious who it could be. The motel manager? Wrong number?

Or someone who knew her?

She picked up the receiver, staying silent.

"Why are you in Tijuana?" asked the robot.

Her handler, Isaac, using his electronic modulator to disguise his voice.

Shit.

"After the mission I thought I'd get a little R&R." Hammett bit back her nervousness. "Spend a few days south of the border. Unwind."

"Does unwind involve you dispatching four men in Los Angeles?"

"Yes," she said, matter-of-factly. "That helped me shake off a lot of tension."

"Protocol is for you to go home after an op. Await further instructions."

"Protocol also says we shouldn't discuss business on public phone lines."

"You didn't leave me a choice."

"There are always choices," Hammett said, determined not to show fear. "And I'm choosing to hang up on you."

"Go home. I won't tell you again."

"Is that a threat, Isaac?"

"It's an order."

"I have some business here. I'll go home when I'm finished."

"Fernando Guterez is not your target, Hammett."

Goddamn. Nothing got past Isaac. It was eerie.

"He is now. I took out Hot Rod. This guy is even worse. Or do we rank baby rapers on some sort of sliding scale?"

"I'll be watching. If you're not back across the border in an hour, I'll consider that going rogue."

"I'll go home after I kill Guterez. And if you send someone after me, they'll join him in hell."

Hammett hung up. She'd been able to control her emotions, but her hands still shook. Making an enemy of the organization she worked for was damn near the stupidest thing she could do. But she also knew she was the best they had, and she was gambling they wouldn't sacrifice her and her formidable skills because of a minor insurrection.

Hammett dropped and did thirty quick fingertip push-ups to burn off the adrenaline. Then she padded to the bathroom, stripped down, and got into a shower of questionable cleanliness. The motel hadn't provided shampoo, only a cheap sliver of soap wrapped in wax paper. But at least there was a private bathroom, a considerable bit of luxury in a place like this. She lathered up, scrubbing off her make-up, considering her next move.

They'd trained her to kill, and she'd taken many lives for her country, without ever rejecting a target. She'd killed brave men who fought against tyranny and oppression, simply because they opposed the U.S. government's foreign interests. She'd killed wives and girlfriends of targets—innocent collateral damage who were in the wrong place at the wrong time. She'd extracted information from U.S. allies in the most painful ways possible, because that was what she'd been ordered to do.

But Hot Rod, and Tex Darling, and Fernando Guterez—these men were monsters. They needed death like the Sahara needed rain. For the first time ever, Hammett was using her skills to do real, measurable good in the world.

So was it worth going AWOL and being hunted by her own organization, just to rid the world of a few profiteering pedophiles?

Hammett turned off the water, shook her wet hair. "Fuck yeah, it is."

She dressed again, sticking the 340 in the back of her belt as Darling had, pulling her shirt over it. Then she left the motel and strolled the streets. They were crawling with activity, mostly young Americans in various stages of loud and wasted. A block away, she found a tamale cart and scarfed down two with some bottled water. Another block later she bought a cheap poncho—the kind Eastwood wore in the Dollars westerns—and put it on even though the post-sundown heat was hovering around ninety. Then it was back to the motel where she strapped on the left-handed and right-handed shoulder holsters she'd liberated from Darling's dead henchmen.

With the poncho on, she did several practice draws, adjusting straps and buckles until she was comfortable. Then she abandoned the motel and went off to wait for Guterez.

The streets of Tijuana hadn't gotten any cooler, but had gotten louder as more partying asshole American kids whooped and screeched and acted pretty much like partying asshole American kids. Hammett knew of Baja's old days, of criminal activity and illicit sex shows and hard drug use. It used to be dark and dangerous. Now it might as well have been Ft. Lauderdale, New Orleans, or Las Vegas.

Some cute twenty-something guy with too many tequila shots in him stumbled up to Hammett and drunkenly groped her ass. She hit him in the kidney hard enough to tinge his piss red, then sidestepped some underage chick blowing chunks onto her micro mini and walked into Jack's.

The scene inside was like the scene outside, only hotter and a bit darker. Hammett pushed through the throng of partiers, found a corner to back into, and checked her watch.

Still forty minutes before Fernando's arrival. She killed time by memorizing egress points, finding six potential exits if things went sour, plus a door marked *No Admittance* that probably led to offices on the second floor. Hammett also spotted four men whom she pegged as bouncers (or maybe predators the way they scanned the crowd), possibly armed.

There were a few other men packing. Slick, older guys, their jackets let out to de-emphasize the bulge of their firearms. Cartels. When things got hot, Hammett didn't know how they'd react. Most certainly Fernando Guterez was connected. But were these his people? Or partial owners of the club, protecting their interests and watching how business boomed? Or local boys just relaxing with a cold Corona after a long day of cocaine trafficking and torturing informants?

A total of eight men she had to keep tabs on, plus whomever Guterez brought with him.

Scratch that. Nine. An attractive Hispanic man with a wide smile and a black eye patch had made his way through the crowd and was staring at Hammett from three meters away. He moved like a panther, both effortless and coiled. Beneath his leather vest, under his right armpit, was the bulge of a weapon.

Hammett kept her expression blank, staring as he approached. When he was within arm's reach, he stopped, spreading out his palms.

"Of all the tequila joints, in all the towns, in all the world, look who walked into mine."

"Keep walking, Bogie," she said.

"It is okay, my sweet *bonita*. I bear no ill will. I'm just happy to lay eyes on you again. Well, *eye*, I mean."

He winked. Hammett was sure she'd never seen this man before. She could also read people very well, and he wasn't lying. This guy apparently thought he knew her.

"Refresh my memory."

He frowned, looking hurt. "Our time in Vegas was not so long ago, was it? The Luxor? The waters at the Bellagio? The bed at the Venetian? Did the agency you work for brainwash you?"

Interesting. He thought they'd had sex and knew she was an operative. He also didn't seem threatening. At least, not in a violent way. But he radiated pheromones, as if he were ready to pounce on Hammett at any moment. Which, judging by his physique, wasn't something she'd normally turn down.

But this wasn't the time, or the place.

"Remind me of your name again," Hammett said.

"A joke, yes? I do not understand your intentions, but I will play along. Heath, at your service."

He offered his gun hand, no doubt intentionally to show her he wasn't going to draw. Hammett took it, and he immediately pulled her close. She dug her free hand into her poncho, seeking the 1911, but Heath merely brushed his lips across her knuckles, then kissed her fingers.

"Still paranoid as always," he said, eye twinkling. "I understand our relationship has not been built upon trust, but believe me when I say I'm not here to harm you."

Hammett pulled her hand away from his warm breath. "So why are you here?"

"Is coincidence not enough for you? This is where I grew up. My home. If anyone should be paranoid, it should be me. Perhaps you've looked me up to finish what we began?"

Was that a threat? Hammett eyed the bulge in his armpit. Unless he was very, very good, she'd be able to draw her weapon before he could.

"To settle old scores?" she asked, her voice flat.

"To make each other cry out in ecstasy, *chica. Por favor*, do not pretend you don't remember. My ego is not so strong that I could handle a rejection like that. Not from you."

Hammett had only just met him, but she was pretty sure Heath's ego could handle quite a bit. But his presence was distracting her from the mission. This Mexican lothario needed to *vamos, pronto.*

"If I asked you nicely to leave, will you comply?"

He smiled, then moved his face closer as if to kiss her. Hammett decided, perhaps foolishly, that if he tried she'd let him, if only to see if he was as good at it as she would have guessed. But before his lips met hers, he whispered.

"Those eight men you spotted. Four who look like bouncers and four who look like cartel. They all work for Guterez."

His visible eye was dark, wide, crinkled at the edges in amusement. He was talking shop, but apparently enjoying himself.

"And who do you work for? Isaac?"

"I know no one named Isaac," his breath smelled faintly of Cuban cigar smoke, which was a turn-on for Hammett.

"But you aren't here by coincidence, are you?"

His lips brushed hers. "No. I am here to assist you."

Two could play this game. She moved her lips to his ear, gave it a soft nibble. "What if I don't need assistance?"

"You are very good, *bonita*. But this is only the first team. Guterez is sending more men. Many more. You have apparently made some formidable enemies. But you still have friends in high places."

The Instructor, Hammett thought. He wouldn't let Isaac take down his number one student. Assuming Isaac was the one who informed Guterez. On the other hand, this Heath fellow might be the one working for Guterez, running a game on her. If so, his next act would be to get her someplace private.

"We should leave," Heath said, his unshaven cheek nuzzling against hers. "Go somewhere private."

Hammett frowned. She'd been starting to like the guy. Not too many male hitters were fluent in seduction. Killing him would be a pity.

"Where do you suggest?"

"Out of Baja, for sure." His eyes crinkled. "Preferably somewhere with a firm mattress and room service."

Then, in a blink, Heath had drawn his gun from his shoulder holster.

He was blindingly fast. Faster than she would have guessed.

Hammett was faster. But as she pulled a 1911, planning to gut shoot the Mexican with one hand and counter his aim with her other, she realized he wasn't pointing at her.

Heath's gun boomed over her shoulder, in the direction of one of the bouncers. Hammett turned slightly, saw the bouncer drop his piece and fall to the ground, red blossoming on his shirt, and then she adjusted her aim and shot at one of the suits, who'd drawn a bead on her and Heath. Two pulls of the trigger and his last thought flew out the back of his head in a red puff of brain matter.

Then Heath tugged Hammett against him, pressing his warm, hard body against hers.

"Round robin?" he said.

She knew the maneuver and nodded. Then they were back to back, each covering 180 degrees of the bar. Hammett took down two more targets as the crowd erupted in screams and panic. The smart ones hit the floor. The stupid ones—who accounted for the majority—stampeded the exits, the impromptu mayhem making Hammett lose sight of the other hostiles.

Behind her, Heath fired three times, then shifted his weight to his left, making Hammett compensate by turning right.

"Got my four," Hammett yelled over the din.

"Gas," Heath replied.

Hammett wondered if that was some sort of Spanish colloquialism for *great* or *nice work*, but Heath continued to turn, forcing her to see the front exit. Someone had lobbed a few canisters of an aerosol weapon into the bar. She assumed it was tear gas, as that was the most common. But then she saw several patrons double over and puke, and realized it was something worse.

Chloropicrin. A vomiting agent.

Used by the Nazis in WWII, it wasn't lethal. But it was able to penetrate gas masks, which then forced soldiers to remove them or drown in their own spew, exposing them to more deadly gases.

Hammett had heard about it regaining popularity for riot control in various cities around the world. During her Hydra training, she'd been intentionally exposed to chloropicrin.

It hadn't been pleasant.

If it had been tear gas, she would have made a try for the exit. But this stuff had already turned half the bar into Mardi Gras on Bourbon Street at 4am, the sound of violent hurling replacing the panicked screams. Even if she held her breath and ran for it, the chances of staying upright weren't good. It hadn't been more than a few seconds, and the floor of Jack's had already become a pukey Slip 'N Slide; people throwing up and falling and then throwing up some more. It looked like a pie fight from a Three Stooges two-reeler, only a lot more disgusting.

Hammett pushed left against Heath's back, spinning him like a gun turret, until she spotted the *No Admittance* door.

"Upstairs," she said, breaking into a jog before Heath answered.

Hammett closed one eye, dropped a shoulder and knocked over a man in her way, hurdled two young girls who crouched on the floor holding hands and crying, and then kicked the door. As she'd guessed, it opened to a staircase, and Hammett took them two at a time, aware Heath was a few steps behind her.

The stairs ended in a hallway, gas starting to leak up through the slats in the wooden floor. Hammett held her breath and sprinted, seeing another door, shouldering through it, and finding an empty office. There was a window on the far wall, and she ran over, jerking it open. It let out onto the roof, overlooking the street. Hammett opened the eye she'd closed earlier, her pupil dilated to speed up her night vision, but she almost needn't have bothered because the stars and moon were out and the sky clear.

She took in her surroundings. Drunk, vomiting partiers were spilling out of Jack's and three sedans were parked in front. At least ten of Guterez's men stood watch, guns out, scanning the escaping crowd for Hammett.

But that didn't interest her as much as something she saw two hundred meters to the west, next to the curb. A black Cadillac Eldorado with tinted windows, bull horns perched on the hood above the grille.

Assuming there weren't many Caddies with horns in Tijuana, that car belonged to her target, Fernando Guterez.

Watching his orders being carried out from what he thought was a safe distance.

He thought wrong.

"You are going for Guterez, aren't you?" Heath, behind her, breath hot on her neck.

Hammett tucked away her weapons, opened the window, and slid through, blending into the night. The roof was tarred, flat, radiating heat beneath her footfalls as she sprinted for the edge of the building. The building next to Jack's was a meter higher, and had a stone lip along the roof. Hammett judged the gap between them to be the width of a small alley. She lowered her head, accelerating—

—and then dove off the edge, hands outstretched for the lip, feet coming up under her to take the impact of the wall.

She judged it right, hitting with her fingers and toes at the same time, then scrambled up the side, fell onto the roof in a shoulder roll, and continued to sprint while eyeing her next obstacle.

Heath, apparently as quick on his feet as he was while flirting, had caught up with Hammett and matched his pace to hers. As their feet beat out a steady rhythm on the tar paper, he turned for a moment, appraising her.

"You are indeed a most capable woman, *chica*." His words came easily. Even though he'd just leapt over an alley, he wasn't winded.

Neither was Hammett.

"You know parkour?" she asked.

Also known as free running, it had been invented in France as a way to best traverse military obstacle courses. The goal was to conserve movement and use the terrain to your advantage, letting momentum guide you. It had been explained to Hammett as taking the path of least resistance, like water in a stream. But rather than appear passive, practitioners of parkour (*traceurs* for men, *traceuses* for women) often looked like extreme skateboard riders—flying and flipping through the air—except they weren't riding anything.

"I know many—"

Heath's words were cut off as he confronted an air conditioner. But like any good traceur, he vaulted it leapfrog style, and landed right in step with Hammett.

"—different things," he finished.

Hammett sighted ahead of her. The next building was two meters shorter, and the jump longer than the last one. Putting on a burst of speed, Hammett launched herself into the open air, headfirst with her hands outstretched, seeing the alley blur past beneath her, and then she tucked and flipped in the air. She timed it correctly, landing on the roof, on her feet, then continued the momentum with a somersault and came up running.

Heath had also opted for flashy, doing a side flip, landing fast but dissipating the higher force of his landing with a shoulder roll. Hammett hadn't met many people, women or men, who could keep up with her. But before she could be impressed they were coming up to another jump, this one to fire escape scaffolding, at least two meters higher than their current level.

"It's too far, *bonita*."

Heath was right. Had she been alone, Hammett would have slowed down and scouted another route. The jump was damn high. But she had a strong competitive streak, and it had been a while since she'd tested her limits.

Besides, she wanted to prove the cocky son-of-a-bitch wrong.

So Hammett turned a cartwheel into a back flip, then another, then sprang off the roof with all the force and speed she could muster, twisting in the air—

—and immediately realizing she was going to come up short.

She stretched, extending her arms and spine, pointing her toes and keeping her knees together to be more aerodynamic, while the reptile part of her brain screamed "YOU'RE GOING TO DIE!" Her fingers brushed the rusty, iron railing, but she was already starting to fall and couldn't maintain a grip, and she glanced down and saw there wasn't anything else to grab and no soft places to land.

If not death, then several broken bones. She'd heard vague rumors of an operative who'd taken a big fall from a building, irreversibly crippled thanks to a miscalculation. Hammett didn't want an error in judgment—brought about by the spirit of one-upmanship—to be her undoing, so in the nanoseconds after missing the grab she was already figuring out the best way to land.

When something caught her wrist, she was as shocked as she'd ever been. And not much shocked her.

"So what is the going rate for saving a damsel in distress?" Heath asked as he hung from the scaffold by one hand, his other clasped around hers.

She stared up at him, at a loss for words.

"The mattresses at the Hotel Solamar in San Diego are quite firm, *mamacita*. They also have excellent room service."

Hammett pulled herself up his arm then hung alongside him, staring into that damn amused eye. She'd misjudged the jump, was surprised Heath had caught her, and didn't know what to say when he had. All signs she was off her game, and should have gotten the hell out of Dodge.

Instead she gave him a slow, soft kiss. His tongue darted out to meet hers, but she'd already pulled away.

Heath let out a big, dramatic sigh. "Even if that is the only thanks I get, it was worth it."

"I'll thank you with more feeling later," Hammett surprised herself by saying. "Help me kill Guterez, and Solamar's penthouse is on me."

Heath scrunched his brow, as if considering it. "The penthouse on you, you on me." Then he smiled. "I like this idea."

Hammett smiled back, taking care to make it look genuine, then she chinned up the fire escape and swung onto the stairs.

Thirty seconds later she and Heath had climbed back down to street level. The Eldorado was still parked at the curb, its engine running. The limo was at least ten years old, but it looked to be in decent shape, and had so many coats of wax polish it could probably be seen from space. Hammett couldn't peer through the tinted window glass, but if she had to guess, Guterez was either alone in the backseat, or with female company, having sent all of his thugs to go after her. He was probably armed, and so was the driver.

"Sneak up on the driver and take him out," she told him. "I'll make sure the doors are open, and that he's not looking at you."

"What is the plan, *bonita*?"

Hammett handed her guns to Heath, then began to strip. When she got down to her bra and panties, Heath gave a soft whistle through his teeth. When she was completely naked, his breath caught.

"*Perfecto*," he whispered.

She looked into Heath's eyes, but his were on her body. "Do you have any blood left in your head to follow instructions, or did it all rush to your dick?"

He smiled at her. "I've missed you."

"Yeah, me too," she dead-panned. "Forty seconds, then take the driver out. Start counting now."

Hammett pulled down her lower eyelids and touched her fingers to her pupils, prompting tears. Then she put on a frightened expression and ran out of the alley, toward the limo.

Nudity was useful for many things. It showed you were unarmed. It projected vulnerability. To some people it was a shock, and to others a distraction. As she staggered to Guterez's car, she had a pretty good hunch he'd let her in, or at least open the window to talk.

Her hunch proved correct. When she was within five meters of the car, the rear window lowered. Hammett saw an older mustachioed Mexican man stretched out in the back seat. On his lap was a Mexican girl wearing whorish make-up who looked young enough to still play with dolls.

"Problema, señorita?" Guterez asked. His eyes were wide, and he looked inordinately pleased with himself.

Hammett fell onto one knee, counting off in her head.

Twenty-two... twenty-three...

She didn't glance to see if Heath was circling around to take the driver, and wasn't sure he'd actually follow her orders. But she went on the assumption that his obvious infatuation, coupled with his need to show off, made him a temporary ally.

"Por favor, señor! Por favor!" she yelled to the limo.

A few staggering steps later and she was at his window.

"Qué pasa?"

"Me violaron. Ayúdame, por favor."

Guterez's amused expression morphed into a leer. *"Dígame."*

Thirty-eight... thirty-nine...

Hammett reached into the window, grabbed Guterez's upper lip by the mustache, and yanked as hard as she could, pulling his head out the window. A moment later, the driver's door opened, and she wondered if she'd misjudged Heath and he'd abandoned her. But then there was an "ummph" and the sound of a body hitting the street, followed immediately by a gun skittering across the pavement.

Guterez was also reaching for a gun, but his bent position, and the minor still on his lap, meant he couldn't get his hand into his suit jacket.

Hammett used her other hand, latched it onto his ear, and tugged until he had no choice but to follow her out the window or literally lose face. When the back of his neck was exposed, she dropped an elbow and snapped his spine as deftly as breaking a board in karate class.

"*Vete a casa,*" she told the girl.

The girl scurried out the opposite door and ran into the night.

"It gives me much pleasure to watch you work, *querida.*"

Heath had taken the driver's seat, and was staring at her through the partition, smiling. Hammett opened the door, let Guterez flop out, and climbed into the back.

"Do you have my clothes?"

"Yes. But must you put them on? It is like hanging a sheet over a Degas. Such beauty should not be covered up."

Was this guy for real?

She decided to find out.

"You said something about the Hotel Solamar?" Hammett said.

He stepped on the gas.

"Celebrate life when you can," The Instructor said.
"It's what you should be doing between ops."

They didn't make it to the Hotel Solamar.

When they were less than a mile away from Guterez's murder, Hammett told Heath to pull over. He parked in an alley and got into the back with her. He reached for the champagne.

She reached for his fly.

She freed him in one, deft movement and wrapped her hand around him, already half hard in her fist.

He groaned deep in his throat, struggling to remove his pants without interrupting the stroke of her palm, the tease of her fingertips. After almost a minute of fumbling, he managed to push his pants down his legs and kick them free. Then his mouth was on hers.

Hammett had always found it easy to tell from a man's kiss how he would be in bed. Some hurried the exchange, as if it was a chore one had to endure in order to get to the rest. Some were soft and romantic, imagining themselves soulful lovers when in reality, they were simply lazy and uninspiring. And then there was Heath.

Heath kissed with his whole body, as if lips and hands and hips and cock were all making love to her at once. And Hammett found herself wondering if, when this was over, she really needed to kill him. As if sensing her thoughts, Heath pulled away.

"You do not seem like yourself, *mamacita*."

Hammett rubbed her thumb up his underside and offered a wicked smile. "Is that a bad thing?"

"Bad? No. But I do not feel the fire, the passion, I felt in Nevada."

An odd thing for a guy to say in a situation like this. He was quite obviously aroused. What more did he want?

She lowered her head to take him in her mouth—

—and he put up an arm to block her.

Hammett hadn't ever encountered *that* before. And while she was off-guard, Heath suddenly had her in a hammer lock, forcing her face into the leather seat, his weight atop her.

He tricked me! He's the enemy! I need to—

Then she felt his breath on her neck, his tongue trailing up to her ear. At the same time, his free hand cupped her hip, his fingers making their way between her thighs, beginning to stroke her.

He's not trying to kill me. He just wants to play.

She closed her eyes, sighed, allowed him to caress and nibble her. But when she felt herself getting close, she bent his finger, leveraging him off her and onto his back on the limousine floor.

Hammett gracefully rolled onto him, locking his manhood between her thighs, but not allowing him to enter her. She pinned his wrists and moved her lips close to his. He tried to kiss her, straining his head up, but she moved just out of reach.

"Oh *chica*, you're killing me."

He tried to buck his hips, but she clenched tighter. Then he smiled and whispered something, either *mercy* or *merci*, and his body relaxed.

Hammett began at his throat, running her tongue across his rough stubble, up his jawline, penetrating his ear. She heard him gasp, and she licked her way back to his mouth, kissing him slowly, enjoying his taste.

In a quick movement, she had moved down his chest, running her teeth over the hair on his chest, catching his nipple in her mouth, giving it a quick bite and making him groan.

She moved lower. No longer able to pin his wrists, but still wanting to keep him compliant, Hammett skimmed her hand down his body and cupped his testicles. She held them firmly, but not cruelly. Heath grunted again, and she scooted backward and rubbed her chin across his tip. His cock bobbed against her cheek, and she gave him a slow kiss, trailing her tongue up his length.

Heath reached for her, and she gave his balls a warning squeeze, again not enough to cause pain, but enough to assert she was in control.

Then she began to tease the holy hell out of him.

She used her lips. Softly. Kissing him from the base to the top. Her tongue. Gently. Following the same path her lips had taken. Her breath, making him slick with her saliva and then blowing warm and cool. Even her teeth, giving him a hickey on his shaft and causing him to hold his breath for the duration.

But she didn't take him in her mouth. Even when his hips began to buck.

"*Lo siento*," she said, nuzzling him with her chin. "I apologize for having no fire. No passion."

"I may... I may have misspoken, *bonita*." His voice was deep, throaty. "And I do hope you accept my humblest apologies."

She quickly surrounded him with her mouth, sucking hard, making him cry out. Then she just as quickly pulled away, watching with amusement as he twitched and bounced.

"Such cruelty will be returned in kind," Heath said, his breath coming quicker.

"Cruelty?" Hammett laughed. "You have no idea."

Then she lowered her mouth again, taking him deep into her throat, and then staying completely still. Just as she'd done while kissing him. When Heath strained upward, she retreated, not allowing him to thrust.

Hammett hadn't teased a man like this in a long while. Probably because she hadn't found any worth the time and effort. The last one she'd done this to hadn't been able to hold out for more than a few minutes. She hoped Heath would do better. Either way, she could still get hers. But she would be disappointed if she couldn't impale herself upon him.

So the question was, make him beg until he comes, or be selfish and ride him?

She chose to make him beg. A treat, because he'd saved her from falling. A punishment because he'd been able to make the jump that she missed.

It didn't take long for his moans to morph into words. First, a string of Spanish invectives that would make a cartel hitman blush. Then, finally, the begging she'd been waiting for.

"Please, *bonita*. I cannot take any more."

Having broken him, Hammett began to match his thrusts, taking him fully into her throat, increasing the tempo to intensify his pleasure.

Heath abruptly stopped, surprising her. "Not yet, *querida*. I want to be inside you."

Not many men could control themselves after a certain point, and she knew Heath was close. It was a matter of pride with her to finish him off.

Hammett bobbed her head even faster, using her free hand to pump at the same time.

"Please," he said. "Please stop."

Any second now. Hammett released his balls, using both hands to stroke him.

"No!"

Heath suddenly jackknifed his legs, bucking Hammett forward, onto his chest. He looped his arms around her thighs, lifted her like he was doing a chest press on a weight bench, and plopped her, face-first, onto the seat. Before Hammett could twist around, Heath had her by the wrists, with his face between her legs.

Hammett had had plenty of men, and more than a few women, go down on her. But never in this position, from behind. Rather than struggle and attempt to escape, she waited to see what Heath was going to do.

What he did was similar to what she'd done.

Namely, tease the ever-loving hell out of her.

He used his whole face—lips, tongue, chin, even his nose, to probe every intimate millimeter of her body.

Every millimeter, except the part she wanted him to focus on.

Hammett tried to shut down her body, resist sensation. She refused to come first. This had become a competition, just like the parkour across the rooftops, and she'd lost that one and wasn't about to lose again.

But Heath was good. Very good. Perhaps the best she'd ever had. And though she knew enough mental tricks to alleviate severe pain, even torture, she couldn't blot out his insistent, probing tongue.

It only took a few minutes for Hammett to begin to squirm and buck against him, trying to get him to hit the right spot. But he was every bit as cruel, taking her right up to the edge, and backing off.

Hammett felt the wave or orgasm building in her, and receding as he pulled away. Building and receding. Building and receding.

It was wonderfully, exquisitely terrible. She had become a slave, bound to his will, unable to focus on anything but his incessant, relentless teasing.

Hammett almost blurted out, "Just let me come and I promise not to kill you," but right before

she reached that point, Heath loosened his grip on her wrists just enough for her to twist out.

Like a snake striking, Hammett whipped her leg around and brought her hands to Heath's throat, finding his carotid and jugular. She put just enough pressure on the points to prevent blood flow to the brain, a less conventional choke hold.

Heath looked surprised, then confused, and then his eyelids began to flutter as unconsciousness overtook him.

But Hammett didn't want him knocked out. She just wanted him compliant and couldn't go toe-to-toe against someone stronger. So as he slumped back to the limo floor, Hammett straddled him, releasing his neck just as she sank onto his cock.

Heath blinked, apparently not sure what had happened. Then he gripped her hips, and Hammett rode him hard as she'd ever done before, using her muscles to make him explode first.

The problem, of course, was it felt just as good to Hammett as it obviously did to Heath. He matched her thrusts, his strong hands pushing her down on him, his body surging up into her, and Hammett knew she didn't have longer before she lost control.

"*Chica*... oh, *chica!*"

Heath began to spasm, and confident she'd beaten him, if only by a second or two, Hammett allowed herself to go over the edge. She ground against him as she came, screaming in her throat, her thighs locking, feeling the passion surge through her in burst after burst.

When she couldn't take any more, she slumped forward, her breasts pressed to his chest, damp skin against damp skin. For longer than she cared to think about, she merely lay there, feeling the gentle rock of his breathing, the sensation of him softening inside her. She inhaled deeply, taking in the scent of his skin, and his hair tickled the side of her face.

This was different than the male escort she'd had the previous night. This was something more. Something real. A connection to another human being. A kinship. An understanding.

It was bewildering to her. Hammett felt something with Heath. Something she hadn't felt in…

Ever.

But Hammett had spent most of her life trying not to feel. And as emotion washed over her, making her want to—cry, of all stupid things—Hammett pushed up from his body, then reached down and grabbed Heath's head by the hair and bashed it into the floor of the limousine.

Once.

Twice.

Three times.

Heath stopped moving.

Hammett stared down, wondering if she'd killed him. Almost fearfully, she reached down, seeking a pulse in his neck.

Strong.

He was alive.

But should she allow him to live?

This was strange territory for Hammett. Her instinct, her training, told her to finish the job. He knew too much about her.

Shit, Hammett felt as if this man actually *knew* her.

She raised her fist, ready to crush his trachea—

—and hesitated.

Hammett never hesitated.

Instead of delivering the killing blow, she got off Heath, her legs quivering. She found her clothes, her guns, and dressed while she watched his chest rise and fall.

"Just kill him," she said.

But she didn't kill him.

And she didn't know why.

Instead, she left him in the limo, unconscious, and hurried out of the alley, heading back to her rental car.

On the drive to San Diego, when enough time and distance had passed, Hammett tried to convince herself that the reason she'd let Heath live was because he was a really great lay, and it would have been a shame to snuff him out. It had nothing to do with her.

She kept telling herself that lie, over and over, until she began to believe it.

"Pay close attention to anything out of the ordinary," The Instructor said. "Seemingly random events, coincidences, and unexplainable phenomena might be early warning signs that you are about to be attacked."

Hammett slept in the back seat, in a 24 hour Walmart parking lot, and awoke an hour before dawn. She used her car's GPS to find the nearest rental car outlet, and spent twenty minutes explaining to the dowdy clerk that she wanted to return it here, not in L.A. where she'd picked it up. She had to pay extra, which took all the extra cash she had, including a hundred dollar bill she'd sewn along the underwire of her bra. Part of her wondered if she should have bothered returning the car at all—if Isaac had tipped off Guterez, and considered her rogue, she had bigger things to worry about than her expense account with Uncle Sam. But if Isaac had cut her some slack, or had talked to The Instructor to send Heath to help her, then it would be best to play it by the book. She wouldn't want to have to pay for the car out of her own pocket.

The airport shuttle didn't leave for another thirty minutes, so Hammett walked across the street to a 24-hour convenience store and went to the Good Humor freezer for one of her favorite comfort foods, a Chipwich. She compulsively checked the date on the wrapper to make sure it was fresh, and then brought it to the smiling Indian guy at the counter.

"Back so soon," he said, ringing up her ice cream.

Hammett had been so lost in her own thoughts she'd almost missed it. "Excuse me?"

He patted his ample belly. "I can't eat more than one, but you are so trim and fit and can eat two."

The cashier obviously thought she'd been in here earlier, getting ice cream. But Hammett had never been in this shop before.

It occurred to her that this was the second time in a few hours she'd been mistaken for someone else. Did she just have one of those faces? Or did she have a doppelganger running around?

Paranoia kicked in big time, raising the tiny hairs on her arms and neck, and Hammett pushed quickly away from the counter just as a supersonic round cut through the air where she'd just been and punched through a display cooler, exploding a bottle of soda.

Sniper!

Hammett dropped as another round zipped over her head, and then she rolled into the candy aisle, out of sight of the storefront window. She'd automatically noted the egress points when walking into the shop, but the rear exit could be seen from the parking lot, and no doubt the shooter was already covering it, anticipating that's where she'd run. A textbook move.

Unless the sniper had no line of sight.

Hammett dug out a 1911 from under her jacket and crawled on knees and elbows to the far end of the aisle. She peeked around a display of beef jerky, aimed at the storefront, and squeezed off eight carefully spaced shots.

Rifle rounds that went faster than the speed of sound poked through safety glass like it was wet tissue paper. But the bullets from Hammett's gun were subsonic, and the storefront window was laminated to resist breaking and entering. So wherever she shot, the shatterproof glass spiderwebbed but remained intact, making it difficult, if not impossible, to see through the millions of small cracks.

Thoughts coming on blurringly fast, Hammett put herself in the sniper's position, reasoning that even without being able to see, the shooter would assume Hammett would go for the rear exit. Depending on how powerful the scope was, it wouldn't be easy to readjust focus and find the target, so the sniper's best bet was to wait a few seconds, then fire at the exit.

That's why Hammett ran straight for the front door.

She hit it low, hard, and fast, pushing it open, immediately doing a tuck and roll—

—and getting winged in her right shoulder.

Hammett didn't feel any pain, just a tug, but she knew the pain would come. More upsetting than the bullet was the fact that the sniper had anticipated the move. Whoever was shooting was smart. And trained.

Hammett came up staggering and ducked behind a parked car. Maybe she should have stayed in the store. There was a gunshot, followed by one of the tires exploding a few tenths of a second later. Doing a quick math calculation in her head, she estimated the sniper to be within a hundred and fifty meters.

She glanced at her bleeding shoulder long enough to ascertain an artery hadn't been hit, and then pondered her next move.

Another shot, and the car shuddered with the round's impact.

The gas tank. The shooter was trying to blow the gas tank.

Which is what Hammett would have done if her target was hiding behind a car.

It was a bizarre feeling, almost as if the sniper was reading her mind. Maybe they'd had similar training? Similar experience?

Heath?

Someone Isaac had sent?

Whoever it was, the next thing Hammett needed to do was something neither she nor anyone who was trained to think like her would expect. What was a move no one would ever make while pinned down by a sniper?

Running toward the shooter.

She didn't dwell on it, because she didn't have time to. Depending on how much gas the car had in it, a well-placed round could ignite the fumes and turn her temporary shelter into a bomb. So, going on pure instinct, Hammett sprang to her feet and began to sprint in the direction the shots had come from.

She could do the hundred meter dash in about thirteen seconds, the hundred and fifty in twenty. As she ran, Hammett put herself in the sniper's mind.

The target is gone. Find her. What the hell, she's running right at me? Lock on. Squeeze.

Hammett veered left, and sure enough a gunshot boomed from ahead, but it was a miss. She got back on track.

Eject the cartridge and reload. Locate the target again. Lead her. Squeeze.

A sharp turn right. Another shot. Another miss. Even better, Hammett had seen the muzzle flash, and knew where her attacker was. A van parked at the end of a street at a T intersection, back door halfway open. Less than sixty meters away, she headed toward the van.

Last shot, then I have to get out of here. Eject and reload. Locate target. Squeeze.

Another veer right. A shot and a miss. The side panel door slammed closed as Hammett got within twenty meters. The van was going to bolt.

And go where?

If Hammett had been the shooter, she would have plotted the escape route. Don't drive east into the rising sun; glare could fuck up a quick getaway. That meant west toward the harbor.

So Hammett stopped chasing the van and cut west, anticipating where it would wind up. She pulled her other 1911 and beat the van up the street, skidding to a stop and firing into the windshield at the driver.

The van made a hard right, tires screeching, but it was too top-heavy and rolled. It hit its side, skidding across the pavement, and crashed into a parked car.

Sirens shrieked in the distance, and at least a dozen people, on the sidewalks and in traffic, watched, slack-jawed. Ignoring them, Hammett ran to the van, going in through the rear door, crouching and ready to fire, and coming face-to-face with...

Holy shit. Except for the hair, which was shorter and dyed red, and the gun, a Mauser rifle instead of two .45s, Hammett could have been looking into a mirror.

Her double appeared shocked, eyes wide, mouth slightly open, which was probably how Hammett also looked. Then they both reacted, the woman bringing up her weapon, and Hammett slapping her upside the skull with one and a half kilos of 1911.

The double went down, and Hammett aimed, both fingers on both triggers.

"Are you okay?"

She swung one gun around, to the man behind her. Young, fit, yuppie in a suit on his way to some boring 9 to 5 job, stopping to help. He immediately raised his hands. Hammett saw his car parked a few meters back, a Lexus, still running.

Hammett cleared her head of all the confusion, all the questions, emptying her mind like dumping water from a glass, and immediately reverted to her training.

"She's hurt," Hammett said. "Get her into the car."

The guy didn't move. Hammett fired over his head.

"The car!"

She tucked away one gun and grabbed the rifle, The good Samaritan lifted the unconscious sniper and brought her to the Lexus. Hammett opened the rear door.

"Put her in the backseat, on her stomach."

He complied.

"Do you have jumper cables?"

"In the trunk."

She considered shooting him. It was a practical thing to do, because he'd seen her up close, and he'd no doubt report the car stolen the moment she took off. But the clerk at the convenience store had seen her as well, and so had the store's surveillance cameras. Hammett was trained at keeping her head down when video was being recorded, but when the shooting started that hadn't been her main priority, and her face could have been caught on tape. It would take the authorities a while to sort everything out, but killing him would make them a lot more eager to catch her, and there were at least a dozen witnesses watching. It would be impractical to kill them all.

"I need your wallet and your cell phone," Hammett said. He handed them over, looking appropriately frightened. She put his things in her jacket and pouted, sticking out her lower lip. "Don't fret, lover. Think about the story you'll be able to tell the boys back at the office."

Then, on impulse, she grabbed his tie, tugged him close, and kissed him, jamming her tongue into his mouth, then shoving him backward onto his ass. She climbed into the Lexus, floored it, and took off down the street.

Ten blocks later, confident she wasn't being followed, she pulled into an alley and got out. Hammett took the battery out of the man's cell phone, pocketed it again, and then got the jumper cables from the trunk. Her doppelganger was still unconscious. Hammett patted her down, finding nothing, then hogtied her with the cables, tight as she could.

She needed someplace private to think, and get some answers. Luckily it was still early morning, and the place she had in mind wouldn't be open for a few hours. Hammett did a search on her GPS, set her coordinates, and was there in six minutes.

The parking lot was empty; a good sign. Hammett pulled up to the front door, noting the open and closing times. Assuming an employee got here an hour before opening, she still had plenty of time to get some questions answered. Driving around back, Hammett let herself into the building using the tire iron in the trunk of the Lexus. Once she opened the door, she was greeted by an explosion of welcome noise.

Barking.

Hi, puppies.

Hammett went back to the car, heaved up the sniper in a fireman's carry, and took her into the shelter. She found the shower area where the animals were given their flea baths, and set the woman down on the concrete floor, near the drain. Part of her wanted to go exploring, pet some dogs and cats, maybe feed a few. Perhaps she would, when she finished the interrogation. Right now, she had to figure out what her twin knew.

Hammett used several leashes to better bind her intended victim then searched the office cabinets for pet meds, finding a cache. She did a quick cleaning of her shoulder wound, judged it didn't require stitches, and taped on a bandage. Then Hammett kept searching meds until she found the supply of epinephrine. Dogs and cats, like people, sometimes suffered from anaphylaxis and needed cardiac resuscitation, and the EpiPen worked similarly for all mammals. It took three shots to wake the woman up, and when she roused, she threw up all over the floor.

Hammett used the hose attached to the wall to wash the vomit away, giving her enemy a cold soaking at the same time. Then she shut off the water, sat on her haunches, and stared at the woman.

The resemblance was startling.

"You know how this works," Hammett said. "I ask you questions and hurt you if I don't get the answers."

The woman cleared her throat and spat, then said, "Who are you?"

Hammett shook her head. "You're confused. I'm the one who asks the questions."

Hammett reached over to the sniper's bound hands, stretched out one of her fingers, and bent it until it snapped.

The woman screamed. Dogs howled.

"Did you get plastic surgery to look like me?"

The sniper looked at her, defiant. "No. I was going to ask you the same thing."

"The only work I've had done are these," Hammett patted her breasts.

" They look good."

"Thanks."

"I always wondered what I'd look like with bigger tits. I guess now I know."

This had to be one of the more surreal interrogations Hammett had ever conducted. Like asking questions of herself in the mirror. "Why do you look like me?"

"I don't know. I've got as many questions as you do."

"But I'm asking the questions."

"Fine. You've established that. So will you let me tell you something rather than asking?"

"Technically that was a question, but go ahead."

"I was adopted."

Hammett had also been adopted. Could the sniper really be her sister?

Now it made more sense why Heath thought they knew each other. He'd banged this woman in Vegas, and had confused Hammett for her.

"Who sent you?" Hammett asked.

The woman hesitated, then said, "We're obviously related. And by the way you came at me, I'm guessing we had similar training. If so, you know I've been trained to resist interrogation for as long as possible, because I know when it's over I'll be killed. But something isn't right here. You're obviously my sister, or a clone. And I don't know why I was sent to kill you."

"Who sent you?"

"I'm Clancy. I work for a government organization called Hydra. I was sent by my handler, who I never met. He's just a voice on the phone. Codename: Isaac."

It was a lot for Hammett to absorb. This woman—probably related—had the same training and worked for the same group.

"Who trained you?" Hammett asked.

"He didn't have a name. I knew him as The Instructor."

Curiouser and curiouser. "How did you know where to find me?"

"I arrived in San Diego yesterday. Isaac called, gave me your location at the rental car place. I followed you to the shop."

"What were your orders?"

"Sanction, with extreme prejudice. But I was told to stay at least a hundred meters away at all times. Now I know why."

Because up close, you'd realize you were killing your sister.

Targets didn't have faces or features through a scope. They were just walking bullseyes. But Isaac was apparently worried about a face-to-face meet.

Hammett asked more questions, and Clancy answered. When there was nothing left to say, Hammett took the scalpel from her pocket and did what she needed to do.

"It's only called a safe house when it's safe," The Instructor said. "If it isn't, flee."

The flight to Atlanta had cost six hundred bucks. But Clancy, like Hammett, sewed money into the seams of her clothing, and Hammett had enough for the plane ticket, a mediocre airport Denver omelet, and taxi fare to her safe house in Buckhead, with a bit left over.

Knowing her former employer was gunning for her made Hammett edgy, and returning to one of her safe houses was a risky move. But there was only one way to call off the hit— kill Isaac. Even if he wanted a truce, she'd never trust the bastard again. But Hammett didn't know where Isaac was, or even who Isaac was. Only one person in the world, other than Isaac, had that information.

The Instructor.

Of course, like Isaac, The Instructor was also an enigma. Or so he thought. Because Hammett had figured out how to find The Instructor.

The problem was that the key to finding him was at her Atlanta safe house. And there was a high likelihood Isaac had a reception planned for her when she arrived.

Hammett had the cab drop her off two blocks from her address, in front of a drug store. Inside she bought a Braves baseball cap, a windbreaker, a box cutter, and some cheap mirror sunglasses, and a Chipwich, since she'd been gypped out of the last one back in San Diego.

She put on the hat and glasses, and while eating the ice cream she took a circuitous path to her apartment, spiraling in one block at a time, taking everything in. She pretended to be talking into her stolen cell phone while she walked, stopping often to yell nonsense into it while she was actually checking out parked cars, open windows, and people on the street. When Clancy failed to check in, that would raise red flags with Isaac. If he was smart—and all indications pointed to him being just that—he'd send a team this time instead of a lone hitter. So besides paying attention to singles, Hammett also focused on pairs.

Was that really two guys arguing sports, or were they killers waiting for her to show up?

Was that couple holding hands really married, or were they on the lookout?

This type of recon was slow and arduous, but in the cat and mouse game the odds were better if you played the cat. Hammett wanted to spot them before they spotted her, and that meant taking her time and being careful. But even as careful as she was being, she almost missed it.

Just fifty meters in front of her house, standing at the bus stop across the street; a woman, wearing jeans and a white poncho wrap which made her upper body shapeless, a floppy sunhat, and sunglasses.

Reflective sunglasses, just like Hammett wore.

The woman spotted Hammett a moment after Hammett spotted her. They stared at each other for a moment as cars passed between them. Hammett knew this woman was after her, knew she was armed, and wished she'd had a more sub-stantial weapon than a drugstore box cutter, having ditched her guns before boarding the flight. She had a weapon cache in another part of town, in a safe deposit box in a bank in Five Points, but her ID for that box was in her safe house.

Bringing a box cutter to a gunfight was just plain stupid, and Hammett was considering sprinting away when the woman did something unusual. She shrugged, held out her palms, and mouthed, "What are you doing?"

Almost as if she recognizes me. Does she think I'm Clancy?

Clancy had spilled her guts about many things during their time together, but she hadn't mentioned working with another female assassin.

The woman in the poncho began to cross the street, but Hammett didn't detect any threat in her gait or posture. Hammett matched her nonchalant stance, and was grateful she had the sunglasses on because as the women neared, Hammett got even more confused.

This woman looks exactly like me.

She immediately wondered if it was Clancy, but that was impossible.

Which meant this had to be yet another twin.

Make that triplets.

Hydra.

Hammett considered the name of her secret government organization. A hydra was a mythical Greek dragon with seven heads. Why seven? Could Hydra have actually trained seven identical women to be operatives?

Hammett bit the inside of her cheek, hard enough to draw blood, and let some dribble down her lips. When the twin approached, Hammett dropped to one knee, feigning an injury. A moment later she was being helped up and led to a car parked on the corner, a Chevy rental. The woman helped Hammett into the passenger seat, then got behind the wheel and buckled up.

"Hit me from behind," Hammett said.

"Isaac said she was good. Did you finish her?"

Hammett nodded and then coughed, spattering the windshield with blood.

"Where are you hit?"

"Hospital," Hammett mumbled.

The woman pulled into traffic. "When did you change your clothes?"

Hammett had the box cutter to her neck a heartbeat later. "Drive cautiously, no sudden movements."

The woman stayed calm. "You're not Ludlum."

Hammett patted her down, took a Glock 17 from under her poncho, a cell phone, and a Zippo lighter. She did a quick pull of the Glock's slide to make sure it was loaded, then pressed that into the woman's armpit. "No. I'm, Hammett, your target."

The woman began to laugh. "Hammett? As in Dashiell?"

"Yeah. And your partner's name is Ludlum? I assume after Robert."

"Makes sense. Whoever created Hydra must have liked thriller writers. I'm Forsyth. As in Fredrick, who wrote Day of the Jackal."

Hammett thought of Clancy. Tom Clancy. Their code-names were all spy authors.

"Where do you want me to drive?"

"Turn up here."

"Right? On Alberta?"

"Yes."

"You look exactly like me and Ludlum. You're our sister."

Hammett didn't reply.

"So what did you do for blood?" Forsyth asked. She seemed much calmer than Clancy had been. Then again, she wasn't hogtied and having her fingers broken. "Bite the inside of your cheek? I used a variation on that trick once, in Istanbul. Spit the blood in a man's eye to blind him."

"Where is Ludlum?"

Forsyth made a right turn, her driving slow and steady. "We split up two hours ago. Supposed to text each other whenever someone enters your apartment."

"She's covering the back."

A nod. "If it matters, when we took this job we didn't know you were our sister. We wouldn't have taken it if we'd known."

"But when you got close enough to me, you would have figured it out."

"We weren't supposed to get close. Orders. We rigged your apartment with C-4."

"Sensor?"

"No. We were told you were good enough to spot it. Manual detonation, once you went in."

Hammett hadn't found a detonator on Forsyth. "The cell phone? Dial a bomb?"

"No. The lighter. Don't open it unless you want your place destroyed."

"Wouldn't want that. I've got thousands invested in my clothes."

Forsyth looked at Hammett, then began to laugh. Hammett had said it because she'd sewn hundred dollar bills into every outfit, and apparently Forsyth did the same and got the joke.

"How are you supposed to know when I entered the apartment?" Hammett was curious. Her window shades were drawn, the lights off. She'd been planning on slipping in and out in less than thirty seconds.

"Ludlum has a scancorder."

Hammett had heard of scancorders. They were allegedly devices that used microwaves and Doppler radar to detect a human heartbeat from many meters away, including through walls and concrete. Developed in the private sector to search for earthquake victims in rubble, the military applications were obvious.

"I didn't think those existed yet," Hammett said.

"Officially, they don't. Unofficially, they're cool as hell."

She was chatty for someone about to die. Maybe it had to do with working with a partner for a few years. Hammett had always been a lone wolf. She preferred it that way.

"Have you and Ludlum always worked together?"

"Only for the past three years."

"Recruited by The Instructor?"

Another nod. "You're Hydra, too?"

Hammett stayed quiet.

"Why does Isaac want you dead?" Forsyth asked.

"I had some personal business to attend to. He considered it going rogue."

"Isaac's an asshole."

That was an understatement. It was also personal. If Forsyth had Hammett's training, she'd been taught to offer nothing. Yet both Clancy and Forsyth had given up a lot of intel with very little persuasion. Was it their hope Hammett wouldn't kill them, because they looked alike and were trying to bond?

Or did they actually feel a bond?

Hammett had felt something like a bond with Heath. Enough of one to not kill him when she probably should have. But she didn't know what it was like to chat with a sister. Without wanting to, Hammett thought of her terrible childhood, and suddenly felt an urge to ask Forsyth about hers. Had she had decent parents, rather than a psycho? Friends? Normal relationships?

Hammett had spent her high school prom beating a rival gang member to death with a bike chain, which probably wasn't something many seventeen year old girls could claim. What would it have been like to grow up normal?

"Mathieson is coming up. Left or right?" Forsyth asked.

"Neither. Pull into the next alley, where you call your sister and tell her to bring the bomb in my apartment."

"She won't listen. She'll know I've been compromised."

Hammett knew she could force Forsyth to make the call, but the problem remained. Any weird calls from Forsyth, and Ludlum would be on alert, and much harder to subdue. Besides, even with a weapon, it wasn't easy to maintain control over one person, let alone two. Especially when both had training. Even as Forsyth drove, seemingly at ease, Hammett could see the wheels turning in her sister's head, plotting how to get out of this situation.

The smart move would be to kill Forsyth, impersonate her, and get close enough to Ludlum to kill her as well.

"You'll need help eliminating Isaac," Forsyth said, no doubt trying to remain essential while knowing her minutes were numbered. "Ludlum and I can help. We've been thinking about leaving Hydra for a while. If Isaac is a hard target, a team will have better odds. Do you still want me to pull into an alley? There's one behind the Quickie Dry Cleaning."

Something pinged in Hammett's brain. The things Forsyth said among the banter.

Right? On Alberta? Mathieson is coming up. Quickie Dry Cleaning.

Forsyth was telling Ludlum their location.

Hammett grabbed Forsyth's scalp by the hair, checked the right ear, then yanked her head over and checked the left, finding the earpiece.

Shit. They'd been in constant contact, and Ludlum had heard everything. Hammett needed to—

Forsyth made a grab for the gun at the same time she hit the brakes. Hammett bounced off the dashboard, still gripping the Glock. Forsyth—who'd been smart enough to not only play Hammett, but to also put on her seatbelt—wrenched Hammett's wrist and made her drop the gun, which bounced onto the floor of the Chevy.

Hammett drove an elbow into her twin's nose, breaking it, and then head-butted her in the temple. Human beings had evolved to take head-on punishment well, but they didn't do

318

so good when hit in the side. Hammett's head was fine, but Forsyth's brain smacked the inside of her skull, bringing instant unconsciousness.

Forsyth's body went slack, and the car began to roll, picking up speed as it went down an incline toward the intersection. Hammett was reaching for the passenger door when the Chevy rear-ended the trailer of a semi-truck at the stoplight.

Both airbags exploded, pinning Hammett in her seat. The white propellant powder hung in the air like smoke, clogging Hammett's nostril and burning her lungs. She found the handle, shoved the door open, and plopped into the street on all fours—

—just as a gun was pressed to the back of her skull.

"Hello, Sis. Face down on the street. Now."

Disoriented from the car ride, Hammett still couldn't help but wonder why Ludlum hadn't killed her immediately. Not that she planned to complain.

Hammett raised her hands as if surrendering, and then executed a move she'd practiced so often it was practically automatic; she knocked the gun away from her head with her right hand and caught it in both, twisted her body while pointing it away, and pulled Ludlum to the street, face-first.

Ludlum tried to roll onto her side as they wrestled for the weapon, but Hammett had leverage, and strength, and kept applying pressure until her sister's grip gave and the gun fell to the ground.

Hammett searched for it, then catching movement in her peripheral vision, she bunched her shoulder to take a kick that was meant for her head.

Forsyth. That was the problem with knocking someone out. Eventually they woke up.

Hammett rolled smoothly to her feet and reached into her belt for the box cutter. A kick caught her in the side. The cutter skittered across the pavement.

"You chipped a tooth," Forsyth said, fists in front of her and shuffling on the balls of her feet. "And I thought we were bonding so well."

Movement to her left. Ludlum, scrambling for the dropped gun. Hammett did a quick cartwheel, kicked the Glock away, and hit Ludlum with a right cross.

Ludlum blocked, then tried a leg sweep, which Hammett jumped over. She looked right, saw Forsyth moving in, muay thai style. To her left, Ludlum adopted a taekwondo back L-stance.

"You girls want to surrender?" Hammett asked.

They attacked as one, Forsyth with a flying elbow, Ludlum with a side spinning kick. If they'd both connected, Hammett would have been knocked horizontal. But Hammett threw herself into a back handspring, coming up on her feet in time to block a right cross and a spin kick. She backpedaled, ass hitting the rental car, and turned sideways just as Forsyth smashed her foot through the passenger window. Hammett scooped the woman up, WWE style, and body slammed her onto the pavement.

Ludlum threw a knee at Hammett's face, but Hammett dropped and shoved upward, sending Ludlum soaring overhead. Then she moved to stomp on Forsyth's head, but Forsyth was already kipping up to her feet. Hammett lashed out with her palm, clipping Forsyth in the chin, and then dropped down on all fours to search for the Glock. It had been kicked under the rental car, far out of reach.

Time to run.

Getting back to her feet, Hammett sprinted toward the truck Forsyth's car had rammed into. The driver was standing outside of his open door, mouth agape as he stared at the spectacle. She rushed him, clipped him under the jaw, and then swung herself up into the cab of his semi and locked the doors. Then she studied the control console.

No keys. The driver had taken his keys from the ignition before getting out.

Hammett checked both side mirrors, saw Forsyth approaching on the right, and Ludlum on the left. Ludlum had found her gun.

Hammett quickly searched the cab for a weapon, but there were too many shelves and compartments and boxes. Eyes scanning upward, she saw a skylight on the roof, the windows hinged to double as an emergency exit. Hammett climbed onto the bed, undid the locks, and pulled herself up.

Three shots rang out, and Hammett leapt from the cab to the top of the trailer, sighting a white city bus that was heading toward them.

Parkour time.

Hammett put on a burst of speed, trying to judge where the bus would be when she made her leap, knowing it was going to be tight, flinging herself into the air as bullets tore past, sailing into open air with the street four meters below her, and landing on the roof of the bus as it passed.

Hammett stuck the landing, but the bus's speed knocked her sideways, and she began to tumble toward the edge. She splayed out her arms and legs, stopping the roll but not the momentum, and skidded on her chest until she reached the side, her head peeking over just before she stopped.

Hammett watched the road whiz past for a moment, caught her breath, and then inched away from the edge. She turned back around to look for Forsyth and Ludlum, and spotted them climbing into the semi. Hammett frowned, watching as Forsyth started the truck. Apparently she'd found the keys.

Hammett got onto her knees, sighting ahead. Open road, no traffic lights for a few blocks. She looked back at her sisters, and the semi was now in pursuit. Ludlum, gun in hand, crawled out of the cab skylight.

She needed to get off the bus.

"Hey!" Hammett banged on the roof, hoping to get the driver's attention. At the rear, she began to crawl toward the front, slapping the aluminum roof as she went. She had no idea if the bus driver could hear her, but she kept her center of gravity low in case he did and hit the brakes.

Another pop of a gunshot, and a round buried itself in the side of the bus. The semi roared up alongside.

As she'd done with Clancy, Hammett put herself in her adversaries' minds. They would get close and try to shoot her. If that didn't work, their next move would be to stop the bus, either by pulling in front of it, killing the driver, or blowing the tires. They'd expect Hammett to try to jump off the bus when it slowed down, or get inside.

What wouldn't they expect?

They wouldn't expect Hammett, outnumbered and outgunned, to attack.

Springing up from a crouch, Hammett ran across the roof of the bus and jumped, launching herself face-first at the oncoming semi, arms outstretched Superman-style, sailing over the gap between the two vehicles. Ludlum frantically emptied her magazine, wide-eyed with obvious surprise, her shots failing to connect. Hammett sailed over Ludlum, hitting the trailer on her chest. Hammett bounced, feeling the wound in her shoulder tear open, rolling right off the other side but managing to grab onto the upper side rail with one hand.

As she hung there on the side of the semi-trailer, the street beneath her blurring past at forty miles an hour, the adrenaline kicking so hard she felt her heart would burst, Hammett had a brief, terrible moment of self-reflection.

She didn't wonder what led her to this point. She didn't regret all the horrifying, unjustifiable things she'd done. She didn't wish it all had gone differently. Instead, as she hung there, she had a single, overpowering urge.

She wanted to set the entire fucking world on fire.

Except for the puppies and kitties.

Gritting her teeth, she forced all the pain, all the anger and hatred and fury, into pulling herself back up onto the trailer.

Ludlum stood over her aiming the Glock at her midsection, ready to pull the trigger, but Hammett didn't care. If Ludlum shot her, it would only piss her off even more.

The truck began to slow down, edging for the side of the street. Hammett clenched her fists, stood, and faced her sister.

"Don't move! Hands up!"

Hammett put her hands up—holding her fists in front of her, ready to box the shit out of this identical bitch.

Incredibly, Ludlum didn't shoot. Instead, she holstered the gun inside her jacket and spread her palms out. An odd move, considering Hammett was going to rip off her face and feed it to her. She'd heard of a serial killer who made people eat their own faces, and the rage she felt warranted something that extreme.

"Easy, Hammett." Ludlum took a step back. "We don't have to do this."

"Yes," Hammett said. "We do."

In Hammett's adult years, she couldn't recall ever being scared. She'd been surprised before (it happened often in this biz), worried (once when she'd taken a shih tzu who'd eaten a whole bag of Halloween chocolate to a vet), and resigned to death (the by-product of several enhanced interrogations). But Hammett gave up fear when she gave up playing with dolls. So it was odd to see fear on Ludlum's face, a face that looked exactly like her own.

"Pussy," Hammett snarled.

Then she attacked.

Ludlum was excellent. She blocked the first salvo of punches and kicks, and even managed to send a few back.

But Hammett was better than excellent. The Instructor had told Hammett that, pound for pound, she was the second best mixed martial arts combatant he'd ever taught, including men in her weight class. She kept attacking until Ludlum had no choice but to cover up, and then Hammett pummeled the woman down to her knees.

Sometime during the fight the truck had parked, and Forsyth appeared on the trailer top.

She also looked scared.

"Control your fear," Hammett said, quoting The Instructor. "If you don't, you'll die." Then Hammett added a bit of her own wisdom. "But it doesn't matter. You're going to die anyway."

Forsyth held her ground, adopting a kung fu stance, Shandong praying mantis style.

Hammett didn't bother with styles. She just walked up and beat the holy hell out of her. Hitting and kicking and striking until Forsyth fell to her knees.

"We can work together," Forsyth said, her face already beginning to swell up like Rocky Balboa's at the end of the first movie.

Hammett gripped her hair, pulling her head back to expose her neck. Then she raised her fist to shatter her windpipe.

Suddenly, Ludlum was on her back. And she'd cinched the neck lock, squeezing her biceps to cut off the flow of blood to Hammett's brain.

Hammett spun, but Ludlum clung on. Hammett's vision became narrower, darker, as her consciousness seeped away, and her last thought was these women better kill her because there would be hell to pay if they didn't.

"Learn to tell the difference between friends and enemies," The Instructor said. "And understand that friends can become enemies, and enemies can become friends."

Hammett woke up with her wrists zip-tied behind her and her legs lashed together with—of all things—jumper cables.

She was being lowered into the semi cab, and as she began to struggle her oppressors dropped her into the sleeping compartment and onto the mattress. Hammett continued to thrash, trying to get out of her bonds, and then one of her sisters was sitting on her.

"Easy. We want to talk."

Hammett went limp. "So talk."

"You're our sister."

"Or your clone. I wouldn't put it past our government."

It was broken-nosed Forsyth talking, her voice sounding a bit nasal, as if she had a cold. "Either way, we have a connection. We shouldn't be fighting. I learned that when I met Ludlum."

"We've all had the same training," Ludlum said. "We've all been through the same shit. And now we're being exploited."

"Think of the money we could make if we went freelance," said Forsyth.

"I don't need money," Hammett said.

"Money or not, do you like being Uncle Sam's bitch? At his constant beck and call, doing whatever he orders us to do?"

Hammett did not. But she kept silent.

"Before I met Ludlum," Forsyth said, "I felt like I'd been running on automatic pilot. I did what I was trained to do, and what I was told to do. But things have changed a lot. You've heard how misery loves company? Being exceptional also loves company."

"We were two before," Ludlum said. "With you, we're three."

"Four," Hammett said, figuring she could play these cards until she was dealt a better hand. "There's another one of us named Clancy. She tried to kill me in San Diego."

"Another identical sister?"

"Yeah."

And Clancy, like Ludlum and Forsyth, had apparently bought into this sisterhood bullshit. Genuinely bought into it.

"Where is she?"

"Still in Cali," Hammett said, straight-faced. "Recovering from the beating I gave her."

"But you didn't kill her."

"No."

"So you feel it, too."

Hammett didn't feel anything. But she recognized a potential asset when it appeared before her.

"Sure I feel it," Hammett lied. "Now untie me."

Forsyth and Ludlum exchanged a glance. And then—incredibly—they untied her.

Ludlum climbed off, sitting next to her, and Hammett felt like this had become some bizarre teenage slumber party. What was next? Pillow fights and talking about boys they crushed on?

Then Hammett felt a gun press into her side. Apparently there were still some trust issues to overcome.

"Can you contact Clancy?"

"Yes. Do you really have my apartment rigged with C-4?"

" Why does it matter?"

"Do you two really want to be free of Isaac and Hydra?"

They nodded as one.

"I can find The Instructor. He can tell us where Isaac is. But I need to get into my apartment."

"Call Clancy," Forsyth said, holding out a cell phone. "If she answers, we'll believe you."

Hammett glanced at the phone, then glanced at the gun in her side, and immediately realized what she had to do.

"The best defense is a good offense," The Instructor said. "People can't defend themselves when they're dead."

Hammett recovered a computer hard drive from her safe house in Buckhead—without blowing up.

326

Written on the HDD was the end result of a blunt force attack on the databases of the NCIC, DoD, CIA, SSA, and NSA. A year ago, while in a vulnerable state and realizing that someday she might need to seek out The Instructor—perhaps to enlist his help, or perhaps to kill him—Hammett had worked for dozens of hours with a police sketch artist, and the best facial reconstruction software, to recreate his face in portrait and profile. Then she used a recognition program to manually scan millions of pictures on various government websites, in order to get a match.

The Instructor had done a good job to hide his tracks, but no one can hide completely. Hammett had known she'd found him, but had never looked at the information. This was a safeguard; if interrogated, she truly had no information about The Instructor. But now that she needed to contact him to find Isaac, she was willing to forsake plausible deniability and initiate contact.

But, coincidentally, she didn't have to. Because the moment Hammett walked into her apartment, the phone rang.

Then again, She knew damn well it wasn't a coincidence at all.

"You know who this is," The Instructor said when she picked up the phone. "I take it you know about the others like you."

"I've met three. Why didn't you tell me?"

"That decision was above my pay grade."

"Are there others?

"Seven of you, total."

Seven. Just like the seven-headed hydra from ancient Greece.

"Are we sisters?"

The Instructor chuckled, also out of character for him. "Yes. Did you think you were clones?"

Hammett had heard about a secret government program that involved cloning, but she let the subject drop.

"I also met an operative named Heath."

"I sent him to help you. He says you repaid him by almost bashing his skull in."

"I did more than that," Hammett said, recalling their lovemaking.

"He didn't seem to be complaining. So you know, I tried to call off Isaac. But my political influence isn't what it once was. However, I have a plan to get that influence back."

Here we go. The real reason for his call.

"Let me guess. I'm you're plan."

"You no longer work for Isaac. You work for me."

"Maybe I don't want to work for anybody."

"If that's the case, this will be the last time we ever speak, and I wish you a long and happy life."

It was so incongruous to anything he'd ever said before, Hammett found herself at a loss for words.

"I can't do anything until I find Isaac," she said, after finding her voice.

"I know. And I'm willing to give him to you."

"But there's a price."

"There's always a price. But this one you shouldn't mind. You eliminate Isaac, and then work for me. And I give you something you've always wanted."

She made a face. "What's that? A house with a white picket fence, two point five kids, a dog, and a husband who works at a brokerage firm?"

"I know you hate the world. It's what makes you the best operative I ever trained. How about global annihilation?"

"I'm listening."

"I have a plan, Hammett. A plan to change the course of the United States, and ultimately, all of civilization. It won't be an easy task. Millions will have to die first."

Hammett didn't need to hear more. He had her at *millions will have to die.*

"I'm in."

"This won't be an easy one, Hammett. Isaac is a hard target. He lives in a fortress, armed guards and attack dogs, the latest in security. Plus he just assigned himself a new bodyguard. Her name is Follett. She's also your sister."

"Is she good?"

"Very good."

"Does she know she's protecting Isaac?"

"I don't believe so. As far as I know, Isaac hasn't revealed himself to anyone."

"So... who is Isaac?"

"Someone you've heard of. That's why his death has to appear to be from natural causes. You can't go in all guns blazing, because there would be consequences. No foul play. No interrogation."

"How about he just disappears?"

"Trust me. You don't want the Secret Service following the trail back to you."

"Why would they be involved?"

"Because Isaac is the senior senator from Illinois, and the Democratic majority leader. Samuel Burling."

"A chain is as strong as its weakest link," The Instructor said. "A good team has no weak links."

Seventy-six hours later, Hammett sat at the kitchenette, pouring over the blueprints to Burling's mansion while Clancy—broken finger in a splint—snipped away at Hammett's hair with the skill of a master stylist.

The four Hydra sisters were in Ludlum's safe house, an apartment in the Illinois city of Aurora. Ludlum and Forsyth were on the sofa, surveillance photos spread across the coffee table before them. They'd spent the last two days getting intel on Burling's residence in nearby Naperville, and had gotten some long lens shots of his property from various angles, along with recent satellite photos, and Secret Service and guard details and routines. Clancy had also hacked into the database of the company that had installed Burling's burglar alarm and security system.

"He's got cameras everywhere except the bathrooms," Forsyth said. "Paranoid little bastard."

"Then we hit him in the bathroom," Hammett said. "Did we get the coke?"

"Meeting a dealer tonight," Ludlum answered.

"Kill him when it's done. No loose ends," Hammett told her. "How about the wand, cameras, and earpieces?"

"Also tonight," Forsyth said. "Burling's security detail routinely scans for radio transmissions, but these will run on an encrypted WiFi network, through a laptop. But even with boosters, the range is limited. You'll need to be on the grounds."

"That's my problem," Hammett said. "I'll deal with it."

"Burling has two armed men on premises. One guarding his room. One at the gatehouse. Two roaming. Plus Burling has a dog. Pit bull. Maimed an electrician visiting the house last year. Burling's people covered it up, paid the guy off so the media didn't find out. It's a killer, Hammett."

"That's my problem," Hammett repeated. "I'll deal with it."

But that wasn't her only problem. Hammett glanced at the counter, at the picture of her sister Follett, her hair cut into a Louise Brooks-style 1920s bob, complete with bangs and side curls, taken yesterday while reconnoitering the estate. According to The Instructor, Follett was the only student who scored higher than Hammett in hand-to-hand combat. Also according to The Instructor, Follett was to be recruited, not killed.

That wouldn't be easy. But Hammett had been tinkering around with an electronic device that could help get her close, and if she refused to be persuaded Hammett would also be bringing a Taser X26.

The only thing left for them to do was finish the haircuts, get the drugs and gear, and steal a cab.

"The guards switch at two A.M.," Hammett said. "That's when we'll hit him."

She turned her head to look at Forsyth, and felt the pinch of Clancy's scissors as they poked her ear. Hammett met Clancy's eyes, watched them widen.

She saw fear. And she liked it.

For the past three days, Hammett had been watching her sisters bond. A trend that would likely continue once Follett joined them. And although Hammett joined the conversation occasionally, she mostly felt like a visitor at a zoo, watching strange animals interact behind a thick wall of Plexiglas.

These women had her training, and were very good at what they did. But Hammett viewed their need for camaraderie and acceptance as something odd, something foreign. She didn't feel a part of their clique.

Seeing the fear in Clancy, Hammett understood why.

Hammett wasn't their equal.

Hammett was their superior.

As Machiavelli said, it is easier to rule with fear than love.

"Careful, Sis," Hammett said. "Remember, I'm doing you next."

Clancy stiffened, no doubt imagining the ramifications. Then she nodded and went back to work, her hands having developed a slight tremor.

Hammett hid her smile. If she couldn't bond with her sisters, she'd at least enjoy terrifying them.

"All good plans anticipate factors down to the smallest detail," The Instructor said. "But even the best laid plans go astray."

Clancy drove the quartet half a kilometer away from Burling's estate, and dropped Hammett and Ludlum off alongside a copse of trees that lined the private street. Then she continued to take the stolen taxi cab up to the front gate, dropped Forsyth off, and did a U-turn to come back around.

The night was cool, dark, quiet. It smelled like the Midwest suburbs, a unique mix of woodsy and urban.

Ludlum set up her scancorder, the Doppler radar part similar to a handheld bullhorn, and pointed it at Hammett to get a base reading on her heartrate.

Hammett logged into the encrypted WiFi on her laptop, and three video images came up, each taking a third of the screen. Besides the suppressed 9mm Beretta ankle carries, each of her sisters wore a silver brooch on her Anne Klein jacket. The brooches hid pinhole cameras and microphones, battery powered and transceiving via a dongle. Coupled with the earpiece she wore, Hammett could see what they saw and hear what they heard. They began to walk toward the guard house, moving close to the fence and out of sight, Hammett keeping one eye on the road, the other on the laptop.

"Hey, I know you." Forsyth played drunk like a pro as she stumbled up to the guard's gate. "You in the mood to party, cowboy?"

Forsyth held a half-full whiskey bottle out to the guard. They'd watched the shift change two minutes ago, using field glasses from a hilly vantage point a kilometer away, and it was unlikely the guard had even settled in yet. He was a young guy, under thirty, fit and trim in his rent-a-cop uniform. One of Burling's private troops, not Secret Service.

"You know I can't drink on duty."

The man shrugged and smiled, and in the light of the guard post Hammett noticed a gold wedding band on his left hand.

"I've had plenty to drink," Forsyth slurred and leaned against the booth's open window.

"I can see that."

"I'm not really in the mood for more. You want to know what I am in the mood for?" Forsyth opened her coat and started fiddling with the buttons on her blouse. The lapel of her jacket blocked the camera's view, leaving Hammett with nothing but audio.

"I'm in the mood to get naked, that's what I'm in the mood for." Forsyth said, answering her own question.

"I'm sorry, Ma'am, but you need to keep your clothes on."

"Is that a rule?"

"I'm afraid it is."

"Looks like I broke it." She giggled. "And look at this. I broke it again!"

"Please, put your clothes…"

"Oh, come on. Don't be such a stick in the –" Forsyth giggled, and judging from the bobble of the camera, she stumbled. "Oh, no."

"Are you okay?"

"Oh…."

Hammett heard the sound of a door opening, then more ruffling of Forsyth's jacket and a flash of a uniformed chest.

"Oh, wow," Forsyth cooed. "You really are a stick. But not in the mud."

"Ma'am, I'm…"

"I'll say."

"…married."

The sound of a zipper and jingle of a belt buckle.

"Does your wife do this to you?"

"Ma'am, please."

"Oh, I aim to please."

"I can't…"

"Oh, no. You can. Trust me. Look at the size of this thing."

Another flash of an image, this time a bare, hairy thigh.

"Let me just…."

"Uhh…umm…oh my God."

"Want me to stop?"

"What? No. God, no."

"Worried someone will see?"

"Uh, yeah. Come here."

The sound of a door opening and closing came over the mic, then a flurry of movement and the camera's view cleared, Forsyth having slipped out of the coat. She laid it down inside the guard house, the camera showing not only her nudity from the waist up and the guard's from the waist down, but a nice view of the security monitors behind him.

With a wink directly into the camera lens, Forsyth turned back to her work.

"Nice view," Hammett said into Forsyth's earpiece. Looking past the impressively-endowed guard, she focused on the three screens behind him. Each split to show a dozen different feeds, for a total of thirty six camera views. With this vantage point, Hammett knew where every exterior guard and camera was located.

Things got more complicated inside, one room looking pretty much like another. Although Hammett had committed the mansion's floor plan to her eidetic memory, the rooms on the monitors were labeled only with numbers, and as a result, she could place only the kitchen, dining room and other distinctive rooms into the map in her head. No matter. With the scancoder, they should be able to sort things out.

The only problem she could see was that Forsyth seemed to be enjoying her work a little too much.

"Make it last," Hammett warned. "He's young."

"Oh, yes," Forsyth said around a full mouth.

Hammett glanced at her other two sisters. "Let's move."

Guided by the guard house security monitor, the three chose a spot along the fence partially obscured by the branches of a large oak. They were over in seconds, landing amidst a garden on the other side.

One obstacle down.

At least twenty to go.

She nodded to her sisters, who took position behind her, then reached into her pocket and pulled out the dog whistle. She blew it, the sound silent to the human ear, and then waited.

Seconds later, the sound of running and panting reached them in the darkness.

"Remember, ignore him, don't look him in the eye. We might smell enough like Follett that he'll accept us."

The dog came into view. Even in the shadows, Hammett could see he was a beauty. Black, with a white throat and chest, he looked elegant yet powerful. Not one of the many pit bulls half maimed and scarred by dog fights, but a well-cared-for animal with perfectly formed ears and a beautiful dished face that reminded her of an Arabian horse.

He stepped close, sniffing the air.

Hammett smiled, radiating control and calm, not showing her teeth. Dogs took that as a sign of aggression.

Good dog. Maybe she'd take him with her after they did away with Isaac. Her lifestyle wasn't any more conducive to owning a pet than it had been when she'd dropped Rod's kitty off at the shelter, but she toyed with the idea often. Her sisters could have each other. All she needed was woman's best friend.

The pit bull sniffed, then growled, low in his throat. His body went stiff.

"Everyone stay still. He's going to attack."

Then the animal lunged.

But as fast as the dog was, Hammett was faster.

She grabbed for him, instinctively going for his lower jaw, sticking her hand into his mouth holding tight, forcing it downward to keep him from biting.

He settled back on his haunches, ready to give his muscled body a shake. If he did, she wouldn't be able to hold him, not even her strength and practice would save her from his teeth.

He didn't get the chance. Her sisters closed in around the animal, as they'd planned. Each grasping a back leg, they lifted the solid mass of canine muscle into the air, rendering him powerless to do anything but writhe and growl.

"Quiiiiitttttt," Hammett said, her voice quiet and firm. "Settle down."

In her experience, dogs responded best to calm strength. Except for a rare few, dogs didn't prefer being in charge. A confident pack leader relieved them of the responsibility and made them feel secure. As luck would have it, Hammett was a natural alpha, and dogs seemed to sense it.

This beautiful creature was no exception.

Slowly he stopped struggling. Then he relaxed. And when Hammett nodded for her sisters to lower him to the ground, he rolled onto his back, offering his belly.

Releasing his jaw, Hammett pulled a dog treat from her pocket, one of those smelly ones canines adored, and fed it to him. Then she rubbed his chest and scratched behind his ears.

So far, so good.

When Hammett checked the laptop, she was relieved to see that Forsyth still had the guard occupied, and she had to admit, a little impressed to see how flexible and inventive her sister was. She could also see the exterior guards were clear for the moment.

Ludlum gave Hammett the scancorder, then awaited her order.

"All right, go," she told Ludlum and Clancy.

The pair bounded through the garden, staying among the trees. When they reached the edge, Hammett gave them another all clear, and they dashed for a small retaining wall near the house.

Hunkering down beside the dog, Hammett swept the house with the scancoder and compared the findings with the security camera images from Forsyth's sex booth.

Hammett opened her audio feed to both Clancy and Ludlum. "Burling is in the master bedroom and a single Secret Service agent is outside his door."

"Check." Ludlum whispered.

Clancy echoed.

"Follett is in the next suite, door to the right of the master bedroom. She's lying down, maybe sleeping. Lights are out and I can't tell. I'm also picking up three guards. One in the kitchen, same uniform as two outside. Guy must be getting a snack. No one is in the room with the security camera feeds." Hammett double checked all the guards' positions. "Move. Now."

"Affirmative," both sisters said in unison, creating a strange, stereo effect in Hammett's ears.

Christ, they even all sounded exactly the same.

The two ran for the house, the video feeds from their jackets bouncing with each stride. Clancy made for a patio door on the first floor, just outside a spacious living room area. Ludlum dashed to the front door. Then both of them set about picking the locks.

Hammett looked back to her view of the guard house security monitor where Forsyth straddled the guard, her feet propped on either side of the L shaped desk. Head thrown back and hands gripping his shoulders, she raised and lowered herself over him, one knee blocking Hammett's view of the screen where she'd last seen the exterior guards.

Hammett opened Forsyth's audio channel. "Hey, Jenna Jameson, move your damn knee."

A whistle trilled from somewhere near the house. The dog responded, perking his head toward the sound and whining.

Hammett glanced back at the video from Clancy and Ludlum's camera brooches. Neither was yet inside.

What was taking them so long? Hammett would have been able to pick those locks five times over by now.

"Sorry," she told the dog, and held his collar. Better to have the guards' attention focused on the garden than the house.

When she checked the laptop again, Forsyth was leaning forward, the stud muffin guard taking care of her from behind, the monitors free and clear.

Back on the lawn, the two guards stood together, probably trying to figure out what might have happened to the dog.

Clancy slipped inside, then Ludlum.

Hammett dug into the dirt of the garden with one hand and gently wiped the moist loam on the dog's white snout and front paws. "Sorry, buddy. But I have to give them an explanation of what you've been up to. Now not a word, okay?"

He looked at her as if he understood.

She released his collar, and when the next whistle came from the guards, he bounded off.

Hammett returned her attention to the laptop. Clancy was visible on the security monitor. She sat with her legs stretched out on a sofa, a book in her hands. Her own video feed revealed she was reading The Hunt for Red October.

Funny girl.

Ludlum, on the other hand, was nowhere to be seen on the security monitor. Her own monitor showed a powder room decorated in burgundy, ivory, and gold.

"Ready for you," Hammett told Forsyth.

Forsyth was now standing in front of the guard, one ankle braced on his shoulder. She leaned to the side, peering around him. "That's weird."

The guard continued, as if he hadn't heard a word.

"I said, that's really weird," she shouted. "I'm on the security cameras, I'm in bed and reading. Those images had to be taken earlier today."

Blood apparently returned to the head on top of his shoulders, and the guard untangled himself from Forsyth and spun around to look at the monitors. "Holy shit. Someone must have replaced the feed with prerecorded video, like they do in all those bank robber movies."

Hammett had to smile at the movie reference. Any security system worth its money had safeguards against that. But she'd been counting on the guard's inexperience for her plan to work. Good to know she'd gambled well.

"I'll bet something is just wonky with the system," Forsyth said.

He picked up a radio and hit the call button. On the security monitors, the guard snacking in the kitchen and the two outside simultaneously grabbed their radios.

Hammett gave Clancy and Ludlum each a quiet, "go," and then keeping an eye on her laptop, she headed closer to the house, reaching the spot she'd chosen earlier, a greenhouse sheltered from the rest of the property by fragrant vines of Japanese hydrangea. She entered through the plastic door, the temperature inside at least fifteen degrees warmer, Hammett's nose assaulted by dozens of flower scents; roses, peonies, freesia, lavender, lilies. Less prominent were onions, garlic, peppers, mint, thyme, parsley, basil. And over everything, the smells of mulch and organic fertilizer. She placed her equipment on a tray of geraniums, and dug out her sat phone and voice modulator as she checked the others' progress.

Forsyth was holding the guard's cock as if it was a leash, keeping him from leaving the booth. "Oh, come on. They can handle it. Look how close you are. It won't take long to finish."

She dropped to her knees, took him into her mouth, and the guard groaned.

Good answer.

Clancy approached the master bedroom, the Secret Service agent giving her a nod as if he clearly recognized her as

Follett. "I need to see him," she said, a slight whine in her voice.

"I can't let you in."

"Why don't we let Mr. Burling decide that?"

"He's sleeping."

"I hear a television."

The agent paused, as if listening.

"He's not going to like it if you keep me out. Trust me on that." Clancy played with the buttons on her blouse, clearly suggesting the reason she was there.

The agent sighed, apparently knowing enough about his charge to know she was likely right about the trouble turning her away would cause. "Okay, I'll check."

Easy peasy. Her sisters were damn good. Not quite in Hammett's league, but close enough for government work.

She smiled at her own joke.

Ludlum was meeting the two exterior guards at the kitchen door. "What's going on?" she asked.

"Someone might have spliced into the security camera cables with video of you from earlier in the day."

"What? Like some caper movie?"

"Yeah. We might have a breach."

"Should be easy enough to tell," Ludlum said. "Let's go take a look."

The three made their way down the hall where the midnight snacking guard was about to enter a code on a keypad in a reinforced steel door.

"It would be tough to breach that," Ludlum said.

Hammett watched the guard punch in the numbers, automatically committing them to memory. Ludlum probably had a photographic memory as well, so she could handle it if needed, but there was nothing wrong with having a back-up just in case something went wrong.

They opened the door, and Ludlum and the three guards filed inside.

Checking Clancy, Hammett made sure she'd gotten inside Burling's suite before she made her move. Clancy had, and she was already kissing and teasing a very interested Burling, leading him toward the bathroom.

Show time.

She pulled out an encrypted cell phone equipped with voice modulator, similar to the one Isaac probably used, and punched in the number The Instructor had provided.

One ring.

On the computer screen, Follett's dark form jolted into a sitting position. Switching on the bedside lamp with one hand, she grabbed her phone with the other and held it to her ear.

"Hello?"

"Is Mary Novak there?" Hammett said, using one of Isaac's codes, the modulator lending her voice a robotic sound almost identical to his.

"I'm sorry, she's driving to Nashville for the weekend. Visiting the Opry."

"The Opry is nice. My friend Paula loves it."

"You have something for me?" Follett asked.

"I've left a package for you."

"Location?"

"You'll find it in the greenhouse in the east garden. You need to pick it up now. Don't let anyone see you leave. Understand?"

"Affirmative. But won't the security cameras pick me up?"

"I've taken care of that problem. But you have to leave now. Use the window to avoid the Secret Service agent in the hall."

"On my way."

Hammett disconnected the call, figured she had at least two minutes before she needed to prepare for Follett's arrival, and then she checked her sisters' progress on the laptop.

The guard with Forsyth was on top of her and already grunting his climax. Not good.

"You have to keep him there longer," Hammett said in her sister's ear.

Forsyth nodded. "That's right. That's right."

If need be, Forsyth could always force the issue, knocking him unconscious, then convincing him he'd hit his head. But coupled with Burling's death, the odds of anyone believing this kid happened to have that kind of an accident on the same night were astronomical. This would be a tough enough sell as it was.

Hammett glanced to the others, hoping their timing was better.

The security room that Ludlum had entered was not covered by a camera, but the one on her jacket lapel showed the three guards all checking the cables and her palming a degausser wand that was half up her sleeve. Looking a little bit like a flat curling iron, the wand was powerful for its size, could scramble the security recordings in short order, wiping the hard drives. Of course, degaussing didn't actually erase data, but it changed the alignment of magnetic data storage systems so that the data itself was unrecoverable.

When Ludlum was finished, there would be no record of Follett's four duplicates ever having been at the house. And if the rest of the night went as planned, and The Instructor came through on his end, no one would look deeply enough into Burling's death to realize Follett was in so many places at the same time. Especially since no one but Isaac knew who Follett really was.

On the next section of the laptop screen, Clancy had stripped down to nothing but a thong and draped her jacket in order to give Hammett a good view. For a second, Hammett marveled at Clancy's body, identical to Forsyth's, identical to hers, in every detail; even down to the mole just below the nipple of her left breast.

Amazing.

Then she focused on that bastard Burling.

The man she knew as Isaac.

Completely naked but only half aroused, he looked fairly fit for a middle aged guy. He showed a few signs of his obvious zeal for partying, the broken capillaries crisscrossing his nose, a little puffiness under his eyes. But all in all, he had the waxed and groomed sheen of a metrosexual man with power.

Clancy stroked his still soft length, then fashioned her lips into a pout. "I have just what you need, baby."

"I'll bet you do. I have to say, you're the best bodyguard I've ever been assigned. What branch of the government did you say you worked for?"

"Right now, I'm working for you. And I'm very good at my job."

Hammett shook her head. How many double-cross and sexual entendres was that? Four at once? Clancy knew Burling was Isaac, and Burling thought Clancy was Follett, whom he assigned to guard himself. If it got any more complicated, it would become some sort of Shakespearean farce.

Clancy grasped the necklace draping between her breasts. A small cylinder-shaped piece of amethyst, the pendant wasn't actually stone at all. She gave the end a twist, and it detached from the chain. Then she held out the cocaine to Burling.

"This stuff is dynamite. A nice little pick me up." She toyed with him as she said the words.

He screwed off the cap and pulled out the tiny spoon attached, covered in white powder. "Oh, you know what I like, don't you?"

Clancy giggled, keeping her hands stroking as he snorted the cocaine into one nostril then the other.

Hammett scanned the garden. No Follett, she checked Forsyth. The last thing she needed was the guard she'd been taking care of wandering around when Follett showed.

Forsyth and her Romeo were sitting on the floor, Forsyth pushing her bottle of whiskey to his mouth.

He finally took a few gulps then shoved her hand away. "I've got to go."

"What? I didn't even get mine."

"Some other time, babe."

"Really? You're one of *those* guys? Your poor wife."

"Listen, I'm sorry, but I've got to do my job."

She set down the whiskey. "You're right. And your job right now is to get me off."

In a flash of movement, Forsyth had the guy's back pinned to the floor. Holding his shoulders down with her feet, she lowered herself down onto his mouth.

"Well," said Hammett into Forsyth's ear piece. "That's one way to shut him up."

Hammett figured she had at least another thirty seconds before Follett arrived. She aimed the scancorder to her left. One and the dog, just standing there. Maybe having a smoke. To the right—

—Follett threw open the door and attacked the moment Hammett read her heartbeat, leaping through the air in a Muay Thai cobra punch. Hammett barely had time to lean back, and Follett pulled the strike and actually ran up Hammett's body like it was a tree, placing a foot on Hammett's thigh and driving a knee into her chin.

Hammett tumbled backwards, knocking over a crate of vegetables and spices, the bright stars in the night sky shining through the glass roof joined by the ones swimming in her vision.

She managed to roll into a crouch, reaching for the Taser X26 in her belt holster, raising it and having it immediately batted aside, coming lose from her grip and falling into a bed of flowers. Then Follett began to rain down punches.

Hammett tried to catch a wrist, but Follett was too fast and too strong. Hammett went for a foot sweep, and Follett side-stepped it and then sun-kicked Hammett in the cheek.

She rolled with the impact, coming to her feet, instinctively throwing a punch that hit nothing but air.

"Follett, stop," Hammett said. "Paula just got back from Queens."

Follett paused at the code. "Who are you? Isaac?"

Hammett considered saying yes. But she hadn't been privy to the conversations Isaac had had with Follett, and didn't want to be caught in a lie.

"I'm Hammett, your twin sister. The Instructor sent me. We both work for Hydra."

Hammett was hit in the eyes with six hundred lumens. A tactical flashlight.

"Jesus, you look just like me."

"Light off," Hammett said, shielding her face from the glare. "We don't want to attract the guard."

"He knows me."

"And how will he act if he sees two of you?"

Follett switched off the beam. Hammett kept her hands up where Follett could see them.

"I was ordered to recruit you." Hammett studied her, and didn't see her concealed carry. Which meant it was either in an ankle holster under her jeans, or tucked into her waistband at the small of her back. "Are you armed?"

"Of course I'm armed. And I don't work for The Instructor."

"You do now."

Follett shook her head. "Isaac is my contact. If you really did have the same training I did, you know The Instructor told us to trust no one, including him."

"Things have gotten complicated. Isaac has been compromised."

"And I'm supposed to take your word for that?"

"Not just mine. There are more of us."

"Of us?"

"Us. Sisters. We're septuplets."

"Bullshit."

Hammett's back stiffened. The defiance and mistrust she sensed in Follett were no doubt a prelude to another attack.

"Isaac was my handler, too. He tried to kill me. The Instructor is taking Hydra away from Isaac. That's what tonight is about."

"Why try to recruit me here? Now? Why did you…"

Hammett saw her put it all together.

"This is a sanction," Follett stated. "Are you saying Burling is Isaac?"

Hammett nodded, watching closely for a change in her sister's stance.

"Bullshit. He's just a senator."

"He ordered you to guard him, to protect him from us. You're an assassin, Follett. We all are. How many times have you been ordered to protect a politician?"

"I… I need to talk to Burling."

Shit. Hammett read it in Follett's posture, heard it in her tone. She'd slept with him already. Possibly even liked him. And now an alleged twin she'd just met was going to compromise Follett's mission and challenge Follett's direct orders. Hammett immediately realized she was going to lose this argument, and that Follett was going to draw her weapon and shoot her. After all, it's what she would do if the roles were reversed.

So—tempting fate for the third time in as many days—Hammett ran directly at a sister who was trying to shoot her.

Follett drew like an Old West gunslinger, the weapon appearing in her hand so fast Hammett didn't see the movement. But she'd anticipated it, getting into Follett's head, predicting exactly where the gun would be when it came out, striking at that spot.

Hammett's fist connected with the inside of Follett's forearm, a two-knuckled blow that hit both the ulnar and median nerves. Her hand opened on reflex, and Hammett kicked the weapon away then spun around, catching Follett on the cheek with the back of her fist.

Follett staggered back, putting up her hands to defend herself, and Hammett attacked her body like it was a heavy bag; left kidney, right kidney, stomach, ribs, ribs, finishing up with an uppercut.

Follett slipped the last punch, then lowered a shoulder and sprang forward, driving Hammett to the ground.

Hammett was better at sparring than wrestling, and according to The Instructor, Follett was a near-unbeatable grappler. She immediately proceeded with a full mount, a maneuver Hammett recognized from Brazilian jiu-jitsu. Once in the power position, Follett immediately began to work her knees up into Hammett's armpits, ready to apply a stranglehold or an arm bar.

Hammett couldn't let that happen. If she did, she'd get bones broken at best, choked to death at worst.

Follett was up too high to bridge her over with a raised knee, and she was moving down to cinch the neck lock.

Electrified with panic, Hammett almost made the mistake of trying to claw at Follett's face, which would just give her sister more leverage and a stronger advantage.

Remember, it's not about lifting your opponent. Just lift your own body to escape.

Hammett slipped her right elbow under her sister's thigh and managed to get her left shoulder up. Then she swung her foot over Follett's leg and locked her ankle, at the same time grabbing her armpit and rolling over.

Reversal, Hammett on top.

Unlike her grappler sister, Hammett didn't attempt a hold or lock. She knew she couldn't win on the ground against a superior opponent. So instead she opted for an escape, kicking her legs away, getting to her feet—

—Follett caught her foot—

—and Hammett face planted onto the dropped crate of vegetables.

Twisting onto her back, Hammett reached out one hand for Follett's inevitable mount, the other groping through the scattered vegetables for something she hoped would be there.

Still grasping Hammett's leg, Follett bent it sideways and dropped onto Hammett, knocking away her arm. Then she went for an unconventional move, driving her knee into Hammett's neck.

As unconsciousness zeroed in, Hammett's free hand found what she sought. She squeezed, then flung it, jalapeño pepper seeds, pulp, and juice splattering across Follett's face.

Follett continued to press down, apparently trained to ignore the pain just as Hammett had been. But she couldn't open her eyes with capsaicin in them, and Hammett lifted her leg and to the side—not dissimilar to the yoga position Eka Pada Koundiyanasana 2—and was able to reach the Beretta in her ankle holster.

Hammett shot Follett in the shoulder—the suppressor screwed into the barrel making a sound like a wet cough— and when her sister recoiled she sat up and smacked the butt of the gun into Follett's forehead.

Follett fell backward, onto her ass. Hammett, sore as she was, kipped up and kicked Follett in the side of the head. Then she sighted the dropped Taser, scooped it up, and shot her in the leg with it, giving her a ten second pulse burst.

Follett seized, and when the neuro muscular incapacitation and subsequent pain ended, she once again tried to sit up and attack. Hammett gave her a fifteen second jolt, and finally her sister passed out.

That was one tough bitch.

Exhausted and more shaken than she wanted to admit, Hammett took advantage of her unconsciousness and bound her hands and feet with plastic zip lines. Then she recovered the laptop. A quick glance showed Clancy hovering over a spasming and naked senator, the Secret Service agent by her side calling for an ambulance.

That seemed to be going well. But what else was to be expected when good quality cocaine was blended with good quality strychnine? If Clancy had followed protocol, after Burling began to seize she'd blown more up his nostrils, ensuring his demise. A thorough autopsy would discover the poison if it was tested for, but The Instructor said he'd take care of that end. Besides, this *death by natural causes* bullshit was tough. If they'd wanted something completely undetectable, they should have hired that half-Japanese assassin Hammett had heard rumors about.

Forsyth was still in the security booth, only this time she was wearing her bra and panties and pulling on the rest of her clothing. The guard was passed out on the floor, the bottle of roofied-up whiskey next to him. Shrugging on her jacket, Forsyth pulled a half empty, whiskey bottle from her bag and switched it with the drugged bottle.

All going according to plan there, too.

Ludlum, on the other hand, was still in the security room with her degaussing wand.

"Ludlum?" Hammett said into her earpiece. "Get the hell out of there."

The shriek of an ambulance pierced the night.

"Hurry," Hammett added.

"I got nothing," one of the guards said, Ludlum's camera showing him on hands and knees on the floor.

Hammett heard Ludlum give a dramatic sigh. "The whole damn thing seems screwed up. I'm going to call the security company. If you two figure it out, give a yell."

Back up in the master bathroom, the Secret Service agent was heading out the door.

Shit.

"Keep him there, Clancy," Hammett said. "A few more seconds."

"Where are you going?" Clancy asked.

He paused. "I have to let the guard at the gate know."

Hammett glanced back at Ludlum's progress. "Out through the living room. Now."

"Listen," Clancy's voice trembled. "I know I'm supposed to be able to handle this, but the senator and I, we're close, and I just…" She covered her face with her hands, and when she looked up, tears trickled down her cheeks. "You have to take care of him."

"I need to—"

"I'll call down to the gate. Please. I'm a mess. I can't do this."

Hammett held her breath.

The agent nodded, and switched places with Clancy. Grabbing her phone from her jacket, Clancy slipped it on and made the call, pretending to talk to a man who was passed out on the floor of the guard booth.

Hammett let out a breath. That was too damn close.

The siren grew louder. Red light pulsed over the garden as the ambulance raced past. When they reached the gate, Forsyth motioned it through, wearing the guard's uniform jacket, his hat shielding her face.

The emergency caravan moved up the driveway to the house, and Hammett heard breathing from the edge of the lawn.

"Just in fucking time."

Ludlum followed her voice, coming to a stop next to Follett's limp body. "She dead?"

"Unconscious. Help me carry her. We don't have much time."

Ludlum taking Follett's shoulders and Hammett her feet, they carried her to the gate and slipped through. Forsyth was waiting on the other side with the cab. Two seconds to throw Follett in the trunk and pile in, and they were on their way.

Sitting in the passenger seat, Hammett checked the laptop. Now there was only one feed left to watch, Clancy's. The remaining sister followed the paramedics as they wheeled Burling out the door and loaded him into the ambulance. She climbed into the passenger seat and the Secret Service agent rode in the back with the senator.

Behind the wheel, Forsyth took an alternate route to the hospital and parked on a side street about three blocks away. Now there was nothing to do but wait.

While Ludlum and Forsyth reviewed each step of the op, then chatted about the booth guard's anatomy and their favorite sexual positions, Hammett watched the laptop. She was the only one not surprised when Clancy rapped on the car window ahead of schedule. Ludlum let her in the back seat.

"He's deader than hell," Clancy said.

Hammett smiled. *Shouldn't have fucked with me, you bastard.*

They drove to a safe house in Milwaukee that The Instructor had arranged. And when they arrived, the four circled to the back of the cab and opened the trunk.

Follett blinked at the light of morning, streaming clear and fresh over Lake Michigan.

"Welcome to the club, Sis," Clancy said.

Epilogue

Vice President Ratzenberger sat at the Resolute Desk in the Oval Office. The President was off doing some international bullshit, giving Ratzenberger much-needed private time. He came in here often when the Commander in Chief was away.

Imagining the future.

He put his feet up on the desk, ankles crossed, and dialed the secure number.

"This is The Instructor," came the monotone pick-up.

Ratzenberger frowned. He didn't like this man, or his methods. But he appreciated his results.

"How's our little project going?"

"Hammett and her sisters have been briefed and are on board."

Ratzenberger was surprised. "No problems?"

"I didn't train them to cause problems. I trained them to solve problems."

The Vice President was surprised by their level of commitment in the line of duty, considering what was being asked of them. But then again, what was the point of patriotism other than to make sacrifices for your country?

"And that asshole, Burling?" Ratzenberger asked.

"You mean *Isaac*?" The Instructor chuckled, then used his electronic gizmo to change his voice. "Our people are performing the autopsy. It will be called a cocaine overdose. You not only got rid of a powerful rival, but you've discredited him as well."

It had been a masterstroke to use Hydra to eliminate Burling by telling them he was their handler, when The Instructor had been Isaac all along. Like being a double-agent for the same side. But even if they never found out, and even though their commitment seemed assured, Ratzenberger still had some doubts.

"You aren't concerned this is getting out of control? I saw the things Hammett has done, on the news. She's seems like a wild card."

"There are safeguards in place."

"I know you said Chandler is formidable," Ratzenberger said. "Is five against one enough?"

"One and a half, if you count her handler."

"Can she be recruited as well?"

"Chandler? No. She's... different. The best way to deal with her is to proceed as planned."

"So we're going to do it."

"It's best for the country, Mr. Vice President. We've discussed this."

Ratzenberger bit his lip. This was incredibly risky. But the nuclear strike was an easier and less-lethal alternative to releasing the disease. And Hydra Deux was still prepping.

"Keep me posted," he ordered.

"Of course."

The Instructor hung up.

Ratzenberger leaned back in the Executive chair and closed his eyes.

Soon, the fate of the world would be left to a few specially trained operatives. And Razenberger's legacy, his destiny, was intertwined with that fate.

So many ways for things to go wrong.

So many ways for things to go right.

The Vice President imagined a nuclear strike.

The mushroom cloud.

The burning.

The radiation.

Then he thought of millions of people, blood streaming from their eyes, coughing out bits of lung tissue.

"Dear God," he prayed. "Let me know I'm doing the right thing."

God didn't reply.

ABOUT J.A. KONRATH

Joe Konrath is the author of more than twenty novels and dozens of shorter works in the mystery, thriller, horror, and science fiction genres. He's sold over a two million books worldwide, and besides Tracy Sharp he's collaborated with bestsellers Blake Crouch, Barry Eisler, Ann Voss Peterson, Henry Perez, Tom Schreck, Jeff Strand, and F. Paul Wilson. He likes beer, pinball machines, and playing pinball when drinking beer. Visit him at jakonrath.com.

ABOUT ANN VOSS PETERSON

Award-winning author Ann Voss Peterson wrote her first story at seven years old and hasn't stopped since. To pursue her love of creative writing, she's worked as a bartender, horse groomer, and window washer. Now known for her adrenaline-fueled thrillers and Harlequin Intrigue romances, Ann draws on her wide variety of life experiences to fill her fictional worlds with compelling energy and undeniable emotion. She lives near Madison, Wisconsin, with her family and their border collie.

Peterson & Konrath Bibliographies

CODENAME: CHANDLER
(Ann Voss Peterson & J.A. Konrath)

FLEE (Book 1)

SPREE (Book 2)

THREE (Book 3)

HIT (Book 4)

EXPOSED (Book 5)

NAUGHTY (Book 6)

FIX with F. Paul Wilson (Book 7)

RESCUE (Book 8)

EROTICA
(Konrath & Peterson writing as Melinda Duchamp)

Make Me Blush series

MISTER KINK (Book 1)

FIFTY SHADES OF WITCH (Book 2)

SIX AND CANDY (Book 3)

Alice series

FIFTY SHADES OF ALICE IN WONDERLAND (Book 1)

FIFTY SHADES OF ALICE THROUGH THE LOOKING GLASS (Book 2)

FIFTY SHADES OF ALICE AT THE HELLFIRE CLUB (Book 3)

Jezebel series

FIFTY SHADES OF JEZEBEL AND THE BEANSTALK (Book 1)

FIFTY SHADES OF PUSS IN BOOTS (Book 2)

FIFTY SHADES OF GOLDILOCKS (Book 3)

Sexperts series

THE SEXPERTS – FIFTY GRADES OF SHAY (Book 1)

THE SEXPERTS – THE GIRL WITH THE PEARL NECKLACE (Book 2)

THE SEXPERTS – LOVING THE ALIEN (Book 3)

Ann Voss Peterson Bibliography

VAL RYKER THRILLERS

PUSHED TOO FAR (Book 1)

BURNED TOO HOT (Book 2)

DEAD TOO SOON (Book 3)

WATCHED TOO LONG with J.A. Konrath (Book 4)

BURIED TOO DEEP (Book 5)

SMALL TOWN SECRETS: SINS

LETHAL (Book 1)

CAPTIVE (Book 2)

FRANTIC (Book 3)

VICIOUS (Book 4)

SMALL TOWN SECRETS: SCANDALS

WITNESS (Book 1)

STOLEN (Book 2)

MALICE (Book 3)

GUILTY (Book 4)

FORBIDDEN (Book 5)

KIDNAPPED (Book 6)

THE SCHOOL (Book 3.5)

ROCKY MOUNTAIN THRILLERS

MANHUNT (Book 1)

FUGITIVE (Book 2)

JUSTICE (Book 3)

MAVERICK (Book 4)

RENEGADE (Book 5)

PARANORMAL ROMANTIC SUSPENSE

Return to Jenkins Cove
CHRISTMAS SPIRIT by Rebecca York (Book 1)
CHRISTMAS AWAKENING by Ann Voss Peterson (Book 2)
CHRISTMAS DELIVERY by Patricia Rosemoor (Book 3)

Security Breach
CHAIN REACTION by Rebecca York (Book 1)
CRITICAL EXPOSURE by Ann Voss Peterson (Book 2)
TRIGGERED RESPONSE by Patricia Rosemoor (Book 3)

Gypsy Magic
WYATT (Justice is Blind) by Rebecca York (Part 1)
GARNER (Love is Death) by Ann Voss Peterson (Part 2)
ANDREI (The Law is Impotent) by Patricia Rosemoor (Part 3)

Renegade Magic
LUKE by Rebecca York (Part 1)
TOM by Ann Voss Peterson (Part 2)
RICO by Patricia Rosemoor (Part 3)

New Orleans Magic
JORDAN by Rebecca York (Part 1)
LIAM by Ann Voss Peterson (Part 2)
ZACHARY by Patricia Rosemoor (Part 3)

J.A. Konrath Bibliography

JACQUELINE "JACK" DANIELS THRILLERS

WHISKEY SOUR (Book 1)

BLOODY MARY (Book 2)

RUSTY NAIL (Book 3)

DIRTY MARTINI (Book 4)

FUZZY NAVEL (Book 5)

CHERRY BOMB (Book 6)

SHAKEN (Book 7)

STIRRED with Blake Crouch (Book 8)

RUM RUNNER (Book 9)

LAST CALL (Book 10)

WHITE RUSSIAN (Book 11)

SHOT GIRL (Book 12)

CHASER (Book 13)

OLD FASHIONED (Book 14)

LADY 52 with Jude Hardin (Book 2.5)

JACK DANIELS AND ASSOCIATES MYSTERIES

DEAD ON MY FEET (Book 1)

JACK DANIELS STORIES VOL. 1 (Book 2)

SHOT OF TEQUILA (Book 3)

JACK DANIELS STORIES VOL. 2 (Book 4)

DYING BREATH (Book 5)

SERIAL KILLERS UNCUT with Blake Crouch (Book 6)

JACK DANIELS STORIES VOL. 3 (Book 7)

EVERYBODY DIES (Book 8)

JACK DANIELS STORIES VOL. 4 (Book 9)

BANANA HAMMOCK (Book 10)

THE KONRATH DARK THRILLER COLLECTIVE
THE LIST (Book 1)
ORIGIN (Book 2)
AFRAID (Book 3)
TRAPPED (Book 4)
ENDURANCE (Book 5)
HAUNTED HOUSE (Book 6)
WEBCAM (Book 7)
DISTURB (Book 8)
WHAT HAPPENED TO LORI (Book 9)
THE NINE (Book 10)
CLOSE YOUR EYES (Book 11)
SECOND COMING (Book 12)
HOLES IN THE GROUND with Iain Rob Wright (Book 4.5)
DRACULAS with Blake Crouch, Jeff Strand, F. Paul Wilson (Book 5.5)
GRANDMA? with Talon Konrath (Book 6.5)
WULFS? with Talon Konrath (Book 9.5)

TIMECASTER
TIMECASTER (Book 1)
TIMECASTER SUPERSYMMETRY (Book 2)
TIMECASTER STEAMPUNK (Book 3)
BYTER (Book 4)

STOP A MURDER PUZZLE BOOKS
HOW: PUZZLES 1-12 (Book 1)
WHERE: PUZZLES 13-24 (Book 2)
WHY: PUZZLES 25-36 (Book 3)
WHO: PUZZLES 37-48 (Book 4)
WHEN: PUZZLES 49-60 (Book 5)
ANSWERS (Book 6)
STOP A MURDER COMPLETE CASES (Books 1-5)

MISCELLANEOUS
65 PROOF – COLLECTED SHORT STORIES
THE GLOBS OF USE-A-LOT 3 with Dan Maderak
A NEWBIES GUIDE TO PUBLISHING

FLEE

J.A. Konrath and Ann Voss Peterson

CODENAME: CHANDLER

She's an elite spy, working for an agency so secret only three people know it exists. Trained by the best of the best, she has honed her body, her instincts, and her intellect to become the perfect weapon.

FLEE

Then her cover is explosively blown, and she becomes a walking bulls-eye, stalked by assassins who want the secrets she holds, and those who'd prefer she die before talking.

Chandler now has twenty-four hours to thwart a kidnapping, stop a murderous psychopath, uncover the mystery of her past, retire five highly-trained contract killers, and save the world from nuclear annihilation, all while dodging 10,000 bullets and a tenacious cop named Jack Daniels.

Buckle up. It's going to be one helluva ride.

SPREE

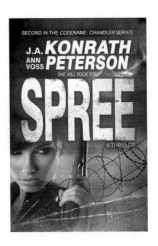

by J.A. Konrath and Ann Voss Peterson

CODENAME: CHANDLER

After having her cover blown and risking everything to stop a nuclear Armageddon, covert operative Chandler figured she might have been shown some appreciation for the sacrifices she made. Instead, the very organization that trained her locks up Chandler's sister, Fleming, for treason, intent on extracting every last scrap of information from her broken body and mind.

SPREE

Despite impossible odds, Chandler launches a desperate rescue mission, recruiting old allies (Jack Daniels and Harry McGlade, from Konrath's novel WHISKEY SOUR), and new ones (Val Ryker and David Lund from Peterson's PUSHED TOO FAR, and Tequila Abernathy from Konrath's SHOT OF TEQUILA) to break into a black site—an ultrasecret military prison on US soil where no one gets out alive. But standing in her way is a squad of deadly psychopaths and a rogue government agency determined to destabilize the nation—and conquer the world.

Buckle up. It's going to be one hell of a ride...

THREE

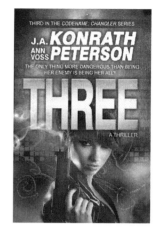

by J.A. Konrath and Ann Voss Peterson

CODENAME: CHANDLER

Time is running out for Chandler, the elite assassin whose mission to rescue her sister from a notorious black ops prison landed her at the top of the nation's Most Wanted list. Burned by her handlers and forced to work with her mortal enemy in a race to preserve the very government that wants her dead, the living weapon has become a ticking time bomb.

THREE

In saving her sister, Chandler unleashed a power-mad American president dead set on controlling the world—no matter how many millions of innocent people he must kill to do it. To stop him, Chandler will go deeper than she's ever gone before, pushing her body and mind to their absolute limits. All the while she is hunted by the one man who knows her every secret, her every hiding place—and her every weakness.

Infiltrating the White House, crashing a bullfight in Mexico City, hijacking a blimp in Toronto…these are just the beginning of the end, as the Codename: Chandler trilogy races towards its stunning conclusion.

Manufactured by Amazon.ca
Bolton, ON

21494426R00205